BLADE HONER
BOOK TWO

MY ENEMY'S HEAD

BY

MARIA KVILHAUG

TLS

ISBN13: 978-1-959350-19-4

Set in: Mjolnir 22pt, Georgia 11/12pt

©The Three Little Sisters
USA/CANADA

The Son said:
"Here you may see a most vigorous Phallus
cut from a father of horses:
And you, Slave Woman, take this Wand to you!
- it will not at all be dull between your thighs."

(Vǫlsa þáttr – The Song of the Wand)

**

Back I turned, and thought I was to have my will
This I thought that I would have;
her desire and her pleasure
…
And near morning, when I returned…
A bitch I found then tied to the bed
of that marvelous woman.

(Hávamál, st. 99,101, Poetic Edda)

***

RELEVANT PRIMARY SOURCE QUOTES

Royal Frankish Annals, 782 A.D: When he heard this, the Lord King Charles [Charlemagne] rushed to the place with all the [Christian] Franks that he could gather on short notice and advanced to where the Aller flows into the Weser. Then all the [Heathen] Saxons came together again, submitted to the authority of the Lord King, and surrendered the evildoers who were chiefly responsible for this revolt to be put to death—four thousand and five hundred of them. This sentence was carried out. Widukind was not among them since he had fled to Nordmannia. When he had finished this business, the Lord King returned to Francia"

Anglo-Saxon Chronicles A.D. 787: "This year King Bertric took Edburga the daughter of Offa to wife. And in his days came first three ships of the Northmen from the land of robbers. The reve then rode thereto, and would drive them to the king's town; for he knew not what they were; and there was he slain. These were the first ships of the Danish [Norse] men that sought the land of the English nation." ...

Ibn Fadlan A.D. 921: "I saw the Rūsiyyah when they had arrived on their trading expedition and had disembarked at the River Ātil. I have never seen more perfect physiques than theirs—they are tall like palm trees, are fair and reddish (...) Every one of them carries an axe, a sword and a dagger and is never without all of that which we have mentioned. Their swords are of the Frankish variety, with broad, ridged blades. Each man, from the tip of his toes to his neck, is covered in dark-green lines, pictures and such like."

..."Each woman has, on her breast, a small disc, tied around her neck, made of either iron, silver, copper or gold, in relation to her husband's financial and social worth. Each disc has a ring to which a dagger is attached, also lying on her breast."(...)

"Every day the slave girl arrives in the morning with a large basin containing water, which she hands to her owner. He washes his hands and his face and his hair in the water, then he dips his comb in the water and brushes his hair, blows his nose and spits in the basin" ...

Ahmad Ibh Rustah 10th century AD : "As for the Rus, they live on an island ... that takes three days to walk round and is covered with thick undergrowth and forests; it is most unhealthy.... They harry the Slavs, using ships to reach them; they carry them off as slaves and...sell them. They have no fields but simply live on what they get from the Slav's lands..."

"They carry clean clothes and the men adorn themselves with bracelets and gold. They treat their slaves well and also they carry exquisite clothes, because they put great effort in trade. They have many towns. They have a most friendly attitude towards foreigners and strangers who seek refuge."

Ibn Fadlan A.D. 921 "They are accompanied by beautiful slave girls for trading. One man will have intercourse with his slave girl while his companion looks on. Sometimes a group of them comes together to do this, each in front of the other.

Sometimes indeed the merchant will come in to buy a slave girl from one of them and he will chance upon him having intercourse with her, but the Rūs will not leave her alone until he has satisfied his urge (...)"

Six men entered the pavilion and all had intercourse with the slave girl."

John of Wallingford, prior of St. Fridswides: "The Danes[Scandinavians], thanks to their habit of combing their hair every day, of bathing every Saturday and regularly changing their clothes, were able to undermine the virtue of married women and even seduce the daughters of nobles to be their mistresses."

Laxdæla Saga ch.12 (A.D. 948): "...She [the slave concubine] answered, "Myr Kjartan is the name of my father, and he is a king in Ireland; and I was taken a prisoner of war from there when I was fifteen winters old." Hoskuld said she had kept silence far too long about so noble a descent. (...) After that he let Melkorka go away, and got a dwelling ready for her up in Salmon-river-Dale, at the place that was afterwards called Melkorkastad (...) Melkorka now set up household there, and Hoskuld had everything brought there that she needed; and Olaf, their son, went with her. It was soon seen that Olaf, as he grew up, was far superior to other men, both on account of his beauty and courtesy."

Tacitus, Germania 7-8 (1st.century A.D.): "And what most stimulates their courage is that their squadrons or battalions, instead of being formed by chance or by a fortuitous gathering, are composed of families and clans. Close by them, too, are those dearest to them, so that they hear the shrieks of women, the cries of infants.

They are to every man the most sacred witnesses of his bravery-they are his most generous applauders. The soldier brings his wounds to mother and wife, who shrink not from counting or even demanding them and who administer food and encouragement to the combatants.

Tradition says that armies already wavering and giving way have been rallied by women who, with earnest entreaties and bosoms laid bare, have vividly represented the horrors of captivity, which the Germans fear with such extreme dread on behalf of their women, that the strongest tie by which a state can be bound is the being required to give, among the number of hostages, maidens of noble birth.

They even believe that the female sex has a certain sanctity and prescience, and they do not despise their counsels, or make light of their answers.

They believe that there resides in women an element of holiness and prophecy, and so they do not scorn to ask their advice or lightly disregard their replies.

In the reign of the deified Vespasian we saw Veleda long honored by many Germans as a divinity, whilst even earlier they showed a similar reverence for Aurinia and others (...)

Snorri Sturlusson, Prologue (Prose Edda) A.D. 1225: "Thus they recognized that the Earth was quick, and had life with some manner of nature of her own; and they understood that she was wondrous old in years and mighty in kind: she nourished all that lived, and she took to herself all that died. Therefore they gave her a name, and traced the number of their generations from her."

Bede - De Temporum Ratione (725A.D.). "...began the year on the 8th kalends of January [25 December], when we celebrate the birth of the Lord. That very night, which we hold so sacred, they used to call by the Heathen word Modranecht, that is, "mother's night", because (we suspect) of the ceremonies they enacted all that night..."

ALDEIGJUBORG
(Staraya Ladoga, Russia)
A.D. 790-791

Forth came earls, men fully wise
all seeking to soothe her pain
But weep she could not, Guðrún;
From bitter grief her chest could burst

Nobly born earls' wives, gold-adorned, they sat with her:
Each one of them spoke of heavy grief
The bitterest loss they knew themselves.
...
But weep she could not, Gudrún,
Filled with grief by the corpse of her prince
Paralyzed by pain at his deathbed

Then said Gullrand, Giuki's daughter;
"Little could you, foster mother,
comfort the young one with all your stories
Show her, rather, the face of her prince."

(Guðrúnarkviða hin fyrsta, st. 2-3,12-13, Poetic Edda)

First Day

When Zivah woke up that first morning in what passed for her new home, she lay still for a long time, listening anxiously to all the sounds of the Hold, not daring to move or speak. The detestable man, who owned her just like he would own his horse or dog, got up, and she listened tensely after each one of his movements until he spoke to her.

When he told her to get up and start working, she obeyed at once, not even daring to look at him as she got dressed and climbed out of the bed. Brushing past him, she hurried into the bathroom and was greeted cheerfully but quietly by Aziza, who approached and embraced her as soon as she cautiously stepped inside that room. As Zivah was to discover, the bath-room was mostly for the slaves' disposal apart from when their masters were to bathe. It was the room where they could be themselves.

Aziza kept her arm around the younger woman while she led her to a water basin and had her wash her face. When Zivah had finished and dried her face with a towel, Aziza pointed further down and asked, "You need to wash down there?"

Zivah blushed and shook her head, noticing that the other slave girl in the room, the one they called Suri, tried hard not to giggle. "No fuck last night?" Aziza asked, smiling. Zivah was going redder and redder. Blushing, she shook her head once more. Aziza embraced her again and whispered into her ear, "Thióðolf Heri is a good man, Zivah, he will never hurt you. You are safe."

Then she made her sit while she combed her hair affectionately. Zivah closed her eyes and felt the generous love exuding from the older woman with every gentle touch and every kind attention she gave to her. Like Mother. She allowed herself to lean a little against her and noticed that Aziza did not withdraw from her at all. It felt so good.

Aziza was wrong. Thióðolf Heri was a terrible beast of a man like all the others and the only reason there had been no "fuck" last night was because Thordís had intervened, miraculously enough. She remembered how her little sister had come to her aid just that moment when she had known that he was going to do it, and she had understood quite a bit of their conversation too, if not all of it. Even though she could make out most of their words, it was hard to grasp the meaning of all that riddle speech.

When the child had turned to her last night and spoken to her, telling her that she was safe and could sleep in peace and that her master had promised not to use her if she did not want it herself, she had not known what to reply, so she had not replied at all, just obeyed the Maiden's command of going to sleep. Because whatever that girl said to her now was in truth a command, no matter how it was worded, and that *hurt*.

Yet when she had lain there in the dark and started to think about everything, Zivah had begun to realize that despite everything else, the man had just *promised* to never take her unless she wanted it herself. Her stepfather had let her know that a spoken promise was something Norsemen took very seriously.

Then up from her pool of chaotic memories from the voyage hither had emerged other memories; images of little Thordís intervening, like a little dancer, trying carefully to maneuver a horrifying situation that was utterly out of her control and her ken. And all this while that Zivah had been surrounded by hordes of beastly rapist killers, though she had not actually been hurt, nor raped, nor killed even once.

Then it had occurred to Zivah for the second time since the raid that the little girl was possibly just trying to protect her in any way she could without offending these men, and might not have that much power after all. Straining her ears, Zivah had heard that her master was finally sleeping, breathing deeply, and had decided to face the child again. When she had turned, she had seen her little sister sleeping in his arms, her tiny face tucked in against his broad chest, his arms placed so gently around the child, so very protective. It was as she had known all the while, Zivah had thought, and bit her lower lip. Her half-sister was one of *them*, and she was not.

"Zivah," Aziza said when she had finished combing her hair and made of it a simple and very tight bun at the neck, "you must carry water to your House-Bond. If he stands when you come in, you bow head and lift basin up to him and stay like that until he is finished. Understand?" Zivah nodded. "If he is seated when you come in with the basin, you bow head and kneel before him, and lift basin up, stay there until he is finished. Understand?"

Zivah felt sick. "Kneel?" She asked hoarsely.

"Yes, kneel. You must kneel so you do not seem above him when you offer basin. But only kneel to the man if he is seated. Norsemen do not like it if you kneel when they are standing."

"No?" She thought he had liked that well enough when he made her kneel before the whole town. "Oh, there are times they like us to kneel just fine," Suri chuckled, but Aziza hushed her.

"No, they think of kneeling as humiliating," Aziza said, "even for slaves. They do not bow even to gods, Zivah, they do not like other people bowing to them either. Only if it is punishment. Or for pleasure. If they are seated, then kneeling is fine for slave, because it is practical. Understand?" Zivah nodded. She was beginning to understand that Norsemen were insane, that much was clear. Aziza put an apron on her that had pockets, and put a towel and a comb into her pocket and told her to offer to comb her House-Bond's hair.

"What Zivah say?" She asked nervously.

"You can say *House-Bond* or *Heri* first, to greet him, and then you say whatever you need to say. Slaves do not speak much unless spoken to, so keep it short and precise."

"What is difference? House-Bond or Heri?"

"House-Bond is the man who owns you by law," Aziza said, "and only him. *Heri* just means lord or master. You call all free men *Heri*, all free men are *Heris* to slaves. So if you call him House-Bond it is more familiar. More like family. In a household everybody call the master House-Bond, even the free folks of the Hold. Even free wife calls her man House-Bond, Zivah. So it is more affectionate. It is good counsel for slave to be friendly with House-Bond."

"And yet *Bond* is a cover word for *God*," Suri added, grinning.

"Zivah can say *Heri* to House-Bond?" She asked.

"Yes, but it marks a distance to him, Zivah. You may want to let him feel closer than that," Aziza suggested cautiously.

Zivah shook her head slowly and went to serve her lord.

Thióðolf woke just after dawn from the commotion of slave girls scurrying about the hall making ready for the breaking of fast. He gently released little Thordís, who was still sleeping soundly, from his arms and sat up. Zivah was awake too and lay with her back still turned, looking into the wall. "Zivah," he said softly. She rolled over, but kept her gaze averted and down. "Heri." She sounded so indifferent.

"Are you very tired?"

"No, Heri."

"Good. You can get up and, uhm, go to Aziza. She will tell you what to do. I promised that you could help out in the hall and court."

"Yes, Heri," she said and put on her grey dress before she crawled out of bed, stood up with her head bowed and went to find Aziza. Thióðolf shooed away the slave girl who came to attend him and put on his clothes and arms himself before he went to sit by the table. Arnulf had already eaten and was outside.

Zivah came out of the bath room, carrying a basin full of cold water.

"Heri," she muttered, her face down.

"Yes," he said.

"Aziza says I water to Heri," she said and knelt down before him with her head still bowed. She lifted the basin up towards him so that he could wash his face. She already knew the slave walk and the slave talk to perfection.

Too perfect.

"You could, uhm, you could address me as House-Bond, you know, Zivah," he said gently, "it is more familiar than Heri. You do not have to keep your head bowed all the time. It is a way of greeting, really, not a permanent condition."

"Yes, Heri," she replied obediently, still keeping her head firmly lowered. He sighed and smiled to himself. *She is a warrior like her sister*, he thought. He was quite certain she understood that a suggestion from him to her counted the same as a command. Yet she gracefully refused as if she had been a slave for years and knew exactly how to. He washed his face, and when he grunted, she put the basin away and produced a towel from the apron that Aziza had given her. Thióðolf dried his face and gave the towel back to her. She still kept her face lowered, but produced the comb.

"Heri," she said, "Aziza says I comb Heri."

"Well, Aziza knows the customs, but I think I shall rather comb my hair myself. It is one of those other familiar things," he said and gently took the comb from her.

"Yes, Heri," the girl replied, unperturbed, head stubbornly bowed.

"You can go, Zivah," he said, and she took the basin and the towel and disappeared. He was quite certain she had not looked at his face even once. Then another and far friendlier slave girl came over and gave him his morning porridge and beer, smiled brightly and spoke amiably to him while lowering her eyes only after a teasing glance into his, "Good morning, Thióðolf Heri."

"Good morning, Suri," he replied, smiling, and gave her a wink, what sent the cute Persian girl away giggling. His gaze followed her until she disappeared into the bath room.

What irony of fate that all the women of Arnulf's court adored him except for the only one who belonged to him. Who happened to be the most beautiful as well as most pitiful woman he had ever been close to. He had never even thought to own a bonds woman for such purposes. Whatever had he done to deserve such puns from the Ladies of the Loom? How the gods must be laughing over the verses of his life of late.

Thióðolf suddenly remembered how Zivah had spread her legs for him last night, obliging him while moving her mind to a different place, hidden away from his reach, and how he had nevertheless started to uncover her body just before Thordís came to tell him off, praise be to the Goddess. The poet groaned and clutched his Freyia pendant for a moment before he hid his face in shame.

Until that moment he had only remembered how content he was that he had *not* raped his poor, recently abducted and still grieving, free-born slave girl. It was a self-restraint which had made him feel truly honorable and noble. He had thought that she ought to be friendlier with him now, more trusting, and certainly grateful. She was not grateful at all, and there was no doubt in his mind that 'Zivah the Untouchable,' as the men had begun calling her when she and her sister were not around, remembered how he almost *did* rape her after all.

The recollection of that fatal, previous day unraveled before him; how he had noosed her, beaten her, made her kneel and thank him for the ugly slave dress, almost laughed when she started to weep in the bath, and then how he had thought that raping her in conclusion to all that would be a good idea for both of them, and that she would probably enjoy it too. There was no saying what he would have done if Thordís had not stopped him, and his silent young slave had witnessed the entire process. And this morning he expected her to smile and call him House-Bond, like a weak man who thought himself great when undeservedly humored by slave girls. What a conceited fool he was. Thióðolf had lost his appetite and his interest in the giggling girls, got up and went outside to draw some air.

He found Arnulf and Hallgrim Hidden Spear sitting on the outside, and went to join them. They both looked at him with amusement in their eyes, making it clear that he was about to be teased. Thióðolf braced himself and sat down after greeting them both. But instead of teasing him, they suddenly went very grave.

"So you are still scorning my gift to you," Arnulf spoke brusquely, glaring at him.

"I am not scorning her, Heri," Thióðolf said, lowering his eyes respectfully to the warlord, trying to hide his embarrassment, "On the contrary I really like her. I am grateful for your gift. She pleases me very much."

"I did not hear any pleasing last night," Arnulf grunted.

"Well, *you* were being rather loud," Thióðolf said, peering sideways at the red-haired warlord.

"Not that loud, and not then. I heard everything. You let a little girl stop you. What sort of man lets a little girl do that?" Arnulf growled.

"The honorable sort," Thióðolf said, "at least where I come from." He straightened his back and looked directly at his Heri for a moment before he averted his eyes. The Heri still glared sulkily at him which was unnerving.

"So you are not going to touch the girl at all, or what?" Arnulf snapped.

"Not unless she wants me to. Really, really wants me to," Thióðolf stubbornly insisted. Arnulf snorted disdainfully. "Are you going to let the rest of us, then? I had hoped you could break her in first."

"No, Heri," Thióðolf said, maintaining his stance, "I am sorry, but you gave her to me. She is mine to command. And I am going to declare her unavailable to other men. Nobody may use her, unless she herself expresses clearly that she really wants it."

"That is remarkably ungenerous of you, after all we have done for you," Arnulf muttered gravely.

Thióðolf clenched his teeth, his mind working quickly. "But you do not understand, Heri," he said, "I am a poet. You have given me a great gift, a beautiful woman who needs to be wooed. And yet she is a slave. How does a man woo a slave? How does a man convince an abducted woman that she can trust him and give herself freely? How, indeed, after having already done just about every wrong to her that he could possibly have done?"

The other two men exchanged glances, shrugged, and looked expectantly at Thióðolf to see how he would answer his own questions. There was a mysterious glee to their eyes when they looked brightly at him, anticipating a lecture of poetic splendor. The skald drew his breath.

"I do not know," he admitted, "but I am eying an opportunity to learn and become a better man. I see a challenge to be overcome. I see a task fit for a warrior. I see poetry come alive. I see my soul's edge being honed on this path, and the honer is hidden, the honer is forbidden, because the honer is a slave. How can a slave hone a warrior? How can I be honed by one whose life and death I own? I shall find out, because I know no fear. Can you not see what a great song this can be? Let the song be sung in its own time. Let my victory be the proof of my worthiness. How can you call this path a gift scorned? Can you not see how I honor it? This is a most sacred story that I have entered," Thióðolf paused and locked his eyes with theirs in challenge, "My slave is not to be touched, and you can tell that to all the men."

The two other men regarded him carefully, obviously rather impressed by his eloquence. And gleefully entertained also, Thióðolf noticed. Then a smile broke out on Arnulf's face, and he turned to Hallgrim, who was also grinning all of a sudden. Arnulf took off one of his gold finger rings and tossed it to Hallgrim, who caught it with his fist.

"You won, Hallgrim, and I agree. He is truly an honorable man," Arnulf chuckled.

"You knew that already," Hallgrim said, "when you made the bet."

"I knew I would lose. And yet there must be a contrary," Arnulf said cheerfully. Hallgrim nodded confirmatively. There always had to be one.

"What have you two been up to?" Thióðolf asked, looking from one to the other, suspecting a plot had been played at his expense. The other two grinned.

"Well, it is like this, my friend," Arnulf said, "that seeing as you always go on about honorable conduct we wanted to test you, and see if you were truly as honorable as all that. That was when we gave you the girl. We made our bet then, about whether you would show yourself truly noble. We both thought you would, but you know there must be a contrary. It is sacred. You know Hallgrim, and you know me. We thought I would certainly be the most convincing contrary in this case, and so I bet against you, and as you may recall I did *everything* I could to corrupt your honor."

Arnulf Heri looked mighty proud of himself. So proud, in fact, that he gave his own chest a good beat. The whole court seemed to be paying attention, and Thióðolf heard suppressed giggles from among the men who were walking by doing their morning chores.

"You are right, Heri, you did a very good job of it too," Thióðolf admitted, sulking only a little, realizing that he had been played good and well. Arnulf laughed and gave his friend's back a friendly slap, what made the bard lose his breath.

"And yet you made it through, Skald," the captain said cheerfully. "You made it through three tests! The tent, the ship and the bed. With the third test passed, you made your honor true. With a little help from our *known* honer, admittedly, but as you said only an honorable man would let a little girl stop him. What besides also served to test our Priestess and see her through as more than worthy for our court. She is a warrior's daughter and has shown excellent courage. And you, Thióðolf, you are truly honorable and worthy of your father's great name and lineage. Which we shall not speak of, except for one thing... a related issue, you might say."

"And that is?" Thióðolf asked, peering around to see gleeful faces everywhere among the men.

"It is like this, my friend, that he, seeing as I was already the contrary when I gave her to you..." Arnulf began, a gleam of mischief in his eyes. Hallgrim chuckled and winked at him. Thióðolf looked from one to the other and knew.

"Oh, no; you did *not*," he whispered before he burst out in laughter.

When I woke up that first day in my new home, I found myself alone in the bed and dawn long past. I had slept so profoundly that I had not even noticed how everybody had gotten up and now went about their chores. The Hold was near empty, except for a slave woman who was tending the fire and cooking pots.

She bowed her head to me, saying, "Good morning, Maiden," and offered me a water basin to wash my face in. Then she helped me dry my face before she produced a comb and asked permission to comb my hair. I just nodded, a bit uncertain about how to behave with her. Even if she was friendly enough she was so submissive, although she was an adult.

Apart from the obligatory greeting, she did not speak unless I talked to her, while I was not used to speaking to adults unless they talked to me first. It was odd, being called "Maiden" every time she spoke to me. Thus we hardly spoke at all, what she did not seem to mind. I noticed how dark her hair was, and her eyes were brown. I thought I had heard the other women call her Suri. Rather than asking her any questions, I just sat there and enjoyed the way Suri combed and then plaited my hair.

After the slave had thus groomed me and adjusted my dress a little, she set a small plate of porridge before me, which I ate heartily and drank down with watered beer. Sated and curious about my new home I went out into the courtyard which had temporarily been occupied by slave women working at laundry.

I found Zivah among them, obediently doing her chores and acting correctly, yet still with that air of aloofness that she mastered so well. I knew her better though, and felt her soul had gone far away, leaving only a fragment of herself within her body, for the purpose of survival. I decided to approach her even though I felt uncomfortable and a little worried that she would reject me as harshly as she had before. But when I stood next to her she only bowed her head like a well-behaved slave does towards a free person, while she continued her work.

"What are you doing?" I asked, just to have something to say to my sister. "I am washing the blood of my people off of the clothes of your people," she replied in our mother's language, still with her head bowed, adding, in Norse, a polite "Maiden." I looked at the laundry and realized that the women were washing the clothes that the Vikings had worn during the raid and the entire voyage, and the water had been tinted with a red-brown color. Zivah continued to scrub old and crusted blood off her pile of clothes, and I found nothing more to say to her, nothing that could bring either of us comfort.

It was the truth, what she had spoken, and I felt that I was being shamed, or that my sister thought I ought to be. I understood well why she felt that, seeing as she was still a slave, but I could not see how I could have done anything in any other way, and the saga was not even finished yet. The story just moved on, and I along with it. I had no talent for pondering about how things ought to be when other things had already happened. So, I left all pondering about matters beyond my power to change, and moved on, as I have always done.

Since all the slave women were busy, I went to the stables and found the stable boy tending the horses.

There were ten horses there, all very beautiful, and I had
never seen such beasts up close before, marveling at how large
they were. The best thing about living in a court full of slaves,
I soon found, was that none of them could refuse talking to me
or answering me no matter how much I pestered them, unless
they could excuse themselves because of chores, which they did
surprisingly often.

The stable boy was called Búi, a pleasant looking young
man of strong build and a Finnish appearance to him, always
very sweet and amiable. His name was Norse, though, and he
said that he did not remember his Finnish name, having been
brought to Aldeigjuborg very young and grown up here in
Arnulf's court. Búi was the only male slave who did not sleep in
the Hold, but on a cot in the stable. He did not seem to mind my
presence or my many questions about the horses. Instead, he
told me how to talk to the horses and how to listen to their silent
speech and many signals, and how to please them. Soon I had
greeted and learned the name of each of the horses and touched
them all. When I revealed that I had never in my life ridden one,
the slave boy simply lifted me up and placed me on horseback
for the first time in my life.

"His name is Frost-Fax," Búi said, "a good horse, for a maiden.
I am sure the House-Bond will teach you how to ride if you ask.
All free people should be able to ride."

"Do you think so?" I asked excitedly, and Búi nodded
encouragingly. "If you like, Maiden, I can take you for a round in
the courtyard so that you can get used to the feel, like. Just hold
on to his mane," and then Búi led the horse in circles around the
courtyard while I tried to get the hang of how to ride a horse,
knowing instantly that this was going to be a favorite sport of
mine.

The men had been out early, and came back only when the
laundry was done and the clothes had been hung out to dry.
Thióðolf and Arnulf greeted me and asked me how my day had
been so far. I told them about my horse riding, saying that I
wished I had known how to ride for real, but nobody had ever
taught me. I already knew this was the right way to ask free
men, giving them a chance to grant my wish as if the idea was
theirs in the first place. They both shrugged and grunted absent-
minded in the way I knew meant that they were going to oblige
my wish in their own time, and I said no more, contented.

Then the warriors cleared space in the court for their daily practice at battle arts, with unarmed wrestling as the first sport. Only two at a time wrestled while the others watched and cheered, or just hung around, chatting, or getting ready for partaking in the sport. Some of the younger ones were playing a curious ball game using wooden rackets with which they threw a small ball back and forth, and others played at tugging a rope from either end, trying to make the opposite party lose their balance.

They also practiced jumping as high and as long as possible, or at aiming with archery, spears, daggers, knives and pebbles, or at throwing several objects such as knives up in the air and catching them again without getting hurt. The best ones made a dance out of it, having the other men clap or stomp the rhythm and chant while they were at it.

Sometimes they were hurt anyway. The dark-skinned slave, Shumayl who had met up with us in Khazaria, was, apart from being good with accounts despite being a man, also a Healer, despite being a man. The little Tunic Man had once impressed me with his deep thoughts of Red Gold, and now I discovered that he also knew surprisingly well such age-old women's chores, but then he had very small hands and had obviously had time to devote himself to everything but combat and heavy exercise.

His head was actually broader than his neck, what for me had already become an unusual feature in a man his age. And Shumayl the cunning slave turned out to be an expert surgeon, as efficient as my mother had ever been and obviously accustomed to mending bones and wounds. While the men practiced, the little man waited in the shadows, from where he quietly watched the practicing men, ready to treat anyone who got hurt.

It was rather obvious that he was accustomed to this daily task, yet he seemed to find the court entertaining enough. I tried to join him once, hoping to learn more about the healing arts from him now that I had lost my mother's guidance, but he looked so uncomfortable with my presence that I quickly withdrew and continued to move about the court. I noticed several slave girls who often stopped to admire the training warriors as well, what always made the men work particularly hard.

It was almost surprising that they made such an effort to impress women who could never reject their commands anyway, but there it was, right before my eyes to see. I saw Sígtrygg hiding behind a pillar, trying to straighten his hairdo and one of the other men helping him out before he allowed the man back into the eyesight of their bondswomen. I had never seen such vain men before. They were even posing and showing off their strong bodies to the slave girls, relishing in their responses of shy giggles and playful eye-councils.

I frowned, wondering if Zivah would ever look at these men that way. Since nobody told me what to do, I simply moved around the courtyard, watching everybody carefully, and suddenly I almost crashed with Ivarr, the boy they had told me was Hallgrim's son by Arnulf's sister. He was a young boy, not much older than me, but considerably bigger and stronger. As is the practice of most Norse tribes, Rus boys are raised by men and begin their training from the age of three.

Even if this one was hardly more than eight years old, he was already strong-looking, and he was carrying a wooden practice blade and shield. I was facing the heir of this court for the first time. We both stared at each other for a moment before I remembered my manners and quickly lowered my eyes. The boy seemed to beam with pride, not even averting his own eyes as he should have before he pranced away while I stood and looked after him, the only other child in the entire court. He was even close to my own age.

And yet he seemed to think I was nothing.

The men watched as the girl lowered her eyes submissively to the boy and then noticed how he cocked his head like a conceited rooster, prancing away, so full of himself they felt like giving him a few good kicks in the buttocks.

"Your son has no manners, Hallgrim," Arnulf Heri said, "Young Ivarr there thinks he is a warrior already, and acts like one who was never taught what is holy." The other men nodded in agreement.

"I thought it was the mother's brother who was supposed to provide such lessons. My son lives in a warrior's hall and all the women he knows are slaves. For the most part," Hallgrim said.

"Hmm, you are right, Hallgrim of the Hidden Spear," Arnulf said, "and as I am *his* uncle and you are *her* uncle now, Thióðolf, what do you say if we match our two wards for a most holy game of mutual interests?"

"I think you speak wisely, my Heri," Thióðolf said and smiled, "I shall have to instruct the she-wolf first."

"Oh this is going to be good," said Njál, and they all laughed.

Poor Ivarr.

MAN-MAKER

"Thordís," Thióðolf called me, and waved to signal that I should come to him. He was sitting close to the stables in the company of four other men, Njál and Hallgrim, Sígtrygg and Arnulf. I walked up to them and greeted them. They all smiled brightly at me.

"Why did you lower your eyes to that boy?" Njál asked.

"Because he is a boy," I replied.

"Why on holy Earth would you lower your eyes before a boy?"

"Thióðolf told me to lower my eyes before men," I explained, wondering why he even asked. The men looked amused.

"Exactly, Thordís: Before men. Is that boy a man?" Njál asked.

"No," I shook my head and looked to Thióðolf.

"You should never lower your eyes before a boy, Thordís," he said mildly, "He does not rank above you."

"He does not? But you said that men rank higher," I objected, but Thióðolf shook his head, and so did the other men. This was getting interesting.

"Why do you think a man merits respect?" Hallgrim asked.

"I don't know, Hallgrim, I am just trying to follow the rules. I thought that he ranked higher than me because he is male."

"So you think that you have to respect people just because they have a Freystone dangling between their legs?" Asked Sígtrygg.

"I suppose so," I replied, wondering why the men were grinning. As far as I was concerned it was a very easy and straightforward rule to follow, and all men and boys had Freystones.

"No, Thordís. The Freystone is sacred, but Freyia's Hall is just as sacred, and in no way less powerful. Anybody can have a Freystone. Even dogs have Freystones, and you don't revere them because of it. It is not the Freystone you are supposed to respect," Hallgrim said.

"Not even Arnulf's?" I asked, and gazed curiously at the men who were suddenly beginning to look funny the way people do when they try hard not to laugh out loud. Arnulf looked really proud, but was also laughing inside, his giant shoulders shaking considerably. Even Thióðolf struggled to compose his features. Everybody was obviously suppressing giggles. I thought they were a very strange lot, seeing as my question was utterly sensible from my point of view.

Even if I was but seven, I had seen a bit of the world already, and it was very clear to me that strong and warlike men ruled the world at large for no other reason than because they could. They were obviously neither wiser nor smarter nor better at running and organizing things than anybody else, but they all seemed to possess a knowledge or cunning regarding how to induce submission in less powerful folks such as myself. As far as I had observed, warriors ruled because they could threaten the rest of us with violence and slavery, and deducting from what I had seen,

I was pretty certain that they used their Freystones to induce respect and submission just like they used any other weapon. The lord stone was clearly a part of the reason why they ranked higher than the likes of me, and there was no doubt in my mind that the large size of Arnulf's sky-seeking stone made his one particularly impressive.

I still thought about it now and then and marveled.

All the men looked as if they were trying to read my mind and succeeded. Now they were once more pulling desperately at their beards while coughing and grunting, and I was beginning to suspect that this was their way of trying to not show openly how funny they thought I was. I frowned for a moment before I decided that this was a way of respecting me, and that they thought I was witty rather than foolish. Hallgrim Hidden Spear cleared his throat and gathered his composure first. I looked expectantly at him.

"I will concede that Arnulf's Freystone is a marvel in its own right," Hallgrim began, and then to my surprise, the revered and mysterious shadow walker began to giggle out loud while the other men burst out laughing, Arnulf most of all. I frowned again before I settled for the pleasing realization that I was keeping my kinsmen well entertained without even trying. When they had calmed down, Hallgrim proceeded, "But having a lord stone is still not what it takes for a man to merit respect from women and girls."

"Is it the strength, then?" I asked, still conscious about the fact that the boy had been considerably larger and stronger than me. There would be little point in even trying to rank above him, at least from a practical point of view, which was the only sort of view I found worthy of assuming. Hallgrim grinned.

"No, Wolfling," he said, "it is not the strength either. Look at Búi, the stable boy. He is very big and strong, and he has a Freystone."

"A large one too, I have heard," Njál contributed, grinning, what caused all the men to cast amusedly sideways glances at Runarr, who rolled his eyes in exasperation instead of going red like he usually did when the others teased him. Even Hallgrim broke into more laughing snorts before he proceeded, "That is true, Njál the Foolish. And yet Búi is a slave, and he must bow his head to you, Thordís Maiden."

"Oh," I said, realizing that this was also true. I already had a number of further questions that I wanted to ask, but said nothing, thinking it wiser not to ask too much since the men obviously thought the most practical and mundane of questions were thoroughly amusing.

"A man merits respect when he becomes a warrior, or else great in some manly skill," Hallgrim explained, "and women and girls are those who judge if he is worthy of such respect."

"We do?"

"Yes, Thordís of the Serious Face. You are a warrior's daughter. Your job is to make warriors."

"You mean by giving birth to them? I am a little young for that," I objected. Hallgrim, coughing and pulling at his beard, looked to Thióðolf Skald, who also appeared to have gotten a fit of coughs.

"Women and maidens make warriors in many more ways than by giving birth to them," Thióðolf explained when he had finished coughing, "Some of those ways are fitting only for women grown, but young maidens have a very important duty of their own."

He paused, waiting patiently for me to ask what kind of duty that would be before he continued, "A maiden's way of making warriors is to make a boy's life miserable. You should not lower your eyes to a boy who has not proven his worth. He is not worthy of your respect. You carry the treasure of the birth-giving womb, and so you are worthy in your own right. Boys become worthy only when they have proved themselves worthy. You are already a symbol of everything we live for, Thordís, you are born sacred. That boy, he is nothing at all before he has proven himself. Your mission is to remind him of that fact at all times, Fierce Eyes. Your chore is to taunt and harass him and point out all his weaknesses, stare him down, laugh at him, refuse anything he asks of you. You should make him feel as if he is wading through the rivers of Hel. You should make him cry! You should torment him every way you can."

"Really? What if he gets angry with me? He is big," I mused, feeling worried.

"He cannot touch you, Thordís. You are a girl. You are precious. He would be the laughing stock of the town if he hurt you, and besides, we would beat him half to death if he touched you in any way. It would only prove him a coward if he touched you. He cannot even mock you with words. Oh no, he has to take everything you say and do to him, he will be powerless to stop you, for you are within sacred right to ridicule him endlessly."

"Why?" I asked.

"That is how a boy becomes a warrior, Serious Face. He must hone his anger during battle practice and strive to become the best warrior he can be because that is the only way he can prove himself worthy of your respect. The lousier you make him feel, the more he will dedicate himself to the battle arts and overcome his fears. That is how a maiden makes a warrior, and he will thank you for it, when he comes of age. Come, come Wolfling, you can sit on my knee and I will tell you a story."

I sat on his knee and noticed that all the warriors were listening in, loving the way Thióðolf Skald told stories.

"When I was a boy, my mother told my sister to make my life a never-ending misery, just as I am now telling you to torment that boy every chance you get. Now, it is in a girl's nature to torment boys, so my sister had no problem at all knowing how to terrorize me when she got started. She was horrible to me."

The men chuckled knowingly.

"Is it in our nature?" I asked, puzzled, having never really wanted to torment anyone before.

"Yes, Serious Face, it is in your nature."

All the men nodded with certainty.

"Why?"

"Because girls will become women, and women want warriors. Your kind are man-makers, Thordís, you are blade honers. You want strong men to protect you, so even as children you set about honing boys into men by challenging them endlessly until they become fit to earn your respect for them. It is in your nature to do that. Women can only respect men who are fit to protect them, both in body and soul. At least, that is how our people think, and if you ask me, we are right. Do you wish to hear the story of how I was honed by my sister when I was a boy, now?" Thióðolf asked.

"Please, yes," I said eagerly. We all looked to our skald.

"I was no warrior yet. I was just a boy trying hard to become one. My sister had no reason to respect me yet, and nobody required that of her. On the contrary, everybody encouraged her, humored her and expected her to act as my man-maker, since making a man out of her brother is a sister's most sacred task. It is so because there is no bond stronger than that between siblings, and a brother's first obligation is always to protect his sister. She is his first and most important Síf, and that bond of blood is more sacred than any other. And so she must make a warrior out of him, and she does that by letting him know, at all times, how far removed from a warrior's skill he still is, what spurs him on to actually grow in strength and skill and courage. You have no idea how she taunted me, how she laughed at me, how she pointed out every awkwardness, every sign of cowardice in me. It felt so unfair! She could whine and weep and ask folks to help her, but if I was too weak or too frightened to get something done, she would laugh at me and call me a weakling and a coward. She could ask men to carry things for her while I had to carry everything myself. When I went through my first stone-carrying ordeal, she followed me and taunted me every time I dropped the rock. She never had to prove her courage at all, since, although a free woman cannot be squeamish, nobody expects her to be courageous. She could mock me endlessly for my own lacks, whereas it was unforgivable for me to mock her, since she ranked as the most sacred and precious of all things a man protects, being a young Síf of our clan. I could do nothing to stop her harassment, because trying to stop her in any way would only have shown me unmanly. I went great rounds to avoid her, Thordís, living in fear of her mockery every day. Ah! How I suffered!"

He laughed, and the men around also chuckled, remembering their own sisters, and Sígtrygg commented, "I had three of them. Three sisters out of Hel's serpent pit, sleeping in the same hall as me. And one female cousin. I thought myself surrounded by rabid she-wolves. There was no end to their mockery or to their demands that I do this or that for them. They treated me like a stinking turd!"

The men all laughed affectionately, looking surprisingly fond of their sisters, as abusive as they had been towards them.

Thióðolf proceeded with his story: "But then came the day when I finally was deemed fit to join the clan's men in a little, well, it was a little squabble with another clan. One of our Sífs had been offended, actually. Not enough to merit death, but just so much that we had to make a point. If a woman is disrespected by a man of another clan, it is not only an offense to a person we hold dear, but also a way of saying that the men of her clan are weaklings, and so we had to settle the matter. Now, we did not kill anyone, but we gave them a good beating that day, and I received my first scar. It was just a scratch, really."

He pointed to a scar on his cheek. "My mother had been a Healer, and my father's body had been covered in scars what origins he had explained to me, one after the other, so I could easily see that the scar had been more than just a scratch. A few inches further up, and he would have lost an eye."

"This is not a scratch, Thióðolf," I said, "This came from a deep cut." There were some raised eyebrows and nods of appreciation of my skillful observation. Thióðolf beamed with pride for me.

"Ah, you are wise in such matters already," he exclaimed, impressed, "but when a man has seen a few fights, this one seems more like a scratch than a cut. But it was my first battle wound, and I was very proud of it then, especially as it was in my face, for everyone to see. All the men patted my back and called me a warrior, which made me feel great. It was nothing to how great I felt when we returned home and my sister greeted me. For the first time ever, she came towards me and averted her eyes before me, called me a warrior and welcomed me home. And then she respectfully asked permission to tend my wound for me, which I, of course, granted her. It was a great day for me, Thordís. I even asked her to fetch something for me, just to see if she would, and she did, smiling! She had never served me before, but now that she gave me the thing I had asked for, I thanked her, and then she lowered her eyes to me, to show that she was willing to obey me."

All the men appeared very moved at his story.

"That was when I swore my first oath as a man; I swore to always protect her and avenge any slights against her, and the same for any children she might have. We became great friends later, and I have always respected her, been grateful to her because she had spent so much time honing me, spurring me into growing courage and skill, just to prove myself worthy of her respect. She made a man out of me. She made me a warrior. She is a norn in my eyes, and a goddess in my heart. I pray I will always be worthy of the respect she now shows to me." Thióðolf turned to me and looked very serious, although his eyes seemed to be laughing.

"Now, you are a warrior's daughter. You are by nature a man-maker and a blade honer," he said. The men nodded enthusiastically.

"And when she is grown, she will be a natural spear enticer," Njál guffawed. Thióðolf and the others glared at him.

"Are you disrespecting our Síf, Njál?" Thióðolf sneered.

"I am sorry, Thióðolf Skald," Njál said quickly and bowed his head apologetically, "I meant no disrespect. It is just that she is pretty. She will become a beautiful woman. Cannot help seeing that, foolish as I am." Thióðolf seemed content with the apology and turned to me again.

"Yes, you are pretty, and the scorn of a pretty girl is worse than everything. Now, that boy over there, his name is Ivarr by the way, he is not your brother, but he is Arnulf's nephew, and you are now Arnulf's fosterling, and so you are the closest thing to a sister for him, and you are required to spend a lot of time honing him. You will never lower your eyes before him again, not until he has proven himself a warrior. You must stare him down, glare at him as much as you like, and if you find it worthwhile, you make his life a misery. If you ever see him doing something you think is awkward or cowardly, you may point it out. Laugh at him as much as you wish. You can even tell him to do things for you."

I shifted uneasily on my feet and peered over at the boy, who was practicing at blade-wielding. He was a tad bit too scary-looking for me to imagine taunting him like they said, and I felt as if I would have to be mean to him, what I had never intentionally been to anyone.

Then Njál the Foolish and Sharp-Toothed squatted down beside me, patted my upper back gently and smiled to me. "Serious Face, our little kit, I mean, our little Wolfling, we men have your back. Do not worry. But you ought to do as Thióðolf says, as we are all telling you to. It is your duty to do so. If you don't, if you act as if he was already a warrior, he will be full of himself and think himself far above his actual skills. We have seen how this happens among other people, where weaklings and cowards prance around pretending greatness, and their women keep humoring them because they know no better kinds of men, and because they are expected to humor men.

"A man will become weak instead of strong, for he will not think it necessary to aspire to greater skill and courage. And then he is likely to die during his first battle. After a fashion, your mockery may save his life."

"So I can glare at him?" I asked, feeling how my spirits lifted. It had occurred to me that I, being but a maiden among warriors, could not glare at anyone anymore, unless they were helpless slaves, which would be rather unrewarding. I rather missed it after that first evening with the Vikings. I could still remember how all these violent and powerful men kept averting their eyes in awe of me.

It seemed like such a novel notion now.

"You can glare at him as much as you like," Hallgrim smiled.

"And mock him?"

"Absolutely," Sígtrygg assured me..

"And he cannot touch me or mock me back?"

"Absolutely not. That is how he learns the self-control of a warrior," Arnulf confirmed.

"Ah," I exclaimed, beaming with anticipation.

"Don't look so gleeful," Thióðolf grinned.

"Sorry, Thióðolf," I bowed my head apologetically.

"I am just joking, She-Wolf," he laughed, "You go and enjoy yourself thoroughly. He may not know it yet, but one day he will realize what you have done for him and thank you in all his prayers forever after. For now, he will suffer, and you will enjoy his suffering. It is in your nature to enjoy this game, your glee is exactly what makes you maidens so good at it. Let him know every day that he is yet but a useless boy, while you are a girl, and so you carry the most sacred well of fate within, and need not prove yourself because you were born worthy. You are sacred and precious, a young Sif of this court. He is nothing, and it is your job to remind him of that fact, so that he will work hard to one day become something of worth. Smile, and be as gleeful as you like about it! Nobody will think any less of you for being cruel to a boy. We men all know the truth. You are making a warrior."

"Oh." I was feeling a little dizzy. And just that moment Ivarr walked past, and I glared at him so hard he startled and stumbled, falling over, upon which I surprised myself by saying loudly, "Did you see how that little boy fell over, warriors? It looks like he just learned how to walk."

The men laughed heartily. Ivarr got to his feet and looked all red and confused before he scurried away. That was for scorning me before, I thought viciously, next time you will be more courteous and there will be no lowering of my eyes before you have proven yourself as a man.

Then I realized that Thióðolf was right.

This was certainly in my nature.

⊕LADE ⊕ONER

"You see, Fierce Eyes," Thióðolf continued, smiling, "it is a sacred trust. Ivarr will thank you for this one day. Oh, Thordís, this may be difficult to see now because you find yourself in a Viking court and not in a typical sort of court that I grew up in, but this game of honing is one that serves to tie deep bonds between a kinsman and his Sif. Our women tend to adore us, just as we adore them, and we make each other strong. I have been many places in the world and never seen any people whose warriors are as strong as our own. Do you know why we are so strong, Thordís of the Serious Face?"

"No. Why?"

"Because our women are strong. Our women are strong and merciless. They have no respect for cowards, and are not required to. Women bear forth the new generations, and because of that, women are sacred. Women give us all the food we eat, all the beer and ale and mead that we drink and all the clothes that we wear. They make our halls splendid, they make the sails of our ships, they raise our children and give good counsel, on account of being wise beyond a man's grasp. They heal our hurts and dress our wounds and mend our broken bones and hearts as well. And they make us happy. They are our reason for smiling, our reason for living. They nourish us in every way. We are born from them. Our children are born from them. Women provide."

I peered doubtfully at the men. The Rus had not treated the women of my mother's people as something holy at all. They had used them and sold them like cattle. But there they sat, grunting their agreements to Thióðolf's speech, and said that women were sacred and strong.

"I know, Thordís," Thióðolf said, even though I had said nothing, "You are too intelligent to not see the discrepancy between our speech now and our actions before, and how things are done here. But Aldeigjuborg is a very small part of our world, little one. It is all you have seen so far, but there is so much more, and so much more diversity. This place is," he looked uncertainly at the other men. He looked a little worried that he had spoken too much. But the men did not look offended. They looked, embarrassed, perhaps. I could not be sure.

"The Rus are uprooted," Hallgrim Hidden Spear volunteered, suddenly grave, "We have lived too long beyond the reach of law and justice, too long without clans, too long without Sífs and children of our own. We have become prey to the weakness of needing to be humored by those who have no other option in life than to humor us if we command it.

"Man is the trunk of the tree, but woman is the roots and the branches. The weaker the roots, the weaker the trunk, and likewise above, and the whole tree topples. I have seen that our strength and our capacity for glory will wane in time if this continues. We need to restore the ancient balance, Thordís. But we have to play it carefully. We have been Vikings for so long we know no other way. I am the first to admit we are very proud men, and there are but a very few among us who are capable of seeing this, but we who sit here with you now do see this, even if it may be hard for you to believe."

I looked cautiously at Arnulf Heri, who, surprisingly enough, nodded to confirm what Hallgrim had just said.

"We have thought that your arrival here must be an opening," said Hallgrim, "something to start with, if you like. So, we would like to educate you in the traditional manners of our people, just as we would like to educate young Ivarr in the same. This is why we now are teaching you the ancient lore even when you yourself can see that it is somewhat out of date in this place."

They all looked carefully at me, and I felt a slight chill. Something within stirred, something ancient and powerful, that told me yes. Yes.

"I will accept your training, Warriors," I said, and they broke out in fond smiles.

"Thordís," Thióðolf said, "We men became warriors a long time ago in order to protect women and children. Norsemen became warriors to defend their Sífs and their little ones from the onslaughts of foreign Vikings. This is the ancient trust of our people. You have seen yourself what may happen to a people who fail to produce warriors capable of defending their women. If we had not become warriors we would have ended up like the river land people, easy prey. You have seen how women are vulnerable. You are open like gates and you may easily be seized by those who will destroy you, and so men must protect. I told you that women are sacred to us, and that women provide. Women have no use for weaklings hanging at their skirts like big babies. Why should they provide for us unless we make ourselves useful?"

36

"Because you force them?" I asked, thinking about their slaves.

"We are not speaking of our slaves now," Arnulf replied, "We are speaking of our Sífs, our own women; our sisters and mothers, daughters and wives. We would be less than men if we forced our own women as if they were our slaves. Even I grew up with strong women as well as slaves, and I was honed by my sister and by my mother and grandmother. If you had already seen how certain other Vikings behave around here you would be able to see the difference between me and them. It is true what Thióðolf says. Our Sífs have no patience with men who are weak. They hone us and challenge us, and when we earn their respect they reward us by showing respect and honoring our rank. We struggle all our childhoods and youths to earn the right to be respected and honored as warriors by our women. But we would never have struggled this hard to become strong if our women were humoring us along the way, like they do in other lands, where weak men prance around and think they are great on account of being humored by their womenfolk all the time."

The men nodded and grunted, and I was all ears.

"Most folks have forgotten why men must be honed and challenged by women," Hallgrim proceeded when Arnulf nodded at him, "I think we are the only people left in the world what remember this sacred trust. In other places, men are so fearful of the taunting of women that they forcefully forbid women from ever taunting men. And the result is that their boys grow into wimps. Their women do not respect them at all. They are just forced to pretend that they do."

"Like our slaves," Njál grinned, and the other men chuckled.

"Imagine that, being so fearful of disapproving verdicts from your own sister or wife you forbid it. That is the down bottom of cowardice," Sígtrygg said, and the men agreed with their grunts.

"I do not mean any disrespect, warriors," I argued, "but all the women in this court appear to be slaves. They cannot disapprove of you, can they? They cannot give verdicts?"

"As said, we are now speaking of traditions, the ancient ways of Norsemen," Arnulf said and snorted dismissively. I could think of a verdict or two for that attitude, but sensed the importance of caution around my lord. He wanted a blade honer, but Mother had told me that men do not always know what their wishes really mean.

For the time being, I would be their blade honer just the same way as I had been their Hel Maiden, entertaining them until I knew better my true standing among them. I had no choice but to trust Arnulf, but I was not going to trust him more than I had to. The men said nothing to their Heri's speech and conveniently let their minds wander towards the related topic of slave women.

"Oh, I have heard some fine verdicts," Sígtrygg the Týr-man said, grinning, "and they tend to be acted upon."

"I hear you. Our girls can disapprove fine," Njál agreed, and all the men nodded and grinned very broadly.

"They can?" I asked curiously, but the men did not seem to hear me.

"Let us just say that we have found ways around the issue of slave and master in this court," Hallgrim smiled, "but it is true that it can never work in the same way. You have seen how we are, being men without roots and home and hardly a Síf in sight."

The men nodded sadly.

"It is different in the homelands, Thordís," Thióðolf continued, "You will not see nearly as many slaves compared to free people there. I come from a different place, a place far to the northwest of North Path Island. The entire west coast of that island is a great mountain ridge going north, so we call that land North Way, and there are some thirty tribal lands there, of which I belong to a place called Hálógaland, far to the north. We have free women everywhere, many Sífs. And our women hone us. We honor the old ways of the blade wielder and the blade honer."

Thióðolf paused and searched his mind.

"You know how we teach you to respect men?" he asked.

"It is very hard not to be aware of that here," I said, and the men began to laugh hard again.

"Our ways are old and have a purpose, a purpose that was devised by very wise women and men a long time ago," Thióðolf said when they had calmed down again, "To make our men into strong warriors we needed to become ruling sorts of men. We could not let those we were to protect order us around. But we had long been the guardians of the Red Gold, and there was a great deal of wisdom among us. When we became warriors and rulers, we swore that we would never accept conceit in our midst. We had seen the soft lives of men in other lands, men who were conceited, men who were laughable and weak, cowardly and sneaky, and yet they believed themselves great and brave and powerful, for their women were humoring them and let them think that they were worthy of respect."

"Why would free women humor their men if they were not worthy?"

"Because they have no choice and expect no more," Hallgrim replied, knowing the story.

"Only if our Sífs could respect us and truly accept our ruling would we be worthy," Thióðolf said, "So, our ancestors devised a path where women are taught what to expect from men, and men are taught to strive to live up to women's expectations. A woman's respect and obeisance is not something that can be forced, but something that must be merited. Our Sífs are living verdicts on our honor and our manliness, our ability to protect them and make them happy. We demand respect from our women because, you see, if a woman disrespects a warrior, she is in effect saying that he is not worthy of her respect, because he is a coward, or dishonorable. She has the right to do that, if she truly thinks him unworthy, but it is a very serious matter, Thordís. It is a matter of life and death, peace and war."

"Why?"

"If a man is taunted by a woman, he will have to prove himself," Arnulf stated, to the grunting agreements of all the men.

"Free women have the right to speak out their verdict on men's honor, and they have the right to avenge any disrespect against themselves," Hallgrim explained, "and they have the right to hone men into greater men. And so a woman can hone a kinsman, or a man what she likes to test his worthiness, and she can publicly taunt a man she regards as cowardly or dishonorable, but she will have to be careful how she does it, and to whom. She must be especially careful if the man is not of her clan. Countless heroes have been born from the honing scorn of women, but even more have turned into corpses from the same thing, and it is not always the man who was taunted what becomes a corpse. Sometimes a taunting woman has found herself bereft of clansmen and unprotected. There is taunting what hones, and there is taunting what only leads to disaster, even for the woman herself. It is a subtle game."

"But what if she is angry with a man outside of the clan then?"

"Even if you are angry and with good reason, it is still very important that you always respect warriors outside of the clan, She-Wolf," Hallgrim said gravely, but then smiled and continued, "Inside the clan you are freer. If you think a kinsman somewhat lacking in honor and manliness, you may hone him, and you would hone him by transgressing rank." Hallgrim winked at Thióðolf, who went a deep red.

"We hone by transgressing rank?" I asked, looking from one to the other. "Little Priestess," Arnulf exclaimed, "you transgressed rank terribly last night, and you know it!"

The men gathered began to giggle loudly, no longer bothering to restrain themselves at all, looking teasingly at me. I peered cautiously from one to the other and had a feeling they all knew about my very rude little intervention in the affairs of a free man and warrior last night. Surprisingly, I could see that they liked well what I had done. I felt my shoulders relax a little.

"When you transgress rank for the purpose of honing a man into becoming a better man, he will respond, at least if he is a Norseman, although there are dishonorable exceptions. He may even be moved to heroism. What also means he could end up dead, so a Síf who loves or needs her kinsman will be wise to think it over first. But in less serious matters we encourage our Sífs to let us know about our failings by way of transgressing rank. As our Síf you are free to do that, though, with us, at least as far as you understand the rules and ways and what you must and what you cannot expect. But when you see men from other courts, Little Priestess, you must be respectful towards them no matter how dishonorably they behave."

"Why?"

"It is as we told you. A Síf's verdict is our assessment of our greatness as men and warriors. But a woman from another tribe or clan or court, that is another matter. A Síf is the mouthpiece of her clansmen. Whatever you do or say to men from the outside can be interpreted as a message from us. We use our women as messengers, you see."

"Why women?"

"Because you can say things men cannot say and still live," Arnulf declared, "It has to do with courtesy. It will not do to harm the soft."

"Oh," I said. I peered at Arnulf and thought it somewhat surprising to hear him speak of courtesy towards the soft. But there are rules and there are other sorts of rules, and rules keep shifting according to place and time of year too, as I kept discovering was the case among these men.

"And so we may use a Síf as our war-Freyia and send her to declare war with another court simply by telling her to glare and never lower her eyes to their men. It is a way of saying that our woman has reason to disrespect them, a way of saying that we think them dishonorable, and that she feels confident that her clansmen can kill them all. We only do that if we really hate those men and want to fight them and know that we can. See?"

"But…" I was a bit taken aback by that sort of responsibility, "What if a woman forgets herself? What if I was to be so angry with some warrior that I was disrespectful to him and did not get to apologize properly?"

"If that happens you may want to run back and tell your clansmen immediately, so that they will not be taken by surprise when the enemy attacks," Hallgrim said gravely. The others grunted and looked quite frightful and gloomy all of a sudden.

"Would you, would I be punished?" I asked meekly.

"Not by us. Your actions are ruled by the fates. We would fight for you. But you might find your kinsmen on the losing side and yourself unprotected and left to the mercy of that man you offended in the first place. So if a man from the outside offends you seriously it will be a very good thing if you could consult your clansmen before you do anything rashly. Leave it up to us and you may just end up with a head gift," Arnulf replied and winked at me.

I felt an awkward, pricking sensation in my face.

"She is blushing," said Sígtrygg, looking amused. They all looked amused. And there was something else too, something in their eyes when they looked at me. Like admiration and... I suspected that they were actually proud of me for some reason. I had seen that light in other eyes before. They looked as if they thought I had accomplished something of importance.

"We heard you are the sort of girl what gets to hold her enemy's head in her hands," Hallgrim said, and they all smiled fondly at me.

"I suppose I was boasting," I admitted, "but my father said I would not lack for head gifts when he gave one to my sister."

All the men seemed to be holding their breaths all of a sudden.

"Your father gave a head-gift to Ziv, to your sister?" Arnulf asked nervously, and I thought his eyes had gone wide for a moment.

"To Zivah, yes. She has actually held the head of her enemy in her hands," I said, feeling proud, seeing as all the men were obviously very impressed to the point of being terrorized by this information about my family life, mighty Arnulf Heri most of all.

"Well that explains a great deal," Sígtrygg muttered, finally letting out his breath as did the other men. They stretched their spines, whistled mutedly and exchanged very meaningful glances. I thought they looked relieved about something. I cleared my throat.

"May I ask what that explains?" I asked.

"Let us just say there is a powerful spell in that sort of gifting," Hallgrim said thoughtfully before he turned to me with those inscrutable dark pool eyes of his, "I should say that I have no problem imagining that you, Thordís Maiden, could get a whole rack of silver skull cups for your collection if you so wished."

"Do you so wish, Wolfling?" Njál the Foolish asked curiously, and they all looked expectantly at me. The whole courtyard had gone silent and they were all listening to our conversation.

They were all looking at me like they were expecting me to surprise them pleasantly. The fearsome Rus Vikings looked as feral as ever, but now I did not think that they were frightening anymore. They were my friends. All this time I had strived to secure their friendliness for the sake of their protection and the possibility that they would not hurt Zivah too much. That moment it dawned on me that I really liked them all. I forgot all the terrible things that they had done when I found myself embraced by them.

Brothers. They were my brothers. As I stood there gazing fondly at their friendly bearded and scarred faces, something strange seemed to happen to my face again. This time my cheeks seemed to pull themselves out to each side of their own accord.

"By the glory of all the gods and goddesses," Njál said brightly, "she smiles!"

"She smiles," the men of the court whispered, and smiled back at me. All the warriors of the court were looking at me, and they were all smiling. Ivarr did not, of course, but he was just a boy. I could not help myself around these funny men. I smiled for the first time since my brother Thorolf died. I looked at Njál's happy face and suddenly thought his vicious fangs were a rather entertaining sight.

"I suppose I would like to have as many silver skull cups as I get to have enemies," I declared, smiling broader and broader.

My new brothers broke out in loud cheers and war dances where they played at bringing me my head gifts, and called me 'Serious Face' no more.

THE NEW SLAVE

After having served her House-Bond his water and happy to not have had to comb his hair, Zivah had helped out in the Hold, and found that it was relaxing to work with the other women, especially as they were all being so kind to her. It was odd to think that she had always taken the affection and kindness of other people for granted. Now she was deeply grateful for every kindness shown to her. It was so precious, so precious. A gift from the goddess.

When most of the men had disappeared from the courtyard, the slaves had started on the laundry. Aziza had told her that she did not need to be there. The women had encouraged her to go inside and rest in her master's bed while the men were out. They had really not wanted her to partake in that work. Zivah had looked at the soiled and stained clothes that the other slaves were carrying to be boiled.

Then she had looked at the others and remembered the way they had comforted her the evening before, and how they had made her feel that she was not alone anymore, that she was one of them. She would honor their kindness and be their sister right back, and besides, she needed to move on. Her mother had told her that it was important to face a deep hurt if one was ever to be healed.

Zivah had drawn her breath and declared that she needed to do this. The slaves had made space for her and watched her carefully and even somewhat awed as she handled the clothes stained with the blood of her people. She had not cried even once. Zivah would not cry anymore, and when the maiden had appeared after sleeping in quite some time, asking what she was doing, she had felt a triumph when she said those words of rejection to the little traitor.

The Sun stood rather high before five giggling women emerged from the Hall where all the free men slept apart from Arnulf and Thióðolf. As far as Zivah could tell there were some thirty men sleeping in that hall. The women still looked sleepy and really needed to comb their hairs. They also walked with some strain and were brawling and giggling as if they were drunk. Now they sat down with the other slave girls, talking loudly and laughing, making the other girls laugh as well.

Zivah noticed that all five of them wore lilac-colored bead necklaces that were similar to the concubines' green bead necklaces, and guessed that these necklaces somehow identified these women as a certain type of slave. They were quite spectacular women, she thought, all unusually pretty, not to say playful and loud. They had obviously had a lot of strong draught last night too. Zivah looked from one to the other, and noticed that the one who was brawling most loudly had deep grey eyes with thick dark lashes to frame them, eyes the shape of almonds, and high cheek bones.

Her hair was dark, almost black, yet her skin was a pale yellow. Her body was small and slim, yet quite strong and very supple. Now she was standing before everybody while talking loudly and moving to illustrate all the points that she was trying to make, while the others laughed so hard they almost rolled over. The other lilac bead women assisted the first one by way of shrieking agreements and confirmatory movements. They were very suggestive movements also, what made Zivah blush deeper and deeper as she began to figure out what they were explaining so merrily.

The excitement was such that Zivah had problems understanding all they were saying, but she gathered enough to know that they were joking and that they were joking about men. She peered cautiously at them and felt chilled when she grasped what they had been doing all night. Or what had been done to them. How they could look so cheerful she did not know, after having spent the night with thirty beasts. The fear gripped her throat when she realized that these women were so used to it they did not even care anymore.

They were laughing about it and making jokes. These people are insane, she thought, insane, insane! They own me. Suddenly the loud gray-eyed woman with the messy hair and lilac beads looked directly at Zivah, frowned and said, "What is up with the new girl? She looks like she is going to puke any moment."

One of the other women leaned over and whispered to the woman, who raised her eyebrows before she turned and looked at Zivah again. There was compassion in her eyes, even pity. Zivah could not even understand how that woman could pity her. She was not the one who had just spent her night being gang-raped in a hall full of brutes.

"Zivah," the woman said, "My name is Miri, and these here are my sisters. Now Harawa, here, she is from Big Tunic Land."

"We call it Persia, Miri, it is not exactly the same," Harawa smiled and nodded amiably at Zivah. "Never mind," Miri said, ignoring her sister while turning to the next one, "And this here is Tziki, now she is from Miklagard, which is like the old Roman Empire or something."

"The land of the Hellenes," Tziki, a sweet-faced woman with dark greenish eyes and chestnut hair giggled proudly and nodded in greeting before Miri turned to the next one, "Now this here is Rada," she proceeded and waved to a dark blonde woman with light blue eyes, "She was born a slave to the Tschudes and knows little more than that about her origin, which is exactly what I can say about myself, only I was born a slave among the Khazars." Rada nodded to Zivah and smiled. Finally, Miri turned to the last of the lilac bead women, the one whose skin was almost as dark as soil and whose eyes and curly hair was a deep black, "and here we have Saxa. Now she had a different name before, when she lived down in Blue Land. She is a Blue Woman, as you can see, or at least half Blue or something."

"My first name was too difficult to pronounce for them, so the men here just called me Iarnsaxa," dark-skinned Saxa explained proudly and pointed at an iron scissor lying close, and Zivah realized that her name meant Iron Scissors in Norse. She frowned.

"It is on account of her iron thighs, you see," Miri explained while Saxa showed off her powerful thighs to the merry delight of the other women. "Only we usually just call her Saxa," she concluded before turning formally to Zivah. "We are the Sheaths of the Hall and we welcome you, Zivah. We are your sisters too, now."

Zivah nodded to all the five women who were now looking brightly at her, trying to let her know that they were friendly. She tried to smile back at them, but it was so hard.

"What is, uhm, what is sheath?" she asked.

The congregation of slaves began to giggle.

"It is the thing sword-men stick their swords into for safe keeping," Harawa said and giggled. Zivah looked at the Persian woman and thought she must be from some place similar to that of Shumayl and Aziza, although she was less dark of skin, but had the same dark hair and dark eyes. Then she figured out what the woman had just said and blushed. All the women began laughing.

"It is joke?" Zivah said, trying to smile.

"No, it is not joke, Zivah," Miri said, "this is probably new to you, but it is actually a title. We are officially the Sheaths of Arnulf's court. It is a very respectable title too, we have privileges and all. Like sleeping in and getting to watch you girls do the laundry."

Everybody laughed again, but not because it was a joke. They laughed because it was both hilarious and true. While they continued working on the laundry, the Sheaths of the Hall entertained them by going through the various techniques of fucking that they had experienced the night before, showing how they had been taken in diverse manners, showing how with lewd movements and detailed descriptions that made all the women roll over in shrieking laughter, seemingly without end.

Each man was named and described and his conduct mercilessly given over to the verdicts of their Sheaths to the near hysterical amusement of the other women. Zivah looked around and saw the few free men who were still in court, and knew that even if they stood with their backs turned, they were listening intently to everything that was going on. They did not seem to mind at all. In fact, she thought she saw their broad shoulders shaking with laughter. She even saw a ring change owner, and knew that the men often did that when they had bet on something or other.

They were all insane.

When all the men returned and took over the courtyard for their practices, the slaves went about other chores, and there was a time in the afternoon when the slave women sat down to spin. The women sat together in a circle and spun while they chanted a strange song. It was relaxing, Zivah found, although she had never spun thread in her whole life before. But the people here seemed to be wearing a lot of textile and not as much leather and fur.

Zivah caught on to the spinning rather quickly and enjoyed the long song that was led by Laimi while the other women chanted the refrain. She did not get all the words because they put their words in such strange order when they sung, more to create rhyme than to create meaning, it seemed to her. It would take a long time before she discovered the key to understand the meanings of the songs by truly grasping all the various forms and meanings a word could take. It seemed to be the form of the word and not where it was placed that mattered.

Whether Zivah understood the words or not it was peaceful work, and all the women started to look drowsy and relaxed. She was starting to feel good now, somehow. This was not quite as bad as she had thought it would be, although from where she had been she was just grateful for anything that was less bad than real bad. At least she was no Sheath.

Suddenly, the women stopped singing. Zivah looked around and saw them all sit there with bowed heads. She looked up and saw that horrible man they called Hialti standing there watching them with leering, rat-like eyes. She met his gaze but for a moment and quickly bowed her head, feeling her heart beat.

If she remembered correctly Hialti was the one who had gotten the lousiest verdict from the Sheaths, and she had heard them call him Rat-Hialti. He really did look like some sort of hungry vicious rat.

"Slave," he wheezed, grinning viciously, and tapped the shoulder of a very young woman they called Tana. Tana got up with her head bowed and followed him. The women immediately resumed their singing. Zivah joined them uncertainly, but kept casting glances at the space where Tana had been sitting.

Tana was not one of their Sheaths. She was just one of the servant girls who did all sorts of chores and slept in Arnulf's Hold at nights. After a while, the girl returned and sat down. She took up her spinning and her singing and nobody spoke about it. Zivah cast a careful glance at the youngest slave woman and saw that she was trying to force back tears, without quite succeeding. Tana spun and her tears ran, but she kept singing until the tears stopped and she was smiling again.

The women next to Tana patted her back, and began singing a song that seemed to have a rather angry beat to it. It was song about how the rat had caught a mouse and thought himself great for that sake, only to be ridiculed when it was pointed out that the mouse had already been trapped. It was a funny song, but nobody laughed while they sang it, and they spun hard and they spun angrily. And the men who stood with their backs turned and pretended not to listen, they seemed to be beating the rhythm too, with their feet.

They were all crazy.

When they took a small break, she dared to ask one of the other girls, the giggly one called Suri.

"Hialti, he fuck Tana?" she whispered. Suri nodded.

"What about Sheaths? They have Sheaths for that?" she asked nervously.

"Yes, the Rus have the Sheaths living in their halls, to spend their nights with. But there is only one Sheath for six Sword-men, so they use us too whenever it pleases them," the other woman replied, "in the day only, though. We work more so we need our sleep."

"Any man? On any slave?" Zivah whispered.

"Of course," the girl said, "they are our Heris, all of them. If a Heri calls you. You must go with him. What the Heri says, you do, because you are a slave." Zivah went pale. "Unless you are a Sheath or a concubine," Suri explained, "Aziza and Laimi, they are off-limits to all men but Arnulf, unless he makes exceptions. In the case of the Sheaths they are only available to the men who own them in particular – unless they make exceptions. The rest of us are fair game to all the free folks whenever they want, but we are allowed to spend our nights in the Hold where only Arnulf has the right to use us."

"Arnulf has the right to use us?" Zivah squeaked.

"Of course. Arnulf Heri is our House-Bond, and we are his slaves. But do not worry about him, Zivah, he never uses that right. Oh, perhaps it has happened, especially with a new, oh dear." Suri paused to worry about how pale Zivah had gone. Then she shook her head, deciding that it was probably better for the new girl to simply know the facts.

"Zivah, Arnulf is not actually your House-Bond and he would probably not use you without asking Thióðolf first. But truly, if Arnulf commands, you better obey at once, no questions asked. He is the lord of everybody here, including your master, for as long as you live in his court. The rules that apply to us generally apply to you as well, unless dispensations are made formally."

"So they can all…" Zivah could not finish her question, already knowing the answer painfully well. Suri sighed, remembering this morning.

"Zivah, you are only safe from being commanded by the other men if your House-Bond declares you unavailable. Which is why you may want to start to address your House-Bond as House-Bond and begin smiling to him. If he makes you his concubine you are safe from these men. If not, you are fair game." Suri smiled and patted Zivah's back encouragingly, "And if I were you I would try to get that one hot on you as soon as possible, for he is a better master and according to Aziza a better fuck than any of these other men here."

Zivah was feeling dizzy. She would surely go mad in this place.

A great cheer suddenly broke out from the courtyard, and the women stopped their spinning and their singing, listening. Suri went to look and returned.

"They are having a party!" She exclaimed, and the women got up, looking excited.

They left their work just like that and ran out into the courtyard together, where they stood by and watched their masters who were suddenly dancing out there, taking turns dancing and jumping and hurling themselves through the air. Zivah had never seen anything like it. The closest thing she had seen were the hunters when they danced the story of a great hunt to come, or one that had happened in the past. But those dances had been nothing at all like this.

The men were standing around in a sort of circle, stomping the beat with their feet and by clashing their swords against their shields, while other men danced within that circle, like acrobats, dancing dances of battle and combat and the slicing of necks and the carrying of heads. And each dancer ended up offering an imaginary head to Zivah's little sister, who stood there beaming, and smiling broadly at them all.

Thunder Goddess was smiling again.

Zivah had not seen Thordís smile since that day when Thunder Wolf died. She had always remembered the last time the girl smiled at her. Little sister smiling at Zivah while she pushed her away, and then she had run, and Zivah after. And then Thunder Wolf had died and Thunder Bear had blamed Zivah for it, or at least that was how it had seemed.

Now Thordís stood there smiling at her kinsmen who were dancing war dances in her honor.

They seemed to think she was their queen. Her little sister was a Viking Rus queen while Zivah was a slave who could be called on and fucked by any of her superiors at any time. She looked around and saw the slave women shout and scream encouraging words to the men who owned them as if they were cows, clapping the beat with their hands, moving their hips, dancing joyfully in response to the games of the court.

Zivah withdrew from the party and went to sit inside the bath room, trying to breathe. She did not even look up when Aziza sat down next to her and put an arm around her.

"Are you sad, Zivah?" Aziza asked. She nodded. The woman who felt like Mother asked why.

"Thordís…" Zivah whispered, "Maiden is sister. Sister to Zivah. Same mother."

"Now I see," Aziza muttered, "oh, gods, Zivah."

Later, when the news had been passed to all the slaves of the Hold and Hall, they came to her, one by one. They said the same things to her.

"Let the Maiden keep her brothers, Zivah. We are your sisters now," the women said.

"We are your brothers, Zivah," the man-slaves said.

The goddess was merciful.

⊗ITY ⊗OUNCIL

A few days after their arrival in Aldeigjuborg, Zivah was as yet left alone by the men, including her House-Bond, who had let Thordís sleep between them every night. The little girl still slept in his arms, what Zivah thought odd, but the child trusted the man even after what he had done to her own sister in the market that day.

Thióðolf Heri seemed to be very fond of her, even to the point of loving her. Rather than leaving the girl over to the care of the slave women, the Rus appeared to want to raise her themselves, and Thióðolf had obviously been given the main role of parent. While eagerly attending his little charge, he ignored his new bonds-woman as much as he could, what suited Zivah fine.

There was no way around the daily morning ritual where she had to serve him his water and towel for washing, and she had to attend him whenever he needed someone else to groom him in any way. They never spoke again while this grooming happened, not after that awkward moment on that very first morning when he had tried to have a conversation with her.

It still felt awkward, being that close and never exchanging neither words nor gazes.

"Why he wants me to serve him?" She asked Aziza on the third day, after leaving her master to eat, "He not like it better than I like it."

"You are his slave and we are Arnulf's slaves," Aziza explained, "it would be very rude of him to demand any attention from his host's slaves unless freely offered by the host."

"I wish Arnulf Heri offer," Zivah muttered.

"But it would be very rude of Arnulf Heri to offer such help when Thióðolf Heri already has a slave to do that," Aziza said, "that would be like insinuating that Thióðolf Heri cannot get proper help from his own slave."

"Rus crazy," Zivah snorted, making sure no men were facing her way while she spoke such words.

"Thióðolf Heri is not a Rus, Zivah. He is... oh I do not remember the place, but he is just a Norseman."

"Norseman all crazy."

"Norsemen, Zivah," Laimi corrected her, "Norsemen are all crazy."

"That is so true," Suri giggled.

"Thank you for words, Laimi," Zivah muttered and repeated, almost wheezing, "Norsemen are all crazy." She shook her head when she saw that she had made the other women laugh heartily in agreement, as if they thought that was a nice thing. She shook her head even more when she noticed that some of the Norsemen who were standing nearby with their backs turned, also giggled, only serving to prove her point.

On that day there was suddenly a commotion among the men, who were washing and grooming themselves with the help of their Sheaths, each other and some of the serving girls. Zivah had to attend her master and could not help but peek around cautiously, watching these men while they were clipping and rinsing their nails, picking out unwanted hairs with something they called tweezers, rinsing their teeth with ointments and pointy little sticks.

They were cleaning up thoroughly before they put on what appeared to be their best and most colorful garments. They were making quite an effort into styling their hairs and beards with combs and by making various sorts of braids. Zivah tried to remember these men from the raid, but the memory of who had done what was fading before the steady flow of new impressions that they kept creating before her eyes.

Now they were fussing about each other, one after the other posing around while the others watched and made helpful comments, assisting each other in looking the best they thought they ought to be. They reminded Zivah of herself and her girlfriends back in the village when they were preparing to go down to the river shore to fish for traveling men. She had never seen such vain men before.

"What are they doing?" Zivah asked of Laimi.

"They are going out to attend the City Council. You are going too."

"I go out of here today?" She felt her blood drain from her face. The court had only just begun to feel a little safe, with its high walls protecting her against that feral community out there.

"Yes, you will be getting your collar today, Zivah. Aziza has made ready a tea for you. It will calm you," Laimi said, patting her back gently. The other slaves were peering carefully at her, obviously pitying her. Zivah drew her breath. Maintain your self-respect no matter what they do to you, her stepfather had said. She was remembering more and more of Thunder Bear's words. She drew herself up to full height and tried to conceal her terror, and kept watching the men.

When the men had finished styling themselves, they all turned their attention to the Maiden. Thordís had new, fine leather shoes and was told to wear her wolf fur coat. Thióðolf himself combed her hair and made some very lovely braids that he could use to put her hair up in a stylish and elaborate arrangement. For jewelry they let her hammer pendant show outside her garments, and after some discussion all the men agreed that the pendant was more than impressive enough and that she needed no further decoration apart from her clothes.

She was given a very beautiful linen tunic of natural, bright colors, and to cover it a woolen dress dyed green, what went well with her red hair, Zivah heard the men say, and she had to agree with them. Never had Zivah seen men who were more adept at styles and colors than these Vikings. They all fuzzed eagerly about the girl's hair and clothes, obviously wanting her to look as impressive and stylish as they thought to be.

"Is Thord, is the Maiden going too?" Zivah asked, sipping the tea that Aziza had made for her and feeling its calming effect, helping her to prepare mentally for this new challenge. She gazed briefly at the collars that the other slaves wore and tried not to feel the shame of having to wear that suffocating sign, that sign which meant that she was nothing but somebody else's property. Try to see it as a sign of your fellowship with the rest of us, Elja, Suri had told her, and the other slaves had touched their collars and nodded in agreement while they looked at her. This sign means that you are one of us.

"Yes, of course. She is getting her own signs of rank too," Aziza replied, "Both of you will be presented to the City Council today."

"They think her look is very important," Zivah muttered and touched her own formless grey slave dress absent-minded.

"She is their Síf, Zivah. She represents the men," Aziza explained, "You should be thankful for that dress in a place like this, Zivah. I would even do something about that hair if I were you."

Zivah made sure to pull her hair back as tightly as possible.

I had been so busy getting dressed and styled and fussed about and ready that I forgot altogether about Zivah, who also had to come. Just as the men gathered by the gates, and I with them, Thióðolf called for her, and she shuffled up to us wearing her grey slave-dress, having pulled her hair tightly backwards in an almost angry-looking bun, hiding all the splendor of that hair. She came up to us and stood there before Thióðolf with her head bowed, refusing to look anywhere but at her own toes when around free men, and stiffened completely when he placed the noose around her neck once more.

My joy in going out all dressed up to see the town seemed to just fall apart and die. Thióðolf cast a regretful glance at me and said, loud and clear so that Zivah too could hear it also, that he had to do this again because it was the law and that Zivah had to be given her appropriate sign before she was safe from being noosed by other folks. I could see how my sister's skin went from paler to redder and back to paler again so fast that she was surely rather agitated, but with great effort she managed to adequately hide her detest for her House-Bond and somehow mustered that queen-like dignity which seemed to carry her soul proudly from within no matter what humiliations she was subjected to.

While Zivah graciously and intently studied her toes, I studied the men who stood around her, and saw once more that they were deeply impressed with her noble bearing. Most of the glances they sent her way now were full of admiration, even respect. But Zivah felt only the humiliation of being noosed and led around in tow like a cow by them, and still seemed to recognize no other glances from these men than the leering kinds that had so hurt her before.

Heavy-hearted, Zivah, Thióðolf and I walked amidst the men, led by Arnulf, who was absolutely splendid-looking in his best clothes and most impressively high hairdo, wearing a lot of jewelry, and true to my nature I was soon enough busy gathering all those new impressions that now were thrown at my senses from all directions. Aldeigjuborg appeared to be a cluster of huge warriors' halls, and each hall seemed to be led by a man who had been elected by the others to represent them. Hallgrim represented the warriors of Arnulf's court, who were, naturally, all sworn to Arnulf. And there were more halls sworn to Arnulf that were not directly connected to his court or his Hold.

There were other great lords living in Aldeigjuborg, powerful and rich men like our Heri who owned a court of his own and besides had the loyalty and service of independent warriors' halls. All these lords kept large estates outside of town. In fact, lords like Arnulf Heri owned all the land and all the ships as well, and all the other men depended on being attached to one of the lords to be able to benefit from those water steeds and fields and trading trips at all. Men had to be sworn to a lord in order to stay safe in that town, and so, it would seem, did little girls.

Now warriors were approaching from all parts of the town, and we were all headed towards a large central hall right by the town market square, where Zivah had been humiliated publicly a few days before. I looked anxiously at her, and so did Thióðolf, but she kept her eyes to the ground and concentrated on maintaining her dignity and heeding the courtesies at the same time. There were a few other women and some men with short-cut hair and shaven faces there by the great hall, all slaves, each one held in tow by a noose.

Only when these other slaves not yet collared could be spotted did Zivah look up at all, looked up and around, saw the other people with bowed heads in their nooses, and the crowds of ferocious-looking warriors all around them, and she swayed a little. Thióðolf was quickly by her side and discreetly provided support, and for a moment she leaned on him because she had no other choice if she wanted to stay upright.

He did not leave her side before he was certain that she had regained her balance and maintained consciousness, and stayed as close as he could while still feigning absolute indifference like he had to. Hallgrim came up to us and stood on the other side of her, looking as uncaring and absent-minded as he could possibly muster, and both men indifferently made sure that the poor young woman was adequately supported.

Arnulf gestured for us to come with him, and we went after him and Hallgrim into the City Council hall before most of the other men, so that we could see that splendid hall while it was still near empty, yet ready for the great council. Well inside, Arnulf was met by another very large man about his own age, a blonde-haired man quite as terrifying to behold as Arnulf had still been when not yet familiar to me. The other large and fierce-looking man was obviously another lord.

For the first time since I met him, I saw Arnulf meet the gaze of an equal, and observed how they both averted their eyes but briefly, and exactly at the same time. The two men embraced heartily and there were some thunderous blows exchanged with their fists to each other's backs. I winced. The force of each blow would have rendered me unconscious. When the two warlords had finished greeting each other with those amiably impressive blows and exchanged some words, Hallgrim Hidden Spear walked up to them, lowered his eyes to the other lord, and addressed him as Hróarr Heri.

Then they too embraced. Tall, sinewy and slender-built Hallgrim only swayed a little when Hróarr gave him a friendly back-slap also. After taking a few moments to recover from all that friendliness, the three of them talked in low voices for a little while, and soon enough they were all casting conspiring glances at me. Finally, Hróarr Heri set his steel-gray eyes on me, a piercing gaze that made my hairs stand on end, before he suddenly marched right over to me and squatted down to be of a height with me.

He placed his enormous hands around my narrow shoulders, and I felt like biting his nose off, right then and there, like a trapped or cornered wolverine. The stranger Heri just smiled humorously. "Quite the little she-wolf, are you?" he suggested teasingly and looked me up and down with great relish, as if I was something too good to be true and very amazing to behold. I was so stunned that I even failed to lower my eyes and greet him until he met my eyes again, and I saw a kindness in them. Not that he was a very kind man. I could see that he was not that kind.

But he had the capacity for kindness as surely as Arnulf had, despite their perhaps even greater capacity for the very opposite. And as I had learned in this world of warriors, friendly affection from men like him was very desirable. I smiled shyly and lowered my eyes.

"Please excuse my bad manners, Heri. I am just a maiden and you are a very fearsome-looking warrior. Your sudden and most fierce presence so close to me simply frightened me for a moment," I spoke quietly, and saw in his eyes that my words and voice were sweet to his ears. I relaxed and smiled again when he averted his eyes respectfully, only after a brief postponement designed to remind me of his very high rank. He leaned conspiratorially towards me.

"You are not just a maiden, Priestess," he whispered, "I know well who and what you are, and I cannot even begin to tell you how pleased I am to see you here among us. But I have to tell you, now, with your Heri's permission, that you must hide that Thunderbolt pendant right away, beneath your garments, and never let it show in public. And when you are presented today you will not speak for yourself, but only speak if you are spoken to, and then only to confirm politely that whatever your kinsmen say about you is true, even if it is not. Do you think you can you do that, Thordís Thorbjörns daughter Thorsgyðja?"

I nodded gravely and said that I could do that, wondering what was going on, but when I looked to Arnulf and Hallgrim, they both nodded urgently to me. This was important. I tucked my Hammer of Greatness in behind my linen tunic, to rest close to my heart and my skin, and not to be seen by anyone. Hróarr Heri smoothed my dress and pulled two of my braids down from my neck to cover my shoulders, hiding the necklace that held my pendant.

"You have enemies here, little Thunder Priestess," he said, "and we who are your friends intend to protect you as well as we can against them. We shall draw as little attention as possible towards your lineage and particularly that pendant. Yes? It is for your protection."

I nodded again.

"Now, Maiden, to briefly introduce myself; I am Hróarr Hóskuldsson Freysgóði, and I am one of the six great Heris of Aldeigjuborg, and out of the six, I am outstanding. Only Arnulf can match me for power in this place. Fortunately for him, we are very good friends. So do not worry about anything and just play your part. Good. You are a clever girl."

Hróarr the Freyr's priest got to his feet as soon as hordes of men started filing in through the entrances, one by one bending down to walk through the low doors, a way of securing the entrances from massive assaults. As I watched all those men entering the hall in such large numbers, I could see how even just one warrior, even if it was but a person who knew how to wield an axe, could defend an entrance like that against many invading foes. When the hall was finally full, there were certainly hundreds of men in there. I had never seen so many people gathered in one building before.

Now, the great hall was crowded with a veritable village of large and imposing men, a few subdued new slaves, mostly female; and me. At the short end of the hall there was a square but elongated, glowing fireplace, and a large oak table was placed behind it. The six lords of Aldeigjuborg, Arnulf and Hróarr among them, were seated in a High Seat each on the other side of the table with their backs towards the wall, facing all of us, and separated from us by the table and by the hearth. Beginning by the front part of both sides of their hearth and ending closer to the congregation in general, two other, more narrow and long tables had been placed.

The thirty representatives of the thirty different warriors' halls in Aldeigjuborg, including the one at Arnulf's court, were seated on benches before those tables, with their backs against the walls. Hallgrim sat down among them at the upper end of the left table, closest to the hearth, what meant he was among the two most important Hall representatives in the entire City Council. The other most important representative was seated at the upper end of the right table and appeared to be bound to Hróarr Heri.

I counted fifteen men on either side, as well as the six House-Bonds, making up a total number of six and thirty ruling men, and these leaders of Viking hordes were all seated strategically with their backs to the walls. I could also see that the floor where these men sat had been raised higher, so that the rulers were not only facing the rest of the public but also looking a little down at us. All the other people, myself included, had to stand around, creating a sort of prolonged half circle facing the ruling lords and chiefs, leaving the space between the two representatives' tables empty, an open court in which to stand trial.

When everybody had gotten to their places, a silence descended on the congregation that truly impressed me, seeing as we were so many folks carrying so many metal items. Then Hallgrim gracefully and quietly got up from his place at the chiefs' table, where he had been seated at the top end, closer to the lords, indicating his very high rank among the chiefs. He was wearing a very long and stately coat that reached all the way down to his ankles, and he had let all his long brown hair fall free, and now that he stood there he had the bearing of a king, I thought, and his dark pool eyes looked round and commanded the attention and deep respect of everybody. I looked at the cunning man and knew that he was pledged to a great and sacred power just as I was. He was also carrying a beautiful wand, hung with amulets.

Hallgrim used the wand to knock the floor three times before he spoke, "In sight of the gods and the goddesses; before the ladies of all verdicts; before the lords of all songs; I, Hallgrim Hidden Spear, declare open the City Council. Alu."

"Alu," the congregation repeated as one, and Hallgrim knocked the floor three more times before he returned to his seat and sat down. Then Hróarr Heri stood.

"This is the first council to be held after the summer's trading expeditions. This day we shall only welcome or reject our newly arrived. Have we any visitors what need to be spoken for today?"

There were a few visitors who now stood forth and presented themselves, and in the presence of all the lords they were welcomed and known and spoken for, and allowed to stay safely for that period of time they had asked permission for. When no more visitors presented themselves, Hróarr stood again, and asked, "have any new warriors arrived who need to be spoken for?"

Then warriors presented themselves before the council, went to stand before the lords, spoke their names and lineages and what Hall or Court they belonged to, and swore themselves formally to the lords who owned said halls and courts, and their lords spoke for them in the council. After that they were all confirmed by those present and judged to be citizens of Aldeigjuborg.

After all the new warriors had been spoken for, it was finally my turn. Hróarr's powerful voice called my name, and just like all the visitors and warriors had done before, I walked alone up to that empty court before all those frightful men and stood as proudly as I could manage, conscious of hundreds of pairs of warriors' eyes studying me carefully, all at once.

I concentrated on the ones in front, the six lords, and met their eyes with a brief sweep of my gaze before I lowered mine and said nothing. They were a bunch of terrifying giants in my eyes, even now that I had gotten used to fierce men. But a lord had to be particularly fierce and outstanding, and these men were dressed and styled to look larger and more terrifying than all the rest, and had the attitude to go with it. Even Arnulf looked positively threatening to me then, and I gulped, barely managing to maintain my own stance as a free and noble maiden.

"Who speaks for this girl-child?" Hróarr asked formally, and looked round as if he did not know already. Arnulf cleared his throat and stood, and just at the same time I noticed from the corner of my eye that Hallgrim also stood, as well as the other chiefs who were sworn to Arnulf, and behind me I heard the steps of my kinsmen from court, as well as all the other men of all the halls sworn to Arnulf, moving forth to show that they would all speak for me.

"I, Arnulf Arnsteinsson Heri, speak for the maiden, as do all men sworn to me," Arnulf said formally, and was immediately followed by confirmatory words from all the men he had just referred to. It sounded like a veritable chorus when my brothers spoke for me.

"The girl is spoken for. Now the words may be spoken on her behalf, unless she wants to speak for herself," Hróarr said. A little astonished, I looked up at the rulers, but when I saw Arnulf's and Hróarr's almost invisible head-shakes I shut my mouth close and lowered my eyes demurely. The offer to speak out was there, even for a little girl, but it had been explained to me before that the offer was not meant to be accepted by a little girl, or by a woman for that matter. At least not if she had any kinsmen who could speak for her and put blades behind words, and thus more power to her claim.

"This maiden whom I speak for is called Thordís Thorbjörns daughter, and she is noble born and a warrior's daughter," Arnulf began, and then proceeded to lie flatly, "I knew her father Thorbjörn well, a warrior of high birth from Gotland. And yet, as you all know, even high birth will not always secure a property if there are older brothers, so Thorbjörn had taken ships in his youth and set up a good trading post down in the Avar Khaganate, where his business flourished, and we traded often and met many a time over many a year. I came to know little Thordís, his daughter, as a Síf of my heart, and for the last seven summers I saw how she had grown from year to year.

When I ventured down south this summer, I was loathe to discover that my good friend Thorbjörn had died, and the maiden was orphaned. She had been left in the charge of some relatives of her mother, and these provided me with the news as well as with a reasonable dowry for the girl, and asked me to protect her in her father's stead. And so I swore, and now the maiden has come to live here in Aldeigjuborg. I shall not take her name from her, but I suggest she be known as Arnulfsfostra as well, for she is to be fostered by me in my court."

I felt my ears burn like fire, listening to such a deceitful story of my origins and my relationship to Arnulf, but I knew it was a way of protecting me, and suddenly the actual meaning of Hróarr's words earlier began to sink in and settle as knowledge in my heart.

I had enemies here.

I gulped and peered up at the ruling lords, wondering which of them would carry ill will against me if they knew of what lineage and history I really stemmed, or if they knew that I was the carrier of the men's hammer. Vaguely, I also wondered why. Father's story had seemed to me much like the legends of old. It had not even occurred to me that some of his old enemies might still be alive and eager to avenge something or other, or to take my legacy from me, like the Uppsala king had once taken the women's hammer from the burnt ashes of its last carrier, my aunt Thora.

"It is odd," an icy voice spoke, slowly, lingeringly, mockingly, up from the table of the six lords, "I find it odd that I first heard a story about a Hel Maiden come to grace Arnulf Heri's voyage, only to be presented with a perfectly ordinary maiden, and told that it was her the whole time. I mean no disrespect to my fellow ruling lords, but I would very much appreciate an explanation."

The icy voice emerged from the mouth of Gunnarr Beak-Nose, and for a moment I met his terrible eyes and froze to the spot even as I remembered to lower my own again immediately.

"Oh, yes, the Hel Maiden," Arnulf said calmly, and chuckled. Immediately, all the men of our court as well as the men of his sworn halls began to giggle as well, and Gunnarr Beak-Nose frowned, looking disappointed. It seemed he would have preferred it if Arnulf and his men had been more inconvenienced. Arnulf smiled overbearingly and looked at Njál, who immediately stood to attention, looking rather puzzled.

"I suppose you just have to tell the truth, Njál," Arnulf said and sighed, looking like he was trying to suppress more laughter. He was a great actor, Arnulf Heri. I had never thought so before I saw him in action. I turned around slightly so that I could look at Njál the Foolish, who now appeared to be thinking very hastily, and I wondered how he would fare, being such a fool, and obviously unprepared. And yet, Arnulf had chosen him to save the day. Then Njál grinned broadly.

"Great lords," the fool began, "I must apologize to you and to all the men, not the least the men of our ships and courts. It is so that when the maiden encountered our slave, Shumayl, he was afraid of her."

The warriors in the hall began to smile, looking expectantly at Njál, who was obviously about to tell a good story. I wondered why he had left out the first part where they had all been afraid of me.

"Of course, our Shumayl is a very little man. He also happens to be very skittish. And he is a Big Tunic Man, well, as big as they go, I assume, and you all know what they are like. They are terrified of Hel, they are, just like the Christians. Now, the thing about our maiden here, well, as you may all see even at this very moment, she possesses some very special sorts of eyes. Whenever she is concentrating, or her intent is directed like a blade towards a target, they turn white and fierce like the eyes of a wolf. Also, Arnulf had given her that wolf-fur-coat, and she was wearing it that day, and the fangs of the wolf's head had scratched her forehead and made her bleed a little. And when Shumayl saw the girl, he thought she was a Hel Maiden, and there is nothing in the world that poor little fellow fears more than Hel Maidens, so he screamed and screamed and ran away, shouting 'Djinn! Djinn! Djinn!' Which is the same as Hel Maiden in the Tunic tongue."

The entire hall roared with laughter, and I stood smiling, though I felt a little sorry for Shumayl now, and glad that he was absent, seeing as the story of his fear of me was rather exaggerated and rendered the man ridiculous in the eyes of free men.

Then, slaves are there to be used, and when we needed him to be the fool instead of Njál, we had made a fool of him, no qualms about it. I hoped the poor slave need never know that he had saved me in this way, seeing as he was no fool at all.

Njál grinned sheepishly, waiting for the commotion to quiet down, and continued, "And then I had this idea of telling everybody what a great Hel Maiden we had got to grace our ship, and if you look at her now and think it over, you may see that she could well look the part, under the right circumstances. And the truth was that we had been raiding a place just before that moment, and you all know what that sort of thing can do to a man's wits some times."

Everybody nodded.

"Rumor passed round like wildfire and soon enough we spent the whole voyage homewards trying to dissolve the confusion as to whether little Thordís really was a Hel Maiden or just a maiden, so to speak. Countless great stories were invented about that girl's origin, it became a great pastime and entertainment for us, and the girl herself, talented as she is, entertained us by playing out all the roles we tried to give her, and she played them to perfection also."

Njál took a breath and peered round the hall, seeing to his contentment that everybody was utterly entertained by his story, proceeding, "And so the many dazzling stories of her were nourished and took on a life of their own, as they always do. Great stories are sacred whether they are true or not. So now you may all better understand how it came to be that people are still speaking of the Hel Maiden who came to grace our ships, although the somewhat less exciting story of the orphaned noble girl is the actual truth."

I held my breath when he finished, and so did the hall, and then another round of cheers broke out, celebrating Njál's story about me, if not my actual one. They loved it. The Rus did not seem to care whether it was true or not. I had come to suspect that my kinsmen were more eager to accept a good story than just a boring true one, for as long as the story was good enough to not offend their intelligence. Somehow, Njál the Foolish had pleased even the sharpest of minds in that hall.

"Can you confirm this story, Maiden?" Hróarr growled, looking sternly at me with sharp eyes. I peeked up at him but briefly.

"I can, Heri," I said meekly, and dared to smile just a little.

"Good," Hróarr said brusquely and studied me carefully, looking a lot fiercer and less kind than he had done before the council began, but I assumed this was because he was now in capacity as lord of the hall. I looked cautiously at the other lords without looking directly at them, all the time keeping my eyes averted and slightly lowered while still able to communicate if they so wanted, paying attention to everything going on in those stone and mask-like faces.

Gunnarr Beak-Nose stared so hard at me that I felt nauseous, and his glaring went on to the point where I could hardly resist the temptation to bow my head, wanting to apologize for whatever had made him glare at me.

I knew with some frustration that the men saw my weakling urge to bow at once, just to placate him, but I noticed well that they also saw my noble warrior's daughter's efforts to not bow like a slave, when I had nothing to apologize for. And when the warlords could conclude that I was able to keep my head high and my eyes low in such a challenging and terrifying situation, they immediately averted their eyes respectfully. All of them did, even that vicious-looking man, Gunnarr Beak-Nose. These Viking lords were testing me in some way or other, but I seemed to have passed the test already, and was soon appraised.

"Arnulf, your young ward is suitably maidenly and suitably warlike," Hróarr declared, "and she is very well behaved and courteous. You can well be proud of her. We acknowledge Thordís Thorbjörns daughter Arnulfsfostra as a free maiden citizen of Aldeigjuborg, protected by Arnulf's court and sworn warriors. She may not be noosed in this town, and may not in any way be offended by men, and is due the respect and courtesies paid to a noble maiden and a warrior's daughter. She may speak her cases at council and she may count on the protection of the City Council, for as long as she honors our laws. Every transgression upon her honor and liberty will be rewarded with death."

"We hear it," all the other lords declared in unison, "Thordís Thorbjörns daughter Arnulfsfostra is spoken for and acknowledged as a free and noble maiden citizen of Aldeigjuborg."

I was beginning to feel what it was like to be taken into the fold for real now, being thus formally and publicly acknowledged. I was one of them by law now, I was a Rus maiden and a citizen, and I could even speak at council! The part about speaking in council was rather exaggerated, of course, seeing as that would be unseemly and indicate that my kinsmen were unable to take care of me and represent my cases, but at least I had the formal right to do so, and now that my right had been declared before everyone I felt that even a formal right mattered. It made me feel a part of their tribe. Our tribe.

When I had been spoken for and accepted, I received my tokens of citizenship and freedom; a belt with a pouch and a proper dagger to hang from it, and a small dagger pendant that was to hang from a necklace made especially for that dagger. They told me that all free women of Aldeigjuborg wore that small dagger, always, a symbol of the protection she had from her warriors, and thus a woman's symbol of freedom.

It was time for the new slaves to be registered. The slaves did not walk forth on their own, but were led in tow by their new masters, their name and the name of their owners and the place they would dwell was duly recorded into the minds of all the men present, and then the slave was made to kneel before the six lords while the thin iron necklace that looked like a collar was fastened around their neck and locked forever, or for as long as their slavery would last, and each collar was inscribed with a rune that gave sound to the first letter of the first name of the slave's master.

The business with the slaves seemed to run swift and smoothly, the people getting bored about the whole thing, but there was a hushed silence when Thióðolf walked out before the lords with Zivah in tow. The silence was, in fact, unbearable, and I saw Zivah struggle to keep herself from swaying and swooning. Gently, Thióðolf held her and made her kneel down while the man with the slave collars fastened hers around her neck. There were three runes carved into her collar, the first letters of her master's two names and another sign that I did not recognize but which I knew, from what the men had explained to me of slave collars, represented his rank or profession and his tribal belonging. I assumed it was the sign for a noble born skald from Hálógaland.

"The slave's name," Gunnarr Beak-Nose wheezed, leering openly at my sister, who fortunately held her eyes to the ground and could not see how viciously that frightful man was looking at her.

"My slave's name is Zivah, and she belongs to me, Thióðolf Grjótgarðsson of Borg," Thióðolf said sternly, his voice quite hard and deep. He was obviously dismayed with Gunnarr's behavior, but was, as far as I know, supposed to be his inferior. And yet, as soon as Thióðolf spoke his name, and spoke it in that way he did, Gunnarr seemed to gather himself up and assume the dignified appearance of a great warlord again. The signals were subtle, but I began to suspect that my friend Thióðolf might be of some famed lineage himself. People did seem to respect him a lot, most of them always averting their eyes first, as if he was a little above them even when they formally ranked the same.

"No concubine's necklace for this one?" Hróarr asked, looking genuinely surprised when Thióðolf shook his head. I saw a lot of men looking stunned when he said no, she would be no concubine yet, and many of them looked at Zivah with pity in their eyes, while others smiled a little, and some began to laugh and joke and leer at her.

Gunnarr Beak-Nose looked positively delighted.

"Still punishing your Eastern Princess?" The man grinned amiably. He looked like he thought that he was sharing a very funny joke with Thióðolf. Before Gunnarr could see Thióðolf's disgusted expression in response to his comment, he had turned to other men around the hall who were eager to meet his gaze and laugh at his joke, the humor of which I failed to grasp, like many others also failed it.

"I suppose I am," Thióðolf said dryly, cutting short their laughter, and lied as smoothly as Njál and Arnulf had before, "The slave is submitting, as you can all see, but I think she will do well learning a little more about why she might just start to appreciate me as her lord. If there is anything I have learned among the Rus, it is that all good things must be shared with all good friends."

At that mockery of a joke, designed to make the vicious man laugh again, Gunnarr Beak-Nose indeed rolled over in laughing fits, and so did all those who seemed sworn to laugh with him, although the rest of the hall was slightly less excited, some laughing politely and others standing grave, just as Thióðolf did. He stood grave next to his humiliated slave girl, who was oblivious to the many discreet but clearly understanding and sympathizing glances that now passed by her and her master.

I understood that Thióðolf was playing a game here, speaking words that did not describe his true actions. Gazing at the men who remained grave, I realized that Thióðolf, Arnulf and all the warriors of our court were doing the same as I did; looking around to make note of who laughed and who did not. And then I suddenly knew that they were testing the men of the hall; to see who among them were akin to us and who were not, while at the same time averting Gunnarr's attention by providing an illusion of camaraderie. Many people in that hall clearly understood what the cunning man was really doing, even as Gunnarr Heri did not.

Neither did Zivah, of course. My sister had just gotten one more reason to hate Thióðolf forever and ever. She understood the words now, I could see it. She understood most of what was being said already, even if she could not yet speak the tongue so well. I only wished she could also understand that the men who now ruled her were playing games that had to do with so much more than just her, and that all Thióðolf ever did was try and make her given misery somewhat less miserable if he could help it. I could see how he worked, because I worked the same way, in acknowledgment of the actual rules and powers that were given as obstacles and blades upon my path in life.

Zivah could not see that yet, too busy being frightened, and too busy condemning those obstacles and blades for their unfairness and their cruelties to actually be able to see how these could be wielded in this battlefield called life. A warrior can make a weapon out of anything, my father had once told me, even out of misfortune. I could not blame my sister for her blindness. She had not been taught the arts of war. Zivah only saw what happened right before her eyes and ears, and for some reason or other she believed that sort of perception to be reliable, and seemed to think that whether she liked or disliked what she perceived was the important thing. Thus she knew not yet friend from foe, and not trap from exit, in this terrifying world of Viking Rus.

Hróarr Freysgodi

Outside of the great hall, Hróarr chatted with Arnulf for a while. I stood next to them and could not help but listen to their forbidden men's conversation, seeing as I was right there.

"How is good Freydís, my friend? And young Solveig and the boys?" Arnulf asked.

"They decided to spend the winter in Gotland with Freydís' parents," Hróarr said, "Many years have passed and there is the old grandmother and the aunt, oh, you know. She was homesick and wanted Solveig especially to see a different sort of life. Our daughter might think all men are Vikings unless she sees something else."

"Nothing wrong with Vikings," Arnulf snorted, "a warrior's daughter ought to appreciate a little ferocity in men."

"The Gutes are ferocious enough," Hróarr smiled, "seeing as almost half of us Rus come out of their stock, the difference is really that they actually have women in equal number as men there."

"Oh," Arnulf grunted and frowned uncertainly, yet added generously after only moments of doubt, "I suppose I can see how that might do a young woman good." Hróarr smiled at his friend, and cleared his throat.

"Exactly. But there are no marriage plans or anything. The girl is still young." Hróarr looked meaningfully at Arnulf, who pretended not to catch his friend's subtle suggestion.

"I have to say I am a little disappointed," Arnulf said instead, "I had thought to ask Freydís for some assistance when it comes to the raising and educating of my little ward here. Not for fostering, but for the learning of womanly arts. I can hardly teach her how to weave and embroider."

"Maybe some of the other Heris' wives?"

"They are not Norse, Hróarr. You know. I want her to know our ways first. She is a she-wolf as you already have perceived."

"Perhaps your slaves...?"

"My ward is a noble maiden and should not have to learn from slaves," Arnulf said sternly, and Hróarr did not press the case.

"I suppose we will just have to teach her the battle arts, then," the blonde giant sighed humorously, and they both laughed out loud for a moment, before they stooped to look at each other and then at me. The two Viking chiefs suddenly scratched their heads exactly at the same time, obviously wondering whatever else they could teach me.

Hróarr was invited home to Arnulf's court with us, and we went into the Hold where we sat down around the table, Arnulf in the High Seat, Thióðolf and Hróarr at either side of the high end, and I next to Thióðolf. Hallgrim sat next to Hróarr, facing me, and next to him sat Sígtrygg the Týr-man, and beside me Njál the Foolish and Sharp-Toothed. The sixth man was one of Hróarr's men, and he was seated next to Sígtrygg. None of the other men were present, having gone to the men's Hall, but the boy Ivarr was, and he sat further down the table next to Njál and dared not look my way at all.

I was taking my duties as his honer very seriously.

The slaves served us and none of them sat, as they never did when we had guests. Even Zivah in her new slave collar served us dutifully and silently. With that face safely directed to the floor at all times, it was hard to make out what she was thinking.

We ate in silence as always, and when the plates and bowls had been removed by the slaves, we sat there with our drinks, and I had watered beer while the men drank proper beer. And after a few sips of drink they all looked at me. Arnulf patted his knee. I obeyed at once and went over to sit on it, a knee large enough to be a proper seat for my tiny frame. This way they could all see me better, and I had begun to grasp that as a maiden, my rank was fluid as water and could move from top to bottom and back again as easily as any stream, so nobody minded it if I suddenly sat in the High Seat at the Heri's command.

"Thorsgyðja," Hróarr said, "Your father was Thorbjörn Thorgrimsson Thórsgóði, of the ancient lineage of the Thunder Priests in Gautland. You are Thordís Thorbjörn daughter Thorsgyðja, the last of your most ancient and divine lineage."

"That he was and that I am, Heri," I confirmed politely, keeping my gaze down.

"Hail to you, Thunder Priestess. I am Hróarr Hoskuldsson Freysgóði," he declared, "and I am to great Freyr the same that your father was to Earth-born Thor. My wife, Freydís Freysgyðja, she is to glorious Freyr exactly the same as you are to divine Thor."

"Hail to you, Frey's priest. You honor me," I said. He had all my attention.

"I am honored, Freyia," he replied, and briefly lowered his eyes to me. I almost startled at being addressed such. The men smiled at me.

"You are a Freyia, of course, even if you will be called Maiden by most for a long time still. But this evening I shall call you by your truest title, for the truth is that I am deeply honored and in awe of being in the presence of an actual Thunder Priestess. We had thought your lineage was exterminated, and yet here you are, carrying a most precious legacy." He paused and regarded me thoughtfully, "Today I told you to hide that hammer of yours.

There are a few reasons for that, Freyia, and the first reason is called Gunnarr Beak-Nose. Did you know that your father, Thorbjörn, slayed Gunnarr's father and two uncles before he vanished into the forests of the river lands, fifteen years past?"

Blood drained from my face and I shook my head gravely. Now that he said it, I remembered my father's story of the cruel Viking captain who had tortured the poor abducted girl just because she cried, and how Father had interfered to defend the girl, upon which he had been attacked by the Viking captain and his two brothers, and how he had slayed them all. And then the Vikings had been uncertain about whether to approve or attack until the captain's young son, Gunnarr, had rallied them and ordered them to kill my father, who had, by the miraculous aid of lord Thor, escaped and disappeared forever. And now I, his daughter, had returned, and I was the only one who could ever be a target for that cruel-looking man's vengeance.

"Do not fear, Freyia," Hróarr said reassuringly. "It so happens that your father had the wisdom to go by a different name when he lived among us. He called himself Grim and he kept that hammer safely tucked behind his clothes just as you do, and so kept attention away from it exactly as you must, and when it was seen by others he said it was but a rather old family heirloom. He even told us that he was a Svear, and not a Gaut. So Gunnarr Beak-Nose would be looking for Grim Svear if he did not think the man was long dead. He is not expecting you to be his daughter, and is not suspecting anything. But it so happens that he might recognize the hammer, and so could some of his men, and other folks in this town who lived here back then and knew your father. Which is why you should keep that holy pendant out of sight whenever you are out of court or around other people."

"I will, Heri, and I thank you," I said, feeling relieved.

"I would advise you to keep it out of sight most of the time," Hallgrim inferred, "even here at court. The less attention towards it the better, for if a thing sings vividly in the minds of men, the song is soon heard far and wide no matter how carefully they try to store it."

"I will, Hallgrim," I said and nodded thankfully.

"Now there is a second reason as to why we need to be discreet about your true identity and the hammer that you keep," Hróarr said, "The fact is that rumors of your father's survival have lived on and grown, both back in Gautland and other places. I was in Gotland this summer to visit my wife's family, and heard those rumors then. They say that when Harald Wartooth had reclaimed Gautland, he gave the women's hammer, the Hammer of Power, to his brother Randvér, king of the Svear, who kept it stored away in the Uppsala treasury.

They say that even now, their successor, old Thorolf Wavy Nose, is always keeping eyes and ears out for any rumor of the men's hammer, the Hammer of Greatness, for it is widely believed that great power will come to the one who is able to wield both hammers together."

"That is what my father told me also," I said quietly.

"Yes. But he might not have been aware of the fact that the Svear king is still looking for him and the hammer, and that he has sworn to destroy all Thunder Priests, and any son that your father may have seeded, or any other male child of his line."

"Oh," I said, and when nobody spoke, I cleared my throat and asked bluntly, "What about a female child?"

"Indeed. It would be very unseemly to kill you, but he would probably marry you, or marry you to somebody, and then he could be in control over any male issue stemming from you. Whether he would then kill the male issue or use it would probably depend a lot on who the father was. Now, I can see that from a woman's point of view the idea of being taken as wife to a king or very powerful nobleman would not be such a terrible fate at all, at least if that meant that your sons would be protected after all. But you would not want that, Freyia. Those Uppsala kings are poisoned by all the treason and sacrilege committed over the last hundred years and more. They would abuse you, and they would abuse your legacy, and even if he married you himself he would not treat you decently because of what you represent to him."

"What do I represent to him, Heri?"

"The enemy, Freyia, the true heir to the Gautland High Seat, as many folks would say."

"Oh," I said and blushed. I hardly dared to look at the men, but when I glanced up anyway it was Ivarr's eyes I met, looking stunned and impressed, and that made me feel a little better.

"It is the truth, Thordís," Thióðolf said, "I have seen the Hammer of Power, shown to me by the Uppsala king. King Thorolf is quite obsessed with it, and spoke of the rumors of your father going east, and of sending spies out to look for him. I did not think he was serious back then, I thought it was a drunken brawl. But he woke up his wife the queen and told her to open the treasury for us in the middle of the night, and then he came out carrying the women's hammer, and spoke of the power that would emerge from the union of this hammer with the men's hammer. He was rather pleased with himself, as if he had already accomplished it. And he told me similar things as what you now hear Hróarr say. We need to be discreet about your identity."

"You may be fortunate, that you are a girl," Hróarr said, "Nobody will expect the guardian of the men's hammer to be a little girl, but if this is widely known people will come searching for you, for even if you cannot pose a threat to them directly, they will be greedy for the control of your womb and all children that may issue from it, and they will try to control the hammer, even try to take it from you. And by people I do not only mean the Svear. There will be many others who would be eager to possess the last Thunder Priestess and the Hammer of Greatness."

At that, Hróarr looked searchingly at Thióðolf, who maintained his calm composure, but I saw that small flicker in his eyes. The others did too, and for a moment I thought that an invisible battle was going on across the table, with men searching for each other's intentions, testing each other's resolve and wondering what they could expect and how far they could trust each other.

For my part, I wondered if I could trust any of them.

"Wolfling," Hallgrim spoke mildly, "You see. You see what your power does to men."

I nodded gravely and noticed that all the other men suddenly tried to hide how embarrassed they were now.

"They cannot help it," Hallgrim said, "none of us can help it. Your power works that way. But we all know that it is only through your affection and love that your power is going to actually benefit us. It is truly up to you who shall benefit from that power. That is the difference between us and the Svear king who thinks he can wield holy powers just because he possesses a couple of keys. The hammers are only keys, Thordís, the power they channel are directly linked to you, to your ancestors and to your lineage and the thunder that flows in your veins. The king may well try and take you and the hammer, but he will never be able to open that divine flow. Only you can do that, and you can only do it in a state of love and trust. If you are frightened or angry, the power will turn on the man who tries to abuse you. It is the absolute truth of things. But that will never stop the Svear king from trying, and if he did, he might end up hurting you and destroying your lineage forever, so you will do wisely to keep safe from him and his spies."

"Yes, Hallgrim," I said obediently and peered doubtfully at them all. They tried to look very mild and reassuring now. It dawned on me that they already knew they depended on my love for them if they were ever going to have even a whiff of that power I carried. Now, that was, in fact, a reassuring piece of knowledge. I smiled at them and lowered my eyes just to let them know that I was not going to think myself above them, just because I was, after a fashion. They all smiled back. Even Ivarr smiled now, nervously, and I gave him a little glare just for sport, noticing gleefully that he winced. I almost thought the grown men winced for a moment too, but if they did, they were quick to hide it, setting up instead their stern and warlike masks of grave and trustworthy dedication to my holy path.

"We will protect you, Thordís Gyðja," Arnulf said, and the men nodded earnestly. I thought their eyes were moist, and felt a stirring in my heart. My brothers said they would protect me with their lives.

I rather loved them already.

The Viking Court

Zivah did not even want to remember that day when they put the slave collar on her and laughed about how she had been and would continue to be disciplined. She returned to court wearing the same iron necklace that all the other slaves wore, and nothing else that could tell the world that she was owned by one man only, knowing fully well that this meant that any of them could command her at any time, and all she could do was wait for it. She decided that she could not possibly spend her time despairing over the inevitable, and every time she saw something that bothered her, she practiced being with the river within, for she was surely going to need that ability any day, and the rest of the time she tried to learn and understand everything.

A few days passed while she learned more and more of the language and the everyday life of the Viking court, which was remarkably cheerful regardless, as if nobody seemed to notice the terror under which they lived. Zivah flinched every time she saw a warrior, expecting to be called at any time. She knew she ought to please her own master if she wanted to be safe from such calls, but she could not bring herself to do it. She just could not. She would rather keep her face safely down than let him see how much she feared and hated and despised him, knowing that if she looked at him she would not be able to hide it. Not from him. He may be a brute and a beast and a rapist at heart, but he was not stupid. He saw deeper than that.

She reckoned he was more likely to punish her if she tried too hard than if she just observed all the courtesies at all times. And even if she did not want to be punished, she could not, she just could not, pretend to like him.

Every day she saw warriors calling upon slave girls and leading them away, often to the stables or somewhere else that offered a little privacy, although not everybody minded an audience, for some reason especially not when they chose Suri. The bonds women never complained. Often enough they even returned looking rather refreshed, and when that happened there was always a deal of laughter and joking, and the woman was often required to tell everything that had happened in detail and whether she had "gone to the waves" or not. Apparently, the waves meant a sort of pleasure that they all seemed to think highly of.

Zivah tried to remember if she had felt anything like pleasant waves before, but could not say she had, and dared not ask. They even made bets about who would get to the waves with whom, and when. Zivah had thought them insane at first, but now she had begun to think that it was just a way of survival. If you live in this sort of humiliating misery, you just have to find a way to rise above it all. These women had found humor. And even if their jokes were often both loud and rather visible, their masters never interfered. They seemed to like it, as crazy as they were.

Sometimes Zivah felt as if nobody in this place was a person of her or his own. People talked of themselves and others in plural more often than not. We. They. Us. If the women had found humor, they had also found sisterhood, and that seemed to make the whole situation bearable. It made a world of difference, actually. It was the only thing that made her live from day to day, even if she sometimes thought her sisters very odd. Zivah would have thought there would be a lot more drama going on, jealousy not the least. But there never was. They did everything together and shared their fortunes and misfortunes at all times.

It was sometimes as if there were just two people living in the entire court – the master and the slave – and since most of the masters were men and most of the slaves were women, the relationship was a complicated blend of mutual affection, desire and even love, as well as the harsh reality of absolute power on one side and no power at all on the other. Somehow they made that into something that often enough seemed to be thrilling for both sides, even though it was still impossible for Zivah to understand how that could be at all.

The first few days after she realized that all the men in court could lawfully rape her any time they wanted to, she had walked tense, dreading the moment that surely would come, just as she had dreaded it on those ships of theirs. Every time a man as much as looked at her, she flinched. But nothing happened, and she began to notice that the men were even trying to avoid looking at her at all, even though they did not always succeed. One day when they were working with rinsing root vegetables outside, Fanged Njál passed by and stopped. The women bowed their heads and he looked them over. Zivah bowed her head and burned, remembering how Njál had been the only one who had treated her kindly all the time, even given her the cat back. She hoped so much that he would not do this to her. Not him.

Not the only one among them whom she had almost started to trust.

"Suri," Njál said, and Suri got up. Zivah expected them to walk away, but when Suri came over to Njál he smiled at her with his fangs and told her to lean her palms against the wall, facing it, right there. Right there in front of them.

They were still both standing, and he mounted her from behind like a beast while he used his hands to feel her up in the front. He even bent over and nibbled her ear with his sharp teeth, and Zivah heard a moan escape from poor Suri. She thought she was going to burn up with shame on the poor girl's behalf, Suri who was always so cheerful. Zivah concentrated on the vegetables but could hardly avoid noticing what was going on and what seemed to never stop.

She peered around to see how the other women responded and noticed that they were trying not to smile. They were so hard to figure out sometimes, her sisters. After what seemed to be an unbearable eternity she could not help but notice that things were speeding up considerably and that Suri was beginning to moan and utter strange, guttural sounds from her throat, what got worse and worse as Fanged Njál was ramming into her harder and harder, completely oblivious of the excruciating pain he was surely causing, and did not even care when Suri began to scream. Zivah felt tears pressing out of her eyes. Then it was over. Njál stood for a while behind the slave girl to catch his breath before he withdrew, and Suri turned and looked up at him with a surprisingly big smile.

"Thank you, Heri," she squeaked brightly and quite loud too, as if she wanted everybody to hear that.

"It is on account of your sweetness, Suri," Njál replied and gave her buttocks a fond slap. Thank you, Heri. Oh goddess have mercy, Zivah thought, we have to thank them after. To her great dismay Njál did not leave at once but stood and looked while Suri went to wash herself, his gaze passing over the group of women who worked with their heads bowed, pretending indifference. He is going for another one, Zivah thought, and wished she could sink into the ground. She had heard many merry tales of Fanged Njál's stamina already.

"Zivah," he called, and her ears began to buzz. She knew she would have to get up, and felt herself waver when she tried to move, as if she was going to faint. But Njál signaled for her to stop her from moving and locked her eyes with his instead. She wondered how they did that.

"Just stay there, Zivah," he said, "I only wanted to tell you something. You see, we thought you would like to know that nobody here is slighting you or anything. It is not as if we do not like you. It is just that your House-Bond has declared you unavailable. No men may touch you here. We men thought you should know, so that you will not feel left out or scorned. We see you are doing a good job with Hel-Hound also. We thought you might like a comb for her long fur."

He tossed the comb through the air and gave an approving nod when Zivah, without thinking, caught the comb with one hand and looked at him with her huge doe-eyes. She met his gaze for a moment more and saw that light in his eyes, the same light she had seen before. Kindness. He was letting her know out of kindness because he understood that she was afraid. He was telling her that she was safe.

She could not grasp it. How could he just rape a screaming girl right in front of them all and then show her this kindness after?

"You will get us one day, River Woman," Njál said and winked at her before he left, just like that night on the ship when he gave little Hel-Hound into her care. Before Zivah could resume her work or even her working mind, Suri dropped down to sit next to her, and sat down heavily, followed by a deep sigh, before she exclaimed loud enough for the whole court to hear; "Oh by all the gods of high heaven, does Fanged Njál know how to fuck!"

All the women rolled over in laughter.

They were really insane, each and every one of them.

One of the first things I learned at Arnulf's house was that I was not allowed to go outside the gates on my own. I was very curious about the town, but had to accept that the men were not particularly interested in taking me there, saying that it was not a fit place for young maidens. I was not even allowed to enter the warriors' Hall. There was, apparently, a whole world out there in which the men did their men things and I had no part of that. In effect, I was stuck in Arnulf's house and the courtyard until Thióðolf began to take me horse-riding.

I was noble born, and as such, I was supposed to engage in the activities of noble women. But Aldeigjuborg was a town of Vikings and their slaves, and there were simply few noble women around to teach me such activities, since almost all the women were slaves or else of little consequence. Most free wives were not Norsewomen, but came from the other kinds of people who lived among us, and I did not know them in any case, dwelling in a Viking warriors' court where I sometimes suspected no House-Bonds would ever take their wives. And so I had very few sensible things to do except hang around, play with the dogs, Zivah's kitten, the chicken, the pigs and the horses, watch the men at their games and listen and ask questions endlessly.

I loved the evenings when the men were at home and I could listen to all the interesting things they talked about. Sometimes we bathed together, and after a while I got used to Arnulf's almost nightly and sometimes daily dalliances with one or both of his concubines, who never seemed to tire of it. It was clear that Aziza and Laimi were slaves, yet I never saw him treat them with anything but kindness and affection, and both of them seemed to adore him in return. Apart from his gentle manners around them in the day, their cries of pleasure every night possibly explained why.

There were evenings when Arnulf and Thióðolf sat with the warriors in the men's Hall, and then I sat at home with the slaves, listening to the distant sounds of men laughing, singing and cheering, as well as the slave talk in the house. I volunteered to help with the spinning and the weaving, which was appropriate for my status even if the slaves did most of the work, but this evening work always made me sleepy.

I was very curious about all the things Shumayl seemed to know about medicine and rune-carving into wax tablets, but the little man never seemed to warm to me, trying very hard to not show how terrified he was of me, even as it was obvious that he was. I knew not why, for he must surely have understood that I was no Hel Maiden after all.

Thióðolf had explained to me that the word he had whispered when he saw me was a Tunic word for Hel Maiden. I wished so much that I could ask him about his homeland, but his attitude towards me discouraged further inquiries, at least for the time being. Although I could harass the slaves all I liked, I refrained from doing so when I understood that they were avoiding me.

Zivah, who hardly ever spoke to me unless she had to, and then only in the polite and submissive manner of all slaves, seemed to find her place among the other slaves, becoming friends with the concubines in particular, although she maintained a certain distance to the five pretty women who served the warrior's Hall and slept there, as if their fate could somehow infect her if she came too close to them. But she was clearly comfortable with all the other bonds-women.

When I saw them working together and chatting endlessly with each other from a distance, and how they went silent whenever I drew near, I sensed that Zivah needed that space and that community for herself, and father had told me that to abuse one's power over others was dishonorable and ought to be avoided. And so I refrained from interfering with the slaves more than I had to. The invisible borders between slaves and free people were set between us, even as we shared both house and bed and table. The slaves themselves seemed more comfortable that way.

Only Búi the stable boy seemed happy to talk to me, and I talked to him whenever the men were out and I had nobody else to talk to, Búi and the horses. I would have talked to him even if others were around, because I liked him, but one day we had been talking together, the warrior called Hialti came and struck Búi across the face, telling him not to be so familiar with Arnulf's noble fosterling. I did not feel quite as comfortable around Búi after that, seeing how he always made sure to be very submissive towards me, and I found that I did not like that.

When the warriors were out and only a few were left to guard the court and did not pay attention to us, I still talked to him as before, but it was never the same after Hialti had punished him. Hialti had a thing for keeping slaves in their places, I had noticed. He could be rather cruel to the slaves when he thought himself undetected, liked to boss them around and take them in the stables. Only Zivah and the concubines were out of his reach, and I noticed that he only ever used one out of the five Sheaths, the one called Miri, who seemed to detest him always.

I had also noticed that Hialti was not particularly courageous during battle training, when he had to face people who matched him or outdid him in strength and rank. I perceived that nobody liked him very much, and that Thióðolf and Arnulf often frowned when he had passed by, looking at each other as if they were sharing dark thoughts about the man. I kept out of his way because he sometimes glared at me and never averted his eyes to me, even though I always respected him in that way.

After a week of getting acquainted with the horses, Thióðolf taught me how to ride. Almost every morning, unless he was required to join the men in some of those mysterious things men did without ever taking me with them, he took me to the hills and fields around Aldeigjuborg, and I was usually riding my favorite horse, Frost-Fax. I loved that horse, and loved riding even more, because it made me feel like I was flying. As usual, I was a fast learner, and Thióðolf taught me many tricks until I could even stand in my saddle.

When the men were practicing in the courtyard, which was almost every day, I was there around them, dutifully making Ivarr's life as miserable as I could, or else playing. Sometimes the men would play the racket ball game with me, and commented upon how good I was at aiming right. I saw that they were also playing at aims, either by throwing knives or pebbles at a target, or by shooting with bow and arrow. I had always been good at aiming straight, but had not had practice since I lived in the village. Nobody asked me if I wanted to try, but one day I went up to a group of men throwing pebbles at a goal and stopped before them, clearing my throat. They all regarded me curiously, and I respectfully lowered my eyes. The men smiled and averted their eyes briefly to signal mutual respect.

"Warriors," I began, "I would like to join you in the aiming game, if you do not mind."

"Well, Maiden, I don't know if it is a game for you, but you may try, of course," one of the men said, called Agnarr. I picked up a pebble and threw it from an appropriate distance for my size, and shot right at the target. The men exchanged glances.

"You must excuse me, Maiden, it seems this be a game for you after all. You are welcome to take turns with us," Agnarr declared, and we all smiled to each other. After a while it became clear that I had a great talent for aiming straight, what caused a great deal of attention from the men because they deemed it unusual for an untrained girl.

Arnulf came and asked if I had played such games before, and I revealed that my mother had taught me how to shoot with bow and arrow, and that I had always been true to the mark.

"Then you have a knack for it," Arnulf said, "and all noble talents must be cultivated. It is most fitting for a warrior's daughter to know the art of the bow. Hallgrim," he called out, "would you care to make a bow for the maiden, fitting her frame? With little arrows to go?"

Hallgrim lowered his eyes to Arnulf and said, "Of course, Heri, I would be honored. Come, little Síf, let us take some measurements."

I went with Hallgrim, who tried out some yew wood forms on me before he began to work on my bow. Hallgrim was the highest ranking among Arnulf's warriors, partly because he was a seasoned warrior of great skill, but mostly because he had the additional skill of good craftsmanship and also because he was a cunning man.

Now, I watched him carefully because I wanted to know how the bow was made, and how it was made differently from the way we did at home. He let me watch and even began to explain what he was doing, and when he noticed my interest, he said it was another unusual thing for a maiden to take an interest in wood-work.

"I take an interest in everything that happens before me at all times, Hallgrim," I informed him gravely.

"Then you are a very wise little maiden," Hallgrim said, nodding approvingly. I looked into his eyes for a moment and once more thought them deep pools that saw everything, both within and without. When my bow and arrows were finished, I tried it out in the courtyard and soon found how to best work with my new bow. As with the pebbles, I was true to the mark almost all the time. I spent some time every day shooting, and soon enough, Thióðolf let me take my arms out when we were riding, and let me shoot at trees and suchlike, from horseback. He told me that he would take me hunting when I was a little older.

I may not have had the same upbringing as most warrior's daughters, lacking in female mentors, but the men taught me whatever they could, whenever I asked, and so I came to know the warriors' way better than most maidens. As soon as I had picked up on all the little ways we paid each other respect or reverence, even though it mostly meant that I had to lower my eyes, I felt at home with the men. I knew that most of them were not very nice men, really, but they were nice to me, embraced me as one of their own, and the Rus Vikings pampered me endlessly for as long as I respected them and their ways.

THE WARRIOR'S WAY

Feeling awkward around the slaves, I stayed with the warriors as much as I could. Every day I watched the warriors at their practice, and my mind had always been such that it picked up every move that others did, until I began dreaming about how to make the same moves I had seen them do. My body began to twitch impatiently, and sometimes it was as if a silent chorus rose from my hammer pendant, carrying a message from my forefathers. You need to learn how to think like a warrior, the ancient voices said, and they said it over and over. One evening as we sat around the table, I decided to broach the subject.

"Heri," I said timidly to Arnulf, "Can a maiden learn the battle arts? Apart from shooting?"

The men looked at each other, then at me, eyebrows raised.

"Of course she can," Arnulf said, "It is not so very common, but we have great songs about maiden-warriors, and some of them were even good in real life. Why? Do you wish to learn such arts?"

"Yes, Heri, I very much wish that."

"Why? Do you want to become a warrior?"

"Not really," I admitted.

"Why not?"

"It seems scary, to go into battle or armed combat," I replied honestly, feeling silly. The men began to laugh.

"And that explains why most girls never become warriors," Arnulf stated humorously, "Most of your lot simply think that fighting is too scary." I hid my face in shame.

"Why are you ashamed, Priestess?" Arnulf asked.

"Because you must think I am a coward," I said, removing one of my hands from my face to peer anxiously at him.

"Of course I don't think you are a coward. You are a girl. It doesn't even make sense to call a woman coward. You are not expected to be courageous in that way. You have other ways of being strong. You are already doing a great job as a man-maker. Poor Ivarr." Both men guffawed at the memory of Ivarr's angry tears earlier that day, after I had pointed at him and giggled when he fell into a piece of horse dung.

"But... then I cannot learn the battle arts?"

"You could, I just don't see why, if you think it too scary. There are always those maidens who are indeed fit to be honed, but most maidens are simply too maidenly for it." He regarded me fondly for a moment before he proceeded, "And you are quite maidenly, Priestess. Are you certain that you are not just bored because we have found no proper chores for you yet?"

"I just want," I went silent. They both looked expectantly at me, curious to know why I wanted to learn the battle arts if I did not want to be a warrior.

I gathered my courage. "My forefathers told me that I need to learn the way of the warrior, to learn how warriors think. I don't want to be a warrior. I just want to learn about what it is."

They both looked amazed, and Thióðolf leaned back, frowning, but with a little smile on his face. His deep blue eyes sparkled as they always did when inspiration had been born within. Arnulf threw his head back and laughed heartily before he patted my back affectionately and quite forcefully, making me spill my watered beer, exclaiming, "Ah, Priestess! That is the best reason a maidenly maiden could ever have for wanting to learn the arts! There is no better woman than one who understands how a warrior thinks! And such training gives noble posture, fit for a warrior's daughter. We shall have you well honed!"

Their excitement was of such a kind that I felt a little worried. Well honed, he had said. It occurred to me that they might just start to treat me the same way they treated Ivarr, and I almost felt like weeping at the thought.

"What are you thinking of, Thordís?" Thióðolf asked mildly.

"I am maybe it is not such a good idea after all," I suggested cautiously. They looked curiously at me.

"I mean," I said, "I actually like to just hone warriors."

"You mean you are afraid that we begin to hone you?" Thióðolf asked, looking sly. I smiled sheepishly and nodded. The men laughed again. "You would not like that, would you? To be treated like Ivarr?" Arnulf asked, chuckling. I shook my head and kept my mouth shut, feeling rather embarrassed. They had begun teasing me already and I was not sure I liked that at all. It was surely a lot more fun to tease Ivarr. From my point of view, that was more or less what he was for, being a boy and all, and seeing as it was my duty to hone him real sharp. But I would not want to exchange my place with him, ever.

I had a feeling it would not sound well to say that out loud, so I made a point out of shaking my head a second time instead.

"Do not worry, little one, we know you are soft, and that you have a very maidenly soul song despite your inborn courage. And here you are, already breaking apart by our exceedingly light attempt at honing you," Arnulf laughed, "so there is no way we are going to hone you the same way as we hone boys, it would not work with you."

I let out my breath.

"Unless you turn out tougher than we think you are," Arnulf suggested languidly, with laughter in his eyes, and I shook my head sternly again, quite certain that I would not be that tough at all. It had not even occurred to me before I tried to put myself in Ivarr's place that I was such a weakling.

I was breaking at the very thought of being treated like a boy. To my delight, my soft ways did not discourage my kinsmen, who still seemed more than happy to teach me. Odd. They looked as if they had hoped for this but doubted it. Arnulf smiled heartily at me.

"Of course you can learn, and then we will see how tough you are, or else just teach you whatever you can learn. That is the customary way with maidens. And even if you are too cowa... I mean, too maidenly to really become a warrior of sword and shield, just knowing ways of getting out of a strong man's grip can be a very useful thing for a girl to know. We would all very much like you to learn such ways. I will teach you myself, and Thióðolf will, is that not so, Skald?"

"That is so, Heri," Thióðolf agreed, "I think all the men will be delighted to teach her." With that, Thióðolf suddenly got up and left us, wearing that sly little smile on his face. He did not return until late at night, when I snuggled into his arms and finally slept, having problems falling asleep without him. I always slept in his embrace.

In the morning, I found my riding clothes laid out for me, thinking that I was going to ride the hills again, and looking forward to it. The riding clothes were boy's clothes, a short tunic with breeches. But instead of riding, Thióðolf presented me with another gift; a little wooden practice blade fit for my humble size, and a small shield. The practice arms were still a little heavy for me, but he told me that my strength would grow to fit them soon enough. Thióðolf and Hallgrim had made them for me the night before, after the skald had left the table, and I was so touched I hardly knew how to thank them.

But when I entered the courtyard wearing my gear, the men cheered me and called me their Shield Maiden, and so many rings were tossed through the air I knew they had been betting on this too. They had just waited for me to ask. For the next few days, I was taught all the basic moves of the sword and shield, while the men cheered me on, thinking it great entertainment.

They were nowhere near as rough with me as they were with Ivarr, since nobody thought I was seriously going to become a warrior, and mainly because I was a girl and they had to be gentle, as they considered such things. But I was a fast learner, my body seemed to have picked up all the moves already just by watching, and with that skill I earned some new respect even though I was clearly at a disadvantage, having started very late compared to most warriors, and being very little.

Yet I was dedicated and attentive, and was honored for that. Not so with Ivarr, whose skills and dedication were constantly harassed no matter how hard he tried or how well he did. He was to be a man and a warrior, and the Norsemen thought that only through constant humiliation would he ever become one.

Me, they humored to no end, which helped me gain some courage. I knew well that I would have lost my courage if they had treated me like they treated Ivarr, a boy who never seemed to break apart, neither at their mockery, or at mine. He just took it, and started over. I really began to secretly respect the boy. Of course, I could not let him know that for a moment.

RAT-HJALTI

Zivah was not sure she would ever really get used to this sort of life, but often did find herself too busy working or watching or learning something new, to ever get to think and ponder much about her fate. There was always something that needed doing, and there was always something going on, and those few moments where she paused to think she was often surprised to realize that she was not suffering. The other slaves had embraced her and treated her with such care and kindliness that all the harshness and hardness of the world seemed bearable. They all said the same. They said a human being, especially a woman, could live through almost any sort of hardships if she only had people around who loved and listened and understood her.

Even after this short time she understood that this was the truth. Each time a slave suffered, she, or he, could tell the others, and then the others would hear and listen and always support, always. There was nothing that was too embarrassing or shameful, and they could joke about everything. They even joked about their masters. In fact, they regularly joked about them as if it was a sacred ritual of ridicule that had to be observed daily, one which also seemed to be one of their most favorite pastimes. It was amazing how quickly the sharing and the hearing and the perpetual, merciless ridicule at their superiors' expense helped the slaves get over their pain and move on.

What Zivah had thought was odd was that their masters never seemed to mind the ridicule their slaves bestowed on them, as long as the formal courtesies were observed in their presence. By now, however, she had long since accepted that Norsemen simply were crazy and that their slaves could not help but be affected a little too. The fact was that the slaves could say almost whatever they pleased about most of their masters for as long as it was not said directly to a superior, and for as long as their masters kept their backs turned.

It had taken her a while to realize that clue. When the slaves sat down to work together on some chores, and most chores required a large workforce anyway, which meant that they were almost always doing things together. Why, then the free men who were present would simply turn their backs to the working slaves and pretend that they were not even there. And when the men turned their backs, the slaves could speak freely.

Zivah could see that the men often listened in, but they never interfered and there was never any consequence either, as far as Zivah could see, although the ridicule sometimes took on extreme proportions. Only after a good while did she recognize that there were indeed limits to their range of joking matters. Nobody ever spoke a harsh or disrespectful word about Arnulf Heri. Nobody ever spoke badly of Hallgrim Hidden Spear, or of Thióðolf Skald.

These three men seemed to be exempted from the slaves' jokes. She still failed to see exactly why, apart from the obvious fact that these three men ranked considerably above the others. Incomprehensibly, when these men were discussed at all, it was always with an approving tone, as if they were veritable heroes in the eyes of their slaves.

She had been quite relieved to find that nobody were beaten or tormented. The only beating she knew of so far was when Thióðolf had beaten her in the market on the first day. Apart from that she never saw anyone getting beaten or hurt apart from all the fucking, which often seemed rather hard to Zivah. But she had come to terms with the fact that it probably did not hurt as much as it looked like it should, and that the louder the shrieks and screams and moans of the women the greater was the possibility that they returned to the work circle with flushed and contented faces, ready to let the others know all about that man's capacities. And if there was less noise, they usually returned to entertain all the others about the man's lack of such. Loudly.

Fortunately, nobody ever fucked Zivah. She had felt shamed one evening when the slaves were alone in the Hold apart from Thordís Maiden, who was sleeping, and all the slaves had gone quiet for a moment before Laimi cleared her throat and asked directly, "So, how many times were you raped, Zivah?"

Zivah lowered her eyes, felt her face burn, and whispered, "I was not raped at all."

There had been an awkward silence then, and Zivah remembered the compassion and pity they had shown her on that first night, when she had been so very frightened, and they had felt sorry for her.

"That cannot be," Tana objected, to the general agreement of the other slaves. Zivah cleared her throat. "It is the truth. Arnulf was going to, three times. He did not. Thióðolf, I wept most of the times and they left me alone then, as if they felt sorry for me."

"Or guilty," Laimi snorted. There was that silence again.

"I did not mean to deceive you, Eljur," Zivah said, for the slave women of the Hold addressed each other such, as sisters belonging to the same masters, "It was the truth that I was terrified and I had seen things, and there had been, I am so sorry if you feel deceived by me."

"We do not feel so, Zivah," Aziza said gently, and she dared to look up and around, meeting their earnest faces, and surprisingly enough the same looks of compassion as before. And where she had worried that the other slaves might become jealous and angry with her for somehow being treated as if she was better than they, she found to her astonishment that they were all happy for her. It was almost as if they admired her a little for it.

Zivah felt their admiration, and to her own surprise, she no longer even knew how to let herself go with the sort of pride that before had seized her when she felt admired. Zivah discovered, now that the world had settled into something remotely stable, that being admired and set apart as special was no longer anything she relished in. She recalled how much she had always enjoyed being admired, watched, desired and loved, but after the raid and the weeks on the Viking ship full of leering and threatening men, she never stopped flinching if a man as much as looked at her.

She would rather fade and become invisible, a faceless part of a large slave crowd, than one who stood apart and was desired by men. She had seen enough of what that sort of desire really meant and was thankful for her gray and formless slave dress which covered up her body. Every day she pulled her beautiful dark golden hair tight into a bun at the neck in the most unattractive way she could muster, and no longer considered her own natural beauty as a very great asset, all in all.

After the revelation of the fact that Zivah from the river lands was the only she-slave among them who could remember knowing actual freedom, and was, furthermore the only one among them who had never been raped, the other slaves still seemed to think that she had been worse off than most of them ever had, what never ceased to amaze her. Zivah stopped complaining and wailing about the fate that had befallen her as soon as she realized that these people who pitied her and felt for her had suffered far worse and for far longer time than she ever had.

As to the Rus-men, their lords, they had taken some getting used to. But Zivah lived so close to these men and saw them all the time, even in their most intimate moments. Even though she could still remember some of them from the raid, that memory seemed to fade and become a dream unreal, and all she really had was the present. And the present was positively crammed with these prowling, oversized, predatory beasts that passed for men.

To start with, she had been surprised at how fondly the slaves often talked about them also. They joked about them, but there was a great deal of affection there, a lot more than she thought she could ever grasp the root of. With all the courtesies that had to be observed it took time to discover the deeper bonds and relations going on at the Viking court at all times. As it happened, she found herself, little by little, not only getting accustomed to these men. She had almost even started to like some of them, after a fashion anyway.

She had come to trust that they would not hurt her, and she had come to understand that even if she could never have born being treated like the other slaves, her friends really did not seem to be suffering so much. Sometimes she could not help but laugh or be awed by the many antics these men kept performing every day. They were certainly not a boring lot, even if they were both insane and shameless. When they took off their clothes to wash in the courtyards every evening, after their exercise, she could not help but notice that they were all amazingly well built. Most of the slave girls leered at them openly.

Zivah had to admit to herself that even she sometimes found their grace and manly beauty somewhat, redeeming. Just a little. She knew that they were pleasing to the eyes, but she still could not really watch their powerful bodies without thinking of the violence they were capable of and which she had seen too much of. And when she remembered what they could use those bodies for, that strength and flexibility so much admired by the other women became more threatening to Zivah than attractive.

Yet, as brutish as they were, it was not as if they did not know how to be charming, even sweet at times. She once caught herself thinking that Njál was cute. Njál with the fangs and the spiky hair and vicious scars. She had seen him in the courtyard practicing his battle arts, and she had heard the tales of how he drank the blood gushing from his enemies throats when he was in battle, after tearing them open with his teeth. He also seemed to be partial to all the slave girls in court, and they always thanked him after, but that was certainly not on account of his gentleness. It seemed laughable, to call that man cute. He was, actually.

Many of them were, once they sat down and relaxed and showed their more human faces. Many of them really were quite sweet. Zivah did not want to admit that, but it just crept up on her from time to time, despite her efforts to maintain her resentment and grudge. It was in fact hard to stay around these men all the time and not begin to like many of them, just a little, despite everything. The way one could, of course, start to like and find fascinating a beast that was both dangerous and unpredictable.

It was one of those late summer days where the last heat seemed to linger in the air. Most of the free folks, including Thióðolf and Thordís, had gone to the river to bathe, and had been joined by four of the five Sheaths as well as the concubines. Zivah had noticed that they had been waiting by the gate for a while before leaving, and heard them call for Miri.

When Miri had failed to appear by the gate, the free folks and the other Sheaths left without her, and Hallgrim seemed to change his mind about going to the river and stayed behind instead. He went to work in his woodshop outside of the Hall. The slave women were busy with laundry, and Zivah was there when Tana was to take a basketful of clean towels and sheets to the warriors' Hall, but suddenly appeared to feel ill, and fainted. The other slaves gathered round, Shumayl first, and his gentle hands brought the youngest slave girl back to consciousness.

"I don't want to go," Tana whispered, her tears streaming, and the slaves exchanged glances. Then Shumayl looked at Zivah. All of them went quiet and looked at Zivah, as if they wanted her to do something.

"You are the one they call Untouchable," Shumayl said to her.

"Oh," said Zivah, blushing, and took the laundry basket.

She had never been inside the Hall before, and dreaded even to look at it, but now that most of the menfolk were out she directed her steps as confidently as she could towards the entrance and saw that the door was shut.

"Miri?" She called, since it occurred to her that nobody had seen Miri all morning and that the Sheath might be inside the Hall. There was no reply, but the door opened slowly inwards. She could not see who had opened it, for the doors of the Norsemen's halls were always so low that they had to bow down to get inside. It was a defense device, she knew. With such a low door, a single man could defend a hall from many intruders, who had to enter one by one and head first, head held low. She had seen how they even slept with their weapons. All about fighting and war, these people. And fucking, let us not forget that. She drew her breath and bowed down while carrying the basket through the door. As soon as she had stepped inside she felt an iron grip around her neck and almost lost her basket.

"Heri," she whispered, and looked into Rat Hialti's leering eyes.

"You woke me," he growled, "just in time."

"I am sorry, Heri. I did not mean to wake you. I was just coming by with the laundry," she whimpered, wondering when he was going to let go of her neck.

"Yes, laundry - and something more. You can put the basket over there," he said and pointed to a table by the wall. Zivah was so nervous that she did not even look around the Hall but moved towards the table and felt to her dread that he followed her. Her hands were trembling when she set the basket down. He was standing right behind her, breathing down her neck. This could not be happening. Not now, when she had finally begun to feel safe.

The dread she felt was blended with an awkward sense of relief that it was Hialti who stood there behind her and nobody else, because he was the only one among them whom she was absolutely sure that she would never like and never trust. So, it did not feel like quite such a betrayal that it was him who finally did what she had expected would happen at some point anyway, being a slave.

The river. The river. The river daughter closed her eyes.

He seemed to like to just stand there behind her and let her wonder what he was going to do to her. He liked to scare and hurt, they had told her. The only thing that kept him from really hurting the slaves was the presence of the other men, who would not accept maltreatment.

Apparently, Arnulf Heri commanded gentle treatment of all slaves and there was a set of rules that the men followed. She knew that from what she had heard spoken when the slaves praised their House-Bond for adhering to ancient rules of honorable conduct regarding the court's slaves. They obviously knew nothing of what he was like when he was out on his summer expeditions. They only saw a just and kind master who had made an effort to keep them as happy as possible.

The slaves praised their House-Bond for his protection, but the protection of slaves could only go so far. Most of the men felt honor-bound to not only heed the rules of their lord but to integrate them thoroughly. Rat-Hialti, on the other hand, bent and stretched these rules as far as he could get away with and had a sort of talent for it. Now, the most detested and by slaves most feared man in court had her trapped. He reached out to touch her breast from where he was standing behind her, breathing down her neck, and squeezed it in a way that hurt. She whimpered and tried to keep it down. Do not let him see that he hurts you, she had heard them say to each other. He likes that. He likes it if you plead and beg and cry and whimper. Then it becomes worse. Look as indifferent as you can. Indifferent. Go to the within place.

All the women knew that place, it seemed.

Zivah tried to think of the river, but was still waiting for the command. If he gave the command she could reply that which they had told her to say. He just kept touching her up and she did not know exactly how far Thióðolf's declaration of unavailability went. She had been prepared for a command, not direct action. Then his hands started to move into hidden places and she could not help it anymore. She flinched. He had her by the throat instantly and flung her towards a bed, where she fell over. She sat up immediately but did not dare to get out of the bed when she saw his stone-cold glare.

"Are you resisting me, slave?" He asked as he approached the bed, opening his breeches.

"Heri, please," she stuttered, "My House, my House-Bond forbids me. Please, Heri, I cannot disobey my House-Bond."

"You cannot disobey, that is the core of the matter, slave," Hialti said, "and if you tell anyone, I am going to make your life utterly miserable. You know I can, and you have not gotten nearly enough fucking since you came here, poor girl. Pull up your skirt and spread your legs."

It was happening so fast, Zivah thought, this was too fast. The man drew closer and she felt a strange sensation of something collapsing within her, something that fell with the absolute certainty that there was absolutely nothing she could do to stop him and that she might as well give up at once. She remembered that feeling from before, when Arnulf had first thrown her on the bed in a similar manner.

This time she would not cry. Her genuine tears might have worked on Arnulf and Thióðolf, but no sorts of tears would ever work on this one, unless it was to provoke further lust. Zivah began leaning backwards, trying to think of the river.

"Hialti!" Miri's voice called out, and the man turned around. Zivah immediately sat up again and lowered her skirt. For some inexplicable reason the Sheath came crawling out from beneath one of the beds, where she had probably been hiding from him all morning, so far successfully, and Rat-Hialti gathered as much, turning red from anger.

"Were you hiding from me beneath the bed, Miri?" Hialti wheezed, temporarily forgetting Zivah. Miri shook her head innocently.

"I was not hiding, Heri. I sleep better there, somehow," the slave woman mumbled.

"Come here," he barked. Miri hesitated for a moment but gathered her courage and walked up to Hialti with her head held very low. Nevertheless he struck her across the face so hard she fell down without a sound, as if she had been prepared and was used to it. She scrambled to her knees and stayed there on the floor, kneeling and with her face low.

Zivah could see that Hialti enjoyed that, hovering above his defenseless bondswoman. They think there is no honor in conquering a helpless slave, so there is no joy in humiliating us more than we already are, Aziza had told her once, when she had asked why the men often overlooked and pretended not to notice little slights of rank and duty from the slaves.

Hialti seemed to enjoy it. He grinned while he looked at the kneeling woman and then at the woman who was still sitting on the bed. Rat-Hialti seemed to think that he had come to a very good place all of a sudden, what with two slaves to torment at the same time and no other men around to stop him. It looked as if an assortment of thrilling ideas were passing through his mind before he probably decided to keep it simple if he was to get anywhere at all. Privacy was not to be taken for granted in a place like this.

"It is your fortune, Miri," he said, "that this sweet girl came here today. I have a mind to let you off for now, even though you have had the audacity of trying to avoid your master.

"I can deal with you any day, Sheath. I think I want to enjoy this unexpected treat instead. Get out and keep your mouth shut, Miri."

"Hialti Heri, that is Thióðolf's woman," Miri said, still kneeling and now leaning slightly forward to touch his foot. It was an appeal, Zivah sensed, although she had never seen that gesture before.

"What are you still talking to me for? Did you not hear my command, slave?" He sneered.

"Heri; Hallgrim and all the men, and Thióðolf, they will be very angry with you if you take that girl. She is forbidden," the woman said, still keeping her face low and touching his foot, "I am just concerned for your sake, Heri."

"How very touching. Do you want me to fuck you so badly that you cannot abide me taking another this day, perhaps? I would usually have expected you to run off at the slightest chance," he said, and started to look seriously impatient.

"Yes, Hialti Heri, please fuck me instead. I will be good, I promise," Miri replied, tugging pleadingly at his foot again.

Zivah could hardly believe these words from the other woman. She had avoided Miri, avoided all the Sheaths, so terrified of even thinking of the fate that had befallen these women, who lived in a hall full of thirty Vikings and slept in their beds. She had kept her distance to them and never accepted their cautious approaches and friendly attempts to talk. Now this woman was volunteering to take her place as Hialti's victim. Hialti let out a snorting laugh.

"Do you two women know what would happen to me if I take Zivah and it is known to the other men, and to Thióðolf? Do you know?" He asked them both, sounding triumphant, like he was about to win a great battle, although his opponents were obviously helpless to begin with. Hialti seemed oblivious to the absurdity of his sense of heroic victory, and proceeded gleefully; "I would have to pay him a fine, Miri. A little fine. Nothing I could not cover. That is the only thing that would happen to me, if they found out. As to you two, I think you can imagine how much trouble I can make for you. You are slaves, and now I think you ought to be a good slave and obey me, Miri. Go out and shut the door and keep that mouth shut too."

"Yes, Heri," Miri muttered and got to her feet, casting an apologetic glance at Zivah, who felt her heart go wild again.

Please do not leave me alone with him, she thought, in vain, of course. Miri left the Hall and Hialti turned to Zivah with a very ugly sort of grin. He really did look like a hungry rat.

"What did I tell you earlier about spreading your legs and lifting your skirt? Did you not hear my command?" His eyes narrowed. Zivah stared at him, and he glared back at her until she lowered her eyes and bowed her head. There was just no way she could not do what he said. She knew it.

Even if she tried to get away and managed, there was no saying what he would do to her then, later. He was a free man, and nobody would stand up for her against him. Zivah remembered something her mother had said to her once, that if you have to do something you do not want to do, then do it with grace. She suddenly felt relaxed, and remembered Thunder Bear's counsel about self respect no matter what happened to her. She was not going to cry and tremble to feed his hungry rat mind.

"I am sorry, Heri," she said slowly, and started to think of the flowing river while she leaned backwards and pulled up her skirt. He was already climbing into the bed without his breeches on and his lord stone pointing at her. She closed her eyes and spread her legs and forced herself back to the flowing river of her heart.

"That's a good little slave," he grunted into her ear, sharp poison words that came echoing through the river flow.

Then something happened above her. It was as if Hialti was flung backwards through the air. She opened her eyes and saw Hallgrim standing on the floor, tall and stately and powerful, and one arm out to the side as if he had just flung something. Hialti was rolling around on the floor without any trousers on, whimpering and looking so scared.

She saw it in his eyes, those leering rat-eyes, a fear she had not ever seen shown in the face of any of the Vikings before. The little rat feared Hallgrim Hidden Spear, and as the shadow walker stood and glared at Hialti, Hialti did not dare to even get up from the floor. In fact, he was kneeling. She almost expected him to touch the other man's foot.

"Apologize," Hallgrim commanded, his voice dark and deep. She remembered that sort of voice. It was akin to the voice used by Thunder Bear when there was no way you could possibly not obey him.

"I am sorry, Hallgrim," Hialti wheezed, his eyes darting to and fro like a panicking beast caught in a trap, "I forgot that she is Thióðolf's woman. She has the same collar as the others."

"Not to me. To her," Hallgrim said. Hialti stared wildly at him.

"You cannot mean that," he whispered.

"I can mean that. Apologize to Zivah." Hallgrim used that voice again. Hialti stared at her, and she stared back, wide-eyed. She thought she was dreaming when kneeling, Hialti bowed his head to her and said, "I am sorry, Zivah."

"Get out," Hallgrim commanded. Hialti obediently scurried to his feet and almost forgot to put his breeches back on before he hurried out of the door. Hallgrim turned to Zivah. He regarded her with those strange, dark eyes of his, and there seemed to be a light of regret in them, and sadness. In her confusion she almost thought she even saw love in those impossible pools of his spirit.

"I am also sorry, Zivah," Hidden Spear said, "and if anything like this happens again, scream. Shout. Kick. Run. Nobody is going to blame you. He would not dare to harm you visibly. If he tells you that he can harm you, he is lying. You are forbidden, even to touch. If you fight, you are only fighting according to the commands of your House-Bond. You must obey your House-Bond before anybody else. If anyone else gives you a contrary command you will not be punished for resisting. It is not true that Hialti can get away with something like that. Because if he harms you, he is offending Thióðolf, and then Thióðolf has the right to kill him.

Do you know what, Zivah? He will. Your man would kill Hialti if he harmed you. We all would. Understand?"

"Yes, Heri," she squeaked, and met his gaze again, "and thank you. Thank you, Hallgrim Heri." She could not believe he had really rescued her. His words of how they would all kill Hialti if he harmed her blurred in her mind, confusing words, incomprehensible.

Hallgrim suddenly smiled at her.

"Do you know, Zivah, that we never expect women to be courageous when it comes to situations like this. We adore them if they are, but we do not expect it, and we certainly do not expect courage from slaves. But there is something that is called a woman's courage."

She just stared at him, so he leaned forward a little, and she felt that peace emanating from him, and saw the light of kindness in his eyes.

"A woman's courage is the courage to know what you feel and be who you are no matter what the consequences may be, in a world where powerful men forcefully require you to humor them even when they do not deserve it. To maintain that sort of integrity despite everything, Zivah, that takes great courage. It is a sort of courage that you and your sister both hold in common and hold in great bounty, and something most of us men here respect, regardless of rank. To be who you are regardless, there is nothing more courageous than that. Come now, child, get to your feet."

He held out his arm and helped her get to her feet. When she felt him so close, and felt his hand closing briefly around her arm, she had the oddest sense of yearning, as if she wanted to lean on him and burrow her face into his chest. The yearning was so powerful that she had to force herself not to, lest he started to think she wanted him to...

Before she knew more he had placed his large arm around her and pulled her close, and she burrowed her face into his chest anyway. They just stood there for a little while and she felt his steady heartbeat against her ear. He reminded her of her stepfather then, the way he had sometimes comforted her by simply being there, holding her, and saying nothing at all. Tears streamed down her face and she could not help but whisper the word.

"Thievs." Father.

"You had a good father, girl," the man replied quietly, as if he would know. Zivah was too dazzled by the protective comfort given to even think of how he could know that. When she felt utterly calm, he released her gently. They both heard some strange sounds from the outside, as if something was being crushed against the outside wall.

"I think we must go out now," Hallgrim said, and to Zivah's surprise, he took her hand and hurriedly led her to the door, where he gestured for her to stay behind him before he stepped out. Zivah came after and gasped. Hialti was taking Miri up against the wall of the Hall, and he was holding her by her hair and banging her head into the wall with each thrust, grinning viciously at the two of them. When he noticed Hallgrim's glare, he slowed down a little and called out, "What, are you grudging me a little pleasure time with my bonds woman also, Hallgrim?"

"I am rather thinking that there is no need for cruelty, Hialti. The slave is obliging you," Hallgrim said. Zivah looked up at the man and saw the anger hidden there, but he was not going to do anything, because there was no rule that said Hialti could not take or even punish his slave.

"Oh, well," Hialti said, "I will finish soon," and continued taking the woman, but stopped banging her head against the wall. For some reason, Hallgrim did not walk away, but stood there and waited until the man had finished his business. Zivah noted with horror that Hialti somehow seemed to get excitement from the fact that he could do something like that in front of them and they could do nothing to stop him. Hallgrim stayed and Zivah stood watching the ground, knowing that this was a way of protecting Miri against worse hurts, and when the man had finished, he looked a little embarrassed all of a sudden and left quickly.

Miri stretched her back and held a hand to her forehead, turned to Hallgrim and groaned, "What, are you waiting for your turn, Hallgrim Heri?" She smiled as she said it. Smiled and bled from the nose, Zivah noticed, and wept. The Sheath smiled and wept and bled and was making a joke.

"You know me, Miri," Hallgrim replied, smiling back, although there was sadness in his eyes. "Are you very hurt?"

"Rather, Heri. If this continues I think I am going to go up in one of those towers and just let myself fall, Hallgrim. This is too much. Nobody can rule me if I am dead."

The slave girl looked straight at Hallgrim when she spoke, and Zivah knew that Miri was deadly serious. She saw the reaction in Hallgrim's face too, his recognition of how serious his bondswoman was.

"That is true, Miri. But look, do you see little Hel-Hound there?" Hallgrim said, pointing.

"I see her, Heri," Miri said, and the three of them looked at the young, female and increasingly rather bloodthirsty cat running across the courtyard, chasing a screaming mouse. Hel-Hound suddenly caught the mouse, took it in her mouth, placed it gleefully on the ground, and then used her paw to hurl the little one into the air. They gazed at the playing cat, which was beginning to earn her name.

Everybody in the whole court, including the hounds, loved that cat and treated her with great reverence also. The free men often said she was a holy sort of beast. She had even stood up to all the large hounds of the court from the very first day, defending her own, and now all the dogs were treating her as if she was the puppy of their pack.

Hel-Hound reminded Zivah of Thordís, sometimes, when she observed the girl running about among the men. A kitten steadily earning increased respect and growing affection from large and wolf-like hounds.

Yet it was Zivah she came to whenever she wanted to cuddle. Only to Zivah. Hel-Hound seemed to have no interest in any other two-legged creature. Zivah smiled. Folks had started to call her Cat Mother.

Hel-Hound, her fosterling, threw the mouse up in the air again.

"I heard that her kind eats rats too," Hallgrim muttered darkly, "We only have to wait until she is a little bigger, Miri. Just a little more. Then there will be a deal of rat hurling too. Miri, you have the rest of the day and night off. If you want to sit in the tower and not fall out of it, you can. In fact, you have my permission to stay up there for as much as you want until the Hel-Hound has done her job, and nobody will bother you up there. Take as much beer as you want with you. Take Zivah for company. Keep it going, Miri, just a little while more. You may find the conclusion to all this surprisingly rewarding."

Zivah frowned, wondering what it was that he was really saying. Norsemen spoke so often in riddles that she had a hard time knowing what they really meant sometimes. Miri knew, and she saw how their eyes met in mutual understanding.

"I thank you, Heri," Miri said, "and I might take you up on that offer. There is one more thing, just so I do not take that fall after all,"

"Yes, Miri," he said mildly, and Zivah saw the emotion that ran across his face. He loves this woman, she thought, astonished. He really loves her. How is that even possible here?

"I would like to sleep in Hallgrim's arms tonight. Just sleep. I need some holding," Miri muttered.

Miri did not look at him when she asked, she was looking away, and she was not even asking him directly, she was just saying it, the way slaves and inferiors must speak to make free men listen. Hallgrim shrugged and grunted in response, and Zivah knew that the slave girl's request for comfort would be granted.

Two Slave Girls in the Tower

When the defender and embracer of slave girls walked off, she went over to Miri, who was still clasping her own head, moaning with pain. Zivah placed her arms gently around her and held her for a long time, and said nothing, wanted nothing, except to stand there and give comfort, swallowing her own grief and struggling to hide her sense of guilt, her wish to apologize, and her feeling of powerlessness, her inability to ever atone for what the other woman had suffered in her place.

She had wanted to speak of it, wanted to tell Miri how bad she felt, but somehow she could hear Mother's voice echoing through her mind. Guilt can become a demand, the Healer had once told her. If you show that you feel guilty for somebody else's suffering, if you show them that you feel incapable of helping them, you are in fact not helping them, not even offering real comfort. Then you are instead hurling at them a demand to be forgiven, denying them your shoulder to lean on. You are but craving even more from them, when what they need is to be held and heard.

Miri relaxed into her embrace and leaned her hurting head against Zivah's chest and stood thus quietly for a while before she smiled and exclaimed, "By the goddess of all blooming things, Zivah, what a lovely and well cushioned chest you have here. If I can come and rest my head on your bosom now and then I will gladly stand in for you any time. Now let us observe the Heri's orders and grab as much beer and food as possible and have a party. Bring those chest-cushions of yours."

Zivah could not help but giggle. The two young women ran into the storage room, grabbed a few containers with beer and something Miri called wine, and some bread. They were both giggling excitedly, and tip-toed around as if that would make them invisible, but the other slaves had already sensed that something was going on, that it was private, and let them alone.

Zivah cast an uncertain glance at Aziza, who just nodded to her, confirming that she could take an evening off with her new friend. Then they climbed up into one of the towers where they stood and looked out at the world while they drank and talked and, as soon as Zivah got the hang of it, sang brawly songs together.

At some point, Zivah cautiously asked her why she had done it. Miri could have just stayed in her hiding place. She had not had to stay there and take the blow, or alert Hallgrim in the first place. Then Miri turned to her and smiled, and touched her cheek gently, speaking surprising words, "Oh, Zivah, you have no idea what you mean to us girls, do you?"

Zivah looked dumbstruck, having no idea at all, and Miri laughed and hugged her.

"I am not going to tell you, exactly. But do you know, Zivah, do you know that you have something about you? A power, of sorts. Something holy, something that lives so strongly in you that even the most ruthless sort of folks will think twice before they try and crush you. It is an innocence perhaps. Yes. It is a sort of innocence. A precious sort of innocence that radiates from you, Amber Eyes. It is holy, Zivah, what you are carrying within that well-shaped frame of yours. And sweet Elja, there is nobody in this court who wants to see that taken from you, nobody!" Miri paused to frown and added, "Except Hialti. But darling, I would fuck Hialti any day if that could save you from him. Come to think of it, I am fucking Hialti almost every day anyway, so you do not have to feel so very guilty about it. Have you not realized it, River Land Woman? We are looking out for you, sister."

Her eyes were so sincere when she said it, and Zivah frowned and shook her head uncertainly. She had no idea what Miri meant, but she felt honored by the message that came along with these words. The message that she was very well-liked, and that many folks at Arnulf's court were looking out for her, many more than she had thought before.

"Why did you stay out there, Miri?" She asked, "You must have guessed that Hialti would be angry. You could have gone and, kept away a little."

"Let somebody else take it instead? No, Zivah, this is my call. I am the only girl here that Hialti cannot hurt."

"I think he was hurting you a great deal back there."

"Oh, he tries. But Zivah, there is nothing a man can do to me that will really, truly hurt me."

"How can you say that?"

"Because I do not care what he wants," Miri said, "I do not care what he thinks of me either. I can kneel and put my arse up and down in any direction required and I do not care, Zivah, I am past humiliation. I only wept back there because my head hurt."

They drank in silence for a little while, and Zivah did not know what to say. Miri looked at her, a little glimpse in her eyes, and asked, "Do you pity me, oh queen of the river lands?" Zivah quickly shook her head, before she changed her mind and nodded. It was better to be honest, she had found. People were uncannily perceptive around here.

"It is all about where you come from, sweet girl," Miri said, "You may be surprised to learn that when I came to Arnulf's court I felt beyond fortunate. I was very happy here, Zivah. I had been made their Sheath even before I came here and I already knew my men. My House-Bonds."

"You knew all thirty of them?"

"Thirty? Do you think I have thirty House-Bonds?" Miri giggled, "My goodness, Zivah, now I get why you are pitying me. Do you think all thirty of them fuck me every night?"

"Can you blame me if I thought so?" Zivah felt a little curious now.

"No, no of course not, they are a bunch of horny beasts, our masters," Miri laughed heartily, "but Zivah, we are five Sheaths, and we are shared by six men each. The same men. And nobody else is allowed to even touch us, Zivah, apart from these six. Not even the other warriors of the Hall. Nobody can call on me during the day like they do with the serving maids, apart from either of the six to whom I am bound. I have six House-Bonds, and I live with them, eat with them, fuck with them, sleep with them, drink and party and talk and sing and dance with them. We are like a family. We even sleep in the same large bed, and the men take turns sleeping next to me. I am like their concubine, only the other way around. Where Aziza and Laimi must share a man, I have six at my disposal. And I used to be happy!"

Miri banged her fist in the wall, getting a little drunk.

"You are their slave," Zivah whispered uncertainly. Miri talked about her six men as if they were married or something. She spoke of family.

"Yes, you know what, Zivah, even if I have been a slave for as long as I remember, it does not mean I am no woman and have no heart. I loved my men. They loved me. But after Bóðvarr, he was such a sweet man, Zivah. He could crush the neck of a horse with his bare hands. All hails to Bóðvarr!" Miri cried and raised her cup to drink. Zivah took another sip and, brawling, agreed that Bóðvarr the sixth House-Bond sounded like a very sweet fellow, what with the strong grip and all. She was starting to go insane too, no doubt.

"Bóðvarr died less than two years ago. I had five years of happiness, Zivah, five years of true companionship with my House-Bonds. And then Bóðvarr went and died on us. From a damn arrow. An arrow. And after some months passed they needed another warrior for the hall and another to fill up the six, and in came Hialti. Hialti! Rat-Hialti! He destroys everything, Zivah. Everything. He is getting worse and worse. He poisons my relation to my men. I am losing my respect for them. Even for Hallgrim. Oh, I shall bow my head and open my legs and all that but I am NOT GOING TO RESPECT THEM ANYMORE ANYWAY!"

She screamed it out for the whole court to hear.

Zivah tried to hush her down, asking her why she could no longer respect her men, and Miri looked at her and shook her head, "Because they cannot protect me. What sort of men cannot protect their woman against abuse? I am a slave, so he has the right to abuse me, and there is nothing they can do to stop him.

"Now I despise them all. We used to be so happy together. Now all I do is want to die or get drunk."

Zivah threw her arms around the other woman again and decided to try out that drink called wine, now that the first beer flask was empty. And then they both got really drunk.

There was a point when the girls had gotten the bright idea to piss while sitting on the fence up there. They had been trying to aim and all. Zivah could hear the sound of her own abandoned laughter a long time after, and later had the vague memory of people looking up at them, astonished, and Miri saying, "Well Zivah, that is the first time anyone here ever heard you laugh, and if I may say so you have the sweetest sort of laugh I ever heard. Look at them people. Look at them. Men and women both adore you, Zivah, do not doubt that. Laugh, because it makes them happy. They want more. Here, I will tickle you."

She had tickled her and Zivah had begun to laugh again, while Miri praised the goddess for her laugh by raising her hands, exclaiming that hers was a laugh that sounded like the joyful chatter of birds.

Zivah told her that she was mightily sure the people who were looking were just trying to get a peek at their buttocks and that she ought to think less of her laugh and more about how to piss straight down from the tower without hitting any of the Heris, seeing as that might get them into trouble, what caused them both to giggle hysterically while they tried very hard to get it all proper. After the slave girls in the tower had discussed at length whether the pissing project had been a success or not, and their voices were getting more and more loud, they both suddenly slumped down and leaned their heads against each other's shoulders. Zivah, pondering, wondered why fate was shifted so unequally in this world of songs.

"What I don't understand about you, my fellow slaves," Zivah muttered slowly, "is how you can all pity me. It seems to me that all of you have suffered and still suffer far more than I have ever done."

Miri looked tenderly at her and murmured sleepily, "Oh, but Zivah, we slaves who live here; we all came from nothing. We will rejoice in anything that can make our lives into something more than nothing at all. But you, oh Zivah, poor girl, my poor sister. You had something precious! You had freedom, and family and a sweetheart of your own! You had thoughts for the future and folks what loved you without wanting anything back! Then you lost everything!"

Miri actually began crying, and Zivah's heart shattered from within.

"Oh, my poor child," the Sheath wept, took the younger woman's hand compassionately, squeezed it and looked earnestly into her eyes, "There is not one of us slaves here who cannot pity that."

The wise woman's drunken head drooped, and she slept, even as Zivah sobbed, "I never even knew what I had before it was gone."

Zivah saw how Hallgrim squatted down next to them and looked at Miri with tenderness in his gaze. She saw how he traced the lines of her cheek so very gently before he carefully lifted her and threw her over his shoulder so that he could climb down from the tower with her.

Miri would sleep in his embrace that night.

Zivah vaguely recalled having asked Miri about the riddle-speech regarding Hel-Hound the cat. Miri had just smiled slyly at her and said that there was a reason why Hallgrim had earned the nickname Hidden Spear, and then she had placed a finger over her lips to signal that she must not speak more of this. Then Zivah felt the strong hands of her own House-Bond and did not even have the presence to flinch when he lifted her. It felt good to be touched, suddenly, good to feel those big strong hands holding her.

His hands were so very warm. But she said nothing, just hung there across his shoulders while he climbed down with her, carrying her as if she weighed nothing, and placed her carefully into the bed. Thióðolf Heri tucked her in. He actually tucked her in. Zivah kept her eyes closed and felt that, felt the way he made sure that she was comfortable and well covered. She wondered how much he knew, as to why they had the party.

Images of him and all the kindness he always showed to everybody, herself included, floated past her inner eyes. A kind man. She knew it, deep down, and sometimes she even knew that the only thing she wanted was for him to acknowledge how much he had hurt her, so that she could forgive. He would never acknowledge that, because he would always think it had been his right to do so. And then the memory of how he had beaten her in the market and humiliated her before the whole town because of that stupid dress flashed vividly through her whole self.

With that image in mind, Zivah managed to restore the grudge that she had already spent so much effort nurturing. It would be such a waste of so much effort if she was to let go of that well-funded and time-consuming grudge too easily. She would still not speak to him more than she had to. Before she slept, Zivah thought about Miri, the woman who was slave to six pirate warriors, and Hialti with them. She took it for me, she thought, my sister suffered in my place. I am protected and she is not, but she was the one who protected me nevertheless. My Elja threw her body in as a shield for my sake, just so I would not have to experience even once, what she has been through hundreds of times and then some.

She thought of the words spoken earlier that day, about the courage of women. Zivah held her hands to her heart and thought that Miri, the lowest of slaves, was the most courageous woman she had ever known.

Later that night, she woke from her drunken slumber when her master entered the bed and began settling next to the soundly sleeping Thordís. Zivah, facing the wall as she always did, with her back to the two of them, could feel how he was still seated in the bed, regarding her. Then she sensed how he leaned over and felt with some dismay how she did not actually feel threatened by that movement at all. And her heart beat so hard, but not from fear, when his hand finally brushed gently, but hesitatingly past her cheek.

She made a point out of flinching.

Thióðolf her House-Bond quickly withdrew his hand.

So there. It will take more Atonement from you than this, she thought stubbornly, although it pleased her, the feeling she now got; that he had finally understood that not giving her over to other men and not using her against her will would not be enough to atone for what he and his peers had made her suffer. It was a start of sorts.

It was not enough.

Her cheek burned for a long time where the tips of his fingers had brushed past, so very softly.

The Mare on the Mound

Norsemen were not fond of kneeling. They did not even kneel to their own gods. But even a Rus Viking warrior of the first rank would kneel to Death anytime. Hallgrim Hidden Spear knelt by the great mound and bowed his head like a slave, waiting for his Freyia to use him as she pleased. While he sat, he made his mind quiet and his ears open, and sensed the presence of all the nine. The very gentle ladies were watching him from the shadows.

"Hallgrim," she said. It was the Mare's deep, hoarse voice.

"Freyia," he said, still with his head bowed.

"I would have asked you to stand up," she said, "but I am taking so much pleasure in the sight of a kneeling man, I think I shall have to be satisfied first. This is not a Contrary thing."

"I am yours to command, Freyia," he said and tried to hide his smile. He had become a little worried when she said she was taking pleasure in the sight of him, what had probably been the Bone Lady's intention. She had a talent for wickedness, but that was only as it should be. He waited, silencing his mind. There was a silence, the sounds of night and darkness and the shadows of the burial site. He could feel her ice cold stare, taking pleasure in the sight of a kneeling man. She had the strangest tastes, that one. She let out a deep breath.

"I am satisfied now," the Mare declared huskily, and Hallgrim got to his feet. "Hidden Spear," she said, "What are you seeking here at the doors of death? Why have you called me? I have long been left to roam alone in the shadow lands."

"I was under the impression that you had your sisters with you," Hallgrim said, cutting short the ritual words. They were too well acquainted to bother with all that now. She snorted.

"Sisssssters," she hissed, sounding annoyed, "I see those bony old wenches all the time. We are all weary of each other. Has it ever occurred to you that we want to have a man sometimes? Someone to play with?"

"It has, Freyia. And I think I have something in store for you. If you will help me. I think this is a sort of task that you may very well enjoy."

"I have a feeling I shall despise the whole act," the Mare hissed, moving into the Contrary.

"I am sure you will," Hallgrim said, adapting immediately, "I think this will be the most detestable act you ever engaged in, if I am one to speak, hardly worth your time at all, Freyia."

"Now you have utterly lost my interest," the Mare growled excitedly. She was a very lustful sort of creature, and she walked the paths of the Contrary just as he did. Hallgrim could sense the excitement all around him. The Sisters were around, listening.

He could smell the fur of their wolf-hounds and the ground bones of their body paintings. The most kind and gentle ladies were hungry for a man. Fortunately, he was not a man this day. He was the shadow walker.

"Freyia," Hallgrim offered, "There is a man what you may take a great liking to. He is a lower ranking warrior at our court. He hurts the women. Not only the women. He hurts slaves. Helpless folks. He is a part of my Sixer group, and I share everything with him. We used to be content. Our Sheath used to adore us. He has been hurting our Sheath to the point where she wants to die and no longer respects her men for not protecting her. He destroys all that is holy. He wreaks havoc on every bond and tie that once made our court great."

"This man," the Mare said, "sounds like a man of great dishonor and cowardice. I already like him a great deal. But what is this to me? I cannot abide women at all."

"I know, Freyia, and I would not have bothered if you could abide them, or if I did not think that you would like the man. The fact is that this man has been with us for nearly two years and has, as yet, not gone far enough. He has managed to keep his sneaky and most hurtful councils hidden from the sights of free men. But I hear the stories. I see the pain. I see what this is doing to our court, and to people that I-"

"Love?" She asked teasingly. He could feel her grinning.

"You are perceptive as always, Freyia."

"I am Death. I do not perceive at all. I just like to finish the verses. With a question." They both chuckled at her words.

"Of course, Freyia. But I am asking you. I am asking you to make this man expose himself. I want him to expose what sort of man he is in front of everybody in a manner that will surely get rid of him forever," Hallgrim said.

The Mare seemed to consider it a while.

"What will we get, then?" She asked, eventually.

"I thought you could have the man," Hallgrim replied casually.

"The whole man?" He heard her smack her lips approvingly.

"We would appreciate something to make a silver skull cup with," he suggested modestly, "but that too is yours to give or not. You shall have the whole man. He will be our gift to you. For our Atonement. For our compensation. For your pleasure and entertainment."

"We would not be partial to that at all," the Mare said huskily. There was a silence again, and Hallgrim finally dared to look up to the burial mound, where she was sitting. In the light of the full Moon, she sat on the top of the mound, her torso naked, as if she could not feel the chill of the autumn night. The pale light of the Moon revealed her countless serpentine tattoos. He saw her terrible eyes reflecting light in the darkness, and the flash of white fangs when she smiled.

She moved from her spot then, moved like a large wild cat, so graceful and so strong and ferocious. Hallgrim stood still, allowed her to draw close. She sniffed him. He felt her cold hand on his chest. It never ceased to surprise him, how huge and strong her hands were. Her nails felt like claws, but the touch was gentle, even loving.

"Cold blood," she said, "Hallgrim of the Cold Blood. I say you will turn blind shortly, Dry Meat."

"Then I am honored," he replied calmly.

"You are welcome. But there is an issue involved. It is my sister who says so. She says so inside my head, I think. At least I keep hearing her jabbering away inside my otherwise rather empty mind."

The Mare scratched her head uncertainly, and sent a gaze upwards as if she was trying to check back into her mind that way. But then, the Kindly One had always been quite mad.

"I am ready," Hallgrim said, forcing back a smile.

"If this man is to expose himself, he is going to have to do something dishonorable in front of all the court," the fanged priestess spoke slowly.

"Yes," he agreed, breathing deep.

"It means that some of those you love may be hurt in the process."

"How hurt?"

"Just as much as it takes," the Mare grinned.

"That is a sacrifice I am willing to make," he said confidently.

"You are such a hateful person to me, Hallgrim."

"I know, Freyia. I love you too. May I kiss you?"

"My kiss is Death," the Mare declared gravely, but there was that lustful glimpse in her strange eyes.

"I am Hallgrim of the Hidden Spear, and I am about to go Hel-Blind," he replied. The Mare regarded him with amusement before she leaned forward and kissed him. She had positioned herself on the mound so that she was of a height with him, the clever one. He kissed her back and felt her sharp fangs brush his lips. He let his tongue rinse clean the blood and smacked approvingly, just as she did. Then she withdrew and regarded him thoughtfully. Here was, in fact, a fearless man. She could respect that. She really could. The Lady of Cracked Bones approved.

"You are the Mask of the Hall," she said, "and we shall work through you. We need the name."

"You honor me, Goddess of all Grim Deaths," Hallgrim replied, "That name is not mine to give. You must take it from the women of our court. This is their grudge that I carry forth."

With a stern face the Mare studied the shadow walker again. Gradually, slowly, her generally rather grim expression changed into a horrible mask as she began grinning from ear to ear. Her fangs glittered in the moonlight. The priestess had no patience with Hallgrim at all.

"I think I shall call you Hallgrim Heri," she declared ceremoniously, "for you are truly a great man. I despise you endlessly. I see it now, Tall One. In your hide walks the Lord of all Hidden Deaths."

"You owe me a name-gift now, Freyia," he replied and bowed graciously before he turned and walked away.

"Hallgrim Heri!" She called out. He stopped.

"Freyia?"

"Heri is not a name. It is a title attached to a name long since given."

"You called me Cold Blood, Dry Meat. I shall let you off the hook regarding the title, yet you still owe me two. Freyia; if you make a spectacle for the gods out of this, I shall call it even."

"You shall have your spectacle then, Hallgrim, for I am not the sort of woman what pays up for anything," she wheezed.

They were both laughing fondly when they parted.

THE SHE-WOLF'S RAGE

When the men deemed me skilled enough to try and spar with another, they naturally chose Ivarr since he was closest to my size. He was still a lot bigger than me, and I think they told him to go easy on me, which he did, yet it did not take him long to have me sprawled on the ground, pointing his wooden blade at my throat while grinning broadly.

It was the first time since I started to hone him that he felt that he had some power over me, and it was clear that he enjoyed it profoundly. Being inexperienced, I didn't quite grasp the fact that I had been defeated, so instead of yielding, I tried to stab at him, what made him strike me with the flat side of his blade.

When I tried to grab his wooden blade with my hands, of all things, he gave me a kick, only to find himself hanging in mid-air as Arnulf picked him up by the hem of his tunic.

"You cannot kick and strike a maiden!" Arnulf thundered.

"But she started it! Why can I not kick her if she wants to learn to fight?" he whined, but Arnulf boxed his ears and set him down, giving him a kick, shouting, "There is no better practice for a boy than to try and spar with a girl. You cannot hit her, you cannot strike her, you cannot kick her, you cannot hurt her in any way. The only thing you can do is to par her blows and try and disarm her without hurting her. And that is how you learn a warrior's self-control, boy!"

Thióðolf regarded me humorously and said, "And this is another reason why so few maidens become warriors, Thordís, we simply cannot honorably hurt you, and so you never learn what a battle is really like."

I felt a sudden surge of rage grow within, stood up, faced my mentor, averting my eyes only very slightly, and spoke out loud enough for all to hear, directing myself as much to the warriors as to Thióðolf, "My mother knew what a battle is. She died in it, defending her children. My sister knows what a battle is, she was enslaved in one. All the women of my village knew well what a battle was, when you Rus Vikings raped them and killed their men. Do not tell me that Norsemen never hurt women, Thióðolf, just because you like to think of yourselves as honorable men! That would not be the truth, and you know better."

The people in the court went silent. Even the slaves stopped working and gaped at me.

I knew that I had spoken out of turn and disrespected my superiors. Yet I was still seething with rage. Silently, and still visibly angry, I lowered my eyes and bowed my head to Thióðolf and then to Arnulf, and then to the entire courtyard, thus apologizing for my transgression, while not taking a word of it back.

Before I looked up at them again, I expected to see them angry, expected them to withdraw their protection, to tell me that I was not their Síf anymore. I wondered what would happen when the men of Aldeigjuborg got reason to think me fair game. It was a terrifying thought, but I could not take my truth back. My truth had been spoken, and I would stand for it, even if it cost me everything. I would rather die than take my words back, for they were a chant of my own soul's song. I just knew it.

Then I raised my eyes and waited for my fate to turn. But there was no anger in their faces as they met my gaze, only new respect, acknowledgment, even. All the Viking warriors looked as if they were *proud* of me. My kinsmen stood to attention as if I was their Heri, all of a sudden. They banged their shields three times, in a slow rhythm, to acknowledge my verdict. I knew their way then, that ancient custom which still burned in their soul songs even as they had become removed from their roots, understanding suddenly what Thióðolf, Hallgrim and the others had tried to explain to me before.

They would not ever punish me for speaking out a verdict on their conduct within our own court. I was their Síf, and judgments of honor were mine to give.

I was still angry, though. Thunder was rumbling within.

"Sharp words, shield maiden, and true to the mark," Thióðolf was the first to speak. He pointed towards Ivarr with the point of his sword, "And now, Thunder Priestess, now that you feel just anger surge through your veins, you should direct it at your opponent, there. Let him represent the Rus-men who raped your Sífs and killed your mother and made a slave out of your own sister."

Now be the she-wolf of your secret heart.

I heard my fathers calling to me, their voices rising from my hammer pendant. My kinsmen's hammer. And I felt the transformation like a wave rising from within. Thunder and lightning roared in my veins. A strange power seized me, and I knew it for Thunder, I knew it for the wrath of Thor. I felt it rise from my men's hammer, fill my heart, a power expanding from within, until I no longer knew what I was doing, except that I was raging and wanted to kill, and kill, and kill.

I charged at Ivarr with a scream of rage, forcing him to retreat several steps. The court cheered. I vaguely noted that I was seated astride Ivarr's wriggling body, wanting to tear out his throat with my own teeth, wanting to reach into his entrails and rip them out, wanting to drink his blood and devour his flesh and stab him through. I thought myself a she-wolf, I could even feel my fangs, and I wanted nothing more than to sink my teeth into warm flesh and feel hot blood flow and life fade from my victim. I felt no pain whatsoever. Powerful arms seized me and held me, rocking me, calming me down until I found myself as if woken from a dream, held by Arnulf, watching the entire courtyard staring at me wide-eyed, while Ivarr lay bleeding on the ground.

"What happened?" I whispered.

"The battle-rage seized you, Priestess," Arnulf said, "You were a berserker, just now." He looked proud. Then he turned to the men, shouting, "Did you witness this, warriors? Did you witness the rage?"

"We witnessed holy rage seize the maiden," the warriors responded, clearly awed. Arnulf put me on the ground and made me turn to face the men. He pointed at me. "Never had I thought I would see sacred rage seize a maiden, and one so young, but it has been witnessed. This was Thor's wrath, come upon her. This is yet another proof of her lineage. She is a Priestess of Thunder! She is a shield maiden! She has gone berserk! Through her, holy powers have visited us!"

The men all cried, "Alu!" While they banged their shields in my honor a second time. I still felt dizzy, and Arnulf handed me over to Thióðolf while he went over to Ivarr.

"Ivarr," he said, loud enough for everybody to hear, "You shall not be shamed for this today, because it was not a little girl who took you down. You will hear this, and you know well I would never humor you. This was a sacred power come down in this courtyard. It was a Valkyrie, what brought you down. You will not be shamed by this. You will be proud. Tomorrow, she may be just a girl again, but today she was seized by great powers. This does not shame you, boy. Do you all hear that, men? Nobody is in his right to mock Ivarr for what just happened. No one could have stood against such unexpected, divine power."

All the men cheered again, to confirm that poor Ivarr had not actually been taken down by a little girl, even if he had. There were limits to the humiliation a young boy would have to go through, and this was one of them. Ivarr sat up and looked a little relieved. I could see how terrified he had been, and how quickly he managed to hide that fact. Our eyes met briefly, before he averted his, respectfully, and I cared not for mocking him more that day.

"You ought to get your teeth filed, like mine," Njál suggested to me in passing, grinning broadly to show me his set of perfect fangs, "Then you can really tear out throats!"

"Now, there is only one kind of woman what files her teeth," Runarr said to him, chuckling, "and even you might find that one scary, Njál."

"Nah, I am too thick in the head to fear even that one, brother," Njál replied, and both of them laughed as they walked away, leaving me to wonder who that woman was.

I noticed Zivah, who had been watching the spectacle from the start, and our eyes met also. For a moment she held my gaze, before she gave me a little nod and a brief smile, as if in approval, then bowed her head like a slave and walked away. It was the first time she met my eyes or made voluntary contact since we had arrived.

Zivah sat down with the other women, resuming their needle work. They were repairing a large sail. Even the Sheaths had joined them, for the Sheaths partook in all the work of the court when they were not excused, which was often enough. Nobody harassed them if they did not work in the day, seeing as they had to serve the men all evening and well into the nights. After what happened with Rat-Hialti that day, Miri spent a lot of time sitting up in the tower while drinking beer and singing brawly songs and nobody bothered her. She was very friendly to Zivah after their party, but seemed to need a lot of time to herself, and nobody, not even Hialti, bothered her.

Zivah heard that the other men who shared Miri with Hialti were quite angry with him after what he did. Now that she knew a little more about the Sheaths and their relations to their men, she began to think that six known men was probably a lot better than thirty, or than countless unknown, for example. The Sheaths seemed to think they were privileged, even if they had to live with the warriors, the serving girls who lived in Arnulf's Hold were available at daytime to all the men and would also be offered to guests.

Of course it took a special sort of woman to be able to live among so many men, but the Sheaths, as it turned out, were all quite special sorts of women, who did like to party and drink with their men. Miri's only problem was that even though her beloved Hallgrim was one of her six men, Hialti was one of them too. It had come to a point where Miri could not take it anymore.

She did not seem to care at all, but nobody tried to punish her or discipline her. When they heard Miri brawling from the tower, the men looked at Hialti and frowned. He had behaved somewhat better for a while after that. After what happened with Thordís, Miri climbed down from the tower and sat down next to Zivah, studying her for a while before she spoke.

"The maiden spoke for us this day," she said, taking a sip of her beer flask. The slaves agreed, nodding. All the man slaves had gathered too. It was as if the event earlier had made everybody free for a while. The Heris hardly ever interfered in their work unless they wanted personal treatments from someone, and left all the organization to Aziza, so their masters hardly ever noticed if the slaves took some time off to be together either, as long as food was served and things seemed to be run smoothly all over.

Now Aziza brought out beer to everybody and said that they could all pretend to be working on the sail and that no man was going to bother them this evening. They drank and talked a little, and when the men resumed their training practice, they talked more freely.

"Zivah," Miri said, "I have heard that you think the maiden betrayed you to the Vikings. That she ruled the whole fleet of some hundred Vikings and three ships from the very first day, and that she ordered Arnulf Heri to take you as his concubine. Only he did not approve of you eventually and gave you to Thióðolf. Now she makes a mockery out of you by letting you walk around as a slave while she rules the whole Viking court."

They all looked at Zivah, who felt a sizzling burn in her cheeks. It was not exactly how she had explained it, but now that the words had been spoken she had to admit that it pretty much summed it all up. It just sounded a little silly when Miri said it that way.

"Is it true or not?" Miri asked, and had another sip of beer.

"Yes... yes that is how it was, but you were not there. I was sitting by the riverbank with the others, watching young men being hung from trees and women being raped. Then there was a strike of lightning and my sister appeared in a way I had never seen her before. Never. She looked like a goddess of sorts. Her eyes were shining, unnatural they were, and she seemed to be stepping out of the lightning. She had all the men awed. They lowered their eyes to her. They stepped aside when she came walking, and when she talked to Arnulf Heri she did not sound like a child at all. She presented herself as a, as a priestess of ancient and noble lineage, and then she told Arnulf to put her father onto the pyre, and he obeyed at once. And then she told Arnulf to take me as his concubine, and he obeyed that too, before she had our mother's body burned on the pyre with the Vikings."

She drew a trembling breath at the memory.

"I screamed and wept when their bodies burned, but Thordís stood there and stared at the fire and there was no emotion to detect at all. She was cold, stone cold. She has not mourned her parents or her people even once. After that she let me sit in shackles and ropes with the other captives while she sat by the prow and had them sing praises to her honor."

All the slaves gaped, except Miri and the other Sheaths, who had obviously heard the story many times from the men, albeit in a slightly different fashion. Now Miri leaned forwards and looked at Zivah, locked her eyes with hers and spoke, "Zivah, the child's true depth of grief surfaced this day, do you not think so too?"

Zivah nodded reluctantly. Miri drew her breath and proceeded, "And Zivah, the story that we Sheaths keep hearing from the men starts in a very similar way.

"It has a very different sting to it, and continues quite differently. Do you know what they speak of? The men?"

"No," Zivah said, because she hardly ever talked to the men.

"They speak of how your sister had the help of divine Thor to make a most astonishing entrance that had them all greatly entertained for a long while. Long enough for them to start to really like the girl and feel protective about her. While they sang her praises as you say, they *saw* her. They saw what she was doing and they were impressed by her. They kept watching her as she kept doing what she did, and they could not help but approve, over and over, and respect her for her courage and her unbending loyalty." Zivah frowned, not quite understanding.

"Zivah, do you really think that Arnulf and these other men here would have let a little girl order them about? Do you really think that?" Miri asked. Zivah could not help but shake her head. She no longer believed that for a moment, now that she thought about it.

"Exactly," Miri said, "You see, what they saw in that girl, Zivah, was a warrior spirit who did everything in her might to save her own skin and that of her sister. They saw how she bode her time and considered her options and tried to choose the most sensible path at every turn. Every time she felt that she had secured a little more of their affection, she made a new move to make *your* position less fragile, Zivah."

Miri eye-locked her again, "She did it all for *you*, Zivah. Everybody knows it. The men started to understand it even before they left Khazaria. That she was doing all this work to save *you* from being raped and hurt. They watched her workings and they were awed by her, Zivah, awed by how elegantly and how smartly she played them all, and how loyal she was to you even when you hated her, how protective of her Síf she was regardless. Did you know that she offered her own body to Arnulf instead of yours, so that you would not have to? It was her fortune that our Heri is not that sort of man, seeing as the girl is seven."

Miri paused and looked intently at Zivah, who was speechless.

"Even though they knew that she was playing them, they could not but respect that sort of fighting spirit in a little girl," Miri continued, "her courage and resilience and the intelligence she applied, how carefully she observed and learned just so she could always know how to move them without offending them, ah! She fought like a she-wolf for your sake, and she was just a little child! Her struggle made them love her and respect her so much they finally wanted her to be their Síf. It is because of *her*, Zivah, that not one of them has raped you, and her workings also explain why *you* are living safe and untouched here, under *her* protection, and not in some pleasure-slave-for-rent place down in Big Tunic Land."

Zivah gaped. All the other slaves gaped too. All but the Sheaths, who nodded to confirm what Miri had just told them all. And then each and every face turned to Zivah, expecting a reply.

"I did not see this," Zivah said plainly, feeling tears running down her cheeks, all silently, "I just could not see it. I was so terrified all the time. I was so frightened. All I could see was that Thordís seemed to have them all engaged and doting on her, while they leered at me and wanted, oh goddess, oh sweet Danu, oh gods, Thordís..." She broke down in sobs, and they all sat quietly, waiting for her to finish. The slaves had seen too much of life to bother with passing judgment on each other. "When we came here, that first night," Zivah whispered, "then she climbed into the bed just before Thióðolf was going to take me, and stopped him. I started to think it over then, but when I finally turned to speak to her, she was sleeping in his arms. She has been sleeping in his arms every night since then. They are together, and she is one of them, and I am not. It is all I have seen, and I am sorry if I saw this wrongly and made you all think badly of the maiden, oh gods."

"Nobody blames you, Zivah," Miri said gently, "There is nobody here who cannot imagine what terrors you went through. You could not possibly understand everything that happened around you, but you are my friend, Zivah, and I can see that you, and we, really needed to know this. I am going to tell you something more that the men speak of. They speak of how, when you rejected Arnulf, how your sister turned to him even after he told her that he would not take a child like that, do you know what she did when she could not offer him her body in your place?" Zivah shook her head, and thought her mind was going blank with shock. Miri locked eyes with her again.

"She began giving him exactly the sort of attention he would have wanted from any concubine apart from the thing you need to be grown to do. Did you ever notice that?"

"What?" Zivah squeaked. Miri nodded.

"Exactly. Your sister gave herself to Arnulf, Zivah. She started to adore him and humble herself before him, blushing and lowering her eyes at every turn, and looking slightly frightened of him too. She knew exactly what it was he really had wanted from you, and she gave it. The maiden would have spread her legs for him too if she was older, to save you from him. It was obvious to everybody that she put herself in your place the moment she saw that you could not give that which she had promised him when she asked him to take you as concubine rather than selling you off as any other slave. She wanted to keep the deal, so to speak, and so she did, as far as she could, being but seven years old. It was the only way she thought she could secure your safety."

Zivah was speechless again.

"Oh, there is more, Zivah," Miri continued, "because just as you also rejected Thióðolf that first night here, as far as a slave can reject, of course, well; after Thordís had stopped him from claiming his right over you, then she also put herself in your place. She just rolled into his arms and gave him that which he really wanted most, apart from the fucking."

"What was that he really wanted?" Zivah heard herself ask breathlessly, despite herself. She had never before considered the possibility that her House-Bond wanted anything else from her apart from the fucking.

"Affection. Trust. Forgiveness, I imagine," Miri said, "And your sister gave him that so that you would not have to. She may have grown to love him for real, now, but that night she just gave her love away for your sake. Not her body. *Her actual love.* She even forgave him for real. My friend, I am starting to think it is about time to forgive your sister for having a better mind for playing men than you do."

"Oh gods," Zivah said, but then felt a final surge of resistance to this new turn of truth, "but, you see how close she is to these men who killed and raped and enslaved all her people, can you not see how that hurts me?"

"She is a *child*, Zivah," Miri said, the merciless sister, "I can see how that is hard to acknowledge sometimes, seeing what she is capable of. It is just because she is very clever. It does not matter how clever she is. I have been watching her play and train in the court all day after day, and I see what the men see, and I am impressed by the same things that keep impressing them. Clever and diligent and brave she is, but it is obvious to me and to the men that the maiden is still a small child. She needs affection and comfort, yet she is orphaned and all alone in the world, and she will accept affection and comfort wherever it comes from, because she cannot survive without it. Zivah, even grown folks can hardly survive without that. Children *cannot*, and they know it, so they take whatever affection they are offered, wherever it is offered."

Miri leaned forward again.

"Zivah, I think we can all witness that you, her own older sister, you have not offered it. Instead, you have given her the role of traitor."

There was a terrible silence until Zivah accepted the truth of this counsel. "I feel so shamed," she moaned and hid her face in her hands.

"You do not have to be shamed, Zivah," Miri said, "and it is as I said. Nobody here blames you for not seeing things clearly in a situation like you have lived through. It is about time you stop hating your little sister. That is all. It is about time we *all* warm up to that poor child. She is all alone among grown men.

"They try to give her all the comfort she needs, but they are warriors and they are men. She is a *seven-year-old girl.* There are things she needs that they just cannot give her. We may be slaves, but we are the only women grown here and that girl needs some mothering. Perhaps even a sense of *sisterhood.*"

"Yes, she does" Zivah sobbed, and began drying her tears with the hem of the Vikings' sail. It was the first time she failed to assume that her sister's needs somehow invalidated her own.

"Is it always like that, Thióðolf?" I asked him later, when we were in bed, "Are men always seized by such rage when they fight?"

"Not exactly, no," he said, "but it happens. It happens differently though, mostly. We are better trained, so our bodies remember the moves and the strikes even as we feel like rabid wolves or bears. You were, less disciplined, we could say. Wilder. That made you less effective than you could have been, yet utterly dangerous to a boy of lesser experience."

"I thought I was a wolf," I said.

"You *were* a wolf," he replied. "Is your Follower a wolf?"

"I don't know. I have not met her yet."

"I think you just met her. I think she was within you."

"Do you know your animal Follower, Thióðolf?"

"Yes. She is a wolf, too. The one who named me recognized my Follower even at my birth, and so she gave me my name."

"The Tribes wolf," I said, "Who was she then, who named you?"

"Her name is Huld Wand-Witch. She comes around to newborn children and gives them names if she is asked to do so by their parents. She is a very old and powerful witch."

"Oh," I muttered, beginning to drift off to sleep in his embrace.

Just before I slept I heard my sister whisper from her part of the bed, "Good night, Maid, Thordís."

"Good night, Zivah," I whispered back and felt a tremble going through my whole body for a moment before I suddenly relaxed so completely I realized I had not relaxed like this ever since the raid. It was as if I could finally take off a chain mail coat that had been growing somewhat tight of late.

After all this time, it felt so good.

THE SEVENTH SISTER

After that day, the slaves of the Hold and Hall made sure to
be friendly to the maiden, whose response was very uncertain at
first. Every time the slaves tried to include her a little she threw an
anxious glance at Zivah and made sure to withdraw quickly.

Zivah herself hardly knew how to approach the girl.

"Give it time," Aziza said, "I think the girl keeps away from us
all and you because she does not want to bother you, Zivah. She
has more thought for everybody else's needs than her own. I think
maybe both of you need to take your time."

It was getting chilly. Thordís and Thióðolf and many of the men
had gone out for the day and had brought their horses. They had
all seemed to be in a hurry when they left, trying to hide their
anxiety, and Zivah wondered what was going on. The slave men had
gathered in the courtyard, eight men in all, and Aziza gave them a
bagful of food and drink to take with them when they, to Zivah's
immense surprise, went into the warriors' Hall and closed the door
after themselves, obviously thinking to spend some time in there.
The warriors who were left to guard the court took their positions
outside of the walls.

Suddenly the entire court was completely ruled by slave women. It
was a festive occasion, obviously, so they brought out food and drink
too, and Aziza said that today she would slap anyone who tried to
work at all. Nobody seemed to want to say what was going on out
loud, but Zivah was more and more certain. They were expecting a
visitor.

There was a knock at the gate, and it slid open, slowly. The women
stood in a half circle to meet whoever was about to come through.
And then entered a rather small, thin woman with very bony hands,
very pale skin and the strangest sort of outfit and the strangest sort
of body paint. Zivah thought the woman reminded her of a skeleton.
She was followed by a large wolf-hound. Hel-Hound the cat jumped
out of Zivah's arms and walked straight over to the large hound. The
two met and sniffed each other, and suddenly the strange skeleton
woman grinned and said, "Why, I think the cat is just about getting
big enough."

The women did not bow or lower their eyes to the woman, Zivah saw, and neither did the woman establish any sort of rank between them. She just looked carefully at everyone and averted her eyes mutually, although when her gaze lingered at Aziza, she suddenly smiled and lowered her eyes. Aziza gulped, as if it did not flatter her as much as it should. The woman was led into the Hold and sat down in Arnulf's High Seat just like that, what caused Zivah to gasp. The women gathered round the table and sat down.

"There is one among you who does not know me," the Bone Woman said and looked at Zivah. She got up and bowed her head.

"I am Zivah, Freyia. I belong to Thióðolf Heri."

"The Eastern Princess," the Bone Woman said and grinned, "I heard the men call you the Untouchable One. Or was it the Impenetrable One?"

All the women laughed softly, including Zivah. The Seventh Sister smiled. "Zivah of the river lands, tales are sung about you in town, courtesy of your skald," the woman said, "and I am the Seventh Sister. I am a lady of the cracked and broken bones. To men, I am Death."

"Oh," Zivah said brightly, looking up, "What are you to women, then?"

The Seventh Sister grinned, "To women, I am a good old friend."

The Priestess of Death took a large container out from her leather bag and placed it on the table. Laimi and Suri brought out a drinking bowl, filling it up with the contents of the Sister's container. The Sister blessed the bowl and said, "May the seed wither and die. May the womb close and repulse the seed. May the child conceived be unconceived. Death has blessed the Hel-Runes draught. All women of the Hold and Hall must drink." She peered at Zivah and added, "All the women who are being fucked, anyway."

There was a surge of amusement going on around the table, and Zivah felt confused. Miri whispered into her ear that this drink was the secret as to why little slave babies were not running around all over the place to confuse their masters who would also be their fathers, and Zivah understood. Her mother had known some drinks of that sort, and it had been spoken of during her Moon Blood ritual when she became a woman. Now the women passed the bowl around the table, and Zivah just sniffed it but did not have to drink, being the only woman in the entire court who had no need of it.

When the bowl had passed round three times, it was empty, and they repeated the words in unison: "May the seed wither and die. May the womb close and repulse the seed. May the child conceived be not conceived. Death has blessed the Hel-Runes draught. All women of the Hold and Hall have drunk."

And they all peered at Zivah for a moment and almost repeated the Sister's addition but thought better of it and giggled a little. They started to drink beer instead, all looking expectantly at the Seventh Sister. The Sister asked them about pains, ailments, all sorts of things, providing medicine for all of them out of her bag, and it gradually dawned on Zivah that she was a sort of medicine woman, like her mother the Healer. But where her mother had been sweet and beautiful and gentle, the Sister was quite the opposite.

Zivah realized that this might be the first time she actually saw a Norsewoman, and wondered if her general countenance was common and perhaps the reason why Norsemen preferred getting slave girls from foreign countries.

The Sister looked at her and grinned when she thought that.

"Yes, Zivah of the river lands," she said, "It is true that I am of Norse stock. I am not a Norse woman. I am not any sort of woman. I am just walking Death. And sometimes I am Death to the unborn and to the little ailments that women suffer from. And yes, men find me exceedingly repulsive. You have seen how they all fled the court before my arrival. They cannot bear to even look at me. They think I am very scary, you see. I make them shit their pants. I really do."

She leaned forwards across the table and added, conspiratorially, "I try to keep it outdoors. On account of the smell." Zivah thought the women were going to laugh their heads off. Then the Priestess hushed them down and looked grave all of a sudden. The women went quiet.

"I hear there is a man who hurts people," the Sister said.

The women exchanged glances and nodded. The Sister noticed the anxiety and fear in their eyes.

"The man is given, but we need the name. We were told to take it from the women of this Hold. Who hurts you?"

She looked directly at Miri.

"Hialti hurts me," Miri said. The Sister nodded, and turned her gaze to the next girl, who spoke the same name. She looked from woman to woman and all said the same name. Out of all the men who used them as they pleased, only Hialti really hurt them. Finally she looked at Zivah.

"Who hurt you, Zivah?" The Sister asked.

Zivah hesitated. "I am, I am not hurt. He tried, though,"

"Who tried?"

"Hialti," Zivah whispered, blushing.

"Good," the Sister said and got up from the High Seat, "I have heard the name spoken from the lips of all the women of this Hold and the women of the Hall. I think our dear Hialti will become a very entertaining man to us sisters. Good night, ladies."

And with those words she left them and let herself out.

The women of the Hold and Hall drank and danced and howled in the empty courtyard and were all passed out and sleeping before the free men dared to return and the slave men dared to leave the Hall. The warriors picked up their dead drunk women, tucked them into their beds, and did not touch them that night.

THE COWARD

Autumn was about to turn into winter, and I had become skilled enough in the basic moves of many of the battle arts to begin training at unarmed battle. The men did not want me to engage in wrestling, firstly because they deemed me too small to engage either of them. Even little Ivarr could not be engaged by me, because they said it wasn't proper for a male to wrestle with a female in any case, unless it was a part of Freyia's sport.

But they all seemed to think that I needed to learn how to defend myself against a man, and after a deal of practice I began to realize that they were really preparing me for self-defense in case of a rape attempt, without telling me so directly and while doing their best to make it all feel as if we were just having fun and playing. Yet as I look back, I know that they were deadly serious. They truly wanted me to learn how not to be raped, without frightening me.

There was little I could do against a grown man, I thought, but my kinsmen insisted that there were certainly ways of getting out of a man's clasp even if I was a small and feeble girl, and so they set about teaching me the many little techniques that required a sure aim and speed rather than strength, making it also very clear that the point was not to win the battle but to escape, and escape fast enough to not be taken down.

For my comfort they made it into a play where I often ran around with some man after me, and we were all laughing. Within this frame of playfulness, they still taught me to defend myself both with dagger and without, and for a while I enjoyed the game because it gave me a sense of empowerment to realize that being feeble in body did not mean that I was utterly helpless against a strong man. The training began with Ivarr, and when I had managed to get out of his hold enough times to convince them that I could actually stand a chance, I was facing grown men.

I had become quite adept at wriggling out of their grips, even causing a few men to roll on the ground in pain, when the man called Hialti offered to practice with me. I had always avoided Hialti, without giving the reason why any thought. I just did not trust him. Sometimes, he had stared directly at me in a way that was truly rude and disrespectful, when he thought himself undetected. It reminded me of the way men leered openly at slave women.

I thought that I must be mistaken, since I was just a little girl of no interest to men, and thought that he must think me too full of myself. I always lowered my eyes to him, as was my duty since he was a man grown and a warrior, but he never averted his own to me in return. Instead, he would continue glaring at me. I instinctively felt that he did not just crave my respect, which I always paid him just as I paid all men respect.

He craved something else, and I did not understand it. This confused me so much that I sometimes bowed my head to him also, apologizing for whatever it was that provoked him so, because I felt threatened and hoped this sign of submission would placate him.

When he volunteered to be my partner in self-defense practice, I could not honorably refuse without offending him, but I did notice that Thióðolf frowned and exchanged some worried glances with Arnulf, who also looked doubtful. Neither of them wanted to offend the man by refusing his offer without reason, and so we began, with me running around, he running after, capturing me and taking me down to the ground, where my task was to get out of his grip and hurt him just enough to get away before he could take me again.

I usually enjoyed this game, and the men also thought it great fun and always cheered me on. It was not until that day I realized that they had been very gentle with me, and not exactly created a real rape attempt situation at all. I was too small for that. Not one of them believed that I could actually yet defend myself in a real life situation, but they did not tell me. It felt challenging enough for me.

This time was different. Hialti was not going to humor me by letting me get any blows in at all. His grip was like iron pinning me down, rendering me utterly helpless, and there was not one move, not one technique, that I could possibly employ that did not just make him grin even broader than he was already. I realized that I had no chance at all against him, and suddenly felt how my body submitted and somehow became immobilized from within.

I saw Thióðolf's feet then, knew that he was squatting down next to us, saying in a low voice, "There is still a chance, Thordís, you can still get away, remember the move I taught you. Use it."

I thought that he was trying to get eye contact with Hialti, perhaps to let him know that he should go easier on me, but Hialti kept his cruel eyes fixed on me, and it felt as if he was already inside of my soul, having a feast. I shook my head to Thióðolf's words and felt tears of frustration run down my cheeks, knowing in my heart that no move in the world could save me.

I felt as if I was being devoured.

"If you yielded in such a situation, Thordís, you would be raped," Thióðolf began, but before he could continue to tell me what to do, I felt Hialti's mouth against my ear, saying gleefully, in a strangely hoarse voice that felt like rasping knives into my soul, "Yes, little girl, you would be raped. Don't listen to him. There is nothing you could do, girl. I would rape you and fuck you really hard. Would you like that, little girl? I think you would, little fire-head."

Then he made rutting movements against me. I could feel his Freystone hard against my leg, pushing against me several times in rapid motion, and felt as if my soul shattered.

The word he used, the word fuck, it was a word hardly ever used, at least not in my presence. The word etched itself into my heart and made me feel like I was nothing at all. I knew then what rape felt like, even if I was not in truth being raped, and observed it all as if from afar, as if I was moving to a place outside of myself, removing myself from the indignity of it all, giving up even my will to live.

I knew it was all happening very fast, yet it felt like an eternity in which I knew only my own helplessness and felt utterly worthless. I also knew in my heart that Hialti had raped women and girls countless times, and that he was enjoying it. I was being dishonored by a man who enjoyed dishonoring me, as if he hated me for no understandable reason. I forgot that I was protected by my warriors that moment. I thought myself alone in the world, alone against this horrible man. I succumbed to the helplessness and I felt my soul leave me, not wanting to be present in my body anymore, since it was being fucked.

In truth, it all happened rather quickly, and Hialti had only just spoken those words and made those rutting movements before Thióðolf's foot kicked against his chest, making him fly upwards and backwards, leaving him sprawled on the ground. I was seeing what was happening even though I could no longer feel my own body. With some astonishment I saw that body of mine sitting up, swaying, as if my soul's Hold was still trying to get away, even without myself inside of it. My empty-eyed face was directed at the two men. From my other point of view, the one where I was not inside my body at all, I realized with some astonishment just how tiny and vulnerable I looked from the outside.

That was not how I perceived myself usually. I used to think that I was strong and tough, for a girl anyway. That moment was the first time I understood why everybody used to be so very gentle with me. Everybody apart from Hialti, that is.

I saw what now transpired from several angles at once.

What I saw was Thióðolf move against Hialti, sword in hand, and Hialti struggling to get up before my warrior reached him, managing only barely, unsheathing his own sword. The two men faced each other, and Hialti looked odd where he stood, with his hard Freystone still very much perceivable behind his breeches.

My initial confusion about Arnulf's Freystone had been solved with the experience of living around a lot of men who cared nothing about nudity within their own court. I had learned that Freystones did not either hang or stand on different men, but that they did both things on all of them, and that it would stand up in the mornings to say hello to the world, which was how they explained it to me.

Else when a man got excited, mostly for wanting to play the pleasure games. In Hialti's case, I realized, it happened when he wanted to fuck little children.

I saw my body convulse and vomit, as if it wanted to get whatever he may have placed in me out as quickly as possible. Both Thióðolf and Hialti saw me vomiting, as did all the men, and the tense silence that descended on the entire court was excruciating.

We were not playing anymore.

"You have dishonored our Síf," Thióðolf said quietly, yet his bard's voice filled the courtyard, and was carried by a deep tremble that seemed to come from seething rage, still controlled.

"Dishonored her? We were playing! We were just playing, were we not, little girl?" I could not speak, my soul yet not present in my body, but moving around the place, seeing everything from countless different angles. "It was a joke!" Hialti insisted.

Thióðolf pointed his sword towards me and spoke in a thundering voice, "I do not see my Síf laughing, Hialti. I see a girl too stunned to even cry. I see a girl whose soul has left the flesh and not returned yet, after what you just did, before my face. You call this a joke again, and I will feed your balls to you, Hialti, while you are still alive, and I will make you chew each bit carefully."

Hialti looked a little worried, but maintained eye-contact.

"Maybe she took it the wrong way, but I wasn't serious, Thióðolf. We were just sparring."

Thióðolf cast a deliberate glance at Hialti's standing Freystone, raised his eyebrows mockingly and moved closer, making Hialti nervously retreat a few steps. It occurred to me once more that he was far less tough when he faced a man his own size.

"You told her you were going to fuck her," Thióðolf said, still with that same, intense, composed yet raging voice, loud enough to be heard by everyone, "You told a seven-year-old girl that you were going to fuck her hard and that she was going to like it," and added, "and then you mock-fucked her, didn't you, Hialti? You rutted on her as if she was yours to take. We all saw it."

He raised his voice, still without looking anywhere but into Hialti 's eyes. "Warriors, did you see what just transpired? Did you see how this worthless turd rutted at the maiden? Did you see how he dishonored our Síf? Did you hear his words to her?"

"We saw his deed," a voice called from the men's crowd, the voice of Hallgrim Hidden Spear, "We heard his words. And this maiden," Hallgrim pointed at me with his sword, looking furious, and raised his voice further as he cried, "this maiden is a Síf to us all!"

All the men repeated those words, with hard and thundering voices, "*This maiden is a Síf to us all!*" I heard the sounds of near thirty swords being unsheathed as one.

Hialti looked around for support, and found none, only silent, merciless, wolfish stares, and blades drawn. He realized that he was not going to get away from this, but for some reason did not find it in him to apologize properly, what may have saved his life. Perhaps. Or perhaps he knew that he was already doomed, and so kept defending his transgression.

"I got carried away, man. We were *playing*. Then I went a bit over the top. With such a pretty girl beneath me, I just forgot myself for a moment. You *know* how it is," he whined, looking around for support again.

"I thank my goddess that I do not know how that is, Hialti, to want to fuck a helpless child!" Thióðolf said, still calm, still composed and still looking deadly. Hialti regarded him with a mocking expression. In my life, I have often seen this, when a man knows that he is in the wrong, but is unwilling to admit it, even in the face of death. And so they continue on their dishonorable path, even if they know it can only lead them into the darkest pits of Hel, forever lost in churning streams of sharp blades."

"Well, Thióðolf, seeing as you are protected by a female, you probably just don't know what it is to be a man who knows a treasure when he sees one," Hialti said mockingly.

They glared at each other. This was duel of words, not of swords.

"I am a man," Thióðolf said, his voice reaching a thunderous level, yet still composed, "I am a warrior. I trust in my own strength. Why would I need another man to protect me, even if he is a god?"

He took another step, closer to Hialti, who looked like he was struggling not to turn around and run for his life.

"I protect my goddess, Hialti. As I protect my Sífs. That is what a man does. But you wouldn't know, would you? You, who think that little girls are worthy opponents for you! You always hold back during fights and practice, too frightened to take on bigger men. But little girls, oh, they are yours for the taking. That is a coward's view, Hialti, and a coward you are. Do not think for a moment I have not seen you. I see everything, Hialti. I have seen how you have disrespected my Síf, time and time again, with your staring. You have challenged her every time you saw her, as if she was a warrior your own size, one you could challenge to battle. You are a child-rapist, Hialti, we have all thought you were, and now you have proven it before the whole court and even admitted to it, as if you thought we would sympathize and know how that is. You call yourself a man? I call you a coward, one who picks fights with women and children and slaves who have no means to stop you, and think yourself victorious when you take a small child down. You are the lowliest kind of coward in the world."

The verdict was devastating, and Hialti's mouth opened and shut several times. His eyes seemed to be averting on their own accord, looking around for the slightest sympathy among the men who had been his brothers. He received none. Then he braced himself, got a firmer clasp around his sword handle, and prepared himself for the inevitable. Arnulf intervened. The court's Heri and war-leader stomped across the courtyard, looking every bit as outraged as everybody else, and he went straight up to Hialti without even drawing his own blade. The giant Heri's appearance was so terrifying that Hialti lost hold of his sword when Arnulf made a sweep at it with his great arm. Then he moved so close that Hialti seemed to shrink in terror, looking helplessly up at his Heri as Arnulf gently clasped his large hand around Hialti's throat.

I thought he was going to choke him, but instead, Arnulf spoke: "This man is a lowly and cowardly child-rapist, and he has dishonored our Síf. He dishonored her in her own home. He dishonored her where she thought herself most safe, among her own warriors, all sworn to protect her. He dishonored her openly, before all our faces. He has no respect for this maiden. He has no respect for me. He has no respect for any of you men. You are all sworn to me. By sacred law, my Sífs are your Sífs, and were so from the moment you swore allegiance to me. You have, in effect, Hialti, dishonored your own Síf, and the Síf of all my men. This is not a matter to be settled between warriors. You have not earned a warrior's death. This is betrayal, Hialti, this is the breaking of a sacred oath. You are a traitor, and so I condemn you to the Red Eagle."

Hialti now looked truly fearful, white as death, perspiration running from his forehead. Arnulf kept his fist around the man's throat while he relieved him of all his weapons with the other hand, throwing them to the ground, and then released him, still staring directly into his eyes, pointing with one arm to the gate that led to the street outside.

"Go," said Arnulf Heri. Hialti glanced down at his sword, but Arnulf set his foot over it and nodded towards the gate. Hialti ran towards the gate, struggled to open it since nobody cared to help him, and then ran out into the streets. Arnulf looked around, and I noticed that four men approached him and talked to him before they also went out of the gates, but by this time my attention was fading, and I thought I saw my fainting body being suddenly scooped up into Thióðolf's arms, other men gathering round.

"Return, Thordís. Come back. Come back," Thióðolf whispered into her ears while he rocked her, kneeling on the ground in the courtyard. Zivah had come running as soon as Aziza and Miri let go of the hold they had kept on her arm ever since Hialti did that to her sister. Zivah had seen it and almost screamed. She had wanted to run to her little sister, disregarding all rules of conduct, but the two other women had grabbed hold of her and told her to stay put. This was men's business.

"But she is just a child," Zivah had cried, "She is just a child. A child."

"It is good to hear that you see it that way now," Miri had said, "but this is still men's business. Wait."

Zivah, forcing back a sob, waited with the other slaves, staring wide-eyed at the spectacle unfolding out there and Zivah watched the child lying out like a crushed little thing. She saw how her brave little sister tried to get up and then retched and fell over like a wet cloth.

He had broken her. That rat had crushed her little Thordís. And when Hialti left, Zivah felt the women let her go and she ran out there only to stop and fall to her knees when her House-Bond knelt down just before she did and picked up the girl. She met his eyes for a moment and saw such pain and grief in them. He was weeping. She had never thought that he could weep, but he did, he wept openly and so did the other men, wept without sobs, but the tears flowed down their rugged cheeks as they strove to speak to the child, to wake her up, to make her soul return to her body.

Thióðolf got to his feet, carrying the little girl, and simply went into the Hold. Zivah hesitated when nobody else followed him, but then caught the eyes of Hallgrim who nodded to her, gesturing towards the house. So she followed. She stood and watched while Thióðolf climbed into the bed and sat down cross-legged, still bent over the girl while he whispered her name and begged her to return. He let his tears fall onto her face while he rocked her.

Tears of love.

Thióðolf Heri is a good man, they kept saying. But that did not change the humiliating fact that he owned her like he would own a horse. Zivah had to grudgingly admit that even so, he was perhaps not the worst brutish beast she had ever known. And suddenly the little one drew a breath and opened her eyes, looking into his.

Sif

It seemed to wake me up from the spell of terror; a tear of love on my cheek. I was safe. My own man held me. My own man.

I suddenly knew what that meant.

I looked into his eyes and knew he loved me. And I felt myself return to life. Thióðolf was holding me, rocking me like a baby, while tears streamed down his face, as if he was doing my weeping for me.

"I am so sorry, Thordís," he whispered, "I am so sorry I let you spar with that man. I should have known. I am so very sorry."

I was still speechless, but pressed my face into his broad chest and began to breathe, realizing that I had not really breathed since Hialti mock-raped me. Thióðolf seemed to want to cover me entirely, making a shield with his whole body. I began to feel truly safe again, and my hand searched for his. I felt his large hand close around my very little one, squeezing it carefully.

"That man," I finally whispered, "he has raped lots of girls like me."

"I am sure he has, Thordís."

"Is he gone?"

"He is dead, Thordís."

"But he left," I said, anxious that I might see him again if I ever ventured outside of the walls, wondering if I would ever dare to.

"He will never rape a girl again, Thordís, and you will never have to see him again either. Arnulf's fiercest warriors went after him. He will receive a traitor's death. He will be blood-eagled," Thióðolf said reassuringly.

"Can I watch?" I asked, eager to see for myself that the man could truly never hurt me again.

"No, my Síf. Women, children and slaves, they may not watch that rite. It is a warrior's matter only."

"Oh," I said, feeling disappointed.

"Don't worry, child, we will get his head for you. Then you will know that you are safe." I squeezed his hand and felt truly cherished.

"What is blood-eagled?" I asked. Father had not even wanted to explain it to me. Thióðolf, however, seemed to think that I was old enough to know even if I would be forever barred from observing it.

"They will put him down on his stomach and stretch him out, while one of them carves the image of an eagle into his back, or else into his stomach. They carve the image with a sword. And then they will leave him to die slowly, and the crows and ravens will eat of him before he is even dead." I nodded and let out my breath, feeling strangely comforted by that image.

"If anyone disrespects you the way Hialti did before this happened, you must let me know, Thordís. If a man keeps staring you down, he is threatening you. If you were a warrior, it would be a challenge to fight him. But you are a maiden, and even if you were a woman grown it would be the same thing. If a man disrespects you in that manner, it means that he will do what Hialti pretended to do if he ever gets the chance. You must never let that kind of thing pass, you must tell me."

"It is just confusing to me, the way I have to always lower my eyes to men anyway," I whispered, "I thought I was doing something wrong since he always stared that way."

"You did nothing wrong. You are always respectful, little one, you even lower your eyes more than you need to. You only have to lower them the first time you see them in a day, or after they have taught you something, and after that it is enough to avert your eyes first every now and then. But a man must avert his eyes also, in response to your respect for him. If he does not, he is not an honorable man, and then you must tell me." He hugged me even harder and let out a sob.

"If anyone ever dares to harm you, Thordís, no matter where you are in the world, you call on me. Even if I am dead, I will hear you. And then I will destroy them. This I promise you. This I swear. I will destroy anyone who ever hurt you, even from beyond the shores of Hel."

Men always get carried away by their stories. For a moment I thought to inform him that his promise was impossible. But his words were so earnest, his feeling so genuine, and suddenly I tried something new instead. "I know," I smiled, and closed my eyes.

I felt so very tired.

He stopped rocking me and looked up, and I looked up also, to see what was going on. Zivah was standing by the bed, with her head lowered.

"She does not even cry," Thióðolf spoke, looking at my sister, as if he expected her to explain that to him.

"She never cries, Heri," Zivah mumbled and remembered to bow her head.

"No, she never does," Thióðolf confirmed, sounding puzzled, and used one of his hands to dry a tear. Zivah looked like she wanted to say something, but stopped herself.

"Zivah," Thióðolf said quietly, "you may speak."

"Our brother, his name was Thorolf, he died four years past. Thordís was but three years old, and we found the boy dead, she and I. He was five when he died. And after that our parents were so very sad and we also, and Thordís stopped smiling and laughing and crying like other children. She became like she is now," Zivah explained and hesitated for a moment before she added a "Heri."

"Yet, she has begun smiling," Thióðolf mused, looking thoughtfully down at me. I just watched them talking about me and did not mind at all that they were suddenly talking together after all this time. Even if Zivah was still studying the floor all the while.

"Yes, Heri," Zivah agreed, looking uncomfortable.

"Zivah, do you want to be with your sister?" he asked.

"Please, Heri," Zivah sobbed, "I think perhaps she should be with women now."

"Yes, yes, of course," Thióðolf said and turned to me. "Do you want to go with Zivah, little Síf? Do you want to be with the women?"

I nodded, hardly believing what I heard.

The slaves had only recently begun to warm up to me, and we were still a little shy around each other. The women, particularly, seemed to have taken Zivah to their hearts. I was happy for her but I sometimes wished they would include me also. Just sometimes. Even after they began smiling to me and talking a little to me, I stayed away from them. I did not want to take away that only thing which she was happy about, and it had always been my impression that Zivah thought that anything involving me meant that it was taken away from her. So if her happiness depended on me staying out of that community, I would, even if it made me feel a little lonely.

Now I looked uncertainly at Zivah, who suddenly forgot all courtesies, ignored her master as she clasped her arms around me and lifted me up. She was not at all as strong as the men, and I could feel how she struggled to hold me, but she did hold me. I rested my cheek against her soft breast and thought I had long been without something precious.

Zivah let out another whining sob before she composed herself and carried me off into the bath-room, where many other women had gathered. Zivah sat down in the women's circle and held her sister for a while before she passed her over. They all held the girl-child close to their hearts before they passed her over to the next woman. They were quiet, so quiet, eyes meeting only now and then in silent realization.

The maiden had taken it for them all, and now the terror was over. Finally, Aziza took the girl in her arms and held her for a long time. Thordís just closed her eyes and seemed to enjoy the closeness to a woman so much like their mother. The other women gathered round wondered why the child did not weep like other children. The maiden opened her eyes again and looked straight at her older sister.

"Zivah," she asked, "Was this how you felt all the time? This sort of terror?"

"Yes," Zivah said hoarsely.

"I am so sorry," Thordís said.

"Why are you sorry, Thunder Goddess, my sister, what are you sorry for?"

"That I could not do better for you," the child said, "I thought that you would be fine if only they did not take you, but I did not fully grasp before now how terrible it must have been for you to fear it all the time."

"Oh, child, I wish you did not have had to grasp that," Zivah wept.

"I do not," Thordís said gravely, "not really."

"Yes you do. Why are you saying that?"

"He did not actually rape me, and I had thirty brothers to protect me, and it was over very fast, Zivah. It lasted ages for you and you only had..." the child paused and looked uncertain.

"I only had you," Zivah said quietly.

The girl nodded.

"I am sorry, Zivah," she said, "but it is just that I am too little, maybe. I really tried to do my best. I am so sorry that it did not work."

Zivah reached out for her sister, and Aziza handed her the charge. "Oh gods, Thordís, it worked, it worked and you are the most precious sister I could ever have hoped for. I do not deserve you at all," Zivah cried and held her close; "I am sorry, sister, I am so sorry."

"You don't have to be sorry, Zivah. You are just challenging in your ways, like Father said. You have honored me."

"How so?" Zivah frowned.

"You were my blade honer, Zivah. You honed my soul sharp and made me know my own greatness." The women went silent, exchanging glances.

"Only it was getting a little lonely sometimes," Thordís suddenly admitted, meekly, while her eyes went moist. Zivah burrowed her face into her little sister's hair and held her even tighter.

"I love you," she whispered into the child's ears, again and again and again. And when Thordís finally grasped that Zivah really did love her, and she looked round and saw all the friendly and motherly faces looking at her with concern and compassion and love, looking at her as if they actually saw the child she was, then her tears began to run and run and run, all quiet and void of sobs, as if she had learned how to weep like a warrior. She wept. Thunder Goddess wept at last.

"Tears of gold," Miri said, "these are tears of gold."

Little Hel-Hound came prancing through the door, proudly carrying a screaming rat. The furry cat put the rat down and began playing with it.

She played with the poor rodent for a very long time.

The women watched in silence, exchanged glances and knew.

THE MARE'S GIFT

There was a knock on the door in the middle of the night, and I woke as Thióðolf got up from the bed to join Arnulf at the table, with the four men who had gone out after Hialti earlier in the day. They spoke in low voices, but I had good hearing and strained my ears, peeking out of the bed so that I could follow their conversation.

"We lost him, Heri," one of the men said, and I could hear it was Sígtrygg.

"What do you mean, lost him?" Arnulf wheezed, sounding angry.

"We looked all around for him, Heri. We searched, and we searched. Suddenly we stumbled upon..." Sígtrygg's eyes widened for a moment, as if in terror. It was the first time I saw a Rus show his fear openly, now that he thought himself alone among brothers.

"What?" Arnulf sounded surprised.

"We met the Hel Rune, Heri. We met the Hel Rune and the Mare. The Very Gentle Ones."

All the men around the table suddenly shuddered involuntarily, even Arnulf. He shook his head and then composed himself, leaning over the table and staring Sígtrygg in the eyes. "So you met the Kindly Brides of Gallows Hill and Elfin Mounds? I suppose good old lady Death scared you then? Made you turn and run, did she?"

"No, Heri, not at all. Well, you know the ladies. We felt uncomfortable. But we did not run. The most kindly one spoke to us, Heri," Sígtrygg declared brightly, even sounding a little proud.

"She spoke to you?" Arnulf sounded incredulous.

"She did. She only ever spoke to Hallgrim before. But now she spoke to us, and greeted us, even. She asked us what we were up to."

"And what did you say to her?"

"The truth, of course. Heri, if the Hel Rune asks questions, a man must answer. She sees through a man's soul, that one. She is a great witch," Sígtrygg added appreciatively.

"All hails," the men murmured all together, sounding anxious.

"All hails to the Gentle Ladies," Arnulf sighed.

"And what use did the Great Bride have of that story, Sígtrygg?"

"She was... interested, Heri. She asked questions about the young Síf, Heri." Arnulf and Thióðolf exchanged glances, looking worried. "What kind of questions?"

"I hardly even remember, Heri. You know what the good lady is like. She makes your head swim, as in upstream," Sígtrygg mumbled, seemingly entranced. The three other berserkers who had gone after Hialti, Njál and Runarr, and Agnarr the fourth, all nodded slowly in agreement. Arnulf looked from one man to the other before he sighed and rolled his eyes with exasperation. The four fierce warriors all had the same dreamy, distant expression to their faces. Arnulf smashed his fist into the table to wake them from the spell. "Do any of you remember what you told the Hel Rune about the maiden?"

The men looked uncertainly at each other, clearly befuddled, but after some hesitation, Runarr volunteered brightly, "We told her about the rage, Heri. The battle rage. When the maiden went berserk."

"Did you, now?" Arnulf said sweetly.

"Yes, Heri," Runarr announced eagerly, obviously happy about remembering anything at all. Arnulf glared at them until they all lowered their eyes and bowed their heads. "May the Mare ride you to Hel," the warlord growled, and gestured to the men to get out.

"But Heri," Runarr objected.

"I know! I know! I take the curse back. I withdraw it, by the mighty Thor. No man shall blame another for being fooled by Death. May you be free from the Night Mare! Now will you just go? You can resume the traitor-hunt in the morning."

"But Heri," Runarr said again, "there is more to our tale."

"What more? Are you going to tell me that you told her the maiden was from Hel? Did you swear to hand her over to the Kindly Ones for fostering?"

"No, Heri. It would not have been our place to swear such things, Heri. It is just something she said..." Runarr was actually stuttering.

"I am waiting."

"The Hel Rune said that she would take care of it, Heri. She told us that the Seven Sisters had already noosed him. In the market, before the whole town to see."

"The ladies have noosed Hialti?" Arnulf sounded incredulous.

"Yes, Heri. The Old Mother told us that the Sisters had spied an unarmed man running around town with no slave collar on and nothing else to show that he was spoken for. Seeing as they were in want of a fresh man slave, they saw the opportunity to get one for free. So they noosed him, right in front of lots of people too. It is true, folks told us of it later. We know that the ladies noosed Hialti and announced that this man had no arms and no collar, so he was now their property to do what they wished with, and then they walked off with him. Nobody interfered, naturally, as it was within the law and besides, well, you know the Sisters. One just does not interfere."

"Yes, I know," Arnulf mused, "and I would be a fool to grudge the Very Gentle Ladies a good noosing." He stopped and added disappointedly, "Although it breaks my heart to see our vengeance has been taken from us. He ought to have had the traitor's death."

"But Heri," all the men exclaimed in unison before they let Runarr continue as their spokesman, "The Great Bride said that she would honor your verdict and our right to vengeance. She said that she would send Hialti to the Eagle, after she..." He paused.

The men looked partly horrified, partly awed and excited.

"After what?" Arnulf did not sound angry anymore, only curious, and I saw that Thióðolf was leaning forward, equally curious.

"After she is through with him, Heri. The Old One said she would fulfill your just verdict and send him to the Eagle, after she is through. She also said that the... uhm, that the Great Mare felt... uhm... lustful. She said that her pale sister was eager for a good... uhm, a good ride. You know." Thióðolf and Arnulf exchanged glances, eyes widening. "She said that the Seven Sisters felt, uh, playful," Runarr eagerly proceeded, now that he had gotten the hang of his own mind again. "She said they could all do with a man tonight, all nine of them. The Most Kindly One thanked you, Arnulf, for this offering, and assured us that they would be very kind and gentle."

The men shuddered collectively.

"The good woman told us to go back home and rest assured, and that they would gift us after they had known the great pleasure. And so we left. A warrior must follow Death's directions."

"By all the stinking pits of Hel," Arnulf whispered and sat heavily down in his seat.

I did not understand what they were really talking about, and had gained too much respect for Thióðolf to rudely reveal that I had been disobedient, listening into the men's conversation. So I pretended I was sleeping when he finally returned to the bed, after whispering with Arnulf for some time. But I wondered who those kind and gentle ladies were, who were so lustful and playful, and who besides had the power to noose a man in the marketplace of Aldeigjuborg.

I wondered even more why the men appeared to be so terrorized by all that playful gentleness, being generally very appreciative of lustful females. In the morning, there was a great deal of commotion in the courtyard, and I had not even had breakfast before I was told to come out. Everybody in the household, warriors and slaves, had gathered to behold the sacred sight. They all parted as I came walking through the court, reaching the gate where Arnulf and Thióðolf were standing, looking at something on the ground. I looked down too and had to compose myself quickly lest I gasp like a slave girl.

On the ground was a head.

It was Hialt'is head, and it looked as if it had been torn from his body without the use of a blade of any kind. There was a rune carved into his forehead. Arnulf picked up the head, holding it by the long hair, and lifted it high for all to see. "This is a gift from the Mare," Arnulf said to the whole court, "This is an honor paid to this house from the shores of Death. His face has been marked by the rune of Hel. Hialti the Coward has been claimed by the Kindly Ones."

He raised his voice and chanted, his voice a thunderous roar, "The Seven Sisters have known him for their plaything! The Great Mare has ridden him! The Hel Rune caught his soul! Then he was sent to the Eagle, for so I condemned him!" Arnulf looked proudly around before he proceeded, "And so the Kindly Ladies have honored me and my house and carved the mark of the traitor into his back. Yet before he could offer up his breath, the Pale Mare, seized by sacred fury, pulled his head off from his shoulders with her claws of Death. The Brides of the Burial know their own kind; this was done for the maiden, for the Síf of my house, even as we men would have done the same for her. This is for you, Little Priestess. I offer this gift to my fosterling Síf."

My Heri held Hialti's head out for me to take. I glanced at Thióðolf, who nodded.

There were many privileges to being a girl, I had learned. I did not have to prove my courage like boys had to. I could admit to fear and seek protection without losing honor or worth. I could appropriately weep and wail on many occasions. But a warrior's daughter can never, ever be squeamish. One just cannot make warriors, being squeamish. I had not quite realized what not being squeamish actually entailed before now, but found to my relief that it was easy for me. Looking as calm and dignified as I could muster, I took the bloodied head in my hands, concentrated on not letting it show how heavy I thought it was, and looked into the mutilated face of the man who had humiliated me and hurt so many others worse.

It was obvious that he had died in great pain, his dead face still a grimace of terror. Whatever he had done to other girls and women had been fully returned to him by those mysterious ladies whom my kinsmen anxiously kept referring to as most kindly. And I knew the only important thing. The child-rapist was dead. He could never touch me again. That was all that mattered. I gazed at the warriors of Arnulf's court and saw the adoration in their eyes as they beheld me, holding the coward's bloodied head, a most sacred sight to them.

It began to dawn on me that they actually *loved* me. I felt a strange tug of the heart, and knew that I did love them back, even if they were a bunch of hardened rogues and brutes. A message seemed to emanate from the men of our court, a message that began to settle in my heart and soul, growing into certainty. Nobody could touch me. My warriors protected me. My brothers cared for me, loved me and respected me.

The men's hammer heated my heart.

I smiled and looked out at Arnulf's court, and saw that all my brothers were regarding me expectantly. Then I remembered our customs, and made my voice ready to properly intone the sacred response. I had long since learned the frame of such chants, and knew how to fill it with relevant words.

"I hold Hialti the Coward's head, torn from his shoulders! I thank my Heri for this precious gift! I thank the Kindly Ones, who brought me the traitor's head! I thank my brothers, who have honored me! All hails to the Mare! All hails to Arnulf! All hails to the claws that tore!"

Then I spat into the child-rapist's face, to the loud cheers of the court, to the banging of shields, to the stomping of feet, and my soul rejoiced with its own song. The warriors roared and the slave women shouted and howled with joy, and just as the party began, I felt it in my secret heart; my love for them all, and my utter sense of belonging.

I was one of them.

SHE-WOLVES OF THE SECRET HEART

The Vikings and their slaves had partied the whole day, and come evening most were already asleep or passed out from too much drink. The Moon lord stood high in the night sky before there was movement in court again. Zivah woke up when Thióðolf touched her cheek gently, immediately removing his hand when she flinched.

"I had to wake you, Zivah," he whispered, and she looked and saw Thordís sleeping soundly between them in the bed as she always did. She felt that old dread again, the dread of the moment that would surely come when her master decided that he had waited long enough and Thordís was not there to stop him.

"Nothing like that," he whispered, reading her mind. They had a nasty habit of understanding what other people were thinking, these Norsemen. "But you are being called to the warriors' Hall. Do not be frightened, Zivah, nobody will hurt you. But you must go." Befuddled, she got up and put on her grey slave dress. She looked anxiously at him.

"Do you want me to go with you?" he asked. She would never have thought she would want him to come, but that moment she knew the only reality there was; that his protection was the only thing that kept the other men from using her as they used any other slave. She nodded, forgetting the courtesies, but he did not seem to mind. He looked at Thordís and smiled.

"She will sleep," he said, "We gave her a good draught."

When he noticed how anxious that comment made Zivah, he sighed, "Do trust me just this night, Zivah. Nobody will hurt you. All the other girls are going too. This is for you. I promise. You are not going alone either."

Just as he had said that, she saw Tana and Suri looking out from the bath-room, giving her a nod of confirmation. She went to join them and found that the other slave girls had gathered already and were waiting for some signal from the men. The only women not present were Aziza and Laimi, who were both sleeping away in Arnulf's bed, on each side of the House-Bond. When that was noted, Suri whispered, "Njál told me they were not going to need this. He said they had been protected by their concubine collars. This is for the rest of us."

"What is this?" One of the others asked, and they all looked curiously at Suri, who seemed to be better informed than any of them, but she shook her head slowly. "I really do not know. It was what Njál said to me just before, when he told me to go and wake everybody except the concubines and the girl. And Arnulf. Said Arnulf Heri had to sleep through all this, because it was the sacred law or something. But you know our masters. They are crazy."

The women nodded thoughtfully to this eternal and indisputable truth and looked at each other. Nothing was happening and finally Zivah volunteered, "My House-Bond told me I was wanted in the warriors' Hall."

"Oh really, what a surprise," Suri remarked drily, and they all giggled a little, but Zivah shook her head, "He said it was nothing like that. I think we are all supposed to go there." They exchanged glances and suddenly realized that no masters were herding them anywhere and that they had been given an invitation of sorts, which meant that, as outstanding as it seemed, they ought to go there altogether of their own accord. Curious, they decided to go, and so they went.

The only time Zivah had been inside the warriors' Hall was that time when Hialti had tried to rape her, so she had never really paid attention to the interior. Now that they came indoors she saw a huge hall with six large beds situated three on either of the side walls, all with room enough for almost ten people sleeping with their heads or feet towards the wall, and she thought of what Miri had told them, that six men and one Sheath slept together in one bed and that they kept a spare bed for visitors and for the boy, Ivarr.

Nobody was in the beds now, the curtains were drawn, and the men sat round a long table, similar to the one of the Hold. Ivarr sat there also, furthest down, a way of saying that he was lowest ranking among the warriors. She saw Hallgrim seated in the High Seat of the Hall. The five Sheaths were standing to attention next to him, and on the table in front of the man was Hialti's head.

To Zivah's surprise, her cat Hel-Hound was also there, lying on the table and basking in the attention, seeing as everybody's eyes were on her, or so she thought, conveniently. She purred and stretched lazily, occasionally playing a little with the hair on Rat-Hialti's head.

When the slave women entered the Hall, Hallgrim nodded at them and gestured for them to enter properly and take their places next to the five Sheaths. Miri met Zivah's eyes and winked encouragingly. Hallgrim stood up from his seat and the Hall was quiet when he began speaking to the men.

"Do you all see Hel-Hound there? Hel-Hound the cat? Is she not beautiful? Is she not soft and lovely to the touch? What say you all?"

"Aye," the men agreed and looked fondly at the cat.

"Do you want to touch her? Do you want to feel her? Would you like to hold her and cuddle her?" Hallgrim asked. The men nodded again.

"What is stopping you?" Hallgrim asked. There was a deal of uncomfortable shuffling and uncertain glances exchanged before one of them volunteered, "The possibility that she will not like it?"

The men looked expectantly at Hallgrim.

"Really?" Hallgrim said, "Why does that matter? She is our cat. We own her. We can do anything we like with her, can we not? Anything. We can grab her and hold her and do whatever we want to her. She cannot stop us. Why would we care about whether she likes it or not?"

"Because, uhm, because she is... because we like her," Njál said, "We don't want her to hurt or be angry with us. We want her to come to us because she likes us." The men nodded to that, agreeing.

"She would not trust us after," Agnarr said, the men grunting to that.

"She is a holy sort of beast," Sígtrygg pointed out.

The men nodded again.

"Yes," Hallgrim said, "we like her, we do not want her to hurt or be angry with us, we would like her to trust us and come to us of her own accord and enjoy our attentions to her and we also know that she is a holy sort of beast. We would be men of no honor if we abused our power over her. And men of no honor will receive the Judgment of the Norns, whether it be in this life or in the next. You all know that. You all know that the Judgment of the Norns can be known beforehand. You all know how it can be known. Say it."

The men cast uncertain glances at the women and kept silent.

"Say it," Hallgrim insisted, "Say how the Judgment of the Norns can be anticipated."

"But Hallgrim," one of the men said, "there are slaves present."

"This night is a night of the Contrary," Hallgrim said, "and there are no slaves present here. There is only the truth. Speak out."

To Zivah's astonishment, all the men spoke in unison, "The verdicts of women light the path of the warrior."

"Yes," Hallgrim said, "The verdicts of women are holy. Women speak in the language of gods and norns. It does not matter how powerless they are. Whether she is a Freyia or a slave, it matters not. Her verdicts are and will always be holy. The verdicts of women are the signs that light up a man's path in life, lighting the way towards honor and glory and which prophecy the final judgment on our conducts."

He paused and looked sternly at all the men, who for some reason or other suddenly bowed their heads and covered their faces in shame, even if just for a moment. Then they looked back up at Hallgrim, who continued, "We have offered Atonement, but there is still more that must be paid. Tonight there shall be a rite of cleansing in our court. Tonight we shall hold a ritual of the Contrary. The rite will show us the truth of the norns' verdicts on men like Hialti. This must not be spoken of after. This must be kept in the dark night and our secret hearts. I say this to the warriors and to the women of this Hall and of the Hold. This night is secret."

Everybody nodded solemnly. The women were beginning to feel a strange thrill. To their surprise, all the men suddenly got up from the benches and moved to stand behind, closer to the walls. Hallgrim went over to Miri and took her hand. He led her to the High Seat and made her sit down. She looked utterly uncomfortable there, looking out on the Hall from the place of the Hall's lord.

"This night is the night of the Contrary," Hallgrim said, "and all the tables are now turned. You are not slaves this night. You are the women of this court and you are holy to us. Let all sit by this table now. Miri, you are the Freyia of this night. And you are most beloved."

"Aye. She is most beloved," the men agreed fondly, and there were some muffled comments of appraisal, of how very lovely and good their Miri was. Miri's tears began to run down her cheeks, but she sat there and somehow she looked like a queen at that moment.

All the women took their places around the table and were surprised when the men began to serve them drink. It all felt so strange, but as soon as the men had accepted the Contrary mode, they slipped into their roles as easily as if it had always been so, making the slave women feel comfortable about being served by them. Zivah frowned to herself and realized that she had never really known people more flexible than these Norsemen. They seemed to move between realities as easily as dreamers do. And when the women had relaxed into their temporary roles as honored guests of the warriors' Hall, Hallgrim intervened again. This time, he took Hialti's head by the hair and held it up for all to see.

"Are you ready for the ritual, my Freyia?" he asked Miri.

Miri nodded. Without further speech she got up from the High Seat, as if she already knew what she was supposed to do, and began walking out of the Hall, followed by Hallgrim and the severed head. All the women got to their feet and went after them, and finally the men filed out.

When they came out in the courtyard, Hallgrim and the women made a circle, and the warriors stood outside, like a shield wall creating an outer circle. It was odd, Zivah thought, how the presence of these men around them suddenly felt so very protective, as if they had dutifully volunteered to make sure nobody interfered with the women's inner circle. It was also amazing how quiet they could be when they wanted to. It was so quiet now that she almost startled when Hallgrim spoke in a certain sort of voice that she had only heard once before in her whole life. His voice was deep roar of the throat, working like a spell.

"Now you must be the she-wolves of your secret hearts," the shadow walker said.

Zivah felt dizzy. She saw the change happen in the women, the strange lights that were lit in their eyes. She saw Miri take Hialti's head in her hands, heard her speak words in a language of her own, and how she spat into the coward's face. She saw how the head was handed from woman to woman, and how they all spoke their verdicts on the dead man before they spat into his dead face. And suddenly the head was hers.

She took it, and looked at it and recalled the first time she had received a head-gift.

"I hold my enemy's head in my hands," Zivah said. Speaking it in Norse, she realized how strong and loud her voice was, and noticed how the men reacted. They looked awed. The river woman spat into her enemy´s face and handed the head over to the next sister. She looked up and met Hallgrim's gaze. He smiled to her and nodded approvingly.

She could not be certain, but he looked as if he was proud of her.

When the head returned to Miri, Hallgrim said, "The head is yours, Freyia. You may do with it as you please."

And Zivah remembered how she and Mother and little Thordís had once kicked and struck at the mutilated corpses of their enemies.

"No silver skull cup?" Miri asked gleefully. Hallgrim shook his head. The head was hers. And Miri put the head down on the ground and squatted over it and pissed on it. And when she did, other women gathered and did the same. And when many had pissed on the head they began kicking it and stomping on it and screaming as they did, and a low cheer broke out from the men's circle as they watched their women going wild.

Zivah could not make herself partake in it. Had there been a whole body, perhaps. But with just one head, and so many angry women, she decided to leave it to those who had truly been hurt by Hialti. There was hardly anything left of the head when the women finally broke down in sobs on the ground.

Zivah watched as the men approached, gently, carefully, taking the women in their arms, carrying them towards the outdoor wash-house. Zivah followed and watched. She saw Hallgrim undressing Miri and washing her body, just as the other men assisted the other girls. She saw how they put new clothes on the women and carried them into their beds, whether it was in the Hall or the Hold. They did it so softly and so lovingly.

Even when they undressed them and washed them they did it respectfully and without any leering whatsoever. Finally, Thióðolf stood next to her and did not touch her – nobody had touched her.

He asked if she wanted to wash up too, and she went to wash her hands and arms and face. The others had left and there was only him there now, Thióðolf Skald by the water well and his young slave. She met his eyes for the first time since he made a true slave out of her.

"Freyia," he said quietly to her, "let us go to sleep."

Zivah nodded, and together they walked back into the Hold, where the slave girls were already snoring loudly and the last men had left. She climbed into the bed, moved past Thordís and found her place by the wall. Thióðolf lie down on his side of the maiden and she heard him settle into bed after distributing his weapons as always.

His words kept ringing through her mind. He had called her Freyia as if he thought she was a free woman.

"Good night, Heri," she whispered when the court was quiet.

"Good night, Zivah," he replied softly.

It was the first time they spoke such words to each other.

ℵOT AN ⊛RDINARY ⊙IRL

Something had been going on that night, I knew it, but they had given me a drink come early eve that must have contained a sleep draught of sorts, for I slept heavily and did not wake up until midday the day after. When I got up at last the women smiled at me, and from that day they no longer bothered with all the courtesies for as long as no free men were present.

I felt a lot better that way too. Zivah herself brought me my morning water for my face, and she combed my hair and made some beautiful braids of it. I had not yet seen my clothes laid out anywhere and did not want to harass the slaves, but as soon as Zivah had made my hair, Aziza came with two bundles and put them on the table.

"Maiden, the warriors wanted to give you a choice this day. They said that you could either choose your boy's clothes as before and resume your training in the warriors' court, or else you could choose this pretty dress and be an ordinary girl. No matter your choice they will honor it, and they love you," Aziza said, smiling. I looked at the two bundles and frowned. I was not very good at making choices, I found, when I could not make out what was really expected of me.

"Are you not sure, sister?" Zivah asked. I shook my head and asked her what she thought, what left her look very blank.

"I cannot say, Thordís," she said after a while, "Just the notion of fighting with weapons frightens me so much that I would rather succumb and die, almost. I just do not understand how anyone is able to do that at all. I do not know why."

"I hear you, Zivah," Aziza agreed. "I feel the same way. Fighting is unthinkable for me, the closest thing I ever got were some feeble attempts to get away, of course. I think it is because we are women."

"Mother killed a man to protect Zivah," I objected, and they both looked thoughtful. "I suppose, if you need to protect a child, one may find courage," Zivah pondered, and Aziza nodded.

The two women looked uncomfortable at the very thought of having to fight, ever. I looked at their soft and delicate and impractically curvaceous bodies, and the way they were; their gentle movements, their sweet voices and the tender songs of their souls. They were very womanly women, I thought, more so than any other women in the whole court. They were the sort of women you need to protect, not push into combat; the sort of women who ought to sit within the shield circle, providing healing and nourishment while others fought.

I wondered what impression I would make when I was grown.

"As much as I admire you both, you two just do not have the war chant in your soul songs," I finally snorted, dismissively, "but the question that is pressing right now is whether I do or not. And I am not sure."

"Uhm, I did hear the men say you have a very maidenly soul song and that you cannot be honed like a boy," Zivah said, "but they were still training you, so they must see something or other in you."

"They were," I said, "They also saw what happened when Hialti the Coward got hold of me."

"What happened?" Aziza asked, and both looked curious. I thought they had seen everything that transpired with Hialti, but now I realized that they did not see with the eyes of warriors and could not understand.

"They saw me break, Aziza. They saw me break apart. I broke down and succumbed like a girl," I explained, and felt sad.

It was the truth of the matter. The men probably did not want to dismiss me just like that, because I was dear to them, but the message of the other choice seemed clear all of a sudden. They had seen me for what I was, a feeble little girl who would break apart if she was treated too roughly. And now that I thought about it, I knew it was true also. I could not handle that sort of treatment. I would succumb to it. It had just happened of its own accord, as if the will to fight simply was not there and there was nothing I could do about it.

I was a girl and I had a maidenly soul song and I was not going to get to play anymore and all that made me feel a little angry.

"They also saw you hold your enemy's head in your hands," Zivah muttered darkly. I looked at them both and noticed that something had happened with them since last night. They looked stronger than before and there was a light in their eyes. Aziza nodded slowly.

"Do you remember the battle rage that once seized you, when it meant enough for you, Djinn-eyes?" She asked. I did. But the rage had not returned to me after that one time. I pondered a little more.

"What do you want, Thordís? You keep wondering what the men want, but what about you?"

"I honestly do not know, Zivah," I said, "I have always been so busy catching up with the present that I hardly ever think of what I will do in the future."

"Do you know, Thordís," Aziza said, "that you have an utterly unique opportunity to actually be trained for combat by Rus Viking warriors? What does it matter if you will never become one yourself? These men are the most ferocious fighters in the world, as far as I know. Learn to fight from them and you may well find your capacities helpful in many places and times. Arnulf once told me that many Norse women who have trained a few years with their men are often better able to fight than most men in most other places. Believe me when I say that the skill to defend yourself if need be may come in very handy even if you are never going to be a warrior. And I do think that they want you to know the arts for other purposes as well, they think you ought to be skilled at detecting errors and suchlike. I am quite sure they do not expect you to become a proper warrior, but they are still going to teach you a lot. And you do love training with them, do you not?"

"I do. I am just afraid that they will think I am slowing them down and ruining their battle practice," I said.

Surprisingly enough, both of them laughed out loud.

"Why are you laughing?" I sneered, and raised my eyebrows when both of them immediately bowed their heads and went quiet. I immediately regretted my sneer.

"Please don't treat me as a... as a maiden, sister. Aziza. Not when the men are not even here to glare at us. I just wondered why you both laughed. I really just wanted to know why," I pleaded, and knew that I would never sneer at slaves again when I saw how their shoulders relaxed, now that they knew for certain that the Maiden was not actually angry with them.

"Well, it is like this, Mai... Thordís," Aziza said, "that we laughed because you obviously have no idea how happy the men are every time they get to play with you out there."

I looked at Zivah, who nodded. I regarded the two bundles again. Suddenly I knew what it was. It was a test.

Thordís came out into the warriors' court wearing her boy's clothes and an unusually pretty hairdo, making Thióðolf's heart melt at the sight of her. She had passed the test. The warriors all greeted her with cheers and smiles, and he lifted the girl up on a table so they could all see her when they gathered round. Hallgrim came up to her and smiled.

"Little Thordís, our Síf, we are happy to see you back here with us after what happened," Hallgrim said, "and now we would like to hear why you chose this path and not the other." The girl let her gaze wander from face to face, gathering their undivided attention.

"At first, I was uncertain," she said, "because I have had room to think. I know, now, what will happen to me if I go into combat with a man and lose. I also know that if I go into combat with a man, I am most likely to lose. And I know that there is something within me that may easily break, something that might make me unfit for the battle field. I will even admit that I am not exactly eager to get into either combat or battle fields, my brothers. It may be because I am a girl."

She paused. Suddenly she looked directly at Ivarr, who startled and looked like he wanted to vanish through the ground. Poor Ivarr, Thióðolf thought mischievously. He was being well honed these days.

"Ivarr," she said, and the boy went pale with terror, "Ivarr, it is the truth that if the men and you honed me the way the men and I hone you, I would have succumbed. I could not have handled it. I simply do not have that sort of war chant in my soul. I could never have taken it. I honor you for the courage you show when you get up each and every time to fight again, facing laughter and scorn and taunting every day. I honor you. I think you are going to grow into a great warrior."

Ivarr gaped. Then Ivarr stopped gaping and met the girl's eyes. Thióðolf could see it happen, the transformation from within, the first time a young boy realizes what the vicious honer is really doing for him. He turned to look at Thordís, and saw the same transformation happen in her, the sudden realization that there is more than taunting what can hone a man. He was so proud of her. They all were.

And poor Ivarr looked like he suddenly adored the girl.

"That does not mean that you are off the hook, Ivarr," the maiden added, "I am just saying." She winked at the boy, causing all the men to laugh, and the boy too. "So, I thought that there would be no more point in taking this path at all, until I heard it spoken that you men quite enjoy my presence in your games.

"I enjoy my presence here just the same. That was when I remembered what the choice was. You had told Aziza to tell me that I could either resume my practice or choose to be an ordinary girl." She paused again and smiled broadly at them. "And, after thinking about it for a little while, I realized that I cannot possibly be an ordinary girl, can I?" She looked innocently and brightly at all her brothers, who all broke out in big smiles.

"Ah! Thordís," Hallgrim laughed and took the child in his hands, lifting her up to the sky, "you have passed the test, you ferocious little she-wolf. You shall be our shield maiden, girl, yet we shall protect you like we would any other Síf, except that our Síf gets to bite every now and then. What say you, men? Is that what you also think?"

The warriors roared their agreements, and the girl was sent laughing from man to man, each one hurling her through the air and tossing her to the next man while she shrieked from joy. And just as they had finished hurling the red-haired maiden from man to man, the snow began falling.

TAPESTRY OF FATE

The first snow had fallen and made the world white and crisp, yet it was still not enough of it to prevent us from riding in the hills, so Thióðolf and I went out to enjoy the beauty on horseback. We came to the top of a hill from which we could behold the town and the river, and there we made camp, eating a little bread and cheese while we watched the landscape.

"Thióðolf," I said, "When you told me about the blood eagle, you said it was a warrior's matter and that women and children and, eh, slaves, they cannot see the rite."

"That is correct. It is not for your eyes."

"All of you talked about some Kindly Ladies who had done it."

"Oh. Yes. The ladies," Thióðolf said, looking uncomfortable.

"So how come these nice old ladies can carve a blood eagle and tear apart bodies of living men if these rites are not to be seen by women?"

"Well, Wolfling, you know how you are not exactly an ordinary girl? Well, the truth is that there are women, and then there are… other kinds of women."

"How many kinds are there?"

"Countless kinds, in my opinion, but then I am speaking of character traits. What I was referring to is something else, something that has to do with the soul song of a person. Let us think of the tapestry of fate, Thordís, imagine a great tapestry."

"I am not very good at imagining things, Thióðolf," I objected reluctantly, always feeling as if I was wading against heavy currents of the mind when somebody tried to make me imagine things on purpose.

"It may be because you are always overly present in each moment. Now you are present in this little exchange of words and you will do as I say, because I am your teacher. Imagine a tapestry."

Somehow it was always easier to do difficult things if a respected teacher ordered me to do it. Then it became a rule, and rules were easy to follow. With my battle practice, Thióðolf had begun to pick up on that little trait of mine and now became a little bossy every time I had trouble with something, which always spurred me to success.

I saw a great white tapestry before the unseen eyes of my mind.

"What are you seeing?" He asked.

"A great white tapestry," I said.

"Good," Thióðolf said, "And now imagine that all the white threads that make up the tapestry represent the lives of people. Don't object. It is an order." I obeyed, and imagined it. I saw the entire tapestry come alive with pulsing veins of life that ran through each thread that made the great weave. "I see it, Thióðolf."

"Good. That is the tapestry of fate you are seeing. That is the world. Now, what is wrong with this image?"

"Is it a sail?" I asked, since the imaginary tapestry lacked images.

"It could well be a sail. We could say that the tapestry of fate is the sail that moves the ship of Earth. What do you think of it?"

"It is a boring sail," I said, "not like the sails on the Dragon ships. There are no images. It is just white."

"Exactly. It is boring, because all the threads are white. The norns are great artists, Thordís, why would they weave a boring tapestry? Do you really think they would do that?"

"Fate is not boring," I said, "Life is more colorful than this white sail."

"Exactly. So what would you do, if you were a norn?"

"I am not a norn. I am just a girl, or so you men keep telling me."

"More fool us, then, girl. Of course you are a norn."

"I am?"

"By nature. You are a girl. Your kind spurs all fate. Fate begins in your womb."

"Oh."

"You don't need to understand these things yet, Thordís."

"Thank you," I said, relieved.

"Now, since you are a norn, I ask you, what would you do to make the tapestry of fate more interesting, more like great art, more like poetry?"

"I would use lots of different colors and make exciting and funny and beautiful and terrible and sad and scary and nice images," I said excitedly, wondering if my weaving skills would ever come to anything when I spent most of my time with warriors. The slave women weaved all the time, but they were making sails and clothing and other practical things, not tapestries to hang on the walls. Noble women were supposed to engage in that kind of work, but nobody was teaching me. Suddenly I realized that I wished someone would. It sounded fun to make such great and colorful tapestries, describing all the things that I had seen.

"I wish I could do that, Thióðolf. I think I would make really great tapestries."

"It is as I said," Thióðolf chuckled, "You are a norn to the bone. Now, seeing as you are weaving the sacred tapestry, would you make all the threads in the tapestry equally colorful?"

"No."

"Why not?"

"It would become too messy. All the white is needed as a background, to frame the colors, to make the images stand out. There would still have to be a lot of white. Actually, most of the threads will have to be white," I pondered.

"Exactly. And now you will remember that all the threads represent the lives and fates of men and women," Thióðolf said.

"Is this about there being different kinds of women?"

"There are lots of different kinds of people, Thordís, both men and women. Some are colorful because they create great stories that affect lots of people. Others are colorful simply because they are different. And they are sacred, because they make the world colorful."

"Oh."

"So imagine that all the white threads are men and women who live ordinary lives. They may live good and honorable lives, nice lives, exciting lives, or sad and boring lives, bad lives, rich lives or poor lives, but they do not stand out from the crowd. They sing a soul song well known to most. The white threads are most people, Thordís."

"Are they low-ranking folks and slaves?" I asked.

"No, this has nothing to do with rank, Thordís. This has to do with the souls and minds of people, and it does not matter what kind of rank anyone has, or how happy or successful they are. A king of great power can be as white and ordinary as everybody else. And a slave can be very colorful. Just think of Aziza, or Miri, and your own sister."

"Is Zivah colorful?" I thought about her bowed head and grey dress, moving silently around like a ghost fulfilling her obligations, without speaking to anyone but the other slaves if she did not have to, always exaggerating the submissive courtesies when she had to observe them. She who had stood out with her beauty and her temper back home in the village had become but a transparent reflection of her old self. It was only lately that she had warmed up to me and talked to me, but she kept her silence around the men.

"Zivah is very colorful," Thióðolf smiled, and I thought I detected both affection and admiration in his face as he spoke of my sister. He laughed and proceeded: "She is making a joke out of submission, Thordís, what with all the excuse me, Heri and always studying my feet when she talks to me. I think she must know all the details of my shoes and feet by now, but I doubt that she even remembers the color of my eyes. And yet she knows exactly where to draw the line between correct behavior and ridicule. She spites me every way she can spite me without being punished for it. So you see, even as she wears that terrible grey dress, she is colorful. Or one can see that she is colorful exactly because she keeps wearing it."

Thióðolf had tried to offer a new dress to Zivah, a green linen one just like the one she had wanted down at Lake Ilmen, and far more pretty. She had thanked him politely and tucked it away, never to be used. Apart from her night gown, she always wore the grey woolen dress that he had forced upon her in the marketplace, as a reminder to him of what he had done to her. Only when the dress had to be washed and dried did she use other clothes, but always some she had borrowed from the other slave women.

Fortunately, her House-Bond had the wisdom to offer the new dress-gift in private, so that nobody knew about his second gift, as thoroughly and insolently slighted by his slave as the first had been. No one else but Thióðolf and I could claim that she was disrespecting him, since they did not know that she was in fact doing so with this hostile little gesture. Thióðolf knew it, and I, but we never mentioned it, allowing Zivah to perpetually show her little rebellion to us only, without there being any formal and public need for Thióðolf to assert his authority over her again.

Perhaps she knew that he would not punish her if she was discreet about it, which after a fashion meant that she already trusted him more than she would admit. And yet I knew that she had been frightened for a very long time and that she was still fearful of what he could do to her if she angered him. Even so she could not help but punish him in every way she could get away with. I realized that my sister was in fact a very courageous woman, possessing great integrity, and the dignity of a queen, even as she was a slave.

"She may not be easily detectable, now, in the great tapestry," Thióðolf said, "but if you look closer, you can see that the color has only been smudged by the need to hide, because it is too dangerous for her to stand out. But her color is there, Thordís, it is just in hiding. It longs to be seen again. All colors need to be recognized."

I nodded thoughtfully. When I looked more carefully, as Thióðolf told me to do, I saw that my sister stood out among the slaves of Aldeigjuborg, colorful and different. She was still rebelling, even if she did it in the only way she could without being hurt, and yet she was taking a great chance, and she knew it well.

"Am I colorful?" I asked curiously.

"You are colorful beyond words, She-Wolf," he smiled fondly, "You create great songs just by moving around and following your whims. And your color is encouraged everywhere you go, because we all adore the splendor that you bring into this great story which is our lives. There are times us men think you must be the great goddess of all stories, incarnate among us."

I smiled at that and saw before my mind's eyes the image of Thióðolf and the other men, worshipping me on an altar, lowering their eyes to me, their goddess. The very notion was so novel that I began to giggle. I said nothing, though, having a lingering feeling that my warriors did not worship their goddess in quite the way that I was now imagining.

"Are you colorful?" I asked instead.

"What do you think, little fate-weaver?"

He was so beautiful, I thought. He was a beautiful man.

"I think you are very colorful," I said, "I think that is why everybody adores you as well."

"I would not say adore, about me. But liking and respect, yes, that comes to one who stands out in a way that people can recognize and feel inspired by. Most skalds are very much appreciated, and we are always colorful. We are respected because our office is sacred and well-known to all. But our people also respect colors that stand out in unusual ways, because those make the tapestry even more interesting. That is when you find mannish women who engage in the battle arts, women who transgress all the common traits of their gender."

"I have not seen such women, Thióðolf," I objected.

"You have not met such women here, Thordís, because the Rus do not cultivate them, but in many of the homelands, such as in Denmark, there are special orders created by and for such ladies. They cannot live the lives of wives and mothers that most women prefer, because it is against the song of their souls. They do not even want to be witches or priestesses, like most other women are, who have no desire to be wives. They are fit only for the warrior's way, and they can be honed even when they are little girls, just as if they had been boys. We appreciate that, and we respect them, because we always respect true warriors, no matter who they are, and more so because they are unusual and special, and thus sacred. Yet even in the homelands, people often think such women strange, and they often keep to their own. Men sometimes feel awkward around them, seeing as many of them act and even sometimes look exactly like men."

"Do you feel awkward around them?"

"I have to admit that I do, sometimes. I like them well but you see, men may feel awkward because we do not know how to behave with women like that, what with all the courtesies we are accustomed to pay to women. It is like we have to keep two minds around them and switch easily between the two so as not to offend them and also not offend our own sense of honor. But that is just another way of being honed sharp of soul, Thordís. I think what many other men may find a little difficult to grasp is the fact that many of these mannish women even prefer to play Freyia's games only with other women. And many maidenly women like these mannish women well enough, just as they would like a man."

"They do?" I asked, having never heard of such things.

"Yes. Some think that is strange. Well, they do not think it so strange that mannish women have the same tastes as men do, but that maidenly women will like such women in the same way that they will like men. But I think that most maidenly women are attracted to warriors, and as such, they can be as easily attracted to female warriors as they are to males."

"Oh," I said, pondering. I thought I remembered some women from the village who had been great hunters and who often preferred to do such work as most men usually did. There had even been a sort of couple, but I had never paid that any mind at all.

My mother's people had always been very relaxed about the relationships of others, but they had also always been very discreet and private about them, unlike the Rus, who were not at all shy about anything, it seemed, and whose relationships often seemed more like a group effort than anything private. Maybe that was why we were so concerned with courtesies. Come to think of it, courtesies were often the only thing that allowed for some distance to others, some privacy in our world.

"Even if many feel strangely about them, these warrior women are still honored for the color that they bring into the world," Thióðolf continued, "They are also revered for being sacred, since they are always Óðinn's maidens, who marked them at birth to become women of spear and shield and sword.

They are chosen women. I have seen whole groups of such shield maidens, riding together like warriors, and found them a splendid sight indeed. They are in truth priestesses of the Masked One, and every bit as ferocious as the god who rules them."

I was now immensely curious. I had never imagined such things, and loved to hear about all the exciting people that lived out there in the great world.

"It is the same with some men," Thióðolf explained, "There are men who have the souls of women, or who cannot ever aspire to the battle arts, because their soul song is not made for it.

"Most warriors avoid them, unless they take a liking to playing pleasure games with womanly men. There are quite a few warriors who like that kind of games, you would be surprised how many, seeing as women are so beautiful. But taste is different in everyone. Such womanish men are often more than happy to oblige, and yield to warriors like women do. These men are often soft, and must be detected early in life lest they suffer terribly. You know well how little we respect softness in men. We have been brought up to kick and beat and shout all weakness out of boys, to make them warriors the hard way. After such a fostering, it is in the blood, and all a man wants to do when he sees weakness in a boy or in another man is to begin honing him. You know how we hone men, Thordís."

I nodded, knowing well how boys were honed now, and thanked my lord that I was not male.

"But these ones, they cannot help it," Thióðolf continued, "They are like maidens even from childhood, they cannot be honed, and if you try and hone them by treating them roughly, they break apart and become empty, like most girls would."

"Like I would," I said, thinking of how my body had succumbed to Hialti's strength and harsh words as if on its own accord, and shuddered involuntarily.

"Yes, Thordís, they are like you that way, these maidenly boys. You are surprisingly skillful in the battle arts, actually, yet there is something about you that is clear for all to see. Your soul song is maidenly, and you just cannot be honed the way a boy is honed, because it would break your spirit. Even if you are skilled, it is easy for grown warriors to see that you are vulnerable and that you can only learn the arts through gentleness. And these arts are simply not that gentle, what you well learned when Hialti the Coward was acting rough with you. It is the same with these maidenly boys. They are just not made for the warrior's path. Oh, it is common enough to start with. We start training boys when they are but three years old, and obviously it does take some time to harden them up, so we start carefully. When you see a boy react in the manner of a maiden many times, every time, you begin to realize that his soul song is different, and that you simply cannot hone him like you can most boys. They were sent into the world like they are by the norns, and so they must be seen as colors that make the great tapestry more interesting."

"What do you do with them, then?" I asked, feeling sorry for such boys.

"Usually, parents who detect such a soul song in a son will realize that there is little use in honing him, just as there is little use in letting him stay around men who will despise him for not going through the ordeals. In that way it is the same for all boys, they are *all* despised until they have proven themselves, only these maidenly boys must prove themselves in different manners lest they be despised forever as wimps, seeing as they cannot pass the ordeals. Then action must be taken to ensure the well-being of that boy."

"What sort of action?" I asked.

"I know of one boy who was so good at carving things in wood even from an early age, but who cowered in terror during battle practice. His father took him to a grove where he made a prayer, and there he cut off a half of the boy's left foot, and also gave him a proper cut in the face so as to let the world know that the boy had been scarred like a man. Then the boy had become a mutilated one, the one that nobody would tease, and it was decided that he should go and learn the art of wood-carving over in Eire instead.

164

He became a very famous craftsman and translator besides, and nobody ever despised him for not being able to wield a blade that convincingly."

"Oh," I said, "is that how it is done, then?"

"It depends on the boy," Thióðolf said, "In the case I just told you about, the boy had shown talent for woodcarving. But there are those boys who show other signs. A boy who is *very* maidenly, for example, may be made for sorcery. His parents may send the boy to be fostered among witches or sorcerers, because even as we despise unmanliness in warriors, we think that sorcerers are sacred, made not for battle but for sorcery. So they are."

"Are all sorcerers maidenly men, then?"

"No. Not at all. Hallgrim Hidden Spear is a great Seið-man, Thordís, and there is nothing maidenly about him at all. There are many kinds of sorcerers, but many of the most powerful ones are womanly men. I have seen such sorcerers, Thordís, and they carry a power beyond the ken of most. They are *very* sacred, for they create great colors in the world."

"Why are they so sacred?" I asked.

"When men become like women, and women become like men, the norns offer us a mirror in which to see the song of life from a new angle, and that, Thordís, is a very sacred thing. To use that sort of Mirror-Seið is an art that is sometimes mastered even by womanly women and manly men who are not maidenly at all, just because they are sacred."

"What sort of people are they, then?"

Thióðolf looked thoughtful, as if he was pondering whether to tell me at all.

"In the case of women, there are those who wield the Wand. A Wand-Witch knows how to use manly power even if she is a maidenly woman. And there are those men who create our own wombs by witchcraft, so that we can be closer to our souls and know the mind of the norns as well as women do. Such men are called Seið-Wombs. And they are certainly not all maidenly men. Some are great warriors."

"You said *our* own wombs," I remarked, peering curiously at him.

"Indeed," he replied absent-minded, and then proceeded, pretending that he had not picked up my subtle question. "Most colorful people become something special, if they can. There are witches and priestesses and shield maidens, and just by their offices they stand out as different from other women, yet most of them entered these offices because they were colorful in the first place. We adore these women, exactly because they are different, and because they are sacred, even as we love the women who are more ordinary also. It is the same with men. Most free men are warriors, they share the same common chants and the same common beats in their soul songs, and so even most warriors are like white threads for the most part. But we honor as colorful those warriors who have some very special skills or traits that are unusual and admirable, like those who can invoke the battle rage on their own accord, whenever they wish for it."

"My father could do that," I mused, "he was a berserker."

"I am not surprised if he was, seeing as even you possess that talent, child. Arnulf is like that also, and that is why he too is colorful, and likes to have colorful people around him. There are several warriors in our court who are berserkers, six altogether."

"Who are they, then?"

"Apart from Arnulf Heri we have Hallgrim, Njál, Runarr, Sígtrygg, and Agnarr. Each berserker leads one of the Six, apart from Runarr, who must stay with Njál, because the two of them are blood brothers and their rage infuriates each other. The fifth group has no leading berserker, but will be led by Arnulf during battle."

"What about you, Thióðolf? Do you know the rage?"

"I am like that also, even if I do not think of myself as a berserker. My rage derives from... something else. But I can enter the rage when I wish it, and I know how to control it. That was what drew us together, Arnulf and I. We met only when we had to fight side by side and discovered that we were both going berserk. And then there was the fact that I am a skald, and he wanted one. He is a great story-traveler himself. People know their own kind, and those with colorful soul songs will find each other, even as they appear very different from one another. It is like when the colorful threads meet and form into an image in the tapestry."

"Who stands out in *disturbing* ways?" I asked, since Thióðolf had been talking about people who stood out in nice ways only.

"The Kindly Ladies, for one," he said and sighed, "They are very sacred, make great color to the tapestry, and yet they are deeply disturbing." He shuddered.

"Who are they? Are they *very* kind? Why is that disturbing?" I recognized the shudder that had taken all the men when they first mentioned the ladies, and how they had spoken of Death and Hel and terrible, head-ripping claws. And yet, the ladies were said to be *kindly*.

"Well, you know the sacred song about Thor and the giant called Outer World Loki?"

"Of course, you performed it the other day. We all laughed!" I exclaimed, remembering how the entire household, slaves and free, had toppled over with laughter when Thióðolf entertained us with the great song. Even Zivah had smiled, despite herself.

"What did we say about Outer World Loki?"

"You said he was *not that tiny*!" I laughed, because the notion was so witty. Thióðolf smiled and caressed my hair a little, "Exactly. And what did I mean by that?"

"You meant that he was extremely, utterly, gigantically large! Larger than anything or anyone there ever was! Larger than the whole world!" I exclaimed eagerly, showing with my arms outstretched just how big Outer World Loki must be.

"There we go. There are ways of describing certain things by in many ways saying the opposite thing, or by exaggeration or the opposite of that. We do this when we speak of very disturbing matters, because it is a way of not drawing the fear that such things create into our souls or into our houses. It is also a way of placating them. The Kindly Ladies must be placated, Thordís, and a soul can be seized by endless terror if we begin to describe them in more direct terms."

"Are you saying that the ladies are not kindly at all?" I asked, frowning.

"We could say that, Thordís. They are *not that kindly*."

"Just as Outer World Loki is *not that tiny*?"

"Exactly," Thióðolf confirmed.

"But the ladies honored our house and gave me the head of Hialti the Coward," I objected, thinking it a kindly act indeed, "And so they were kindly to *me*!" I finished, triumphantly.

"Yes, but they were not very kindly to Hialti the Coward," Thióðolf pointed out.

"Arnulf's men were not going to be very kindly to him either," I argued, "And yet you don't call *them* kindly."

Thióðolf smiled, and then shuddered again. He had shuddered several times as we spoke. Now he shook his head slowly, "Believe me, Thordís, Arnulf's men would never, ever be able to aspire to the degree of kindliness that the ladies showed to Hialti. The gentle ladies are very… lustful. They take a liking to men who rape children."

"They *like* child-rapists?"

"They like them in the same fashion as they are … *kindly* to them."

"Oh," I said.

It began to dawn on me how Kindly Ladies liked their victims. I had no idea what it meant, for a man to be played with, ridden, and clasped by the lustful brides of the burial mounds, but I had thoroughly understood the part where the Mare ripped off his head with her claws, having held the result in my own hands. I had a feeling that the other ways of describing the things that the ladies had done to Hialti were not exactly about Freyia's pleasures, even if it sounded like it was. Perhaps it was something similar, I mused, but not the same, like a mirror image.

Maybe, I thought hopefully, just maybe, he had been fucked. The thought alone made me smile from ear to ear. I closed my mouth when I noticed that Thióðolf was regarding me with one eyebrow raised.

"Listen, Fierce Eyes, the very Kindly Ladies are women who stand out in ferocious ways," Thióðolf said, "They are like mirrors to men, they do everything the Contrary way. It is sacred. They bring great color to our world, and great wisdom, and that is why we revere them, even as we fear them. They show men what they are, by creating a mirror and a sacred spectacle of all the fears a man may harbor in his heart. And this is why these women are not like other women. They are priestesses of human sacrifice, and they are Death walking in women's bodies. They can do exactly what they like, and transgress all the rules there are. In fact, they are expected to break all the rules there are. They are Death. They lower their eyes to no one. Everybody lower their eyes to them. They can give a man to the red Eagle. They can partake in the Parliaments. They can interfere in the matters of men and the matters of warriors, and not one of us would ever dare refuse them. They make grown men shit their pants, Thordís, they really do."

He paused and mused for a while, making a decision that was not to my liking, "I talk to you of most things, Wolfling, but you are simply too young for these things. You cannot grasp these matters. You will only be frightened, and fear is just not going to settle in your heart as long as I am protecting you. You must wait, and later everything will be revealed to you."

I wanted to argue, tell him that even if I was little I had seen enough of terror and bloodshed without ever succumbing to it. I had seen my parents die, seen the village of my childhood crushed. I had known the battle rage seize me, and I knew what it was like to want to rip out the throat and drink the blood, gorge down the flesh of a boy still living.

I had held a man's severed head up and praised it for a precious gift. I had only known real fear for a moment in my life when I learned that I too could be raped. And yet I was not plagued by terror, and fear had never settled within my soul-stone. How much more scary could it be, to let me hear about the Kindly Ones? I did not say it, but I had a feeling that these priestesses of human sacrifice were somewhat like me.

The ladies know their own kind, Arnulf had said. And I knew them for mine. The colored threads were meeting to make a sacred image.

ᚠIKING ᛋCOUTS

I wanted to ask a thousand more questions about the Very Gentle Ladies, but Thióðolf refused to speak more about them. He said I would have to wait, and not think of them or talk about them, lest I draw them to our house. When I began to sulk insolently, he stared directly at me, which was a terrible punishment for me when he did it, and I bowed my head apologetically and felt sad. But then he just patted my back and told me to find something else to ask about for the time being.

"Thióðolf," I said, "You are not a Rus. Why are you here in Aldeigjuborg?"

"It is a very long story, Thordís, that I may tell you one day. There is more than one reason too. Suffice it to say that I came here looking for something, and then I had to bind myself to Arnulf in order to be able to stay here at all. I was fortunate to know anybody here. You see, I met Arnulf a long time before I came here."

"How did you meet him?"

"He saved my life, the first time I met him. I actually met him down in Big Tunic Land, in Baghdad, some seven years ago. I was new there, and I had not quite grasped all the rules. Unknowingly, I offended some men. Those Big Tunic Men are different from us in many ways, but also very like us. They can be quite ferocious, and they are all about honor, like we are, and not afraid to fight to restore it. They are just like us in many ways; they will rather die or kill than be dishonored. But their ideas of honor are different from ours, especially regarding women."

"How are their ideas of honor different?"

"Well, the most important difference, what I was to find out the hard way, was that they think that their women are dishonored if they dally with men who are not their House-Bonds. I did not understand just how seriously they take that kind of thing. I would of course not take a woman who was married to another man. That is dishonorable, and I understand that. How else is a man to know who his children are, unless his wife keeps to him only? But I could see no reason not to dally with women yet unmarried, or divorced, or widowed. Oddly enough, the Big Tunic Men think a woman is spoiled if she has relations with men before she is married, even after she has been married. I don't know why. Whoever cares how many men a woman has, as long as she is free to choose her lovers, belonging to no man?"

I shook my head affirmatively. I didn't care the least bit. It seemed to me that adults were playing those games everywhere at all times. It was almost as common as eating food, and obviously even more rewarding than eating, if I had interpreted their responses right.

"These Big Tunic Men think differently," Thióðolf explained, "But they protect their women against dishonor just as we would do, only they think that kisses and pleasure games are as dishonorable as rape. If a man makes even the most innocent of advances at a Síf of theirs, they are likely to kill him, and for some incomprehensible reason, they would even kill her, if she went along with it, sometimes even if she was taken against her will. I was rather young, then, and new to the place, and I did not quite understand their rules. And so I got myself in trouble. Fortunately the woman in question was not harmed, since she had done nothing at all."

"Did you play Freyia's games with her?"

"No! Wish that I had, seeing as I got into so much trouble for nothing! I only smiled at her and said hello, and looked into her beautiful eyes, and she immediately withdrew and called for her kinsmen. That was the only way she could save herself after my inappropriate advance, but I did not know it then. Arnulf explained it to me later, when I complained about it.

I had done far more with others already, but this was the first time someone saw me, and I was not even aware of having transgressed before she called out. She had quite a large clan, as it turned out. They were too many for me to take on, and they had the law on their side. I apologized profoundly and tried to make them understand that I was a foreigner and had not understood their customs, and they let me walk away for the time being. But some of her kinsmen were not finished with me, and during the squabble they had seen my Freyia pendant. Then they knew that I was a Heathen, and that it would be permitted to kill me at sight."

"Is that true? Is it lawful among them to kill a Heathen at sight?"

"Yes, that is true. It is true for all those folks who think of themselves as the people of the Book and who think that there is only one god in the whole world and that is their own Full Troth. When I was there I had to pretend I was a Christian, but then they saw my goddess pendant and knew what I really was.

"In any case, these men were raging even more when they started to think that a filthy Heathen had tried to approach one of their Sífs, and they quickly found out where I was staying since I was a Norseman and easily identifiable. Not much later, I had to run through the streets of Baghdad during night with a whole pack of angry men on my heels.

"Suddenly I bumped into a very large Norseman who immediately grasped my situation. Our eyes met and he grinned at me and said, 'Why, a fellow Norseman, are you? Took a peek at one of their ladies, did you? Got yourself in trouble, have you? Need some assistance, do you?'

I said, 'I am, I did, I have, and I do!' Arnulf laughed at that very precise reply of mine and he said, 'Names, we may exchange later. I can see that you are a sort of honorable fellow despite your current predicament. I am, on the other hand, probably the nastiest man you ever met, but there we are,' and then he cut down the first man who attacked us. Arnulf, who didn't even know me then, saved me that night.

"His warrior skills are considerable, Thordís. He killed some of them, and we both fended off the rest, and then he brought me to his place and housed me, hiding me, and eventually helped me get out of that place in one piece. When I came here among the Rus last spring, I managed to get myself into trouble again! Even on my first day here! It is very different here, compared to home, Thordís, and I failed to observe some rules again. That is why I was so concerned with teaching you and Zivah the rules from the moment we met. You must not break the rules here. Breaking the rules can kill you swifter than you even get to know that you are breaking them."

"Did you do something with some women?" I asked. I was a bit confused about Thióðolf, because sometimes when he talked it sounded like he had been with lots of women.

At Arnulf's court I never saw him even as much as look at any of the slave girls, although most of the girls kept casting glances at him and obviously liked him a lot.

"No, it was not about women," he smiled. "The Rus are not very particular about those things, unlike the Big Tunic Men. Just, suffice it to say that a man felt offended and challenged me. We fought, and I killed him. I am rather battle-skilled myself, but the problem was that the man had friends, who now set upon me, and then, Arnulf showed up and saved my skin again! It was the second time he saved my life, and just as before, he took me to his house."

"You said to Hialti the Coward that you didn't need another man to protect you," I said reproachfully. In my mind, Thióðolf was invincible, or ought to be.

Thióðolf the Invincible smiled and kissed my cheek.

"That was an honest boast, Thordís. Hialti the Coward introduced a word duel, and I responded to it. I won the duel with eloquence. Everybody needs others to stand up for them, sweet one. We cannot live independently of each other. No one can. And just like you owe loyalty and obedience to the men who protect you, so we owe each other when we stand up for one another. A notion what leads me on to the next part of this sacred song; When Arnulf welcomed me as an honored guest in his household, then, for the sake of gratitude, I swore my allegiance to him and made an oath to serve him for three years, as his skald and as his warrior. That is why I am bound to him. Although I have asked permission not to partake in any more raids, and he has granted it. I could not do that again, not ever."

"Why not?"

"I do not even know where to begin, Thordís. It broke my heart to see what the Rus, what we did to your people. It is the most dishonorable thing I have ever been a part of, even as I just stood by and watched."

"I thought you did not partake," I said, remembering how he had been unscathed when I first saw him.

"I do not mean to pretend that I was innocent, Thordís, but I had spoken against the attack, to tell you the truth, and yes, I did not actually partake. I even made sure some old people and children escaped."

"You did?"

"It was hardly sufficient. Thordís, I told the men that it was a holy place, a place as yet untouched by war. I told them that it would be a better choice to attack villages where people already have slaves, or already live more or less like slaves, a place not quite so innocent. Then they said that if they were to heed that sort of innocence they might as well give up the entire river land and then where would they get their slaves from now that they have already begun exhausting the Slavic and Finnish lands?"

He looked so sad, all of a sudden, and I left him alone while I pondered his words for a while. I decided to turn from all this saddening talk of my mother's village.

"Thióðolf," I said finally, "Then you are not a Viking, are you?"

"No, Thordís, I am not a Viking. I am just a warrior. I was taught to protect women from Vikings, as are all the men of my tribe. We are Háleygir, not Rus. The Hálóga men are great warriors, greater warriors than the Rus, I think, although I would appreciate it if you did not tell anyone I said that, seeing as we are surrounded by Rus. But my people have never been and still are not Vikings, my Síf. Not yet, anyway."

"Do you think you will become Vikings?"

"I do not know," he said thoughtfully, "There are things happening in the world at large that may change a lot of things, my Síf. To us, a Viking is nothing but a thief and a pirate. And yet, in order to encounter the Vikings that have assaulted our shores over the last centuries we have become great warriors of the ocean steeds. And there has been talk now, for a long time, as to whether we might need our fleets in order to hold back forces that threaten us from the south and that are blocking our ancient trade routes, rendering us in poverty."

"Poverty?"

"North Path Island is not the most fruitful place on this great Earth, Thordís. We dress in fur and leather and eat mostly fish and meat and forest plants, even though we keep herds of cows and sheep also. We have some terrible winters when all we get to eat is preserved foods. For countless ages we have been able to buy other sorts of food and textiles and metals, and other pretty and useful things from other parts of the world, and we have grown used to those things. We have become traders, it is how we live and how we have lived since time immemorial. But now the Christian folks to the south of us are blocking our trade routes and refuse to trade with us, seeing as we are Heathens, and they do not want to trade with Heathens. There is a Christian king down there in Frankland who is called Karl Magni, and he has been combating Heathens south of Denmark for a long time and has proven successful, and he keeps pressing northwards. The Danes are getting rather nervous, and if the Danes fall, then there is not so much to stop them from moving even further north, into North Path Island herself. And we have reason to suspect that the Franks are conspiring with the Christians of England in order to move against us."

"You are the greatest warriors on Earth, you said," I intervened.

"Yes, but they have armies and methods that make it very difficult for us to stop them by way of direct combat, even if they are lesser warriors than we are. In fact, it is almost because they are lesser warriors than we are. They use strategy more than they use their courage, and they fight dirty as if they were women. But we are starting to think that we must approach this problem differently. There is talk that we may actually need to frighten them off a little by way of Viking methods. A little more than two years ago we did a little scouting trip to the shores of England just to see if it could be done, and it can. You see, even if these folks have great armies, their common people do not fight at all. Free men live like slaves in those lands. Not a warrior among them."

"Did you go on that scouting trip?" I asked.

"Yes. Yes, I had to. I was serving on the King's fleet and I was ordered to take one ship with crew and join another ship from Denmark and one from Hordaland. Three tribes were represented, our kings wanting to join forces and see what could come out of it. I was the captain of the Hálóga ship. It was a place called Dorset, I think, and it was the oddest sort of experience. When we had made our beach-landing and stayed there for a few days, uhm, well, there was no resistance from the local farmers at all. And the girls seemed to like us there, when we had shown that we would not hurt them. We felt quite popular, actually, but the farmers had sent for them people who apparently passed for their warriors..." He frowned a little.

"There had been a party on the night before that and there was this local girl that I, well, the same was the case with the Danish captain, and the only chief awake and able to get remotely ready and dressed to meet a representative of the leaders of that place was the Horde captain, who was a young prince, and very proud of his ancestral sword. He thought it would be a good thing to show off his famed sword to the warlord of the Anglo-Saxons, so that the man would understand that he was speaking to a person of high standing even if he was still a bit ungroomed, after the party, to be receiving such. The Anglo-Saxon leader went visibly frightened and barked that all us men had to leave over our weapons to the authorities.

"The Horde prince asked the Anglo-Saxon if he thought we were slaves with no right to bear arms, and when that man continued to insist that the prince himself leave over his weapons along with all the rest of us, the Horde cut him down. Then, of course, the fighting began. If one can call it that. Honestly, cutting them down was as easy as chopping wood, really. And when their puny warriors had been pacified, we could just walk into the towns and steal whatever we wanted right in front of these people and all they did was cower and squeal like slaves. It was sad to see, really, for them Anglos and Saxons what live there used to be like us before, but that Full Troth of theirs has made them awfully weak, and they have developed some very befuddling customs."

"What sort of customs?" I asked.

"Why, they were kneeling and begging for mercy instead of trying to fight, grown men kneeling as if they were volunteering to be sacrificed. That was somewhat confusing to our men. I have traveled in Big Tunic Land and knew that folks there kneel to their gods and to their superiors all the time, but we thought that the Anglos would know better, seeing as they are of common stock with us. You know that we Norsemen only ever kneel to Death. A free woman can sometimes kneel to apologize profoundly or to plead a very unlikely cause before a great lord. But if a free man kneels it is usually because he is signaling his readiness to die, and the one he kneels to, why, he has been given the sacred charge, you see. The Danes, who had been traveling a bit more, had to explain to us Háleygir and Hordes from North Way that the kneeling was not a way of voluntary sacrifice but rather a way of begging for mercy, or praying."

Thióðolf sighed regretfully,

"Only by then, some of my men had already accepted what they thought of as a holy charge and had given those men to Thor by way of axe-blow. We were a little sad to find out that we had been wrong. There is no honor in cutting down defenseless folks. But it was done with the best of intentions."

"Oh," I said, and thought about the men of my mother's tribe who had been sacrificed to Óðinn as a way of honoring their courage, although they probably did not understand that they were hanged and stabbed as a way of being honored.

"Did they understand that, then, them Christians?" I asked.

"I do not think so. I felt bad about it later, but they were being very confusing to us. It was as if they went crazy when we appeared. I only made a little grimace at one very annoying, fuzzy little fellow who kept jabbering at me, and he fainted! Then there was the kneeling, and when the Danes who knew better had managed to stop the sacrifices, their priests kept offering us their cross-symbols, which we thought was a way of saying thanks, so we accepted their gifts. But when we accepted their gifts they started to howl, and they kept calling us Dee-ah-boh-lus, which is a name for their gods below, we had heard. They were rather puny and wore really boring clothes and hairstyles, while we are big and stylish and brave, so many of my men assumed they thought we were a sort of gods from Hel and that they were making offerings to us, what made us feel very proud. The cross-symbol is apparently a very fine offering. Some of the crosses had precious stones and metals in them too. I gave one to my sister and she keeps it on her wall, so beautiful it is."

"I thought they only had the one god above," I said.

"I have never really understood that part myself," Thióðolf said and scratched his head, frowning. "In any case, the Danes have lived close to these folks for a long time, and when we had a celebration later and we bragged about their offerings and how they had called us Dee-ah-boh-lus, we were told that we may have misinterpreted some of their rituals. As it turned out, the crosses they had kept waving and holding up to us had not been meant as offerings but as a way of warding us off.

"Apparently, the Dee-ah-boh-lus are a sort of dangerous gods from Hel that suck the souls out of Christian folks, and they thought we were that sort of gods. It was a bit disturbing, really, but after some moments of general remorse we could not but cheer up again. How could we fail to see the humor in how these funny people had thought we were something more than human?

"It amused my father to no end when he heard of it. It was a great story, and we made great costume dances and songs about it later, what had our Sífs roll around on the floor screaming with laughter."

We both laughed.

"So you were a Viking, then, after all?" I asked when we had stopped laughing.

"I suppose I was, now that you are saying it," he frowned, as if that notion had not occurred to him before, "but I did not kill anyone and we did not act anywhere near what the Rus are doing here. We are not planning to become slavers. We are just thinking of how to make a statement and how to reclaim our trade routes. We need better ships, and the Rus have the best ships in the world, adapted to both river and ocean voyages. This is partly one of the reasons I am here, but we shall not speak of that now. I do not know how it will all turn out. Look now, Thordís, it is getting dark. We may talk more of these issues another time. Shall we to our horses?"

His way of asking was of the sort that meant I had to just agree, although more questions had risen from our talk than answer so far. But I relaxed, knowing that this was how it should be. Knowledge unfolds in her own time, and she usually does so little by little.

A Barbarian in Baghdad

Preparations for the Winter Solstice celebrations had begun, and Arnulf's court was to hold a great banquet for both warriors and household. Arnulf asked me if I wished to play the appropriate role of the Síf of the house, and as soon as I agreed to that I was given over to the care of Aziza and the other women for the time being. They taught me all the things that needed to be made and done before Yule and, most importantly, how to brew the mead.

They told me that the brewing of mead was not a slave's work at all. Brewing was supposed to be done by the House-Freyia and the Sífs of the house. There was only one Síf in the whole court and that was me, and I had to learn how to do it. The fact that there had been no free woman in Arnulf's court for so many years meant that nobody had performed the sacred ritual in honor of the rebirth of the holy daughter Sun either, because slaves could not perform that ritual. And so I was set in motion, to be the priestess of the Solstice and the brewer and server of mead. Obviously, the slaves were the ones to teach me most of it.

Zivah had been so nice to me ever since that time with Hialti, and so had the other women. It seemed like they had forgiven me for being better treated by the men. I think they had just realized that we were all ruled by the same lords no matter what titles we had, and now I was one of them almost as much as I was one of the Norsemen. But I feared for our sisterhood when the fabric for my Solstice dress was brought out on the table of the Hold that first day of preparations. It was the most beautiful fabric I had ever seen, so beautiful I almost gasped before I remembered that I was not supposed to gasp, ever, and heard my slave sister do my gasping for me. The fabric was so soft to the touch, so shiny and precious, and the color was a lovely sky blue, the same color as my eyes when they were not in my wolf spirit. It had come all the way from Persia via Baghdad and Khazaria.

"This fabric is called silk," Aziza said. Zivah and I exchanged glances.

"Is that the fabric that is made by countless little sprites what live in the east?" I asked.

"Yes," Aziza smiled, "yes, Maiden, but I do think the sprites you speak of are in fact little animals, spinning threads like spiders do. But it is true that they make the silk threads and that they live far to the east of here." I gulped and looked at Zivah, who had gotten a vulnerable look about her face. I went over and took her hand.

"Zivah," I whispered, in our mother's language, "I can ask for a more ordinary dress. I do not need to wear silk."

"Thordís," she whispered back, "I shall not say this did not touch me in some way, but I do not grudge you the silk dress. I do not, really. It brought back memories. That is all. I have changed. I am not the same Zivah you knew back then." And then she switched over to the Norse, for she no longer liked to speak that language, the one she had spoken when she was still free.

"Sister, there was a time when nothing would have pleased me more than the wearing of a silk dress, and there would surely have been a time when I would have grudged you wearing it instead of me. But I no longer want to stand out and look beautiful. I have found that looking beautiful only makes of you a more spectacular target for men's violence."

"Zivah, you were the most beautiful of all the women on the Viking ships, and yet you were the only one who was not violated," I objected.

"That was all thanks to you, my sister," Zivah said and raised her voice, making sure that the men who were nearby and who stood with their backs turned to us could hear her, "Even if I was not violated, I suffered the devouring leers of men for so long they became like sharp, piercing arrows penetrating my soul and breaking apart my heart. I do not think I could ever again appreciate the attentions of men. I would rather not be so visible."

"Oh," I said and felt at loss for more words. It was true what Thióðolf had said, that my sister was a very courageous woman who would rebel in any way she could get away with, being a slave. It would seem she had caught up on the fact that she could speak quite freely as long as she observed the courtesies, and that even her slave verdicts on their conduct were holy to my kinsmen. I tried not to smile, realizing that she was starting to feel a lot safer, speaking harsh truths out loud like that. Zivah's face suddenly softened, and she held up the silk against my face.

"It is different for you, Thordís," she said, "You can afford to look beautiful. I love you. I would love to make your dress for you. Aziza, may I?"

"If the maiden agrees," Aziza said. Of course I agreed. I would have agreed even if I did not already know how good my sister was at making lovely things. And Zivah made me the most beautiful dress I had ever worn in my young life.

While the dress was being made by Zivah, Aziza and the other women taught me what sort of foods were to be made and most importantly how to brew the mead. My sister and I exchanged glances when the honey was brought out and we recognized it as honey from our own village. Zivah shook her head when I opened my mouth to comment on it. I decided to ask something else instead, as soon as the mixtures had been blended and all we really did was stir anyway.

"Aziza, how come you came here all the way from Baghdad and became Arnulf's first concubine?" I asked.

"That is a very long story, Maiden," Aziza replied, "Are you sure you would want to hear it all?"

"I love to listen to people's stories." The other women brightened up, ready to hear the story, even if most of them already knew it.

"Well, I shall shorten it down somewhat anyhow. I was born a slave, because my mother was abducted from her homeland and made slave when she was very young. She came from a country far to the east, from a river valley that she called Indus. That is why I have this dark hue to my skin and this blackness of hair - I inherited these colors from her. It was common to be thus colored in her homeland."

"Did she have green eyes also?"

"No, she had almost black eyes. But when she was abducted and taken as a slave, many men took her on the way, and one of them must have had such eyes, since I was born with them just after she came to Baghdad. Even though she was pregnant, she was very beautiful, and she was bought by a man who ran a pleasure house."

"What is that?"

"That is a place where Freyia's games are played. Men come and pay for having pleasure with slave women. It was not the worst kind of place though, it was very sophisticated. We were something they called courtesans, whereas in other places we would have been called whores."

"What are whores, then, and courtesans?" I asked curiously, having never heard of them, and recognizing that these were foreign words. Suri and several of the other women began to laugh. "We are whores and courtesans, Maiden," Suri said, "after a fashion anyway."

"Oh," I said, but the dark-skinned Sheath called Saxa shook her head. "It is not the same at all," she said, "A whore is a slave who is rented out for pleasure games to various clients so that her master can earn a lot of money. That makes a world of difference and you know it, Suri."

"Oh well, I know it. I know it as well as you do, Saxa," Suri said, "but you also know that many folks would not ever see the difference."

"Many folks are big fools," Saxa said, and turned to me. "Most of the women here at court are used by many men, but these men are not clients and they have not rented us. They are the same men, day after day and year after year, and they have become our companions as much as they are our lords. To be a whore or a courtesan, Maiden, that is an entirely different thing. Most of us here used to be proper whores, and I think we can all testify that nobody ever wants to be rented out to various men. It strains a woman's soul, to be used by so many men who have no interest in her otherwise, and to have to serve a never ending line of new men and pretend to like it."

"They have to pretend to like it?" I asked.

"Yes, because when a client is willing to pay up he does not want to think that he is raping the girl, does he? But she is a slave, and so she has no say in the matter. It is rape, of course, but the clients like to think that they are making a fair deal, and the whore must pretend that she is willing lest she be flogged or killed by her master. For the most part, the girls go along with it because it feels better to laugh and smile than to admit how much they really suffer."

"I never pretended to like it," Suri said darkly, "but it did not help me. They just gave me to them clients what enjoyed that sort of thing."

Zivah and I shuddered and Aziza added thoughtfully, "I think that whoring is one of the oldest forms of slavery in the world." She paused a little and frowned before she resumed her story, "and a courtesan is really just the same thing, only she is more fashionable and expensive. So you see, being courtesans, we were somewhat privileged and lived in very splendid surroundings. My mother, and later myself, we learned a lot of arts, such as singing and dancing and the giving of massages, bathing, telling stories, the customers were rich men who paid a lot to be entertained for a whole evening by courtesans."

"Were you more like the Sheaths of the Hall then?"

"Not at all. The Sheaths of the Hall are very fortunate compared to the courtesans of a pleasure house even if they do not have the same sophistication."

"But you said you sang and danced and all that."

"Yes, but every evening we had to serve a new man. The Sheaths of the Hall have six men each, and they have only them, returning to them regularly, and they are as much companions to them as they are courtesans. It is nothing like being a whore, or a courtesan. They actually have a steady relationship. Like a marriage with several men. Is that not so, Miri?" The Khazar Sheath had just entered the Hold in order to get some more vessels of beer for the Hall and had stopped to listen to our conversation while she poured herself a small cup.

"It is so, Aziza," Miri agreed, "Maiden, we Sheaths live with the warriors, eat and drink with them, celebrate with them, and lay with them. We are slaves, yes, but we are very familiar with our men and they with us. Maybe you cannot see it so well from the outside, but inside the Hall we relax a lot on all those courtesies. It is not like in a pleasure house at all. It is more as if we have six House-Bonds each. Few women can claim themselves as fortunate," Miri grinned. After Hialti died and left her with only five House-Bonds, Hallgrim Hidden Spear included, she had transformed into a very happy woman. She laughed and smiled all the time now, and did not drink quite as much as before, although she had a good eye to all strong beverages.

"I only have one House-Bond, and I have to share him!" Aziza laughed, mock-complaining.

"By all the gods, my Elja," Laimi giggled, "Arnulf Heri is more than enough for both of us!" All the women began to laugh.

"Is that because of his very large Freystone?" I asked curiously. Having eavesdropped on slave women on many occasions, I had noticed that they sometimes talked about the size and worth of men's Freystones, and it appeared that a generous size was rather appreciated, why I did not quite know. Aziza laughed again, "Not only the largeness of it. It is more because he has a lot of Frey's power in him, so he can be quite demanding.

"He is very generous towards us in all ways and he makes us very happy every time." Laimi nodded dreamily to what her Elja said.

"I know that," I said and grinned, "Sometimes it is hard to sleep when he makes you two very happy."

Laimi and Aziza rolled over laughing, to the merry accompaniment of the other girls, who began copying the pleasure sounds made by the concubines almost every night. When they calmed down, Aziza dried her laughing tears and suddenly looked all serious, "Arnulf Heri keeps us two well employed, but I will tell all of you that he is also the first and only man who ever made me happy."

"Did you not have many men then, when you lived in the pleasure house?" I asked.

"I had so many I lost count. But I was there to please them, and they did not care about me at all. They enjoyed all the entertainment, but when it came down to pleasure, it was always clear that they despised us for being soiled, dirty women, and they cared not for our well-being."

"Were you very dirty then?" I frowned. It was hard to imagine Aziza being dirty and soiled. She always smelled of rose water and was always so very cleanly. Aziza and the other women laughed again.

"We were very clean, Maiden, we bathed all the time," she said, "but the men of the Caliphate think that women like us are soiled anyway. They think we are soiled for having received the seed of many men."

"Is their seed not sacred then, down in Big Tunic Land?" I asked, frowning again. Just like the men, the women kept laughing at almost everything I said even when I was being dead serious, but I had grown accustomed to that and patiently waited for them to calm down enough to answer me.

"Well, they think they are polluted whenever their seed spurts so I don't think so, although it often appeared as if they thought it sacred nevertheless. Apparently it is only sacred for as long as it stays outside a whore's womb," Aziza said uncertainly. The women looked at each other.

"Honestly it is hard to say, Maiden, exactly why they think we are soiled, but it was the truth, and not only with the Tunic men, but also with all other visitors from many places. Our customers were of all the three faiths, Christians, Moslems and Jews. None of them had any regard for us even if they wanted our entertainment and our bodies for their pleasure. A lot of them did not like women such as us."

"So they wanted to play with someone they didn't even like? Maybe they are thick in the head," I mused, what made all the women shriek with laughter again, agreeing fully with me even though they found it funny for some reason or other. Finally, Aziza wiped her tears again and explained, "It is about their religion, Maiden, their Full Troth. They think the holy game of Freyia is a sin even when they pay to play it."

"What is a sin?"

"Something that they think their god disapproves of."

"Why do they do it then?"

"Well, some of them admitted that man is sinful by nature, but all of them were very certain that it was us dirty women what tempted them into sin and because of that they despised us and could feel a little less guilty for enslaving us, raping us and treating us like trash."

"Oh," I said, "Maybe they are not so thick in the head then, seeing as they know how to compose a story so convenient to themselves." Somehow my comment sent the women into another round of shrieking, sobbing laughs. I knew they did not think me silly, but witty, although I never knew when I was going to appear witty to them or not. All I knew was that I kept making grown folks very happy and that was fine with me.

"Indeed," Aziza said, still giggling a little, "And these men came and went in an endless stream. I was taken the first time when I was but thirteen, and since then I was a courtesan like my mother. She had held on to life for my sake all through my childhood, but when she saw me becoming like her, that is, when I began to work, she began to fade with grief. You see, to be used by so many different men, day after day after day, it takes your spirit away eventually. My mother came to a point where she realized that life would never become any better, and then one day she just went and jumped out from the roof of the house and into the street, and died." All the women suddenly went silent.

"I am sorry, Aziza, that must have been terrible for you," I whispered.

"It was very terrible. But I was only a slave and could not even grieve properly. I continued to work in that house for several years, and do you know, even though I lived in Baghdad all my young years, I never got to see the splendor of that city until Arnulf saved me and gave me quite a tour. Before that, until I was seventeen years old, I was never, ever allowed to go out of the house. We had a space on the roof and in a courtyard so we could get some air and listen to the sounds of the city, but that was all. You have no idea how many times, when I was a little child and had to do common chores, I tried to peak down on the streets and imagine what life was like out there. It was like being in prison."

"What is a prison?" I asked, carefully storing all the new and foreign words.

"It is a place where they lock you up and you can never come out of it. You are trapped."

"That sounds horrible."

"So, it was. Now, I will tell you how I met Arnulf. He had come to do business in Baghdad, and he spoke a little of our language. He had heard of such houses that we worked in, and he was very curious to try it out, especially after he had understood that Baghdad women were mostly unavailable. He had sold all his slaves so he felt a little lonely at nights. He told me later that he was getting a bit desperate about the whole thing, what with women being all covered up and it being impermissible to even speak with them."

"Covered up?" I asked.

"Oh yes, Maiden. Free women in Baghdad must either stay at home or else walk outdoors wearing a very big towel of sorts, almost like a tent. If she does, not she may be mistaken for a whore or slave."

"Why can she not just wear boy's cloths like I do?"

"That is forbidden. Maiden, free women here in Aldeigjuborg are not much better off, really. They cannot walk outdoors alone either, and have to wear necklaces that show who they are lest they be noosed and raped and enslaved. The Rus do not mind talking to women even if they do not know them, and they are a lot more relaxed about the body. I have seen free women undress and bathe with men and nobody cares. Norsemen do not think the body is neither sinful nor dirty."

"Not one bit," Miri remarked, causing a new round of giggles.

"Thióðolf told me that he had been doing quite a bit of courtship in Baghdad, and only gotten into trouble once," I said.

"Well, Thióðolf Heri is very clever when it comes to women," Aziza said and giggled again, and so did all the other girls for some incomprehensible reason, apart from Zivah, who just frowned.

"I am sure that he could always find his way around many locked doors," Aziza giggled again, "Arnulf is less subtle… and less discreet, I suppose. So, he decided to go and rent a slave for pleasure, and because he had some success in his business he decided to try out one of the best places, having heard of their splendor. He got himself all dressed up like a, like what we would call a civilized person, only you do not have a word for that."

"What is a civilized person then?" I asked.

"I don't know how to describe it to you in a way you can understand. It is just that the people of the Caliphate think that you Rus are very not civilized. They call you by another word you do not have in your language. They call you barbarians."

"What are barbarians then?"

"Barbarians, well, barbarians are people like the Rus. Beastly folks. Vikings. Norsemen. Wild maidens like yourself, and wild men."

"Do you think we are wild? Like wild animals?" I asked, astonished, and to my further surprise, all the women began to laugh again. I had a feeling they really thought we were beastly and wild barbarians, even those who did not come from Big Tunic Land. Even Zivah had begun to laugh now, in agreement, and she was surely not from a civilized land herself. But our tribesmen had been rather more gentle than the Rus.

I frowned.

"You Norsemen are like wild beast to us," Aziza declared amiably, surprisingly enough to the merry nodding of every head present.

"It is true," Suri grinned appreciatively, "Norsemen are rugged men, big men, tattooed and scarred and beastly men. Wolfish men and bear-like men. Your men are veritable beasts."

"Thank the gods for that," Miri volunteered, shrieking with laughter like the rest.

"Oh," I frowned, and understood vaguely what they meant, when I compared my kinsmen with other men that I had seen and known. It is perhaps true that we are a beastly lot, at least if seen from the outside. I tried to think of a man I knew now who was not beastly and could only think of one. Although none of the men-slaves were tattooed or scarred, Shumayl was the only man I knew that did not possess any of the characteristics the women had just described. He was not big or wild or scarred, not beastly, nor rugged, and he was not even wolfish or bear-like. He was rather the opposite.

"Is Shumayl civilized?" I asked.

"Shumayl is very civilized. The poor man was not even born a slave, but was for a long time a learned and respected physician, so you can imagine what he feels like, being a slave among barbarians."

"I am not sure I can imagine it, Aziza, I have never known any civilized people."

"You don't have to imagine it, Maiden," she smiled, and I sighed from relief.

"Aziza, Shumayl is very… small. Is it common for men to be so tiny in Big Tunic Land?"

"No, Maiden, Shumayl is particularly small, even for a Big Tunic Man. But your people are also particularly big, so the difference becomes very great in his case. But Shumayl has a great mind, Maiden, and he is very knowledgeable. You should talk to him, seeing as you are so curious about everything."

"I would love to talk to him," I said, "I have seen that he knows a great deal of Seið and runes and the healing arts. But I think he is afraid of me, Aziza. I don't know why, but I think he believes I am a troll from Hel. He called me djinn the first time he saw me. They say that is almost the same as a Hel Maiden, only that Big Tunic Men are afraid of them." Aziza laughed.

"Shumayl had great trouble accustoming himself to the Rus-men in the first place. But you were probably the first Rus-maiden he has ever been near. You are very different from Baghdad girls, Maiden, and I think that if I was not already accustomed to their ways, I might have thought you a djinn as well. Even Arnulf's men thought you were a Hel Maiden when you first came among them. My House-Bond told me so."

"It is true, but they were not afraid of me. Reverent, perhaps. But not frightened."

"Our people are afraid of everything that has to do with Hel, Maiden. The Big Tunic Men as well as the Christians believe that Hel is a terrible place full of very bad and dangerous creatures, and many believe it is a place of punishment for very bad people. They think it is, oh, you do not even have a proper word for that either. We call it evil. It means something very bad, and angry and cruel, and dangerous and poisonous, something that will devour you and destroy you or make you do terrible things to others."

"Oh," I said, utterly amazed at such a novel idea about Hel, "but that is terrible, Aziza, your people must be very much afraid of death, then, if you think that is what Hel is like." And again, incomprehensibly, the women rolled over laughing.

"There are many very brave men among us, Maiden, and women too," Aziza said, drying her laughing tears, "but that is because they also believe that there is another place one could go, if one has been good and obedient to god. Good and god-fearing people will go to Heaven when they die."

"Which of them?" I asked.

"Which of what, Maiden?" Aziza asked.

"Which heaven will they go to?"

"Uhm, god's heaven, Maiden," she said uncertainly.

"Which god's heaven?"

"The one god, Maiden. The Big Tunic Men believe in only one god. Our word for god is Allah, and there is only one Allah. They believe that Allah, that is God, is merciful and loving to those who believe in him, and that he will let the souls of just and god-fearing people enter into his heaven, which is called Paradise."

"Oh, I remember this. But why do they fear their god, then?" I asked.

"I could not say for certain, Maiden, this was not among the things I learned in the pleasure house. But I think they are afraid lest he punish them and send them to Hel, perhaps. I certainly was frightened. I was a whore, and if there was anything many of those men who used me never ceased to tell me, it was that their god hates whores, so I have to admit I was very happy to learn, when I came among the Rus, that Hel is a place for justice and Atonement before rebirth or a higher heaven, and that the judges are female. More importantly, I learned from the Hel Runes. Oh, I am not allowed to speak of them to you, Maiden, please excuse me. But they know the truth of many matters, and assured me that there will be no punishment for having been raped a thousand times. On the contrary, all blame is laid on the rapists and on the men who failed to protect us against them."

There was a silence then, while the women nodded thoughtfully to what the first concubine had said. There were some agreeing comments, confirmations of how much solace many of these slave girls had found when they discovered the Norsemen's concepts of death and afterlife justice.

I wanted to ask more about the Hel Runes, the Kindly Ones, but she was a slave who had already disobeyed an order to not talk about them and so I did not press the issue and thought instead of what she had said about that god what hated whores.

"Is that what you believed would happen when you die, Aziza? That you would be punished for being a courtesan, even if you were a slave and never even chose to be that?"

I was going to say whore, but sensed that Aziza preferred the other word for the same and tried to honor her.

"That was how I was taught by my masters and those who abused me, Maiden. My mother taught me differently, for she was not a believer in the Big Tunic Land faith. She was a Heathen like us, and believed in many goddesses and gods. She told me that the soul is reborn countless times and that each life is the fruit of the one lived before. It is quite similar to what you Norsemen believe, although you seem to think that you have many other choices also, and that the Judgment of the Norns and the Atonement you must pay will allow you to choose to be reborn or to live either where you wish or where you are welcomed, or invited. I have heard them say that the dead may be reborn within the womb of holy Earth, or within objects, inside a mountain where the ancestors dwell, or as an elf or a Follower, or as any other kind of sprite, or as a ghost, or in some god's or goddess's heaven, or even in the various underworld realms, or as a human being or any other living being."

Aziza thought a little and added, "I like the idea of that, Maiden. I would like to atone for any dishonor I may have caused on myself and others, knowing well that the ladies would never judge me for having been born a slave and used by men, and then I would like to choose my next life, and make it into something better than this has been. I would never be punished for the fate they spun for me, for all fate is a song, a tapestry, a story, and they must make all kinds of stories to make the great world song into poetry. I do not have to suffer in shame because my fate was what it was, or is what it is. All I need to do to get an easy judgment is to deal with my fate in a gracious manner, and acknowledge all that has transpired."

She paused to let us all consider her speech a while before she continued, "I have become quite the Norsewoman in regard to faith, Maiden, because of what I just told you, and even more because it is the only faith I have ever encountered what allows us women the same dignity and honor and justice as men. You see, the Big Tunic Men believe that a woman is only worth half of what a man is worth, and that she is worth nothing at all if she has been used by many men. And even though my mother did not believe in an eternity of punishment in Hel, she did believe that she and I were being punished for something in a previous life, and that being reborn as a woman was part of the punishment. I very much prefer your people's views on these things. They ring truer to my soul song."

We stood in silence for a little while, stirring the brew, while I thought of all the strange things that she had told me. The world had become very big, and so very varied. They must be having a laugh, I thought, the norns, creating so much diversity. It was the first time I really considered the possibility that nobody really knew anything, even though everybody took their own beliefs for granted.

What was true to one could be false to another, and nobody could ever know the truth. It was a good story they had made, the norns, this great world song of such extreme diversity, composed like an intricate riddle to be solved only by living it through. The poetry of it awed me. When I told the women of my thoughts, they looked astonished for a moment before they all laughed heartily and Miri the Sheath told me that I had spoken like a true Norsewoman. I frowned, uncertain about what she meant by that, seeing as I had thought myself nobly objective, but Miri just shook her head and laughed a little more before she left the Hold, carrying a lot of beer.

"Shall I resume my story, Maiden?" Aziza said finally, "About how I met Arnulf and became his concubine?"

"Yes, yes," I said eagerly, for Aziza's story was among the more interesting stories in this world. I had already made up a very strange looking long-house in my mind, to go with the pleasure house of her story. I wondered what it had smelled like in there. Aziza always smelled like a flower, and so I thought perhaps it was flowery.

"It was so that Arnulf dressed up like a civilized, let us just say that he got himself a very big and fashionable tunic. Then he came to the pleasure house and demanded to be served. We often had foreigners coming in, which is why I can compare men from many different places. Yet we had never had a Rus before. You have seen how we all think you Norse folks are beastly, even those of us who have not come from civilized places.

"This is because there is hardly a more barbarian people left on this Earth, Thordís, and they also look the part. The big tunic simply did not help, it only made him look even more terrible. All the women were terrified when they peeked through the curtains to have a look at the barbarian customer, and the owner was too frightened to even refuse him. Do you know what I did then?"

"No! Tell me!"

"Of course. I looked at him, just like the other girls, and I just knew that he would be different from all the rich and perfumed, fat old men who normally used us. So, while all the other girls cringed in terror when he came in to take a pick, I just went over to him and began to kneel down and kiss his feet before him like I was supposed to."

"Did you? The men hate that kind of thing," I shuddered, hating the very idea myself. I would have been so embarrassed if anyone knelt before me to kiss my feet.

"Not the men I was used to," Aziza said, "But Arnulf knew our customs well enough and didn't mind, but he did something utterly novel. Before I could even get down on my knees to greet him properly, he stopped me and made me stand up, so that he could look into my face. He actually met my eyes, and I saw something I had never seen in any man before. He looked as if he was curious about me, about who I was, and what I was like.

He looked into my eyes like that, and then he told the owner that he would take me, and I led him to the quarter where I was to entertain him. He was absolutely baffled by everything and seemed more interested in the interior than he was in me at first. I could not know that he had never been to such a place before, but it was clear that everything was very overwhelming for him. He spent a lot of time just looking around, touching and sniffing everything, even tasting things. I almost began to laugh, the way he used his nose and mouth as if he was a beast. That kind of behavior was outrageous."

"Do they not smell things in Big Tunic Land then?" I asked confoundedly. I thought it only natural that one would always smell and taste things one had not seen before to get acquainted with them, just as one would touch and look. Even Zivah raised an eyebrow then. Our people had always known the wisdom of sensing with all the senses a new thing.

"Not at all! It was a very barbarian thing to do!" Aziza laughed, before she continued her story, "Then he turned to me and seemed to notice my presence again, and he smiled at me, understanding that I was trying not to laugh at him. He didn't mind at all. He sat down, and I began to do all the things I was supposed to do, what with playing music and singing and dancing, and he just sat there looking astonished, and I realized he had never seen that kind of thing before.

"When he began to look as if he was bored, I led him to the bath and we bathed together for the first time; I washed him and gave him massage, and all the time he just let me lead him because he clearly did not know what was expected of him anyway. He was so very big and strong, larger than any man I had ever seen before, and with all his tattoos and scars. Most other girls would have been terrified of him. I was just fascinated, having never seen anything like him before. He acted so politely all the time, never even leered at me. He kept studying me and meeting my eyes, like he was actually interested in me, and not just for humping me. I had never experienced anything like it. He treated me with great respect, almost as if he thought me a kind of goddess. I now know he did think of me as a goddess, but in those days I did not know a man could see a slave, not to say a whore, I mean a courtesan, as a goddess. We did not even have goddesses, although my mother had told me about them. Now another thing transpired. He had worn a cross, so I thought he was a Christian barbarian, but when he took his clothes off before the bath, he had been very careful to hide something from me. But I was just going to move his clothes when suddenly I discovered his Thor's hammer among them, and I picked it up out of curiosity. Then he suddenly touched me for the first time, looking very worried, took the hammer pendant away from me and looked me into the eyes, shaking his head and putting his finger towards his mouth, saying, haram."

"What does haram mean?"

"It means forbidden. Very forbidden, to the point where you can be killed for it. I understood that it was a Heathen object, and very much forbidden in the Caliphate, and Arnulf looked so distressed about me discovering it that I decided to make him trust me. I went over to a drawer where I kept my jewelry and found what I had been hiding ever since my mother died. My mother had marvelously enough been able to hide an heirloom of hers ever since she was taken as a slave. It was the image of her god Shiva, with six arms."

Everybody suddenly looked at Zivah, whose name sounded conspicuously like the god that Aziza spoke of. Aziza went to her little shelf where she kept her own things and took out a small figurine. It was made out of something called ivory and came from a very large beast living down in Blue Land. The figurine was the most exquisite piece of craftsmanship I had ever seen both before and since. It was the image of a god that was half man and half woman, and who had six arms. We all gathered round to look at the precious deity and reverently lowered our eyes to it.

"He is a very ancient god from Indus," Aziza said, "although he is also a she, as you can see. The sacred image was very much forbidden in Big Tunic Land, but she had managed to keep it safe. Perhaps the god himself had made it possible, because she would have been flogged if she had been found out, and so would I. For the first time ever in my life, I showed my god to another, looked at Arnulf and put my finger over my lips, shaking my head and said haram. Some divine power passed between us then, connecting us. We looked at one another and knew that we shared a dangerous secret; we were both Heathens. We knew it both, that we could trust each other, and that we also liked each other very much."

Aziza smiled, "Then we played the pleasure games, of course. That was why he had come, after all. It was the first time in my life that a man had striven to please me, Maiden. He did it so well also. He seemed to be interested in my responses, and followed my signals. I had never experienced the like. All the men who had used me, not one of them ever thought for a moment about who I was and what I might want. They saw three words when they saw me, beautiful, available, whore-slave. Then they made up a little story inside their minds about what those three words meant to them and acted accordingly. Not one of them had ever made love to me. Arnulf did, and I did not even regard him as a client then. I went with it with all my being, so that I might enjoy such love once in my life." I looked round when she paused, as did Zivah, and to our surprise all the women seemed to nod in recognition, eyes moist all of a sudden.

"I wept with joy when Freyia's waves took me for the first time in my life, and even more when he kept maintaining me in those waves," Aziza said. "That was the most touching gesture, that he saw that I was happy, and then strove to make me happy for as long as possible. Until then, I had only once, almost, reached a state of pleasure, and showed it, only to be struck by the client who told me that I was a dirty whore. He had been so nice to me until that point, acting as if he was pitying me and trying to make me feel good, and then when I actually did feel good he was furious and thought me soiled and unworthy of more pity. So it meant something to me, when Arnulf only encouraged it. And my soul was transformed after, Maiden. He made me feel pure. He made me think myself a goddess. He has never once rebuked me for having been a whore, he just does not mind. The Rus are free in that sense, very free. There are lots of things one could say about them that are not good, but for a slave-whore who had always been despised as impure and soiled, to be treated like a pure and beautiful woman. It was the most touching gesture for me, and I felt healed. He has made me think of myself as clean, pure and worthy. Where I had wept with joy when the waves seized me, I wept with grief when he left, thinking that he would never return. But he did."

Aziza paused to catch her breath, and the whole room was quiet, staring at her, so moved. Only Zivah looked nauseous all of a sudden. She had obviously not had anywhere near the same experience with Arnulf Heri when he had approached her in that tent. All that time I think Zivah had hated him for that night, but now it did occur to us both that he may not have taken her, eventually, simply because she really had not wanted him to do so.

I could see her stoop to think about that, frowning. I really wished that she would mellow up to him soon, seeing as they lived in the same house. She never ever spoke to him or even looked at him, and he left her alone, pretending that she was not even there, which was, I knew, his way of respecting her and never bothering her. I wondered if Zivah would ever grasp that.

"Did he make you wait long?" I finally asked, remembering the courtesies. When the storyteller pauses, the listener must ask to show that interest is there.

"Not very long," Aziza replied, smiling again, "He had already decided, I know that now, and he just needed some time to get enough money together to purchase me. He came to the house dressed even more splendidly than before and placed a purse full of gold coins in the hands of the owner, and then he simply went into my quarters, pointed at his hidden pendant to let me know that I should bring my god with me, and as soon as I had packed my god, he just picked me up and threw me over his shoulders as if he was abducting me, and carried me out of that house, and I never once looked back."

"Just like that?"

"Yes, just like that. The owner was too terrified of him to do anything. Even the guards stood by and pretended that they did not even see him. They just stood there with the coins and gaped as Arnulf left with me over his shoulder."

Aziza smiled broadly, eyes shining, and I clapped my hands excitedly. I thought this was the best abduction story ever, and all the girls sighed with delight, except Zivah, who concentrated on my silk dress instead.

"It was like a dream come true, Maiden," Aziza said happily, "All the girls dreamed of such things, that one day, one man would see them and love them and save them from that place. But it never happened. Until Arnulf came and just took me. He may not have been anything like what we girls imagined when we dreamt of such men, and I learned quickly that he was a very hardened man, a slaver and a pirate. But he saved me, and he has treated me with care and affection, even with deep respect ever since, made me his concubine and let me run his household. He has shown me great honor, making me his first concubine and his housekeeper."

She paused, peering at Zivah, "I thought them very beastly in the beginning, but I got used to the Rus eventually, and I am a lot happier here than I was in the pleasure house of Baghdad," she said.

THE COURTESANS' COUNSEL

Aziza's story of abduction and love had touched everybody. Even Zivah, grudgingly, had to admit that it was a moving story. But when the women spoke of their happiness in Arnulf's court, my sister got a painful look about her face.

"I suppose it is because you have never known anything better," Zivah muttered sulkily from her corner. Everybody turned to look at her, and she looked back at them all with her large doe-eyes, moist with tears. "Where I came from, women chose who they wanted to be with. Always," she said, "and the men were gentle towards us, and wooed us. There were no orders and no commands and no... random rutting all over the place with diverse victims."

"Victims, you say," Suri asked teasingly, but Laimi put a hand on her arm to silence her. I had begun to suspect that Suri never minded being taken at all, and especially not in front of everybody. I had heard her brag that she got some every day, if she wanted to.

"You know what she means," Laimi said, "and there is no blaming her. Zivah has known freedom and a place where slavery did not even exist. Zivah, even the Norsemen would never treat their own women like they treat us slaves. You see how they are with the Maiden. Even when she is a woman grown they will treat her with the same respect, even more so. Nobody will give her commands of that sort, not even her House-Bond."

"How very reassuring," Zivah said dryly, and looked at me, "I am very happy for my sister in that regard. It does not change the fact that most of us are but sheaths to them, of sorts."

"Well, we are slaves," Laimi continued, "it is different with us. Zivah, most of the women here have always been slaves. They are used to it, and they are used to always grasping at any chance to be happy and forget the past." She turned to Suri, "but even if we are all very happy about Hialti's recent departure, even you can surely remember what it is to be made a victim by a man, Suri. It is not that long ago."

"No, it is not. Hialti made it less bearable, I will grant you that," Suri said, but quickly brightened up, "Now that he is not here anymore I am well entertained most every day." The others giggled.

"You all seem to think that Hialti is the only man here who ever hurt you," Zivah said, looking about with a challenging stare, "but you are being used like animals by all the men, most of you anyway, and there is no excuse not to obey, unless you have the bleeding mark or the collar of the concubine or the Sheath. Even then you cannot ever just say to your men that you feel indisposed. You just have to take it, and you do not even seem to realize just how hard they are with you."

"I should say it needs to be hard," Suri giggled, "if one is to get to them waves anyway." Many of the women nodded in agreement, and Zivah shook her head dismissively, resuming her needle work.

"You have never been in a place like this," Aziza said, "and it must be shocking to see well. The Rus are not shy. A slave must obey. Zivah, Arnulf Heri would not tolerate mistreatment."

"Ha!" Zivah said darkly, "Do tell that to my tribeswomen."

The slaves exchanged glances. Then Aziza spoke as gently as she could, "Zivah, dear, I understand you have seen things that shocked you. But we are here now, we are in their home. If you had been where the rest of us had been before, then you would have seen all this differently. You see, Norsemen are very concerned with the importance of having happy women in their houses. Even slave women. They think that happy and satisfied women bring about good fortune to their court, and that unhappy and resentful women bring about bad luck. I understand you may think that they are indiscreet and rough. I was a bit shocked too when I first came here, even though I had grown up in a pleasure house. And sometimes it looks rather rough, but these things often look far more violent than they feel, I assure you."

I looked at the concubine and cleared my throat.

"Doesn't it hurt?" I whispered, giving voice to thoughts I had pushed far away. All the women looked at me with surprise, as if it had not even occurred to them that I, the free Maiden Síf of the Viking court, had ever worried about whether my brothers hurt them when they took them so roughly. Zivah gulped and looked at me as if she both pitied me for having had such thoughts all on my own, and felt guilty about it. But she had worried about the same thing, I knew.

"No, sweet Maiden, it rarely hurts," Aziza said reassuringly and looked helplessly at Suri.

"The men notice if it hurts," Suri said, directing herself both to me and to Zivah. "These Rus-men, you see, they pay attention. They are real warriors, and that means they always pay attention to absolutely everything. It may look very hard, but it can feel very delightful. The truth is that such roughness is often the only way for many women to reach the waves of Freyia. It is so for me." Surprisingly enough, more than half of the women present nodded to that.

"The men know," Suri said, "The men know who among us needs it to be hard and who needs it more gently, and do you know what, Zivah, Maiden? For the most part, these men choose us or treat us accordingly, depending on what we like. We may be their slaves, but we are their women also, and they think it is really important that their women are satisfied. They really do want us to go 'mmmm.' Our waves are holy to them."

"Why would they care at all," Zivah muttered grimly.

"That is both because they are like that, and because of their beliefs," Aziza said, "Pleasing a woman is their way of pleasing the goddess, who they think works through our wombs, so to speak. They think that if the goddess is left unsatisfied, she will bring misfortune on their court. It is a very old sort of belief, for even my mother told me something similar about her own people. Mother said that the goddess power must be tamed lest it becomes destructive, for there is nothing more powerful than that. She said the divine power must be tamed and channeled and led to flow in fruitful and life-giving ways. If she is not tamed and not led to flow with passion, she will cause floods or droughts and pestilence and famine. When Arnulf once explained to me why he thought it so important to please me, he said similar things. He said the goddess spins all fates, and the happier she is when she spins, the better the fate, he said. That is why they try to make us happy, because they think the fate-weaving goddess works through the wombs of the women that they live around."

Zivah and I exchanged glances.

"My mother told me similar things regarding great Danu the river mother," my sister said thoughtfully, "She told me..." Zivah looked at me, "She told us that it is important to make great and free flowing channels for her divine power to run through us and our homes in ways that please her, and she said it was also equally important that those channels be made, lest her power run wild and destructive. I have never heard of how that power was channeled through the wombs of us women depending on how well their men could tame us and rule us and satisfy us. That notion seems like something invented by men to excuse why they rule us so unjustly." She looked about, testily, and the women considered her words.

"Maybe that is so," Suri said finally, "but seeing as the case is that men rule us anyway, why, if they think that making us happy is just as important as ruling us, then I will not be so stupid as to object."

The other women started laughing again, agreeing wholeheartedly with Suri. They were practical women, the slaves, I could see that now. They had to be practical if they wanted to be happy.

Zivah was more concerned with being right, though, and sighed, exasperated, shaking her head.

"It is hard for you to see it this way, Zivah, because you have not seen what happens when men rule women just as ruthlessly as our men rule us, yet have no concern whatsoever for women's well-being," Laimi said, "and if you had seen that sort of life, you may have been able to appreciate the Norsemen's take on things. It is true that these men pay attention to everything. They are taught to pay attention to every subtle signal. It is true that they try to adapt to what each of the girls seems to prefer, even if it does not look that way to you when they give their commands."

"That is why they like to take Suri where everyone can see," Tana giggled, "because they know how well she likes that."

Suri just smiled sheepishly and shrugged.

"I find that very hard to believe," Zivah said dismissively, "seeing as they clearly did not care if they hurt the women of my people when they abducted them, and seeing how they treat you all here. I have found that women will often make up stories to cover up how bad they really feel about things. I can understand how that is necessary if you are to even survive."

"Zivah, it is the truth I speak," Suri said, "You see the commands of the men, the way they make eye-contact with a girl and then just nod their head towards wherever they want to have them, and then you see the girl obeying, and sometimes it looks violent to your eyes."

"That is exactly what I see," Zivah muttered, and Suri sighed. She drew her breath and spoke, "You need to look deeper, Zivah. Both slaves and warriors here know the subtle language of the eyes, the face and the body. We all speak in silent manners, what you have yet to learn completely. We serving maids often invite the men, Zivah! It is not as if women cannot have pleasure that way. On the contrary, all the girls who have lived here for a while know that even if we can hardly reject being used for pleasure, we can at least behave in a manner what will help us get exactly what we want, the way we want it, and from whom we want it and even how not to get something or someone we do not want."

"Oh really, how is that working then?" Zivah asked, with disbelief.

"Well," Suri said cheerfully, "whenever I want a good fuck from a man I pay him special attention. I let my gaze linger on him, and when he looks at me I smile and bow my head and scurry away. Or I offer him beer or water without having been asked, and when he thanks me I smile and do the eye thing. It always works! And if I want a really good fuck, then I try to be imaginative about how I approach them, within the courtesies, of course. You see, they love to be entertained. The more entertained they feel, the better the reward!"

All the women smiled slyly and nodded. They all knew these procedures.

"Especially if it is Njál," one of them cooed, and they all giggled.

"Njál is the most obliging warrior in the whole court. It never fails with Njál!" Another said, and they all started howling with laughter again, cheerfully agreeing that Njál was a great giver of good times to many women.

"How do you think it works?" Zivah looked curious now.

"Why, within short while the man in question will come and give me the command," Suri said contentedly, "That is how it works. We all do this when we want a bit of pleasing."

"So you actually want them to do that to you?" Zivah asked, and all the women broke out in new laughing sobs at the incredulous look on her face.

"What do you think we are?" Suri guffawed and clapped Zivah on the back, "We may be slaves but we are also women, Zivah. We all like to have pleasure and we happen to belong to a whole bunch of very handsome and well-built men! Have you not seen how gorgeous they are? My goodness. They are the most beautiful men on Earth, I am sure! They are strong and well-shaped, attentive and fearless and clean. They are well groomed and charming too! Really, Zivah, can you not see this?"

Zivah chose not to answer that question, and nobody pressed her, even as they all nodded dreamily to what Suri had said. They seemed to respect her ways and demanded only that she respect theirs in return. And they really did think that their men were awfully attractive.

"When that is said," Suri added, "it is true that we have no choice. A free man gives the command, we must obey. It is the truth. But it is also the truth that we are rather fortunate with the men who command us, seeing as they actually want us to like it. You are privileged, Zivah, but from our points of view it is like this; if you have to fuck anyway, you might as well find a way to enjoy it."

"Are you saying that you always invite them before they pick you?" Zivah frowned.

"Oh, no, they sometimes come of their own accord. But have you seen what happens when the men come to pick a girl?" Suri asked. Zivah shook her head.

"Zivah always keeps her eyes firmly planted on her work whenever a man comes round," Laimi pointed out, matter-of-fact, and they all giggled. Zivah blushed.

"They stand there and look at us and try to figure out which one of us might want him there and then," Suri proceeded explaining, "and so we let them know if we do not want it at all by keeping our heads down, but if we do want it or if we do not mind anyway, then we let them know by way of subtle glances until they decide. They may not always get it right but they do not hurt us even so. I think only Hialti always chose the woman who looked the most unwilling, because he liked to hurt. And you see what they made of that one in the end, the other men."

"Oh," Zivah said, and kept quiet.

I had listened a long time to all this grown up talk and found myself returning to something Aziza had said earlier.

"Aziza, why did the men you had before Arnulf never give you any pleasure? It can hardly be that difficult, from what you tell me? " I asked.

"You have no idea, Maiden," Aziza said, "I will not even bore you with the details. Even if there were men among them who knew how to ride the path well enough, it did not matter to me. I could not... it is just hard to feel pleasure when you feel despised and soiled. I was ashamed all the time, Maiden, and even when I was not ashamed it seemed that the man thought I ought to be. Shame and fear and no trust, it makes it impossible to let go. We must let go of ourselves if we are to experience Freyia's pleasures. You cannot let go if you feel ashamed or dirty or despised, or have other reasons for distrusting the man and his thoughts about you."

"Why do you not feel that way here then?" I asked.

"Maiden, where I come from, a woman could spend the rest of her life feeling shamed because she had been raped or used as a whore. It is the same among many other tribes. Not among the Rus. Here, women often get over it quite swiftly because no one ever blames them or thinks them impure. Besides, we are treated with kindness here in Arnulf's court; the men are very kind to us, always. Most of us have not been treated thus kindly by masters before. Arnulf is a very good House-Bond, with a good influence on his men. There is Hallgrim also, who is a good example to them all. As is your mentor, Thióðolf."

Aziza grinned and cast a glance at Zivah, who still flinched at the very name of the man who owned her.

"Zivah is not the first to be untouchable even here," Suri said and nudged her elbow at a girl who so far had said nothing, one called Lila. She was a little shy, but quickly brightened up. "Oh my goodness," Lila said, "I was brought here and sold on the market in Aldeigjuborg. I had been a slave before but never to people such as these, and I was so very frightened! I cried and wailed so much when one of them first ordered me into the stables. That was Agnarr what wanted me then. I could not help but weep and after trying to calm me down a little, he just let me go. Then there was another who tried, and again I was so frightened that he just let me go. And after that, nobody ever as much as looked at me, seeing as I was doing all my other chores like a good serving maid. I went two years here without ever being picked! In the end I had been so long without a man I just could not stop myself, and I was not frightened of them anymore. So I went up to Agnarr and offered him a cup of beer and when he thanked me I looked at him, and he looked a bit puzzled, so I smiled at him and said I hoped he would like what he had not tried before, and then he ordered me into the stables just like the first time. Only this time I had a great council with him!" She smiled brightly, "and after that I could not help but notice just how, uh, handsome they all are, even with all those scars and scary images on their bodies. On their really nice bodies."

The women grinned and nodded, and I thought some of them almost drooled at the thought. "They pay attention," another woman said, and everybody nodded meaningfully.

"It is on account of their warriors' training," one girl said. "That is what Fanged Njál told me anyway. He said that even a fool like himself has been trained to look deep and listen well to the subtle signals of an opponent. They use that training on everything else too, not just their opponents. They notice everything. I think they read our minds sometimes. And they know when to speed it up, like." The women giggled and snorted and made all sorts of funny movements, imitating the act. "Not to say how they listen in when we talk about them!" Lila said, what caused more giggles. "It is true," Suri said, "They really want to hear our verdicts on their conducts. They use our verdicts to improve, which means they are getting rather good at it!"

Again, the women shrieked with delight, seeing as their men really made an effort to please them, and there was a shine to their eyes now that told of passion and desire and, I suspected, even a sort of love, a collective sort of love, what intrigued me. Zivah saw the same and felt outraged.

"My goddess, you speak of these men as if they were your lovers and not your owners," Zivah exclaimed, still refusing to accept anything the other women had to say about the men she hated so.

"Well they are," Suri said, "They lover us all the time, you know." All the women laughed again, while Zivah gaped and shook her head over and over. The other women smiled dreamily as they thought about the many strong and entertaining and skillful men who displayed their abilities every day in Arnulf's court.

I began to vaguely understand why the slave girls kept casting leering glances at the men when they were practicing their many and varied arts related to battle, and especially when they took off their tunics and one could see their powerful chests and shoulders. I was just a little maiden yet, and did not know exactly what Freyia's pull felt like, but even I found these men quite fascinating to observe already. I thought them sweet, well-shaped, pleasant to the eyes and always very funny to be around.

Aziza drew her breath, and there was a tremble in her voice, an old hurt revealing itself when she spoke again, "Zivah, you cannot possibly see this from our perspective. You are the only one among us who can honestly say that you have come from a better place than this. Not one of us can say the same."

Zivah looked around and saw the other girls confirm what Aziza had said with nods and gravely serious faces all of a sudden. Aziza proceeded, "If you had lived lives like we have lived before, then maybe you would have seen how precious this is to us, to live with men who never once even think the thought that we are impure or soiled. I think all of us here can witness and testify that a woman can be used in all sorts of ways but that there is nothing that is really humiliating to us until we are being branded as dirty and soiled and less than human for being used so. That is the only thing that can really hurt us, Zivah.

That poisonous arrow of disdain directed against us, the message that we are nothing worth, that we are but shameful trash and rotten garbage, because we have been raped so many times. That is the only thing that really hurts a woman's soul, Zivah. Nothing else can hurt us so. If you had known that sort of world where women raped are branded as dirty and worthless, then you too might have appreciated coming among men who think that the goddess is manifest even in a slave girl. You have no idea how important that is to those of us who have known that sort of pain!"

"I suppose I cannot," Zivah said, "and I respect you all, my sisters. It is just that I cannot see it this way. I just cannot. All I know is that I resent this." She touched her slave collar and looked sad, "I cannot help it, my friends. I just cannot accept that I am not free. I have no slave chant in my soul song. I cannot but detest the men who made a slave out of me."

"I know that feeling, Zivah," Laimi said, and then the laughter subsided and we resumed our work, all thoughtful.

After a while, my sister held up the sky blue silk dress that she had made for me. I put it on right there before them and they all cooed and gasped delightfully at the way I looked. I could not see myself, but I felt it. I stood there in that blue silk dress, and for the first time in my young life, I felt like a beautiful maiden, and then I blushed profoundly, being so little used to that feeling.

"Oh, sister," Zivah whispered proudly, "you can be the beauty now. I think you can handle being lovely to the eyes better than I ever could."

The Maiden with the Mead

Ivarr could not even remember there ever having been a House-Freyia or a Síf at Arnulf's court. His mother, Arnulf's sister Guðrún, had died when he was but one year old, and after being fostered by the lady Freydís for two more years, he had returned to court still a toddler, the only child among Vikings and their slaves. Boys had to learn the battle arts from the age of three and were raised by men, so there was nothing uncommon about it, except for the total lack of other children, as well as a total lack of free women.

He knew that the men had been lenient around him when he was still very small, and he had been allowed to sleep in the Hold with the serving maidens at night for several years. Now he could hardly remember a time when the men did not hone him and hone him harshly, and when he did not stay in the warriors' Hall. Yet, he had still been the one dear child of court until this summer. It had been quite a shock for him when Thordís came round.

Only a year younger than him, and yet she was treated like the most precious little puppy of the whole pack, allowed to snarl endlessly at him while the men urged her on and laughed with her at his expense. He knew it was a way of honing him, but it was really hard to accept that some times. She made him feel so stupid and clumsy and inadequate. Only when she had let him know that she secretly admired him for his courage every day had he started feeling somewhat different about her. But that had already been so long ago he hardly remember how proud she had made him feel.

Now she was yet again the center of attention, their precious Síf, chosen to be the priestess of the Solstice celebration, an incarnation of the Sun Maiden herself, while he was just a stupid worthless boy of no consequence. Arnulf, wearing the headdress of the Ram with two large horns on them, took his place in the High Seat of the Hall, and all the warriors gathered round, seated in order of rank on either side of the table, and Ivarr at the far end of the table, being lower ranking than all of them.

The slave women had decorated the Hall with old tapestries made by his mother and grandmother and had prepared a lot of food and drink for the banquet, and now they too gathered round the table to stand behind the men. Thióðolf Skald stood next to Arnulf, ready to lead the ritual and instruct the very young priestess. When everybody had settled and gone quiet, the door opened, and in came Njál the Foolish and the Sharp-Toothed, carrying a dark bundle what everybody knew was the maiden cloaked in black. He placed the dark bundle gently onto the table so that all could see it, and the girl sat down beneath the cloak.

There was a hushed silence before Thióðolf Skald sang forth the first verse of the ritual, a verse he had composed himself for the occasion,

> She slept in the darkness of Darkness itself
> in the cave of Night and Night's sisters
> Laboring, pain-ridden in her dying light
> The three times burned did rise.

The folks of the Hall tried hard not to giggle when they saw the shape beneath the cloak rise to her feet, still covered. Arnulf stood, impressive in his Ram's crown, and lifted the large Thor's hammer that was generally kept away among the holy objects, only to be used for ceremonies such as these, and Thióðolf Skald intoned the second verse,

> The Thunder Warrior wears the horns of the Ram
> when he breaks through the Wolf's belly
> Opens the cave of the Serpent's lair
> To retrieve the Golden Maiden.

Then Arnulf removed the cloak to reveal the Sun goddess. The entire Hall gave a collective gasp. They had gotten used to seeing their little shield maiden run about in boy's clothing and mud in her face most of the time. Nobody was used to seeing her like this. She was wearing a most exquisitely sewn sky-blue silk dress, held together with a lovely belt in which Aziza's housekeeper keys had been hung, so as to indicate that Thordís was the House-Freyia for the time being.

On her chest hung that very particular looking Miöllnir pendant, the Thor's hammer that was said to be countless ages old and worn by the ancestral mother of her ancient and famous lineage, the Thunder Priests of Gautland. She usually kept her pendant tucked in behind her clothes so that it would not draw too much attention, and the courtesies demanded that nobody tried to look at it either. Now it was free for all to see.

It had power, that pendant, even a stupid little boy like Ivarr could see that. It was almost odd to see such manly power exude from a little maiden's chest, but there it was. He had heard men say that the pendant had been forged by the lord Thor himself, or by that heavenly smith called Völund, but nobody was entirely certain. Thordís Maiden was the last of her great and ancient lineage, like a living legend.

Her hair had been washed and combed and was now hanging in lovely red-golden locks down her back and sides, framing that pretty face with those scary wolf-eyes. On her head was a golden ring, the symbol of the Sun goddess, and in her hands were the silver serving spoon and the beautifully carved drinking horn that his mother had once owned. Ivarr knew that his mother had been the last woman to perform this ritual at Arnulf's court. The items looked very large in Thordís' little hands, but she seemed to have a firm grasp on them nevertheless. Thióðolf intoned another verse, what caused chills to run up the spines of everybody,

The warriors gather on the Shore of the Soul
Covered in hoar-frost they wait for the blow
Sleep-walking, paralyzed, force yet to be known
They wait for the blow of the Sun of Old.
The bard's voice grew into a veritable war cry,
Rally the Warriors of the Shield of the Heart!
Rebirth the wolves of the Thunderer's charge!
Wake the Sleeper in the Song of the Soul!
Blow the breath gently from the Sun of Old!

There was a stunned silence before Arnulf spoke thunderously, "The warriors greet the Hall's Freyia!"

"All hails to the Hall's Freyia!" The gathering cried as one.

The girl remained on the table for the duration of the ritual, because she was so little that nobody would have seen her if she had performed it from the floor. There on the table she was seen by all. She gazed down at the congregation and Ivarr could see how the most hardened faces of the warriors softened and tears began running down scarred and bearded cheeks. He could feel it himself, a strange yearning, as if he and all the others had been longing for the goddess so deeply and so long they had forgotten about it until she suddenly stood there before them.

When the maiden saw their reactions, her white wolf-eyes transformed into a light blue to match the color of her dress, and it seemed as if great love was slung out from those soul-mirrors, a love that seemed to hit them all like the breath of the Sun goddess whom she incarnated. It was as if rays of love and light extended from her whole being like great blasts of Sun's rays.

They adored her, and she adored them right back. And the warriors wept freely. They were supposed to weep, they had to weep because the tears were sacred, and the goddess would gather strength from them, making her know that she was wanted, giving her the will to try and rise out from the depths of darkness. The entire Hall wept for the loss of the Sun Maiden, and wept in hope for her return. They wept as one, men and women, free and slave. It seemed impossible not to weep.

"The goddess has awakened," Thióðolf chanted powerfully, "Our tears have made her stir. She calls for the aid of the great Lord! She calls for the aid of Thor. Alu!"

"Thor! Alu!" Everybody cried, calling the name that would save the goddess, and the sacred word for all oaths, and also for all precious beverages. In ordinary circumstances, Arnulf would have performed the next stage, but the maiden happened to be a Thunder Priestess, and carried a hammer that was far above the one the Heri carried, the oldest of all Thor's hammers.

Today their Síf was their Priestess, their goddess and their Freyia, and no person in that hall was more sacred than her. She raised her hammer for all to see. Fortunately the silver chain was more than long enough for her to raise the pendant high, where a man grown would have had to take it off.

"I invoke the might of the Thunder Lord!" She cried, her voice surprisingly strong and melodious, "I invoke the Heat Rider! I invoke the Son of Earth! May he slay the Great Wolf of winter! May he enter the Hall of the Sun! May she open her gates to the Thunder warrior! May he carry the goddess home!"

She placed the hammer against her heart and intoned the last words of the incantation, "May he live long in the glowing Síf's embrace!"

"Alu!" The hall cried, "All hails to the heavenly Freyia! All hails to the Son of Earth!" Now the slave women came with the cauldron full of golden liquid. The most sacred, most precious mead, the libation of the Sun Maiden, the source of all inspiration and all sacred songs, was placed on the table.

They chanted over it, the song of the precious mead, hailing the Earth mother, who had born it, and the Sun Maiden, who had revived it, and the lord Thor, who had restored it. The men roared their deep, rhythmical song from their throats and kept beating the table, while Thióðolf and Hallgrim and the maiden priestess chanted the words of praise and the women intoned with their ululating cries.

When the chorus had stilled, the maiden took the serving spoon and filled the horn while Arnulf helped holding it, seeing as her hands were still little. Then she took the horn and raised it with both her hands for all to see.

"I wed this drinking horn to the great gods," the young priestess chanted, "For our inspiration; I wed her to Óðinn! For our might; I wed her to Thor! For our victory; I wed her to Týr! For safe voyage; I wed her to Njorð! For fruitfulness; I wed her to Freyr! For the sealing of our oaths; I wed her to Bragi, the god of all promises!"

The hall cheered, invoking the names of the six great gods. The priestess turned to Arnulf. "I greet Arnulf, the Hall's Heri! May you be prosperous and just, and may courage and wisdom always swell in your chest," she chanted, and gave the horn to Arnulf. The Heri lowered his eyes to her, for this night she was a goddess, and emptied the horn at once. "I thank the Hall's Freyia," he said reverently and gave the horn back to her.

She filled the horn again, this time for Thióðolf. "I greet Thióðolf, the Hall's Skald! May your words make more words for you, may your deeds make more deeds for you and may wisdom always flood abundantly from your soul-stone!" And Thióðolf lowered his eyes to the goddess and drank the horn down. "I thank the Hall's Freyia," he said, looking immensely proud of his novice. It was he who had instructed her in the first place on how to perform the ritual.

She filled the horn yet again, and turned to Hallgrim, "I greet Hallgrim, the Hall's Cunning Man. May your wisdom grow ever greater than it already is, and may you continue to bestow true courage and insight to our men." Hallgrim lowered his eyes to the priestess and drank his fill, thanking the Hall's Freyia.

212

She turned to Sígtrygg; "I greet Sígtrygg, a warrior of lord Týr! May your fortune bless the entire court and bring victory in every matter. May you continue to bestow skill in battle to our men." Sígtrygg drank and thanked the Hall's Freyia, who turned to Njál. "I greet Njál, the Hall's greatest Fool! May your foolishness continue to inspire and enlighten us, and may your sharp fangs sink deep in our enemy's throat." And Njál drank and thanked the Hall's Freyia. After that, she served all the warriors, proceeding according to rank, greeting each of them by name and by the title of warrior, offering them each a blessing for strength, for courage, and for wisdom.

Ivarr knew that even if she had been instructed, the words she spoke to each warrior were words she had prepared herself, words to encourage each one of them to gather strength so they may all assist the great lord in his battle against the powers that would devour the goddess. And the closer she came to the last and lowest ranking of them all, the more Ivarr dreaded the scorn that would surely come to him alone, seeing as he was no warrior at all and could not possibly be of any assistance to great Thor and the Sun Maiden. He braced himself. He would have to just take it as he always did. Yet, he sat watching her with increasing anxiety and increasing admiration, for she was so very beautiful and a light seemed to radiate from her and he felt her heating rays stronger and stronger as she approached.

Finally she stood before him, having filled the horn once more. He lowered his eyes submissively as had all the men on this special occasion, and looked back up at her, bracing himself for the sharp words of the honer. The maiden smiled slyly at him and offered the horn to him and spoke a whole verse, composed especially for him,

I greet Ivarr, who will one day become a warrior of this Hall!
May you grow strong with the precious mead!
May the golden liquid strengthen your heart!
May honor and manliness swell in your chest!
May you become one with the great Thor!
And so I bless you in the name of Freyia.

Thordís the priestess winked at the boy. Ivarr could hardly believe the honor she had just paid him. He just gaped at her for a moment and had to force back a sob. His hands almost shook when he took the horn and whispered, "I thank the Hall's Freyia." He drank the whole cup.

When she turned and started walking back across the table, his eyes were not the only moist eyes that followed the girl, nor the only ones filled with renewed love for her. Ivarr felt such a tug in his heart when it occurred to him that he was the only one among them who was of an age with her. The shock of that realization made him feel dizzy all of a sudden.

She is my man-maker. He had lived among grown folks so long that the meaning of that vague anticipation he felt could not possibly be lost on him, even if they were both very young. Ivarr watched as his blade honer returned to Arnulf and filled the horn for the last time. She had to fill it to the brim and drink her share too, for where they had become one with the mead and one with each other, she was the vessel of all of them, and in her they were all united.

"Our strengths have been gathered. The strength of all is now in one cup. The maiden is the vessel for our power. The mead is the might of the vessel. The might of the Hall is gathered in the Maiden," Thióðolf chanted, and the girl lifted the horn and drank.

She struggled a little, seeing as it was a strong drink for one so young, and mead was trickling down her cheeks as she forced down the entire contents. Then she looked a bit dizzy and almost lost her balance. Ivarr heard some of the warriors go "aaaaaaw," seeing as she was a rather adorable little goddess. The girl turned to face them all and forced back a hiccup. Instead of laughing as they usually would have, the warriors roared the final chant in her honor;

We have been united in the holy Vessel!
Our strength has been united as one!
All hails to the Sun Maiden!
All hails to the great goddess!
All hails to the Hall's Freyia!
All hails to our Síf!

The warriors began to bang the table rhythmically with their fists, and sang with those deep and thunderous roars they knew how to produce from the depth of their throats. The mead ritual was completed and the drunken girl swayed, only to be gathered in Thióðolf's arms. She had never drunk so much undiluted brew before and was soon fast asleep, noticing only vaguely that the party had just begun, with warriors and slaves engaging freely together in joyful celebration.

Now even the slaves were allowed to drink of the mead cauldron, and Ivarr celebrated for a while longer, but soon fell asleep himself, being not that much older than her, really. To Ivarr's delight, he woke some time later and saw that he had been placed next to Thordís in the same bed. The curtains were drawn and nobody could see them. The beautiful maiden was sleeping so soundly, and before he drifted back off to sleep, he put his arm gently around her, just to feel what it was like. She smelled like rose water and sweet honey mead and she was so very soft to the touch he almost gasped from the sensation.

She did not wake from that deep slumber, and he let his arm rest, and held her close. It was so odd, feeling her breathing body so close, her soft hair tickling his nostrils. Now that she did not run about in boy's clothes and a practice blade, she seemed so fragile all of a sudden. He remembered that one time he had seen her truly vulnerable, crushed beneath the vicious weight of Rat-Hialti, and his heart broke at the thought. She may be tough around the court, surrounded by doting brothers, but the world was full of men like Hialti also. Here, now, with his arm around her, he felt like he wanted to keep her safe within his embrace forever.

She would have laughed so hard if he told her that. Not because she did not know how vulnerable she really was but because he was just a boy and she had real men to protect her. There was only one way to turn the tables. Ivarr felt the strength that grows from determination. The maiden could be his blade honer any day, because one day she would be his spear enticer, and maybe even more than that.

He would take her scorn like a man and laugh hard at himself until nobody else cared to laugh at him anymore. He would accept all her mocking glares without even flinching, until one day she just might feel like lowering her eyes to him and call him warrior after all. Ivarr wished he was not quite so young, seeing at it could take years. Years. He was not yet nine years old. But no matter how long it took, one day he would show her that he was worthy of her respect. And then Ivarr slept.

THE SHEATHS OF THE HALL

The Yule celebration that had started with the Solstice went on, and there were rituals to be held also publicly among the Aldeigjuborg citizens. I was too small to attend, the men thought. I suspected it was because some of the Kindly Ladies were supposed to attend it, and for some inexplicable reason the men did not wish to tell me about, they did not want me to meet the very gentle ones. This meant that the men left us alone for days on end, leaving only a few warriors to guard us, but these did not make any demands on any of the slaves at this time.

It was the time of dark forces where the strict rules of rank were loosened and even slaves could sometimes feel almost like free folks. It was also a time when the norns saw fit to make verdicts on the past year and spin new threads for the next, and that was always a good time to keep women particularly happy and content, seeing as the power of the norns is channeled through the women of the Hold and Hall. When the men were out one night, all the slaves gathered in Arnulf's Hold to eat and drink together, having for once an evening off, without the demands of their masters and with leave to not work on any chores at all.

I was the only free person among them, but they had gotten used to me by now and had begun to see me more as a child than as one of their superiors, and so they no longer lowered their voices around me. The male slaves gathered at the end of the table to play chess while the women chatted, and as women are wont, they soon enough talked about men and their assets, or lack of the same. Even the Sheaths of the Hall had joined us for once.

As soon as the Sheaths had gotten a little drunk, they were happy to share their opinions about which of their men were the best lovers and what kind of Freystones they had, what made the evening very merry since all the women clearly liked to talk endlessly about men's manly qualities, often rolling over in laughter both when they admired and when they disapproved of something.

By now I had figured out that if the slave women liked a man or some of his deeds, they laughed because it made them happy, and if they did not like something, they laughed because it felt good to openly ridicule those who treated them unjustly without being punished for it.

Now that they were talking and laughing, the Sheath called Harawa suddenly turned to Zivah and spoke, "Zivah dear, is it true that your House-Bond has not touched you even still?"

"It is! It is!" Some of the serving maids eagerly volunteered, seeing as they slept in the Hold with us and knew well what was going on. Zivah blushed.

"It is really odd," Harawa pondered, "because Thióðolf Heri has not touched any other girl in this court either. I am starting to wonder if he is one of those men who like other men."

"I have tried to entice that one even from the first day," Tana contributed, to the sad nods of several other girls who could sympathize, and sighed, "He is really hard to get. "

There was general agreement around the Hold. Thióðolf was frequently offered water and drink and other treats from the slave girls, who kept smiling at him, but he never responded with the desired command. He just thanked them politely and smiled back, and the closest thing they ever got was the occasional compliment on something, or a little chat.

Even if there was nothing more, it was worth it, the women agreed, because he was so good at those compliments and so good at those chats, they always walked away feeling like they were flying, as if he had revealed something lovely in them that they had not even been aware of before. The women giggled and looked at Zivah, who looked deeply embarrassed. I frowned and scratched my head, thinking about the time when Thióðolf had told me about the colorful people and the maidenly men. Besides, Búi was nodding in agreement and sighing with the women, as if he had exactly the same experience with the skald.

"I would not know," Zivah said, "I have not asked."

She did look thoughtful.

"I should say not," Aziza said, "Thióðolf seemed rather intrigued with me when I was sent to his bed last spring. Do you not recall, Zivah, how I told you that Thióðolf Heri is a very good fuck?"

All the women began laughing again.

"Zivah no want fuck," Suri howled and caused the merriment to reach new heights. My sister looked a little inconvenienced, but then she started laughing too. I was mystified until I gathered that she must have said something along those lines on her first evening here.

Zivah surprised us all when she asked, sounding genuinely curious, "Is it true then, Aziza? Is he?"

"It is true," Aziza confirmed with a big smile, "that man knows his way around women. He took his time! Even when I had climbed into his bed all naked and told him that I had been commanded to please him, why, he still made certain that I really wanted it first. I never met anyone like that! And when he saw how excited I was, he went on pleasing me endlessly before he even began riding Freyia's path. And I can vouch for his skill and his stamina. He lasted all night! I was exhausted when morning came, and Arnulf told me I could sleep in, which I did. My House-Bond was very happy that I had been well satisfied. And I would be very surprised if I was to hear that Thióðolf preferred men."

I looked at my sister, who had gotten a look of disgust in her face. She still hated him. I had once heard Arnulf comment on that, saying that Zivah could hold a grudge like a proper Norsewoman. He had sounded like he admired her for that.

"I do not know, Aziza," Tziki said, the Sheath who belonged to Njál and Runarr and four other men,

"Runarr has ridden me quite enthusiastically several times even though he prefers to hump Búi most of the time." Everybody giggled. Both Zivah and I looked curiously at her now, and then at Búi, who had gone all red down where he sat with the other slave men.

"He is a warrior," Búi said, gathering his courage, and there was admiration in his voice, "Runarr is a great warrior who needs to show that he is a part of the Six every now and then. They unite in your wombs, you know. They unite as brothers in the shared vessel that is the Sheath. But even if he does his duty when he must, he really does prefer other men, or, that is, he prefers me." The young slave man who was being used like a woman positively beamed.

"You do you not mind, Búi?" Zivah asked, and the stable boy smiled and shook his head, "Not at all, Zivah. I prefer it that way myself. I enjoy watching the men as well as any slave girl does."

"Oh," Zivah said, blushing again. I knew she liked Búi well, because he reminded her a little of her sweetheart back home, gentle and good looking and sweet as he was. He did not look like a girl at all, but after having lived a while with Rus warriors he did not seem very manly to us either. "Only I have to always be, uhm, I have to always be the woman, so to speak," Búi added and grinned sheepishly, "Seeing as a warrior cannot ever submit to the lord stone. That would dishonor him. But I do not mind, really. I am a slave so I have to submit anyway. Nobody cares if I submit to a man. It is different for Runarr."

"It is shady even so," Tziki volunteered, "the men tease Runarr a lot about it. He has to be very careful. Even if everybody knows, it is something they do not want to see all the time. Which is why Runarr and Búi are so careful about not showing their love too openly, in front of others. Runarr sneaks out in the night to be with the boy and returns before dawn to our bed. We all know it and we hardly ever speak of it. But Runarr does get to hear it when they are in a festive mood sometimes, and then he just has to accept all sorts of nasty teasing. He has to just reply as witty as he can and laugh with them to save face."

"Their love?" Zivah asked, incredulous. Búi shrugged and blushed and smiled again and said no more. Everybody exchanged smiles and knowing glances. There was love between that slave boy and the warrior, even as odd and strange as it could seem to most.

"Do you not think that we slaves can love our men, Zivah?" Tziki teased.

"I do not know," she said uncertainly, "I do not know how it is possible to give love freely to one who owns you like a goat."

"So you would be surprised if I told you that I love all my six House-Bonds?" Tziki asked.

"I do not mean to disrespect you, Tziki. I have a hard time understanding how," Zivah admitted.

SOILED AND DIRTY WHORES: TZIKI'S STORY

"Well, let me tell you a story. What say you, Hold, do you want to hear a love story?" Tziki asked, and everybody brightened up. Laimi and Aziza made sure everybody had enough to drink, and then Tziki began her story, "I do not remember much of my early childhood. I think perhaps I was raided, or else born a slave. I do not know. I was not among Vikings, though, not among Norsemen. Oh, no. I was a whore in a rather shady pleasure house in a shady part of the great city that you all know as Miklagard, although they call it Constantinople. We spoke Greek. I was brought to that pleasure house very young, and I was taught how to please men even before I could actually be fucked. I just attended the older whores and such. As soon as I was old enough, as far as they were concerned anyway, I was taken day and night by endless streams of new men."

Zivah looked at her with an expression of pity.

"Oh, yes, you may pity that part of my life," Tziki said, "there were times when all I wanted was for it all to be over quickly. I even hoped that a customer would just kill me one day. I was happy to see that most whores die young, often from illness, sometimes from violence and often enough from suicide too. I could not bear it anymore.

"It was not just what they did to me all the time, the way I felt as if I was nothing but a hole into which they could squirt. No, it was worse than that. If you recall what Aziza told you about being told she was dirty and soiled and shameful, well, that was also what I got to hear.

"The people of Miklagard are Christians, and there was nothing those folks liked better than to let me know how worthless and dirty I was. I remember how I kept scrubbing myself, feeling so very dirty. People spat after us in the streets if we ventured outside the pleasure house. Even the same men who used us in the pleasure house would spit after us and call us dirty whores if they saw us in town.

Their women hated us so much, maybe because they were scared stiff from the thought of ending up like us, who knows, or because their lousy men came to us for pleasure. They should have thanked us, if you ask me. Not to mention their priests, who were our most eager customers in secret. They were most aggressive towards us, when they did not fuck us, and they hated themselves after, and they hated us even more."

Tziki drew her breath, because the memory had made her somewhat agitated, and she wiped off a few tears before she continued.

"I was, I think, no more than sixteen years old, and I already felt tired of life. This was some six years past. One day, the strangest sorts of customers arrived in the pleasure house. There were six of them, and they were taller and bigger and looked scarier than most! Njál had not yet gotten his teeth filed, though, and he did not spike his hair yet either, so he could still pass relatively well among civilized folks. He was very young, but he spoke Greek fluently. Still does."

"Njál speaks another tongue?" Zivah asked, frowning.

"Yes. Fanged Njál is very clever, you know."

"Everybody says he is so foolish. He even says so himself," Zivah objected. The women smiled slyly.

"Njál says that a man has to be very clever to be a fool among Norsemen and live," Tziki explained patiently, and continued her story, "So Njál and Runarr and the others came to the pleasure house and just walked in, looking at us all. Njál saw me and came to sit beside me while the other men took up positions along the wall and completely ignored all the women and the host too. I thought they looked and acted so strangely I did not even know what to do. I just sat there while Njál sat next to me. I got this strange, unusual feeling of being, what shall I say, being comfortable. In a way I had never felt comfortable around any customer before. I sat there, and he sat there, and he turned to me just a little and grinned at me, and I could not help but smile back. He is such a charming fellow. When I turned to face him I noticed that he was studying me very carefully and, uhm, sniffing."

"Sniffing?" Zivah exclaimed.

"Yes, he was smelling me! I thought it was so odd. Like he was a sort of beast, only he tried to hide it a little. I thought he was going to rent me like most men would have, but after a little while he went up to the others and they talked a little, about me, I guess, and then they called out for the owner. My master came up and looked very nervous, and Njál looked very stern when he spoke to him.

"He said, 'I was told to come here if I wanted to find soiled and dirty whores.'

"The owner went all red and stammering and stuttering, and Njál started complaining, 'Hear now, man, I have been looking everywhere, and I have looked at all these women here, and I keep failing to find soiled and dirty whores in this place. I feel that I have been lied to. All my brothers here feel the same.' All six gloomy, giant Vikings nodded, very gravely, to that."

The women began to giggle, some even spilling their drinks. Unperturbed, Tziki proceeded, "The owner started to suggest that soiled and dirty was a figure of speech, upon which Njál said, 'Look here, my good man. Do I seem to you like a man who is capable of understanding such double meanings? I am a very beastly sort of fellow and I have a simple sort of mind. I wanted to see your soiled and dirty whores, but these girls smell like rosebuds. Especially that one,' he said and pointed at me, and then he made a gesture for me to come over.

"I came over to him, and Njál held me in front of him, facing the owner, and said, 'Look at this girl. Do you see a soiled and dirty whore, or do you see a perfectly clean girl?' The owner went all red again and was utterly speechless. There were men there who could have thrown out most clients, but these men were, as I was to discover, already knocked out and thus pacified by the Vikings, which was why the owner was so very frightened. The owner agreed that I was rather clean, and once more tried to explain that soiled and dirty was a way of saying that we led sinful lives, upon which Njál said, 'Why, I lead a very sinful life, man. Are you calling me soiled and dirty?' The owner went, 'No, no of course not!' Njál set his most piercing glare at him and asked, 'Are you taking me for a fool?'"

The slaves were almost howling with laughter by now.

"The owner was so terrified now," Tziki said gleefully, "and suddenly he exclaimed, 'You can have this girl for free, for free!'"

The women were toppling over, and even Zivah had to suppress a few snorts. Tziki continued, "Upon which Njál said, 'My good man. If that is your offer of compensation, I am satisfied. Come here girl, let us go.' So we left that house. We just left it, and I never saw that place again. They actually stole me!"

Tziki smiled and waited for the laughter to subside before she continued her story of her abduction, "We left very quickly and walked until we came to the harbor, where they had a ship waiting, full of Vikings, ready to depart. I was too stunned to be frightened. I know that many of you were scared of these men to begin with, but I had seen too much of soft and civilized weaklings and their capacity for cruelty to ever judge a man by his looks, and when we came to the ship, nobody touched me or even leered at me."

Zivah flinched a little, and Tziki added, "I know what they are, Zivah. I know that they have ways of subduing slaves that were not always slaves. They are very practical men. I was already subdued, and what they wanted was for me to like them, seeing as they wanted me for their companion at home. They treated me so gently and were so friendly with me! I had never been treated with such respect before. Njál had me sit down inside a small tent on the ship and sat himself down in front of me and said to me that unlike the seed of the men of this city, his seed and the seed of his brothers would never soil me and never make me dirty. Instead, they would be libation offerings to my divine body. He asked me what I would feel about serving the same six very clean men every day for the rest of my life and feel cleansed after each time, instead of countless new customers who all soiled me. I laughed and said that I would be delighted. We talked, and Njál was making me laugh all the time! Nobody had ever tried to make me laugh before, but these men did. I laughed and laughed and laughed. And they did not even touch me to begin with. On that rather long ship voyage, I moved around freely and they just talked to me a lot, my six men in particular. They got to know me, and I them, and they started teaching me their language. And when we finally reached Lake Ilmen they put up a tent on an islet and made a bonding ritual, where I was made their Sheath. Then they all took turns having me. All six of them, one after the other, while the others sat round and pretended not to watch."

Zivah looked nauseous. Tziki shook her head, trying to make Zivah see what had been most important to her.

"Zivah, I was used to being fucked by ten to fifteen new men every day! Here I was, I was almost married to the same six men, and only to them! They were nice to me, Zivah. They made it feel like it was a wedding of sorts, and I was their common bride. They were friendly and kind and they tried to please me!"

"Did they?" Zivah muttered, trying to engage. Tziki shook her head, "After what I had been through it was a bit hard to please me at first. I was just happy that they made me feel liked and cared for, and I did not mind letting them have me even if I took no actual pleasure in it. Little by little I started to like having them close, even if I still did not get any waves or anything. I just liked to feel them in me and holding me, because they were the same men returning to me, who talked to me and laughed with me and always kept me well entertained, and besides seemed to care about what I thought about them. I learned, with time, to really enjoy their attentions. Little by little, I discovered that I too could get great pleasure from this, and seeing as it took me a long time to get there it did not hurt that they were six men either!"

The women laughed, but Tziki was not quite finished, "And before you think they all take me every night, it is not so. I usually only have to deal with two of them each night. My men take care not to exhaust me, now that I am able to reach the waves somewhat swifter than I once did. Little by little I grew from just liking them well to actually love them. I really do love them. You see only lords and masters, Zivah. But they are my companions and my friends and my lovers. We are a family."

A Lousy Whore: Miri's Story

There was a silence after Tziki's speech. Zivah looked like she did not know what to say. Then Miri cleared her throat.

"I can tell you my love story too, if you like," she suggested uncertainly, and Zivah nodded eagerly.

"My memory of childhood is like Tziki's," Miri began, "I hardly remember anything at all. I was taken by men so young I no longer remember what it was like. I was hardly more than fifteen years of age when I no longer felt like living. I was like an empty shell. I no longer cared what anybody did to me. I just lay there and drifted off into a peaceful place that felt like clouds, and it mattered not what anybody said or did. I know that this displeased my masters, who tried to discipline me, but nothing could reach me anymore. I had found a way to not feel any pain at all, so they could not reach me. I was given to some men who did not care if I was lifeless."

She paused artfully, and the entire Hold was quiet now.

"When Hallgrim found me, I had been laying in a bed in a tent for some time, legs spread, to be taken by paying clients. This was down in Khazaria by the slave market at the river crossing."

All the slaves shuddered collectively. The silence was excruciating. Then Miri told her story. Her way of telling it was such that it pulled us all into it, as if we had all been there, seeing what she had seen, feeling what she had felt. This was Miri's story of love.

She had drifted off into the clouds of her mind as usual and barely noticed when one man entered and another left. It had become so easy for her. She needed only close her eyes and then she would be gone, floating in that soft space that lulled her and comforted her, like a mother. Nothing and nobody could harm her there. She went there as often as she could, until going there was almost all that she could do. The rental slave girl had a name once, but she no longer remembered it. She hardly even remembered that she had a body.

It did not belong to her anyway.

She had been out there for days and nights on end when there had been some disturbance, something that seemed to pull her out of those soft clouds. Not wanting to go back there, she resisted the pull. Then it was as if there was somebody there with her, somebody sharing her floating existence in the faraway place, someone else taking part in that space within her, for the first time. Then she had opened her eyes.

The very tall man was seated next to her on the bed, with his side to her. He did not even turn to look at her when he noticed that she was awake. He did not touch her. He did not even try to speak to her. He hardly even looked at her, except from a few sideway peeks that met her eyes rather than leering at her body. What strange eyes he has, she thought, like dark pools of starlit sky. She suddenly wondered if he knew how to go into skies like that. It almost startled her, that she had actually wondered about anything at all. She thought she had forgotten that art.

"My name is Ha-hl-greem," he told her in the Khazar language, and she noticed that his accent was foreign and his name too. For the second time since she had forgotten how to, she wondered about something.

"Where are you from?" She tried to ask, but her voice failed her. She tried to feel her own tongue and could not. The tall foreigner turned slightly towards her and offered a cup of water. She had no strength to lift her hands and watched while he leaned even closer to pour that liquid into her mouth and she wondered if she would be able to remember what water tasted like again too.

"Of course you will, child. Drink. If you cannot taste it yet, you will feel it in other ways."

"Where?" She tried to ask, "Where will I feel it?" Still no voice emerged from her, but the tall man smiled.

"Feel," he said.

The slave felt a strange sense of being expanded.

"That is water for you," he said, "and I am from a place far north of here. I am going to start to walk back north this very night, so I have something to ask of you."

She managed to nod, relishing in the novel sense of being curious.

"Girl, you cannot stay here. And now that we have shared a private heaven with each other, I am duty-bound to save you from this fate. I have little to offer you, but for now, I have two options for you that are surely better than this joke of a life. So tell me right away, child. Do you want to die, or would you rather like to come with me?"

She regarded him, puzzled.

"I can assist you either way," he added helpfully.

She looked at all his weapons then, all sorts of weapons that he could use to save her from this life. There had been a time when she had tried hard to get a hold of such a weapon so that she could kill herself with it. There had been a time when she had tried to provoke her masters so much that they would kill her, after they had made sure to keep all sharp objects away from her. Nothing had worked. Then she had found the clouds. And suddenly, somebody had found her there.

A man like all the others, she thought, still watching him.

No. He is not like any other man, she realized.

"May I come with you now and keep the other option open for later reconsideration?" She asked, and heard her own voice speak those words out loud. The unusual man smiled again and took her hand. When she tried to stand up, it became apparent that she had no strength to stand or walk at all. The very tall man lifted her up like she weighed nothing and threw her over his shoulders, which were massive compared to his slim frame. Power seemed to exude from him, and the girl slumped there, surrendering to her fate.

It was night outside, and a full moon. In the pale moonlight she thought she saw all sorts of frightful sights, what could almost appear to be dead human bodies, writhing as if still in pain. They were all men, and she thought she could recognize some of their faces, her most recent masters, wearing terrible grimaces of pain.

She blinked her eyes. It could not be.

A wishful dream, perhaps it was, like the ones where she finally got back at them. She had known such dreams before, too, another art she had long forgotten and now suddenly rediscovered in the presence of this man. It was as if her past was coming back to her in rapid paces, just as her new master was moving incredibly fast for walking so calmly and so silently. She hardly had time to make out the gory sights.

"Where are we now?" She asked, her head hanging down behind him while she tried to adjust her eyes to the darkness, still uncertain that the terrible sights she thought she could see in the gleams of moonlight were real.

"We are in the darkest pits of Hel, obviously," Hallgrim Hidden Spear replied, "but do not worry, child. I am way-wont."

The man who knew his way around carried her hastily away from that Underworld and into the lush nearby forest.

Thus carried away by the tall stranger, the nameless Khazar slave girl hung thrown, feeling, for the first time she could ever remember, the thrill of senses awakening. The sounds, the sights, the smells and the very freshness of the open air overwhelmed her all of a sudden, and for a good while she felt dizzy. His hands closed gently around her ankles where they hung down his front and then he squeezed a certain spot above her heels and kept his fingers pressed there as he continued walking. She felt as if he was pushing waves of calm alertness into her body through that steady pressure. The dizziness faded.

She was breathing, she realized. Breathing and sensing.

He seemed to be walking endlessly through the night, and all the while she was absorbed in the constant exposure to a world she had never known, a world without humans in it, and she felt no fear at all. After a long time, he finally put her down in what appeared to have been his camp all along. It was a very small camp, and there was not another human being in sight. She was lying on a blanket, cushioned from beneath by soft moss that he had gathered before.

He pulled down a casket hung high up in a tree so as to protect the contents from prowling beasts, and from that casket he produced both meat and herbs. She lay there and watched while he made fire, cooked a soup and prepared several sorts of medicine ointments. Hallgrim fed her the soup, and with each spoonful she felt life returning to body. Their eyes met.

"What is your name, child?" He asked.

"I don't know. I don't remember," she replied and peered curiously at him. "Did you purchase me? Are you my master, now?"

"I suppose I am. I paid a bloody price for you."

"You can call me whatever you like then, Master."

"No," he said, "You shall have your name back or be nobody."

"I already am nobody," the nameless one replied.

"Then you are free," Hallgrim said.

She knew not what to say to that. When he reached his hand out to her, she took it, and realized that this time, she could stand up, albeit unsteadily. Hallgrim moved a little away from her, she noticed, and actually surprised her, not to say disappointed her, when he said, "Nameless one, you will have to take those clothes off now."

She stood and watched the dark ground before her. It had only been a dream, then, after all. The slave began obeying, but stopped herself.

"You said there was another option but to come with you, and that I could reconsider that option," she spoke slowly.

"Yes. That offer still stands," the well-armed man said.

"Then I think I shall rather accept that."

"Before you opt for swift death, do trust that I shall not touch you or employ you in any sort of service to me on this night. It is just that nobody stinks here. If I am to carry you any further or even bear to be around you. You really do need to wash. You need to put on new clothes. And you need assistance, because you can hardly stand at all, girl. I swear on all that is sacred that I am only going to assist you."

She peered suspiciously at him, but nodded and let him assist her. He carried her into a nearby stream with a natural pool. It was cold, but she sat there and felt the water enclose her. The little streams tickled her body, and his warm hands, so close when he used a sponge with foaming soap to rinse her, they took such care not to offend her even as he tended to her, and they seemed to radiate a heat that, miraculously, had the effect of calming her down and making her feel warm despite the cold water.

Then he dressed her in new clothing, soft clothing that warmed her and comforted her, the way soft clothes had always been the only thing that had ever comforted her before. He seemed to notice how she clung to the new clothes, relishing in their softness, wanting to hug the clothes back, and then he covered her body in many thick and soft blankets. She slept within a cave of soft textiles and furs, soft and harmless things that could embrace her.

It felt almost like having a mother, she imagined. When she woke at dawn, nuzzling in her deep cavern of covers arranged to protect and warm her, she saw the strange man, the one man who had ever cared for her, curled up to sleep very close to the fire, wearing no form of cover at all but his tunic.

He had even given her his cloak.

They moved north through the wild forest for days on end. On the second day, she walked a little, and with each day she walked more, became stronger, more resilient. She began copying his movements as he walked, learning how to thread silently, how to follow her feet. She watched him use his equipment and his skills to hunt and dig for roots and plants.

She began using the ointments he gave her for the purpose of treating whatever illnesses the men who had used her may have left in her, and drank his brews. At nights, he tucked her into her little fortress of covers that he carried for her all day, and slept without any cover himself. They hardly ever spoke, not more than they had to. As they moved on, the nameless girl surprised herself by her own increased interest in the surrounding world, and in the direction and goal of the crooked path that they were following.

"How far north are we going, Hallgrim Heri?" She asked one evening by their campfire, having learned his people's word for master.

"We are going to Rusiyah, to Aldeigjuborg."

"Rusiyah?" She frowned, searching her mind, that mind which, somehow, was now steadily and increasingly remembering all those forgotten things. And now she remembered that Rusiyah indeed lay north, to the furthermost end of the world, people had used to say.

"Walking?" She asked, incredulously.

"A little stroll never harmed anyone," said Hallgrim Heri.

One chilly night, he gave her a brew that made her feel drowsy at first, but after a little while it was as if her whole body relaxed so thoroughly that her mind felt calm and free. She felt the pulse of the Earth beneath her and knew why Hallgrim always called it holy. Holy Earth, he said, whenever he referred to their common mother. And out of the blissful peace of her mind streamed memories. Memories of the woman who had been her mother. She saw the woman who had once held her close better than any blankets ever could, and heard the word.

"Hallgrim," she whispered, peeking timidly out from her soft cave.

"Yes," he replied, shuddering by the fire.

"My name is Miri. I just remembered."

"Greetings, Miri."

"Greetings, Hallgrim Heri."

"Your name. Slavic or Khazar?"

"I think... I do not know, Hallgrim Heri."

"I think your name derives from Miriam. She was a sibyl of sorts, who led her people out of slavery."

"Oh," she said.

"Or else it is Slavic and means Peace."

She went quiet. Nobody had ever paid this much attention to anything that had to with her, or said such beautiful words about her true name. Now Miri watched how he was heating his hands by the fireplace and realized that her master was freezing and that it was probably not the first night that he did, without ever depriving her of her protective cave of softness.

"Hallgrim Heri, if you want to share my cover, you do not have to kill me first."

"I am very pleased to hear that," he said, but hesitated for a few moments before he shrugged and moved to settle down beside her, sharing their blankets and furs. Apart from carrying or assisting her with something, he had not touched her at all for what began to appear like weeks, and even now he kept an appropriate distance. He would not force himself on her. Miri, after a little while, curled up closer to him, and then closer, until he reached out one arm and pulled her close. He just held her there, in his arm, and she fell asleep with her face resting on his chest and did not wake until dawn.

After that, they slept together every night, and close, but Hallgrim never made a move on her. They talked more, though. He told her of his people, and taught her words all the time. She picked up quickly. He said she had a very bright mind, what nobody had ever told her before, and probably never bothered noticing either. And finally one evening he told her of what sort of life he usually had to lead. After listening to him and asking questions, she looked thoughtfully into the fire.

"What are you pondering now, little Miri?"

"I am, I am thinking of my place among you."

"Of course."

"You cannot own a slave for yourself, then?"

"No, Miri. I have to share. We can only have one."

"What sort of woman is she, then?"

"She died some time past," he said quietly. "She was a good woman. We are in need of another one. I am meeting up with my brothers very soon now. Then you can see them for yourself."

"Is this why you brought me here? So that you and your brothers can use me the way the others did?"

"I would say not at all, Miri. We would be more like your husbands, and other men than the six of us will not use you. That much I can promise, at least. That we will treat you with kindness. But of course, you will be used again. If that is not acceptable to you, I will not demand that of you. If you do not wish to be our Sheath I shall speak to my Heri, Arnulf, and ask that you can work in his Hold as a serving maid, and that you be exempt from the demands of men on account of the great damage you have suffered. That is the best I can offer you, Miri, but it will be better than what you had. Either option would."

"I can decide?"

"You do not have to decide at once," he said.

"But I can decide?"

"You will be the closest thing we ever get to have a wife," he told her, "Obviously it will not serve any of us to have a Sheath who would rather not be our woman. I dare say that a degree of mutuality never hurt in a relationship."

"A relationship. Of my choosing. My, am I moving upwards in the world," Miri giggled.

Hallgrim turned and just looked at her, astonished.

"What?" She asked testily.

"We are going to have to work a little on your manners when you move among free men, sweet Miri. I think you may be exactly the sort of wife we need." He smiled, "and I just made you giggle."

"You did," she agreed, giggling a little more.

She looked into the fire again.

"Hallgrim Heri, nobody ever gave me a choice before."

"I know. I suggest that you use it. Take your time. Get to know us. By the time we reach Aldeigjuborg, you will know, if not before."

"I will. I mean, I will use my choice. I would say you stand a good chance, at least if your brothers are similar to you. Nobody ever made me laugh, either. Nobody ever went into those clouds to find me."

"Miri. I did not save you from that place because I wanted you to be our Sheath. That is simply the only thing I have to offer you, apart from the serving maid option."

"Why did you save me, then?"

"Because you moved me."

She had not known that anybody could be moved by the likes of her.

The day after, they finally caught up with his feral-looking brothers. Miri froze to the spot when she saw them. Hallgrim may be taller than all of them, but these men were all broader and bigger in frame than he was, and one of them was positively a giant and looked somewhat mentally retarded also. When they spotted them, the men stared lustily at her, and Miri knew that her time of freedom was over. She stared into the ground and wished that Hallgrim had no brothers at all.

Knowing their customs now, she knew that she was just as much their property as she was his. Hallgrim made her stay behind while he went to talk to them, and after a brief exchange of greetings and words, she saw the men all glance at her with pity in their eyes before they looked another way and hardly even looked at her the rest of that day. They left her alone, kept out of her way, and if she encountered them closely anyway, they smiled shyly and scurried away. Not one of them approached her in the night, but she curled up in Hallgrim's arms nevertheless, feeling that he was the only thing that could ever protect her.

It surprised her that she trusted that he would, also.

They walked on north, for days on end, and Miri observed the men, listened to their speech, accepted their kindly offerings of food and drink and appreciated the distance they maintained from her. The men never used her and never made her work. She was just there. They were the strangest men she had ever met. Little by little, she relaxed, and stayed with them by the campfire at nights, listening to their stories and their songs, watching their faces and their movements. Little by little, she began liking them, especially the somewhat dull-minded giant they called Bóðvarr.

He was the sweetest thing, and one day he came up to her, shyly shuffling his feet, and offered her a giant handful of early blue berries before he hurried away, blushing. He returned to his brothers, who all peered curiously at her and smiled encouragingly, showing rows of teeth with blue berry stains all over. Miri felt as if she had just been given a wreath of flowers for her wedding gown.

One day they arrived at a beautiful and very big lake. Miri later learned that it was the Lake Ilmen. There was a full moon that night. The men undressed and bathed, and Miri watched them and wanted to bathe too. For a while, she hesitated. They were men, after all. And then she decided that if these men wanted to take her, they could do so whenever they wanted to, and yet they had not, so far. Somehow, they were giving her the impression that her opinions about them mattered to them.

Miri undressed and bathed right there with them and found that it was magic. They were seven human beings under the pale moon and the water felt like soft velvet on her skin. For the first time, she smiled at them, and they smiled back. Seven bodies made a circle beneath the Moon, reflected in the water, and their hands met.

When they came up from the water, she could well see that they were all excited, but by then she had decided, and no longer feared them. They had made camp by that beach before bathing, and there they sat by the fireplace, and it was as if she really woke up for the first time. She talked to the men. Miri found that she had started to understand their words, although Hallgrim could speak to her in Khazarian. She sang with them, and they told her that she had a beautiful voice. After having shared laughter together, the men went a little quiet.

"Miri," Hallgrim said, "we would like to know how you feel about things. There is still time, we can wait a little more for you, but here by Lake Ilmen there is a slave market, and if you are as yet uncertain if you want to be our Sheath, we may have to purchase another one tomorrow, before we get home."

Miri looked from one to the other, meeting all their gazes. They returned her gaze with looks of fondness. They like me, she thought. She wondered what there was to like about her, but then of course, there was always that thing which men liked anyway, as far as she had experienced. She glanced briefly at Hallgrim and then at sweet Bóðvarr's partly innocent look of happy expectation.

"I cannot promise that I will actually enjoy it," she began, "but I am quite certain that I will not mind it. If we reach that market tomorrow, I suppose this night would be a good time to test it out." The five other men brightened up, but Hallgrim looked searchingly at her. There was a question in his eyes. Her heart warmed at the realization that he really wanted to be certain that she agreed. But having been a slave all her life, Miri could not resist milking such opportunities.

"If I can have as much drink as I feel like drinking, I will take all six of you on right away," she declared generously and glanced suggestively towards the barrel of strong mead that the men had purchased from a small village they had passed the other day. She had wondered why they did not open it right away, and now she suspected that they already knew exactly how to tempt her. Miri set up a strict face and folded her arms.

"After the drinking, mind you," she demanded sternly.

Her House-Bonds-to-be laughed heartily and opened the barrel.

They had drunk a great deal, and there had been the bonding ritual, where the men were formally united as brothers in her, their vessel. Then a bed had been made out by the southern end of the fireplace with some covers making out a sort of half-tent.

Miri sat there and watched the men doing all the work while she drank to her heart's content and then how they sat down expectantly around the fire and resumed their drinking too. Their new Sheath could not resist testing them a little, and sat there a while longer. Nothing happened. Miri sighed.

"A girl has got to do everything herself in this place," she grunted, and made her House-Bonds laugh again. Miri had not lifted a finger to work all the while they had been with her. They looked at her with those fond gazes again, growing fonder each time. Her men had laughed a lot this evening, and she discovered that she liked to make them laugh.

Miri got up with a demonstrative, disdainful snort that sent them into yet new fits, and went into the tent cover.

In there, she swiftly removed her clothes and lied down. She tried to feel for the peace, but found none. Her heart skipped a beat when the first man entered, but she relaxed at once when she could see that it was Hallgrim.

"By order of rank, I gather," she remarked, trying to keep up the joking tone, and her First House-Bond nodded to confirm. Hallgrim was still distributing his weapons. She knew he did not want a slave's help with that. Then, still without taking off his clothes, he lay down next to her and gently covered her body up with a blanket. Then he put another over the first, and then a third to top it. He put six blankets around his Sheath and smiled at her. She was snuggling within all that softness again, starting to feel safe. It moved her, that they had made sure to put all the soft blankets there, in her bed. She turned to look at him. They were laying on their sides, face to face.

Miri was not used to this sort of thing.

When they had thus been studying each other for a while, Miri cleared her throat and said, "So, Hallgrim Heri, my previous owners always told me that I was a lousy whore. I usually just passed out, as you may recall."

"I recall that, Miri," he said, but somehow did not laugh this time.

"I will make an effort in your case," she promised, with some effort, "Only you cannot expect me to know what you want and how you want it, really, and as I said, I was always too lousy a whore to learn how. You have to tell me."

"What sort of point are you trying to make, Miri?"

"Well, you must tell me what position you want, what hole, all that."

"Miri, you are not a lousy whore anymore," he said mildly

"Oh, I doubt I shall ever be good at it," she snorted.

"You are not a whore at all."

"What am I now then?"

"You are our Miri, our woman, our hearth."

Miri went quiet.

"Miri," he said after a while of silence, a silence that oddly enough had seemed to be bridging a gap between them.

"You are a courageous woman," he said.

She just frowned.

"Your kind, Miri, you who are lower than the lowest of all, your kind walk naked and unarmed and defenseless through this world, and yet you walk. Yet you keep walking. Miri, brave she-slave; you have walked through the darkness of darkness itself and you still know who you are, and you care not to hide it. You fear nothing."

"I fear losing you if I do not comply," she whispered.

"I know, child, and I am sorry. Even I am not free. Miri..."

Then he began touching the skin of her cheek very tenderly. His fingers seemed to be searching for her, for Miri, his woman, his hearth. Nobody had touched her like that before.

Miri went quiet for a moment before she cut short her story, "I was so used to drifting off as soon as a man touched me that I almost did. But Hallgrim knew how to reach me in that world, and after he had, I did not leave my body to be in the clouds. I was right there with them and met their eyes and held them. I could not yet enjoy it the way I now do, but I did not mind it, and I was present. They were kind to me, very gentle. It took a long time before I could truly enjoy it, but when I did, I did. I even like it when they are not so very gentle now."

She looked at Zivah. "I loved these men eventually. I have loved them for seven years. It was only the last two years that were a bit harsh on me, seeing as Bóðvarr died and Hialti took his place. I feel like Tziki does. They are my men, just as I am theirs. They are my companions and my friends and my lovers. I have never known a better life than this, Zivah. Many of us women here never have. I became alive for the first time when I came among these men."

Zivah met Miri's eyes.

"It sounds like they choose women who come from worse places," she suggested uncertainly, and the others smiled and nodded.

"Of course," Miri said, "Of course they do. They are not stupid. They know that they have to choose women who can appreciate what they have to offer compared to what we might have had before. That is the only way this is going to work. If you were to be picked as their Sheath, you would have suffered. But I think you can see, now, my friend, that we do not suffer. I think you can see now that we feel as if we have been rescued and given a good life."

"I can see that now," Zivah said and looked sad.

"Now, Zivah," Miri said, "Why are you so hateful towards Thióðolf Heri? I heard that he rescued you too."

"Rescued me? I do not see it that way at all," Zivah said, "As far as I am concerned he made a slave out of me."

"No, he did not," Miri said, "It was Arnulf Heri what made a slave out of you."

"Then Thióðolf did," Zivah said, "He did not exactly free me, after I was given to him."

"He could not free you even if he wanted to," Aziza volunteered. "Firstly because you were a gift to him and he could not scorn a gift from his Heri, and secondly because there is no other way to keep you safe in this place."

"Thirdly because he wanted to own me," Zivah said ironically. "Only my sister came in his way, did she not? Now he is stuck with me. I do not know for how long he is going to put up with this. I keep expecting to be given over to some other man any day. Or that he finally rapes me, seeing as that is his right. Why else would he keep a slave girl?"

"Honestly, Zivah, do you really think so? Are you not able to see what a good man he is?" Aziza asked. All the others nodded in agreement and looked expectantly at Zivah. Her tears began to run and she shook her head determinedly and spoke.

"I cannot see that, no. Not from where I stand. All I see is a pirate and a killer who partook in the destruction of my people and who beat me in the market place and made me kneel in front of everybody to say sorry because of that stupid dress! He was leading me in a tow around my neck like a cow. He and Arnulf had planned to take me right there in the bath on the first evening, after he had beaten me, but when I started to cry they stopped, probably because of Thordís. But later, he was just about to rape me that first night when Thordís stopped him. He had thought she was sleeping and put her in another bed. Why would I ever like him? I despise him. I cannot help but despise him and hate him. Oh, there is more. Before all that, he had let me think that he was going to save me and treat me well and keep me safe and take care of me. When I tried to show him that I appreciated that and liked him well, he told me to call him Heri and bow my head and said he would strike me if I showed my anger. Then there was all the rest. He gave me hope and took it away so viciously. I do not think I can ever forgive it."

"I believe you misunderstood the matter in the bath, at least," Aziza said gently, "They were not going to take you there in the bath. They just wanted to bathe. They thought perhaps you would like to get a bath too, since you were, well, you were covered in blood when you came here, and you were clearly exhausted. They were just trying to be nice."

"Arnulf had his Freystone ready," Zivah sobbed at the memory.

"I would try that one out any time!" Suri declared, generating a boost of laughter around the table and a deal of head-nodding and grinning. I was quite relieved to realize that I was not the only one who was impressed by that one. It was confusing the way people always laughed when I tried to talk about it, but apparently this was the common thing to do when speaking of such matters, especially if I was the one who spoke of them.

"Arnulf always has that one ready, Zivah, but it was not meant for you. They just don't mind being naked in front of others, surely you must understand that now," Aziza said. Zivah gazed uncertainly at them. Aziza smiled and nodded to her to let her know it was the truth. They really had not planned to rape her in the bath.

"As to the noose, that was a way of protecting you. If you had not been noosed, anybody else could have noosed you instead. The men feared that their enemies would do such a thing just to provoke them. You see, if anyone had noosed you, it would have been a lawful claim and nobody could have saved you then. Thióðolf had to noose you and then he had to have you collared lest you be fair game in this place, Zivah. He had no choice. If you had looked at him when you first came into court that day, you would have seen how embarrassed he was about the whole thing," Laimi explained.

"Embarrassed enough to beat me, it seems," Zivah snorted dismissively.

"Zivah," Miri said and put an arm around her shoulders, "I think you have completely misunderstood what happened back then."

"What is there to misunderstand? He beat me and humiliated me before the whole town just because I did not accept his gift."

"Yes, he did, because if he had not, then the town council would have devised far worse punishment for you, Zivah. Did you not hear his story of the Eastern Princess?"

"I did not. Not properly anyway," Zivah said and shook her head again.

"We all heard about it. The insolent slave girl who threw her master's gift onto the ground. Are you aware of what they would have done to you if your Heri had not saved you?"

"Saved me?"

"He saved your life, Zivah. Do you know the law here? If a slave is insolent to her master in front of other men and slaves, the City Council has the right to demand public punishment, and there would have been nothing he could have done to help you."

"What kind of punishment?" My sister whispered.

"Public flogging, mostly. You would have been flogged to death. For a pretty girl like you. You might as well have been raped by a hundred men in the marketplace just to make an example of what happens to pretty slaves who disrespect their superiors, and then they would likely have flogged you anyway."

Zivah stared at her. Miri nodded gravely to her and continued, "Your House-Bond saved you. He made quite a speech about how you were the captured princess of an eastern kingdom who had never known slavery before, and because of your royal status you had difficulties understanding just how low you had come in life. They could sympathize with that, Zivah. He spoke so well for you that they let it pass. It was hardly to be believed, but they let it pass. They didn't believe a word of it, of course, but they thought the story was so good they let it pass anyway."

Zivah looked a bit uncertain, but had not yet quite grasped the core of the issue. All she could remember was that terrible moment when Thióðolf had broken what little trust she had left in him.

"He beat me!" She cried, "He beat me and humiliated me in front of everyone!"

"Of course he beat you," Miri said, "He had to. If he had not given you at least a little humiliation they would have craved a lot more. He beat you to save your life, Zivah. It was the only thing he could have done to help you out of that situation. That, and the speech. You would never have gotten away with it without both."

Zivah went silent for a while.

"Did you not understand his speech? I thought you understood the language quite well even from the start," Aziza said.

"I did not hear it. I just waited for him to kill me. I was not capable of hearing anything. There was just a lot of buzzing in my ears." She pondered a little and looked uncertainly from one to the other. "Are you saying that Thióðolf really saved me?"

They all nodded solemnly and Zivah broke out in a fit of sobs and tears. Laimi and Miri reached out for her and held her while she cried.

"What am I going to do?" She finally asked, looking horrified, "I have been terrible to him! I mean, as terrible as I can be, being a slave." One of the other Sheaths looked as if she was about to speak, but Aziza stopped her, "Zivah, you have gotten this far, and now you know that he is not quite as horrible as you have thought. In his mind, you are now honing him, and he loves that as they always do, so I advise you to take it little by little."

"What do you mean, honing him?"

"Zivah dear, he likes you, and he is really sorry about what happened, and he would like to make it up to you. He needs to prove his worth to you, and he does not expect you to go easy on him, not even now that you are seeing him in a different light. My advice now is that you only open up little by little. Play with him a while, until you both feel that he has earned your trust again.

Don't make it easy on him now just because you know better than you did before that he is not a bad man. You already started. Allow him to prove himself to you. He is a Norseman and they are all about proving their worth to women. Even to slave women. Let him suffer a little more. Test him, challenge him. Ease up little by little. He will love you for making it difficult. Just mind the courtesies."

"Oh, I see," Zivah said, brightening up, clearly understanding the game of honing in her heart, if not with her mind. She was a woman after all. But after some thought she started to shake her head again, the way she often did when there was something she just could not accept.

"I still cannot, I still think these men are very strange," she said, "Even if he may not be so bad, he is still a Norseman and, these people are so ruthless. Now when I live here, I often find myself liking them, but then I think of what I saw them do out there, what they did..."

Miri slapped her face lightly, and Zivah blinked in surprise.

"Zivah, Zivah sweet sister, this life is your fate. Why do you struggle so hard against it? It will do you no good now. They are your men now, whether you wished it so or not. Accept that, and you will find peace of mind. Then you might see what a gift fate has given you in the midst of all your grief. Try to see them and know them for what they are. See them, Zivah, see them and then you will learn to like them also."

Miri looked intently at the amber-eyed girl.

"They live in songs and stories, Zivah. They go into one song and play one part there, and then they go into another song and play another part. They are like dreamers. They just go along with the story. It does not matter what story it is, they must always do their best and play their part fully. They think it is their fate and that it is their sacred duty to simply act their given part as well and thoroughly as they can, always."

The slaves of the court nodded thoughtfully, as one.

"I think they are crazy," Zivah whispered.

"It is the truth you speak," Miri laughed. "They are absolutely mad!"

All the slaves began laughing hard again, both women and men. Even Shumayl laughed, I noticed, and nobody minded me, even though I surely belonged to the crowd of mad masters.

I thought it was perfectly reasonable to think of life in terms of stories and songs. If that notion amused them so, we had surely entertained them well and made a good story. Thus I did not mind their laughter. As if to confirm my reasoning, when the laughter subsided, Miri leaned over and patted Zivah's back reassuringly.

"Our men may be utterly insane, sister," the seasoned Sheath grinned, and winked at Zivah, "but they are never, ever boring."

NIGHT OF THE MOTHERS

Three days after the Winter Solstice, the reborn Sun Maiden had grown to such strength that people could see how the day became longer, and Yule was about to end, giving way to a new year. When Zivah inquired about the Yule celebrations, she was told that everybody now knew that great Thor had succeeded in his mission to save the golden goddess from the wolf's belly, strengthened by the Holy Communion where men came together as one in the maiden's vessel.

This had been the purpose of the Solstice ceremony where little Thordís had done such a great job as a priestess. Now, Zivah was told, the norns had been moved by the Thunderer's courage and by the dedication of the people, the Kindly Ladies moved by their joint efforts to spin yet another turn of the year-wheel. That was, apparently, not something anyone could take for granted, and there were countless other rituals that had to be made to secure the continued workings of the Ladies of the Loom.

For such reasons, during the sacred nights of Yule, the men had gone to various banquets outside of court and participated in ceremonies and sacrifice to celebrate and strengthen both the goddess reborn and the hero who had rescued her from the darkness. The slaves were not told anything directly, but Zivah heard of Thor's grove and the grove of the She-Bear. When Thordís had cautiously asked if she could join them, by way of mentioning her desire casually while they were around, the men had failed to shrug and pretend they did not hear it, which would have meant yes, but had instead turned directly to the girl and said no.

She was too young to join the sacrifice, they said, and there were mysteries transpiring yet not for her eyes. The girl was a little disappointed with that, but Zivah heard the men speak of the Hel Rune and the Mare and the Seven Sisters, and could well understand that a little girl may not be ready for whatever these women tended to do during rituals. As far as she knew, they performed human sacrifice and they had also been responsible for Hialti's rather grisly end.

Listening to the speech of the men after, she heard that the Very Gentle Ladies had been lustful as always, but also unusually ferocious and not at all kindly, and that the Atonement had gone down particularly ungracefully. The men looked very relieved at that. Zivah frowned and shook her head dismissively, not quite grasping the point of their riddle-speech. All in all, she thought, the truth kept confirming itself; Norsemen were crazy. She had to smile just a little at the thought, seeing as it was also true that the insanity of their masters kept their slaves well entertained.

After the Solstice she had been told to make an easily destructible image of her departed mother or other ancestral mothers. Everybody did the same. All through the Yule-tide, men and women, slave and free, had been making little figures out of any kind of destructible material from straw to baking dough, representing their ancestral mothers. The figures had to be destructible because they had to be destroyed three days after the celebration, so as to no longer channel their fateful power in such concentration as they had to be channeled during the three-night-long turn of the spindle.

The celebration of the mothers was not an alien concept to Zivah at all. Mother had kept a shrine in honor of all the Healers who had gone before her. Not quite unlike the Norse approach, where they believed that the spirits of ancestral mothers were still with their descendants, following them and steadily inferring with the runes and threads of their fates. She heard spoken that they were called the woman Followers who walk beside us, as opposed to the animal Followers who walk before us or the woman Followers who spin fate from within. Apparently, these ancestral woman Followers were in league with the norns, and fate worked through them as they interfered with the threads of fate while their people walked through life.

"Arnulf told me that it is important to honor the mother Followers and seek their counsel," Aziza explained, "lest they teach us by honing us the hard way, carving twisted runes into our fate's wood."

It was hard to start this sort of work, Zivah found, and then she saw her little sister approaching, looking glum and sad. They sat together for a while, and suddenly they began talking about Mother for the first time since she died. For so long, all Zivah had been able to remember when she thought of Mother was the way her face had been smashed in by that axe and how she had been smelling and feeling her blood on her dress all the way until they reached Aldeigjuborg.

Now the two sisters remembered everything their wise and gentle mother had been and done and said, and were soon laughing and crying at the same time. Then they decided to continue memorizing the life and teachings of their mother the Healer while working on recreating her image. They made a doll out of straw and textile and created that image together, like true sisters. They wept while they worked, talked and repeated words of wisdom that Mother had spoken to them both. Finally they sat there with a beautiful doll with golden straw hair and looked reverently at her. She would be Mother and all the mothers before her too, the river land sisters' contribution to the New Year Earth shrine.

Thióðolf approached when they had finished working and grieving. Zivah bowed her head and pretended indifference as before while he admired their work.

"It is a beautiful image of your mother," he said and looked thoughtfully at Thordís. "Wolfling, do you not wish to also honor your clan's mother, the first Thordís? Is she not the great divine Follower of your Thunder Priest lineage?"

"Thióðolf," the girl spoke slowly, "there can be no other images of her, than me."

Then she appeared troubled, excused herself and walked off, leaving Zivah alone with him. Thióðolf looked puzzled, astonished even, and turned to Zivah, who could see no way of getting away from him without being rude.

"Did you understand that comment at all, Zivah?" He asked.

"Yes, Heri," she muttered, "Father, her father, Thorbjörn, said that she was the first Thordís reborn," and when he looked eager to hear more, she added, "He said that her rebirth had been prophesied. The maiden was born with all the signs of who she really is."

"What sorts of signs?" He asked, sounding urgent.

"Uhm, the prophecy said that the ancient Thunder Priestess would be reborn during a thunder storm as the ninth and only living daughter of her father with a woman from the east, and seven days before the Summer Solstice, when the lineage had reached an end. He said she would be carrying the mark of Thor above her heart and that she would possess the eyes of a she-wolf. Thordís was born with all those signs. He said she was the first and the last of their line."

She peered up at him briefly and noticed how his eyes widened a little at her words, and she saw there was awe in his gaze as he knew her words for truth. Before he could meet her eyes, she quickly lowered hers again. His eyes were so very deep blue and so very soulful.

Sincere, she thought, he is very sincere.

"I see," he said, "Thank you, Zivah, you have given me great tidings today. And it really is a very beautiful doll you made there. But I am sure your mother was also very beautiful, seeing as how lovely both her daughters have turned out. You have a good eye for making lovely things. I would have liked for you to make me a new tunic one day, perhaps from that fabric I already gave you more than a Moon circle past," then he walked off too. Zivah looked at the doll, smiling to herself. They said a suggestion from her Heri meant the same as a command, only not quite as urgent and with the intention of familiarity. Nobody else had heard his masked order, so he would have no other excuse to punish her than his own pride.

She would gladly dare him. There would be no tunic for him yet. If challenges were what the warrior wanted, he would get it. If it was not, why, then he would reveal what sort of man he really was. That was good honing.

For the night celebration, all the warriors now moved into Arnulf's house, crowding it. Where the Solstice had happened in the men's Hall and the ritual had been centered on the men, the New Year celebration had to happen in the Hold, and the ritual was now centered on the women. To Zivah's surprise the entire Hold went into something they called Contrary mode, when the rules were replaced with what they referred to as "the other sorts of rules."

A bunch of crazies, they were, but they made her laugh. The women, even though they were all slaves, sat down around the table while the men, most of whom were free, stood behind. She had thought that such table-turning was a very secret and hidden custom happening at night when the lord of the court could not see it, but now it was happening in the open and everybody seemed to expect it, even Arnulf Heri. Even more surprising, the men started to attend the women, serving them drink and food. She looked cautiously at Miri, who smiled and shrugged, suggesting that she just relax and enjoy this rare treat. Zivah almost startled when Hallgrim served beer to her and called her Freyia.

"This is a night where womanly powers are honored," Thióðolf spoke, being the skald of the court and the one to speak forth during most ceremonies. He seemed to notice that Zivah was confused, and continued speaking as if the words of explanation were a part of the ceremony.

"No human ranking system matter to the ladies who whisper verdicts to us from the shores of Hel," he said, "they who pass their judgments on our conducts from within the dark womb of holy Earth. Slave or free it does not matter. The womb-carriers channel these powers. The womb-carriers must be honored as vessels through which norns speak of sacred laws. This night all women are sacred, and must be honored."

"Alu," the men agreed, and the slave girls beamed and accepted the offerings with relish. Arnulf placed an old clay Earth Mother figurine at the middle of the table.

"All hails to Earth, the great and the powerful," Thióðolf chanted, and everybody called out the same words, creating a chorus of refrains as he continued chanting. "Ancient mother of all the worlds' lineages; we honor you and we greet you on this sacred night. You raise all life and take all life back into your sacred womb. You are Death and Life and Fate. We know you as Life Struggle. We know you as Leaf Island. We know you as the Ship of Freyia. We know you as the Origin. We know you as the keeper of the sacred mead. We know you as the mother of gods and men. We know you as the Replenishing Goddess, who revives all life, spinner of the Flax and weaver of the Linen, and the rune-carving Hand. May the spindle turn and new fate be spoken forth from out of your ancient ocean cave, the Hall of Freyia, the Hall of Hel.

Yours is the cauldron of inspiration, yours is this world of songs. We honor the great songs born out of your darkest and deepest well, we honor the words and the verses and lead sacred lives within the great story woven and sung and carved into the Tapestry of Destiny. May you turn the spindle and be fruitful once more and bestow your countless sacred blessings upon us. May you flourish in the embrace of the high gods. May your formidable birth-giving power increase and fill us all with new life."

He paused for a moment before he chanted the incantation, "Holy, holy, holy is Earth, holy the mother of men! We, your descendants, honor you and greet you."

"Holy, holy, holy is Earth, holy the mother of men! We, your descendants, honor you and greet you," the chorus chanted.

Then they all placed the images of their mothers, grandmothers and Followers around the Earth mother figurine. The table had become an altar for the time being and would remain so for three days, until the images had to be destroyed and the powers freed. Sweets were offered to the Mothers, sweets and mead and beer placed in their laps, and all the slave girls seemed to glow with pleasure at the unusual reverence paid to them. The Norsemen referred to all offerings as Atonement. Zivah had a feeling that this table-turning was a sort of atonement too.

Being the highest ranking female in the court, despite being a child, Thordís was placed in the High Seat, and cushions had been placed there to allow her to sit higher and make her appear a little more like a proper House-Freyia. Arnulf came to stand next to her and spoke to the table.

"I speak now to honor the great mothers who have brought us together in this court, and who were in turn brought together by this court's great protector, the Follower soul of my grandmother, whose name was Bera, the She-Bear. We will remember Bera on this night, as we will remember all our mothers."

Arnulf made a sweeping gesture that seemed to embrace all the people of his court, "All of you, household and warriors, have been uprooted, taken from your homes, and many of you do not even know where you come from. I know that there are those among you, both slaves and warriors, who have never even known their mothers."

Many of the slaves began to weep, and Zivah noticed that several warriors' faces were also wet, although men seemed to sob less than women on a general basis. Tears streamed, and that was more important than sobbing. Arnulf respectfully waited until the last sobs appeared to have ceased, and until the men had dried their faces before he continued, "but all of you have been able to create an image of a mother or ancestral mother whom you know in your heart is your Follower in this life, and so we can honor them all.

If we had been a clan of the homelands, we would have shared our mothers, we would have honored the same Followers. But we have come from many different places, and so we must make our mothers come together, and create our own clan."

Arnulf placed his giant paw to support the shoulders of his Síf.

"There is no clan without Sífs, and no clan without a Freyia," Arnulf spoke ceremoniously. "Women are the vessels that carry the clan's united power. This night we also honor Thordís Maiden. Here, see our Síf seated high! Here, see our sacred vessel! Our little Freyia has made us into something more than a Viking band. She has made of us a clan."

There was an awed silence as everybody's gazes moved to rest on Thordís, who had gone a deep red and looked like she wished she could sink through the High Seat all of a sudden.

"I have heard that our Síf is of sacred and prophesied birth," Arnulf said. "I have heard that she carries within the soul of an ancient goddess, a woman, a priestess who started a lineage of great and legendary renown thousands of years past. Their women knew the Red Gold of the Thunder Lord, and had the power to hone men into Thunder warriors. So, the men of her clan were Thunder warriors, great powerful men what channeled the power of Thunder. Invincible they were in battle."

"Our Síf is the first Thunder Priestess, reborn as the last, chosen by the lord Thor, the last of her great and noble lineage. Now she has come here to us, to the Rus, to a people uprooted, to us men who have lost our Sífs and lived long without anything that might unite us and make us great. For so long, we Væringjar have been little more than bandits. But just as Bera showed the way to Aldeigjuborg, so Thordís keeps lighting the path, and I spy openings in the great song of Rus. We Rus come from all sorts of tribes. We have been lawless men, clustering together because we have had no other options. Now I can see the creation of a tribe. I see the creation of a people, beginning with restoring this court to the state of a proper clan. We honor the Thunder Goddess, in whose power it is to make of us a clan, a tribe, a nation. That is our hope, a small seed of hope; yet to be planted, yet to unfold."

All the men stared at Thordís, expectant, and the girl looked rather shocked, obviously not prepared for this sort of approach on this evening. The maiden looked helplessly at Zivah and then at Thióðolf, and Zivah noticed that her master also looked a little worried. Even Hallgrim frowned for a moment. Arnulf smiled and ignored their worried looks, as if he had expected nothing else for now.

"Now let us celebrate the mother who did establish this town of Aldeigjuborg, this town of the Rus," he said, raising his voice, "She was my father's mother, and her name was Bera. Grandmother Bera was a she-bear in maiden's form.

She lived in a small fishing village off the coast of Svíthióð. She had no lineage to speak of, but she was a daughter of the land, and her heart was that of a she-bear, and hers a valkyria soul. She was a great blade honer!"

He looked round, certain that everybody's attention was on him and his story, "When Bera was young, Vikings came to her village and raided it. Bera was taken with other young women, and brought into the ship of the Sea King. The ship was a part of a fleet that had been ruled by Sea Kings for many generations. The Sea Kings were powerful captains who owned large fleets of ships. They had become great kings in their own right, even as they had no land but Aegir's hills, and no halls but Rán's steeds. Theirs was a moving land. Theirs were the ocean waves and the river streams. They were Vikings, who lived by theft and raids. They were hard and ruthless men, the men who stole Bera from her home and made a slave out of her. Cold-hearted, cruel and of little honor. And she was a beautiful woman, Bera. The young woman was sent from man to man, to be used by all the men aboard the Sea King's ship."

The women around the table shivered collectively.

"Bera did not cry and wail like other women do," Arnulf said proudly. "Bera maintained a queenly stance even as she yielded to the men who claimed her. She met their gazes and she talked to them. She knew each one of them and looked into their souls. Bera made them treasure her, for she knew no fear, and knew that dishonor could only happen if she herself allowed it. So, what had begun as rape became libation, and the men knew her for a goddess. When Bera yielded to the Vikings, she became their queen. They strove to please her, where before they had thought her there to please them. She made them feel loved, and they began to love her back. Their cold hearts thawed in her embrace. Freyia's power ran through Bera's veins."

Zivah felt her spine chill as she heard the story of Arnulf's fearless grandmother. She recalled her time on the Viking ship and wondered how any woman could ever have had that sort of courage. It seemed as if Arnulf thought that the men who had taken his grandmother were far worse than he and his own men had ever been. Then she noticed that everybody was looking at Thordís again with a particular sort of expression. Oh gods, she thought, oh gods.

They think that Thordís is just like Bera. They were right. She suddenly knew it. Thordís would have done what Bera did. Zivah knew not how she knew, but she just knew it for truth, as did all the others. Even Thordís herself seemed to realize that she was exactly like Bera, and blushed a little where she sat, lowering her eyes to their verdict on her. How could that sort of thing even work?

How could they revere a woman that they had all raped and humbled and made utterly powerless? The simple conclusion that they were crazy just did not suffice anymore. Thunder Bear's voice seemed to echo through her mind all of a sudden, some of his last words to her providing the answer: These people respect nothing apart from self-respect. No matter how humiliated you feel – if you can maintain your self-respect, they will respect you, even in your humiliation, even in your helplessness.

Arnulf looked proudly at Thordís before he continued his tale of the She-Bear, "When they reached the place in the east where they were to sell the slaves, no man aboard the Sea King's ship could bear to part with Bera. She had moved freely on the ship, and brought light and love into the hardened hearts of men. The Sea King himself treasured her, and she was crowned the Sheath of the Hall, even if the hall in question was a ship." Everybody looked at the Sheaths of the Hall, who all beamed with pride now, knowing that they carried the same title as the court's Follower, who was practically a goddess.

Their men seemed to pick up on the same and suddenly they all roared proudly, "All hails to the Sheaths of our Hall!"

The women's tears flowed freely.

"Now Bera became pregnant, and the men knew that her child was theirs. They did not wish their child to be born a slave, and so they freed Bera and asked her to be their Freyia. Bera loved her men, and accepted the charge. She bore a son on a stormy night, off the shores of Finland, a strong and healthy boy with reddish hair and blue eyes. The seed of the Sea King had conquered the seed of all the men who had honored Bera's sacred hall, for the boy was made in his image. Now, the name of that Sea King was Arn, after the eagle that was his Follower what flew before him. Yet the boy could not take the name of the Sea King, for he was the son of all the men aboard the ship. That is the way of the Sheath. But since everybody also knew the truth, they called him the Sea King's son. His first name was Arnsteinn, the Stone of the Eagle."

The men grinned at the pun in Arnsteinn's name, knowing that it really referred to his father Arn's Freystone, and then they roared, "Hail to Arn's Stone, the Sea King's son!" Everybody laughed at that.

"Bera and Arnsteinn went with the Vikings on all their journeys. Bera and her son would often stand at the prow, and the boy would ride the neck of the dragon," Arnulf proceeded, and everybody looked at Thordís again, who blushed. She could not possibly have known to what perfection she had indeed played her role when she first came among these men. Zivah recalled words spoken before, words that her father had spoken to his daughter, her sister, words that she had secretly listened to and partly understood.

She knew that her sister would always know how to move among powerful men. She was guided by that men's hammer, perhaps, the one what carried the memories of her ancestral fathers - men of power who knew what made men like themselves move to action.

"Arnsteinn grew strong and healthy, and like all boys who grow up among Vikings, he became a ferocious warrior even before he reached full manhood. He grew big and he grew strong, and the only thing he ever feared was his mother Bera's verdicts."

"All hails to Bera, the greatest of Sea Queens!" The men roared proudly, as if fearing the verdicts of their mothers more than any other thing was perfectly within the range of proper manly honor. Zivah found that somewhat hard to believe. Arnulf continued, "The town of Aldeigjuborg was yet but a small settlement in those days. Vikings, shunned by the homelands, and with good reason, would go here to stay on land for a while, without the harassment of kings' fleets and armies to force them onto ever new adventures. From here they could enter the River Lands, or reach down to the great places of the world where men know how to build great cities, yet must, inevitably, lose touch with their warrior souls. Now Bera began to grow weary. She was a woman, after all, and when she asked her son to build her a house in Aldeigjuborg and set men there to guard her, Arnsteinn obeyed, for all men must honor their mothers."

"All hails to the mothers!" The men roared again. It really was true.

"So this court was built to honor the Freyia of Vikings. She was the first to own these halls," Arnulf said, glowing with pride now, making a sweeping gesture to indicate the Hold they sat in. "From here she began to work with trading, having a skill for it that her menfolk lacked, and so she gained even more respect, for she made this house prosperous. The town grew around it, and all men knew that Bera the Sea Queen was its first mother. She is not only the Follower of this court. She is the Follower of Aldeigjuborg. She was the first Rus-woman. She has become our divine Follower, the goddess of the Rus. In the Grove of the She-Bear, we still honor her, as all citizens do." The men nodded solemnly, and Zivah understood where they had been all day. Before the Night of the Mothers, every Norseman in town had gone to Bera's grove to honor her memory, for she was the founder of Aldeigjuborg. Arnulf must be a very powerful man here, being her grandson, she pondered.

"Arnsteinn married a woman abducted off the island of Burgundarholm. When Bera saw the girl, she said to Arnsteinn that this was the wife for him, for she saw in the girl's soul song her own soul's likeness. The Burgund girl's name was Tyra, for she had been marked by lord Týr, and true to her name, victory always followed her. She was my mother."

"All hails to Tyra of Burgundarholm!" The men roared.

"Tyra was a large and beautiful woman, born to match my father, Arnsteinn the Sea King's son. She and Bera convinced the Rus to stop raiding women from the homelands, and to attempt more friendly relations with folks there. We have prospered from that decision. We have reached a point where even a very high-born nobleman from the northernmost parts of North Path Island will visit our court and live among us."

Everybody looked at Thióðolf and smiled amiably at him, and he looked just a little inconvenienced, smiling and shrugging. He looked a little shy, she thought. It was sweet. She had not known that he was but a visitor from the homelands either. Or that he was a nobleman for that matter.

Now that she heard about it, the many subtle and sometimes even obvious differences between him and all the other men seemed to explain themselves. He really was different because he was from a different place. She had noticed how he also had a different accent.

"Where Arnsteinn, my father, was hard and ruthless, Tyra, my mother, was mild and just," Arnulf continued. "She gave birth to me and to my sister, Guðrún. My dear sister died a year after young Ivarr was born to her, and so she is also honored today among our Holy Mothers. Seven years have passed since our last Síf died. We have not had a Síf in this house since then, not until now, and we have missed them sorely. I grew up in this court with my mother, my sister and my grandmother, she-bears all, and they all honed me into the man I am." Arnulf raised his drinking horn, "I greet my mother Tyra, and I greet my grandmother Bera, and I greet my sister Guðrún. I hail their memory, for they were great women, and they made me a man, and honed sharp my soul's blade!"

"All hails to the blade honers!" The men roared.

The first speech was finished.

Ivarr was the second to speak. The boy looked shy too, and tried hard to keep his voice even as he spoke, "Guðrún, Týra's daughter and Bera's granddaughter, was my mother. I cannot remember her, for she died when I was but a year old. Good Freydís fostered me for the next two years, and after that I have been raised by men. But I honor mother Guðrún, and wish that I can one day avenge the slights against her, offered by Gunnarr Beak-Nose, who was her House-Bond, yet not my father, thanks be to the norns. All hails to Guðrún!"

While the men cheered Guðrún, Zivah looked curiously at Ivarr, wondering who his father was. Then Hallgrim patted the boy's back affectionately after he had spoken, and she had a clue already. Now everybody took turns saying the name of their mothers, supported by the roars of the men who always hailed each name that was spoken. When the turn came to her mother, Thordís stood up and touched the doll that represented the Healer who had descended from the Old River People.

"This is an image of my mother, and Zivah's," she began, "I cannot speak her name, for she was a healer, and among her people, the healer gave up her name and was called only Healer. But she was our mother, and she was a she-bear as well, who protected her daughters with her life. She was a wise woman and highly respected among her people, and she taught us how to shoot with a bow and how to mend wounds, both of the body and of the soul."

Zivah wept when their mother was hailed, and there was a moment then when she suddenly felt as if she was actually a part of that clan Arnulf claimed was about to be made. Everybody, free and slave, seemed to think the same thing. There was a great uniting power in the Mothers' Night. Then she noticed that Hallgrim was peering curiously at her. When she met his glance briefly, he just nodded thoughtfully to her, what only left her mystified. Then the banquet began, and the men brought out all the food and drink, and soon enough the Hold was a merry place.

Other kinds of rules were abroad on this night, and the Sheaths of the Hall saw an opportunity to sit and chat with Aziza, Laimi and Zivah, since no man had the right to claim any of them this night, unless they wanted it. It was the same with the serving maids, but seeing as they slept in the Hold at nights and were busy working through the days, they were not taken so often that they wanted to miss the opportunity to choose their own man.

For once, it was the men who stood passive and waited until a girl nudged him and made him walk away with her, eager to please her, what caused a great deal of amusement and happy and lewd songs all around the house. Zivah thought this an odd way of celebrating the Holy Mothers, remembering the sacral songs and rather more serious processions and grave-faced reverence paid to the mothers from back home. It was very hard to grasp that these people really thought that all sorts of beastly rutting was actually sacred, but that was the truth and Zivah had only just begun to figure it out.

She wondered what other sorts of sacred ceremonies these men engaged in that they did not want little girls to watch just yet, seeing as they clearly did not think this sort of ceremonial savagery was anything she needed shielding from. Gods, they were a crazy lot. She could not help but laugh with them, though. They were rather entertaining, as brutes go.Meanwhile, the women who had more than enough of blade-sheathing every night pretended not to notice what was going on and laughed and joked with each other.

Not one man made a demand from them that sacred night, not even Arnulf, who seemed to find a night off with his comrades rather well-deserved himself. When Suri finally dared to throw herself at the House-Bond, he sent one slightly guilty glance at his concubines, who ignored him and continued their talking with the Sheaths, and left to please the girl, to the great joy of all bystanders. Zivah had to stop Thordís from running over to spy at them, seeing as the girl had always been rather curious about Arnulf's manly virtues.

She still mentioned them every now and then, as if the memory of the sight of his erect lord stone never ceased to awe her. Now she was continuously disappointed because Arnulf, feeling somewhat embarrassed about her keen interest in them, mostly kept his business behind the bed-curtains or in the privacy of the Hamam. Zivah thought the girl a little too curious for her age, really. When the men took off their clothes to wash in the yard she was always there to look at them with a fascinated expression. The men never seemed to mind and only laughed a little when they noticed the little maiden watching them.

Nobody rebuked the girl for her curiosity, but she did notice that they tried to be a little more modest around her, especially after what happened with Hialti. Zivah remembered Hialti and feared that someone might one day mistake the child's interest for anything but innocence. They did not seem to make that mistake, though. It seemed that they thought it only natural that she would be curious, and true enough they never allowed her to touch them below the belt, and they never touched her below her belt either.

It was not up to Zivah to educate her, and if the men of the court thought that there was nothing to it, there was not much she could do except stopping the child from making the worst blunders. Thordís accepted it when her sister held her back from running after Arnulf and Suri, having never once abused the fact that she was free and Zivah was not. She shrugged and went to sit in Thióðolf's lap until she fell asleep. That was another very odd thing about the Norsemen, she thought, that these brutish warriors seemed to think it only natural that free men take care of their children themselves. The men only left the most basic things like feeding and common dressing to their slave women, and apart from that they did all the raising of both the boy and the girl. She had heard they had raised little Ivarr from the age of three.

As soon as the girl was asleep and he had put her to bed, Zivah noticed how the serving maids started to look at Thióðolf. Oh dear. Suddenly that girl Tana approached him, shyly, and nudged him in the side. He went red immediately, and to Zivah's joy he looked directly to her, looking embarrassed, guilty, even. As if he was worried about what she would think if he took another girl. All this time that she had been at Arnulf's court, her House-Bond had not touched anyone at all, at least not in court.

She had wondered how he managed, seeing as all the other men appeared to need a lot of the stuff. Now he met her eyes and there was a question in them. What was she supposed to do? She could not go over there and take Tana's place. She could never do it that way, before everybody, and especially not now when he had already been picked. That would not be fair to Tana. And Zivah was not ready for that yet anyway.

She shrugged and returned to her conversation with the others, and noticed from the corner of her eyes that her House-Bond smiled at Tana and suddenly picked her up, threw her over his shoulder like a Viking and carried her over to an empty bed, the girl shrieking with delight. When he put her down there, he closed the curtain to the loud dismay of men and women who had been curious to see how Thióðolf wielded his Frey's power. Zivah thought of Thordís and wondered if that sort of thing ran in their blood or something.

Not long after there were moans of delight from that bed that made everybody laugh and sing the louder. Zivah bit her lower lip and cursed herself just a little, and him. What else could he have done, without offending Tana on this day when slave women got to choose free men?

Now that she sat and knew that he was making love to another woman right there in the same room, she tried to feel for it, and suddenly knew that somehow, this place had, over time, caused the demon of jealousy to go quite dead. It was something about how they were all together anyway, like the many limbs of a great and very strange and ceaselessly entertaining beast.

Nobody really owned anything alone here. She could not grudge neither him nor Tana the pleasure, at least not when she did not offer or receive it herself. That was all. She had changed. Zivah stretched her arms and smiled, wondering what tales Tana was going to tell the morning after, and whether they would prove as tempting as she had started to think they might. A new year, she thought. This is going to be all new.

SHUMAYL AND THE ANGRY CALIPH

I had noticed that Shumayl often prayed to his god in that fashion the Rus despised, kneeling on the ground. As long as he was discreet about it, everybody pretended not to notice. Sometimes, I had noticed, especially if most of the men were out, and sometimes at nights when the men were celebrating indoors, he stood in one of the towers looking out towards the southeast and the crisp starlit winter nights.

One night between the two sleeps, I had to go out to relieve myself, and on my way back to the Hold I came very close to the watchtower. I heard that Shumayl was singing in his language, singing with a low voice, yet still it could be heard, a beautiful and haunting song. It was, I sensed, a way for him to praise his god, and I was a little curious about it.

He also made medicines, I pondered, and since I had grown up making the same, I wanted very much to talk to him and see what he was doing. He was always so very anxious around me that I did not want to force him, seeing as he was a slave who could not refuse me if I asked. And so I did not ask out of respect for him. He had a dignity to him, Shumayl, I had often noticed. Not the warrior's kind of forceful dignity, what comes from skill and strength as much as from self-respect and self-control. He possessed the sort of dignity that simply comes from soul's integrity and may be carried by anyone regardless of how feeble they may be, or how void of worldly power. I understood why everybody actually liked him and respected him even if he was a very little man.

One winter eve when I was getting really bored from all that spinning the slave women did night after night while they gossiped, I regarded the dark-skinned man thoughtfully and figured that if he was in fact a civilized man, and he thought that I was from Hel, then he was probably just frightened of me and needed some friendly urging. I walked up to where he was seated, preparing his blends. To my surprise, he did not even notice that I was there at first, and I was able to stand behind him and look over his shoulders for several eye-blinks before he even realized that I was there. He almost flinched when he finally discovered me. I hid my astonishment so as not to shame him.

I had overheard people saying that those civilized people had very dull senses, and now I had gotten proof of that. Maybe that was why they were so fearful. It must be rather intimidating to live in this world without all your natural senses intact.

The slave lowered his eyes to me.

"Shumayl," I said, "why are you afraid of me? I never hurt you."

"No, Maiden, you have never hurt me," he conceded.

"I would never hurt you, either. I am wondering why you fear me. I am just a little girl."

"You are like no girls I ever knew, Maiden," Shumayl said and smiled shyly, "I just don't know how to be around you. I am sorry if I offend, Maiden."

"You do not offend," I said, "But you surely do not still think I am a djinn anymore?"

"No," he smiled cautiously and met my gaze for a moment, "I do not think you are a djinn, Maiden. I, the first time I saw you looked different from now. You had very special eyes, and with the wolf head. You looked fearsome, Maiden. I had never seen the like in a maiden so young. For a moment, I thought you a djinn."

I beamed with pride, seeing as a djinn was the same as a Hel Maiden for all I knew, but I was also relieved that he no longer saw me that way. He seemed to relax a little, and I decided to proceed getting to know him better.

"Shumayl, are you civilized?" I asked. He looked astonished, and then smiled broadly for the first time, "I suppose I am, Maiden. How did you learn that word, if I may ask?"

"You may ask anything, Shumayl. I learned it from Aziza. She said that the Big Tunic Men are civilized people and that you think we are beastly barbarians." I noticed that Thióðolf raised an eyebrow, but as he was pretending not to listen in, he said nothing. Shumayl looked anxiously towards the free men in the room, but replied dutifully,

"It is true that we think of ourselves as civilized, Maiden, and that our people regard your people as not civilized. Do you know what civilized means, though, Maiden?"

"Not really," I said, looking at Shumayl's humble frame, "I thought perhaps it only meant that you civilized people were kind of puny and afraid of big men with tattoos and Hel and such. So maybe civilized people are just a lot more frightened about everything than we are?"

Now Thióðolf was grinning, as were the other men who had visited the Hold that evening, and even Shumayl looked amused.

"That could perhaps be a way of saying it, Maiden, but it is not quite how we look at it in Big Tunic Land, which, by the way, we call the Caliphate."

"How do you look at it, then?" I asked, and now everybody around the table looked curiously at Shumayl, who blushed a little at all the attention and looked fearfully at the warriors. Thióðolf nodded reassuringly at him, saying, "Speak freely, Shumayl, nobody here will harm you or punish you for speaking the truth about how your people look at things. We are all curious about your lot."

"Well, first of all, being civilized means that a lot of us live in very great cities and towns full of buildings that are somewhat larger and taller and more complicated than your buildings, and these numerous cities and towns are interconnected and ruled from a central power, in our case the Caliphs. Within that society, we have a lot of very complicated ways of arranging things. It is all just a lot bigger and more diverse than your society is. I should say that even though I am a very little man, there are many big and strong men in the Caliphate as well. We have great armies and have conquered many pieces of land, from Persia in the east to Iberia in the west. Our warriors are as fearless as yours are, the only difference is that all men are not warriors among our people."

"What are they then? Are they hunters?" I asked curiously, having almost forgotten a world in which all free men were not also warriors. Even where I came from, all men were hunters at least.

"No, very few are hunters, just as relatively few as are warriors. A lot of our men are simply workers and peasants, and they are not warriors. They are a little more like slaves are here, even if they are not actually slaves, but they have little power."

"Oh," I said, exchanging glances with the others. It sounded odd, a world where free men were neither hunters nor warriors, but lived almost like slaves. "Who are the warriors then?"

"Well, there are many soldiers who are paid to partake in wars, and often they have no other professions. There are noble warriors who lead them. Sometimes, ordinary men are forced to join the army even if they are not really warriors, and they often make poor soldiers, yet sometimes it helps an army to just be full of men, even if they are not all that great at fighting. We find ways of making all kinds of men useful in an army even if they are not good at direct combat."

"This is the civilized way?" I asked, wondering what kind of armies these civilized people had, full of frightened and inadequate men who were almost like slaves.

"Yes, this is the way of the civilized world, including the Christian Franks," Shumayl said, "and it often turns out to be a quite successful way of winning wars, even if your people think it odd. For your kind, I think, being a warrior is a way of being alive, for men." We all nodded in agreement and waited for him to proceed. "Most of us Tunic Men, as it is with most civilized men, prefer to live in peace and rather have armies to protect us."

"Like women and children?" I asked, incredulous.

"Yes, Maiden, from your perspective, most civilized men prefer to be protected by warriors rather than being warriors, like women and children here. We do not assess a man's worth by his warrior skills, Maiden, we have other ways of assessing such."

"Like what?"

"Well, in my case, as you can see, I am not made for the warrior's way. I have not that chant in my soul song, as your kind like to say."

We all nodded cheerfully in agreement to that also.

"Yet among my people I was a great man, once. I was wealthy and highly esteemed because of my knowledge and my skill."

"We have such men too," Thióðolf intervened, "Sorcerers and good craftsmen are highly respected among us, even if they are no warriors."

"Yes, Heri, but our people do not value sorcerers. My kind is not thought of as sorcerers, but as our words for these are scientists or philosophers. We have many levels of scientists and philosophers, and all kinds of other professions highly valued, yet without being warriors. It is true that we also value many kinds of craftsmen, like you do. It is only that we have a lot more kinds of crafts than you have here."

"Shumayl, it sounds like many healers among your people are men," I said. He said that was the truth of the matter. Where he came from, most healers were men and they learned the healing arts through the reading of painted runes. I looked helplessly at the warriors.

"Well, it makes sense, does it not? Seeing as these civilized men do not have to be warriors," Njál suggested, "that means they can spend a lot of time learning other things what requires just as much dedication and time. And them civilized men have smaller hands than we do, mostly. In battles where there are no women, the men with the smallest hands often perform the best surgeries." The men nodded thoughtfully to his words. Njál was a wise fool, as often as not.

"What is a scientist and a philosopher, then?" I asked, leaving the matter and deciding to try out the foreign words.

"Well, Maiden. There have been many great civilizations before ours, where men grew to study all nature and became very knowledgeable about most matters. They wrote great works with runes onto sheets of leather or a fabric known as papyrus, where they collected all their arts. They studied the nature of the stars and the sky and the properties of Earth and the human body, medicine and music, all things divine and mundane."

"Our people studied those too," I said. "In the era of the great stone temples, they studied all these things. Only, women studied them also. We have kept the knowledge in many sacred songs, some forgotten and some remembered, and we call it the Red Gold. It helps us to know the gods behind their masks."

"Hmm." Shumayl gazed curiously at me. He was a knowledge-hungry man, that one, and this new knowledge enticed him and puzzled him.

"It is the truth she speaks, Shumayl," Thióðolf said. "We have many songs explaining the legacies of our distant ancestors, who knew more about the secrets of the many worlds than anyone does today. They hid the knowledge in riddles, in poetry, but there are many who still can decipher most of it."

"How interesting!" Shumayl exclaimed, genuinely enthusiastic, "I should very much know these songs," he said, "but your people never wrote down your knowledge, did you?"

"No," I said. "Not as far as I know." I looked uncertainly at Thióðolf, who shook his head affirmatively. I thought he must wonder, like I did, if civilized men had bad memories since they needed to write it all down. We refrained from commenting it out of respect for him.

"Please, Shumayl, you were explaining those civilizations," I said.

"Well, Maiden," he said, "then I must speak of the people who came before us, they who lived in great and ancient lands known as Egypt and Babylon, Persia, Greece and the Roman Empire, as well as a land to the east where Aziza's mother came from. Her land, Indus, is a part of a very ancient civilization, where we find kingdoms like Taxila, Hydaspes and Kambojas. We call it all Indus, after a great river there. All these civilizations studied the stellar and worldly properties and achieved great knowledge, what you refer to as the Red Gold, and they carved their runes about their knowledge into great collections of papyrus or leather or clay tablets, what we call books, so that even if people forgot the tales their descendants would be able to look into these books and learn the lore of the past."

Shumayl paused to see if we were following, and we had all grown utterly quiet. I could see that some of the sillier slave girls were looking utterly blank, but the rest of us were thoroughly fascinated. I nodded eagerly to encourage him.

"Now, many of these civilizations are gone, or at least reduced to very little compared to what they once were," Shumayl continued, "and I have noticed that even you Norsemen speak of centuries where the old ways dissolved and many a society was broken apart. This also happened with the great civilizations, as they broke both from within and from countless foreign invasions. The knowledge of old was partly lost. When the Caliphate was established, our caliphs decided to restore the glory of the past, and they gathered the wisest and most knowledgeable men among us and told them to travel all over the world and purchase the books of these old nations. They are still doing this, collecting books from all over the world, taking them home to the Caliphate, where we translate them into our language, Arabic, or else into Persian, and study them."

My father had told me many stories of how our ancestors had traveled around the world to exchange knowledge, so the notion was familiar to me, yet I had not known that people were still doing it, and I had never thought of the idea of carving it all down as runes. It must be heavy to carry all that knowledge on sheets instead of within the mind. Yet it occurred to me that maybe those civilized people were not so pitiful after all. At least they valued knowledge like we did.

My father had been the last to guard all the knowledge of our Thunder Priest legacy, because all the others had been murdered. His knowledge had all been inside his mind, and now he was dead. That moment, it occurred to me that if he had written his knowledge down, then I could have studied it like I would have if he had still lived.

"I have studied many such ancient works, Maiden," Shumayl said. "Among them the works of many great physicians, and so I learned about the healing arts. I follow partly an eastern tradition known as Ayur Veda, and partly a western tradition building on the works of a very wise Greek known as Hippocrates."

"You learned healing by reading runes?" I asked, frowning. My mother had always said that the only way of learning about healing was to practice and follow a more experienced healer in her practice. If we read any runes at all, they were the invisible runes carved into the plants' soul songs, or the soul-runes of the sick, all of which we could access through stillness of the mind.

"Yes, Maiden, but of course we did practice also," Shumayl smiled, clearly understanding my position. "I had a teacher of the arts who was not only my teacher in medicine, but in all kinds of things pertaining to knowledge and to our god."

"Is that the god who is supposed to be the only god in the whole world?"

Shumayl smiled. "It is how the Big Tunic Men believe, yes. We believe there is no god but the one God. There are many ways of believing even among us. My teacher imparted on me something that is akin to your Red Gold, that is, a deeper understanding of the faith. I believe that although there is but one god, he is present in everything and everyone. I believe that it is possible for a man, or a woman for that matter, even a maiden like yourself, to become united with God even as we are still moving in this world. We have to rid ourselves of all impurities of the soul and act with purity in the world, and through so doing, and through great love for god, we will know him even in ourselves."

"There are such mysteries among us too, Shumayl," Thióðolf said quietly, after an awed silence and many a blank look around the table, "and I respect your particular way of faith very much."

He turned to me and spoke, "Thordís, some of these matters are too difficult for you to understand yet, and even more difficult to explain to you like this. I am sure there are many other things that Shumayl can tell you about Big Tunic Land."

I nodded obediently, but remained quiet for a while, trying to take in what Shumayl had just said. I touched my heart and pondered many words that had been spoken before.

"How did you come here to Rusiyah, then, Shumayl?" I asked. "It sounds like you were a wise man and a sage among your people. How come you became a slave among the Rus?"

Shumayl lowered his eyes a little and a painful expression crossed his face.

"I am sorry, Shumayl, you do not have to answer me," I said, even though I knew I should never apologize openly to a slave. He was not a slave right now, for me. He was my teacher, and I honored him. The wise little Big Tunic Man seemed to recognize the respect I paid him and met my gaze again, his eyes shining with a quiet sadness. Everybody, me included, politely looked another way, pretending not to notice his private hurts. But Shumayl humored me.

"It is no secret, Maiden," he said humbly, "I got into trouble with the authorities. My teacher openly rebuked the caliphs for living ungodly and extravagant lives which we in our tradition believed were contrary to the faith. My teacher rebuked the great Caliph Al-Mahdi all too openly and all too feverishly, and suddenly he and all his students were accused of, it is something we call heresy, a great crime."

"What is that, then? Heresy?" I asked.

"It means that you are thinking the wrong thoughts and speaking them out," he said, and we all looked to one another, incredulous.

"A man can grasp the point of punishing the committing of dishonorable or unlawful actions, but how is it even possible to control how people think or what they speak of when they sit among equals?" Hallgrim asked.

"I dare say it is not possible at all," Shumayl said, "and yet our rulers try very hard. There is already an endless row of dead men, who died because they spoke the wrong words to the wrong people."

Everybody frowned and shook their heads incredulously. It seemed so meaningless, and highly impractical, Arnulf pointed out. One would have little else to do then, than killing and killing for an eternity, seeing as people are wont to think their thoughts and speak their minds anyway.

"Is it like not minding the courtesies?" I asked.

266

"Uhm. You could perhaps say so. Caliph al-Mahdi had his way of believing in god, and if anyone disagreed with him or rebuked him, he got very angry and he would accuse us of the wrong thoughts.

Also, despite his claim to being defender of the faith, the Caliph, uhm, well, we criticized the Caliph for living an ungodly life with, uhm, drinking wine and having unlawful intercourse with countless slave girls."

Shumayl's voice had lowered considerably with that last comment, and there was an embarrassed silence as all the free men present went a little red. When he was sure they had not been overly offended, Shumayl carefully proceeded, "and this was dangerous. We would have been executed, all of us. Our properties were seized. Some of us fled. I had to leave my family with relatives and I fled to the north. There I was captured by Khazar slave hunters."

Another flash of pain crossed his features and he paused to catch his breath, as if the fright of that event still resided in his heart. I wondered if he did not know about the great tremble despite being a healer, but chose to ask a different question to help him out of his discomfort. I recalled something Arnulf had said about the Khazars and their imported new religion.

"Are they the people what likes to enslave their neighbors?" I asked.

"Excuse me, Maiden?" Shumayl looked a little perplexed.

"The Khazars," I explained patiently, "Arnulf said they enslave their neighbors because it says in a holy book that they can, if they are Jews."

"Uhm, oh, I see what you mean," Shumayl said and almost began to laugh, but thought better of it, seeing as I was free and he was not.

"Well," he said instead, "I doubt that most Jews enslave their neighbors nowadays, Maiden, even if their holy book permits it and blesses it in certain ways. The Khazars, well, they are not Jews as such, they have just converted to the Jewish faith. They are still quite, well, they are more akin to the Rus than to other Jews in many ways, you see, even if they are darker and smaller than you. What I mean is that."

He paused and bit his lower lip.

"Do you mean that they are barbarians like we are?" I asked. I remembered the Khazar traders standing next to the Tunic Men traders and knew by that visual memory their difference and likeness to us Rus. The Tunic Men had been dressed in colorful and exquisite clothing that was beautiful but obviously not meant to last for even one hike through the forests. The Khazars had more sensible leather and fur clothing and looked more like us that way.

"Yes..." Shumayl cast an anxious glance towards the warriors before he proceeded, "Yes, Maiden, the Khazars are also barbarians. But it is true that they are very eager to enslave all their neighbors that they can get away with, and are very happy to have a divine permission to do so. They are a pragmatic kind of folk, you see, and not of the most compassionate kind.

In truth I saw more horrors among them than I have ever seen here, Maiden. I thought I should surely perish among the Khazars, but then Arnulf, I mean the House-Bond, came downriver and saw me there. You see, he spoke our Tunic, our Arab language. He saw me and started talking to me, and swiftly figured out that I was a learned man. He bought me and he has treated me well all the time, allowing me to practice my skills and honor my faith as much as possible. I am blessed."

The rest of us exchanged glances, wondering how a formerly great and highly respected sage could feel blessed about being reduced to a slave among foreign people. Shumayl clearly understood our confusion.

"It was hard for me, coming among the Rus, and being a slave among them. I mean among you. I had been raised to think of your kind of people as lowlier than us, so it was terribly humiliating to be a slave to barbarians. Besides, your kind is ferocious in so many ways, and I have often been afraid. It took me a long time to get used to your ways. It is the will of Allah that I am here. When I lived in Baghdad I thought myself great, yet I thought only of myself and my own and pretended humility where I was in fact proud. Whereas before I only healed people who could pay me a lot of money, and made my wealth from them, I now heal anyone for free, asking nothing in return, and hopefully I can provide some comfort to people whose misery is greater than mine. God is in everything and everyone, Maiden, or so I believe, and I see his works in every fate."

Shumayl drew his breath and spoke with a new strength in his voice, one that reminded us of the fact that he was a sage, not just a slave, "I have been challenged, and I could well have lost my faith and succumbed to fear and misery, but I have not. I have kept my faith and chosen to deal graciously with the fate that was bestowed upon me. I hope that in my death, Allah will embrace me and appreciate my dedication to serving him and serving those who suffer, and to live in love. For love is all there is, Maiden. Through this fate of slavery, my god has honed me."

Just that moment, it mattered not that he was a slave. We did not understand his particular ideas about humility and pride, and surely love must be balanced by fury, but we understood the essentials. Shumayl was a man who had accepted his harsh fate and dealt graciously with her, allowing his fate to hone him rather than break him. He had embraced his fate with love and looked beyond her harsh appearance and into the hidden soul within. That took warrior's courage, and the norns, or his god, would judge him kindly. Around the table, we all lowered our eyes briefly to acknowledge the fact that we had been well taught, and that we had been gifted with another great story.

TRANSGRESSIONS

The snow fell heavily for several days until the whole world was covered in a thick blanket. We could not ride in the hills anymore because of it, what grieved me because I had loved my little outdoor adventures with Thióðolf almost every day. Everybody spent more time indoors now. But Thióðolf asked me if I knew about skiing.

"Of course," I said eagerly, "Father taught us."

"Us"?

"Yes, me and Zivah. He taught Zivah since she was very young, and later he taught me also."

"Zivah knows how to ski?"

"Yes, she is very good at it."

"Ah!" Thióðolf's eyes lit up. Zivah was just passing by carrying a pile of cloth and tried not to notice him.

"Zivah, will you come here?" He said gently, and Zivah obeyed, approaching us with lowered eyes.

"Heri," she said and stood with her head bowed.

"Just stand there, Zivah. Don't worry. I am only going to measure you." He came closer to her than he had ever been since we arrived in Arnulf's court, and I could see that she was straining herself not to flinch. I wondered why she was still so terrified of him, seeing as he had never behaved roughly with her since that day in the marketplace. Thióðolf measured her and let her go, and then he measured me. After a few days, he presented us with a pair of skis and a staff each, and Zivah's eyes widened in surprise. I could see how she tried hard to hide her delight when she realized what we were going to do.

It was not only us who were going out. Arnulf loved skiing, and had taught both his concubines. A few of the warriors came with us. Father had told me that most Gauts did not know the art, but that he had learned it in his youth and thought it great sport. Thióðolf revealed that where he came from, back in Hálógaland, people did not just ski for fun, but because it was often the only way of getting around at all during winter.

"I come from the land where we think all skiing started," he said, "The mother of our land, great Skaði, invented the art and offered it up to her descendants. We have called her the Goddess of Skiing ever since."

As soon as we had gotten to a place of many nice hills and slopes where we could enjoy ourselves, the other warriors left us to stay in the distance, keeping guard, and suddenly I found myself among something akin to a family. Arnulf and his two women, and Thióðolf, me and Zivah. Zivah kept close to Aziza and Laimi and continued to avoid Thióðolf as much as possible without offending him, but this behavior had become so normal for us now that we hardly even noticed.

Despite her distance to her master, she was clearly enjoying herself, and everybody was quite astonished at how good she was. She loved skiing and never tired of sliding down hills, struggling back up only to slide down again, over and over. When she thought herself undetected, one could even see that she was wearing a big smile, which was the first time ever since we came to Aldeigjuborg.

She was feeling free, if only for the time being. And there was a point where she stood on a hill a little distance from the rest of us and she threw her head back and obviously enjoyed the feel of winter air in her face. Her hood fell back and revealed her long flowing hair, which had loosened from that tight bun she always wore and now fell down in cascades, like a fountain of honey mead.

We all stood watching her then, and she knew nothing of it. And then we heard a soft tune emerging from her. She was singing. I had almost forgotten what a beautiful voice my sister had. Arnulf and Thióðolf both looked so moved, their eyes went moist, and suddenly Arnulf turned away and muttered huskily, "Now I know what I took from her."

I looked at the Heri and thought I saw a strain in his face, a strain of one most unexpected emotion; remorse.

I quickly averted my eyes lest I shame him.

When we had enjoyed ourselves for a good while, we gathered at the top of a hill to eat and talk. After a while, Zivah began to look impatient, casting glances at her skis.

"You can go ski more if you like, Zivah," Thióðolf said.

"Thank you, Heri," Zivah mumbled, and immediately got up to tie her skis back onto her boots. Just as she was about to set off again, she stumbled and fell in the snow, and that happened right next to Thióðolf. He moved to help her, taking hold of her arm and pulling her up to a standing position. To my horror, Zivah immediately pulled her arm free of his grasp and glared up at him, staring him directly into his eyes, looking furious.

They all saw it, Arnulf and his concubines, and they all turned to look another way, as if they did not want to behold the shocking and utterly unpardonable spectacle of a slave who dared to glare at her master and refuse his help. Thióðolf looked astonished for a few moments, before, to my absolute bafflement, he lowered his own eyes to her.

Then he bowed his head to her.

Zivah's eyes widened in surprise, and some strong emotions seemed to pass through her features before she suddenly turned and slid away on her skis to take a turn down the hill without even apologizing first. Thióðolf stood staring after her with a strange and dreamy look on his face, and Arnulf came up to him, grinning, giving his friend's back a few encouraging pats.

"She will yet hone sharp the blade, that one," the giant Heri said and laughed, and I saw how Thióðolf actually began to turn a bright red while he smiled as if a good thing had just passed.

What had just transpired was incomprehensible to me, and swiftly all the things I knew about Rus Vikings, slaves and their rules came together in my mind and formed a conclusion of its own, and the terror of it seized my being so powerfully that I suddenly broke down in sobs and cried violently for the first time in my life, ever. I was not well accustomed to weeping, and yet now I did it as if I was a master of the art. I was rolling in the snow, howling and wailing, until strong arms lifted me and I found myself in Arnulf's embrace. Everybody apart from Zivah had gathered around us, looking concerned, as I kept sobbing and convulsing from despair.

"It is the first time I see you cry properly, Priestess," Arnulf said, "It was about time. What ails you, little one? You can tell us."

I howled again, too terrorized to speak the words that might make real my terror, and Arnulf rocked me a little, not quite as confident about such moves as Thióðolf was. Yet still, he did it, and it dawned on me that I could appeal to the Heri for my sister's sake, because the Heri loved me. I was too deeply steeped in the sobbing waves that had seized me to be able to voice my appeal in the correct manner.

"I fear you will beat my sister to death and that you will give her to the men's Hall after!" I wailed, and was taken over by another violent wave of sobs and tears.

"What? After we beat her to death?" Arnulf asked jokingly, what of course only produced even louder wailing from me. The Heri acknowledged that his skills at comforting little girls were rather limited, and held me out to Thióðolf, who enclosed me in that warm and well-known space that I had learned to trust.

"Why did you think we would do that, Thordís? Do you not trust us?" He asked as he rocked me like he would a baby.

"Yes, but she did it in the open and everybody saw and now you have to follow the rules and make her suffer and then I cannot protect her and then she will just die because I am the only one who can protect her but if I cannot she will not live anymore and I don't want her to be beaten at all!" I cried, unable to stop the rapid flow of words that voiced my deepest fears. The men looked at each other, astonished. Then Arnulf looked at me.

"We will not punish her, Priestess," Arnulf said gently, "We will not speak of it at all." He looked so sincere when he said it that I calmed down a little and looked deeply into his eyes without realizing that I also failed to avert my gaze to my Heri, and he allowed me to look for as long as it took me to realize that he really did not want to hurt my sister, and that he did not have to do it either. When I finally understood that he was truly sincere, I sniveled a little and lowered my eyes.

"Are you sure?" I asked timidly, and looked around into all the faces. It was such an unusual situation, I realized, with the slave women standing there with the men and watching me just as if they were free women out dallying with their lovers, and all of them openly showed their expressions of concern and sympathy. It felt as if we were a close-knit family all of a sudden, and as if our differences in rank did not matter at all. I frowned, because it was as if the entire world had been transformed, and even though the transformation appeared rewarding, it terrified me because all the rules that held my world together were now breaking apart.

I looked uncertainly at their open eyes and the way we all seemed to meet each other on an equal standing, and the way they all confirmed with sincere little nods that it was really true that nobody would hurt my sister even after that terrible insolence of hers.

"But why did you say that she would yet hone sharp the blade?" I whispered, looking at Arnulf, "I thought you were speaking of punishment and that you…" I began sniveling again, "and that you were laughing at the thought!" I wept profusely once more, but not so much with fear this time, because I understood that I had been mistaken.

"Oh, but those were just words of poetry, little Síf," Arnulf said patiently, "I was just appreciating you sister's skills for honing."

"Honing?" They all nodded to confirm what I had heard. Even Aziza and Laimi seemed to know what we spoke of.

"Can slave women hone men for real?" I asked.

"All women are honers, so of course they can. They just have to go about it in different ways because unlike free women they can be harmed if they transgress," Arnulf said.

"She transgressed a lot," I mused.

"Well, that is how women hone, is it not? They transgress," the Heri pointed out. All of them agreed with nods again, as if they wanted me very much to understand.

"You say that slave women can be harmed if they transgress."

"Yes, they can. That is why the honing of a slave woman is such a great honor for a man," Arnulf said and winked at Aziza, who smiled warmly back at him.

"Why is it an honor?" Arnulf looked at Thióðolf, who was still holding me, and gave him a nod, "You are the word-smith, Thióðolf, why don't you explain to her the honor a slave can pay to a man."

I looked expectantly up at my poet, beginning to feel reassured that none of the men I had come to love were going to hurt my sister.

"Oh, child," Thióðolf began, "I am so sad to find that you have nourished such fears all this time. I am so sorry that I have not reassured you better. You are such a clever girl and I think I never realized how worried you must have been for your sister."

Arnulf nodded. "Aye," he said, "my little Síf, none of us men realized that you were still frightened on her behalf. We all thought you knew that your sister was quite safe. I am sorry too, that I have not made that clear to you before. I am so sorry."

I was quite astonished and looked at them both, and then I shrugged it off and wanted to know how a slave can hone a warrior.

"You felt it yourself," Thióðolf began explaining, "the terror when you saw her insolence towards me. It terrified you so much that you cried and sobbed for the first time, you who did not even weep the death of your parents."

I nodded, finding it strangely comforting to have someone else describe my own feelings for me, as if the fact that my feelings had been recognized and spoken out by another was enough to release the fear forever.

"Now imagine how terrified she must have been, Thordís," Thióðolf said. "She has far less reason than you have to think that I would not beat her and send her to the men's Hall. And yet she did what she did, and she did it before the eyes of us all, and she did it on purpose. Can you imagine how much courage that must have taken?"

I shook my head from side to side.

"What is more, Thordís, can you imagine how much trust?"

"Trust?"

"Yes. Trust. She would not have been able to build up that kind of courage unless she actually trusted me not to hurt her. Do you not see? She challenged me to let me prove to her that I was worthy of her trust. It was a trap set out for me, a test, a challenge. It was a perfect honing, Thordís, and utterly generous towards me."

"How was it generous?"

"Because she is giving me a chance, Wolfling, she is giving me a chance to prove myself to her so that maybe one day she can forgive me. It is a great honor because it shows that she trusts me and likes me just enough to give me that chance, and it is an even greater honor because we both know fully that her transgression could have cost her great grief, and so she offered up her trust to me at great risk to herself. She did not offend me, Thordís, she placed her life and well-being into my hands just to see if I would hold her up or throw her away. For a slave to do such a thing is as courageous as going into battle, and it is a generous gesture towards me because it signals trust, and because it gives me a chance to atone and prove myself."

"Why did you beat her that first day then?" I asked.

"Because she was a slave spiting her master within the sight of many dangerous and ruthless men, who could call down the laws of Aldeigjuborg regarding the public conduct of slaves within the sight of other slaves and free men. I had to do something to placate them, lest they demand public punishment just to show their own slaves that they cannot get away with such insolence. You know this. We are among friends now. The point is that Zivah has begun to understand that she is among friends, and so it was a gesture to all of us, to prove to her that we are all her friends and will not hurt her even if she shows openly to all of us how much she despises me."

"If she trusts you and likes you, why do you say she despises you?"

"I am a man, Thordís. I think you would be better equipped to understand such inner opposites than I am. It is just how women are, and I will not pretend to know the why and how of it better than a maiden. The only thing I know is that whereas before she only resented and despised me, she now also trusts me enough to show me how she feels openly, and so she has given me a chance to prove myself. She has set the start of a very sacred quest, and I must expect many more traps and tests before I can prove to her that I will never abuse my power over her again."

"Is it sacred?" I asked, incredulous.

"It is very sacred, the game of trust, and it is another kind of honing," Thióðolf said. "It is an ancient and secret yet much honored game between people of very different ranking, and it must as all great arts be honored. It requires subtle skills to play it, since it involves so many dangers and transgressions. It is a quest and it is a honing. A slave cannot hone like a warrior's daughter, she cannot mock or taunt or speak out in public. She must be far more subtle about it, and so the challenge is also much greater for a warrior, because it is a challenge not of battle courage but of integrity and trustworthiness."

He smiled broadly and peered down the hill, where Zivah was still practicing, not yet quite daring to return. She must be worried still, I thought, and no wonder. I could still not quite grasp that my sister was really this tough, or really this complex.

"Ah!" Arnulf exclaimed, "It makes a warrior's heart sing to embark on such adventures." Both men smiled so happily as if they were about to set out on a voyage to the great halls of the Sun Maiden.

"How come the rules are so different from what you are actually doing when you let slave women hone you?" I asked.

"Well, do you remember when I told you about there being women and there being different kinds of women?" Thióðolf said.

"Mirror images," I remembered.

"Yes. The world is a fluid tapestry, Thordís, we make a structure that is firm, yet what makes the tapestry interesting are all the threads that move in opposite directions without following the structure, so as to make interesting images. We cannot exist well without ways of moving free from the structure, even as the structure is what holds the whole tapestry together.

So there are rules, and then there are other kinds of rules. It is impossible to live without such other kinds of rules. We would suffocate if we did."

"Oh," I said, frowning, "Thióðolf?"

"Yes, my friend?"

"Is that why you lowered your eyes to her? To show her another kind of rule?"

"That is a way of saying it, yes. The intention was to show her that I submit to her verdict of me. I wanted her to know that I acknowledge and accept her feelings about me, and then I bowed my head to apologize for making her feel those things about me. It was also my way of responding to the first challenge she set up for me, accepting her challenge and her honing. Even if she is not a Norse woman, even if she knows not all our rules and other kinds of rules, she understands this language because she is a woman. She understood thoroughly, I could see it in her eyes. She was surprised when I bowed to her only because she did not yet know how well I actually understand her and how highly I regard her. She understands in her heart now that I am ready to abide by the rules she sets for this quest, and I am willing to give her what she wants from me."

"What does she want from you, then?"

"How would I know? I will give it to her anyway, when she deigns to let me know. Before she will let me know I will have to pass all her tests to show myself worthy of her trust, and perhaps one day she will even like me a little."

"You really like Zivah, don't you?" I asked, since it began to dawn on me that he did.

"Yes, Thordís, I like her very much, I really do," he said, blushing.

All of them smiled knowingly. Thióðolf finally set me down to stand in the snow again, and we all cast some glances at Zivah who was still struggling up the hill only to slide down it again, time and time again. She liked the feeling of freedom she got when she slid downhill and the wind made her long honey-golden hair flow, and she looked magnificent now, a master of the skiing art. I could feel the anxiety she was feeling about having transgressed, and it looked as if she wanted to savor those final moments of sensing what freedom was like before she must go to her doom. All that anxiety, all that very real danger, and yet she had done it, just to give a new chance to the man who once beat her. I understood why they admired her and thought her generous.

"When you talked of honing before, Thióðolf, you always talked about our women and our Sífs, and I thought you meant that only Norse women were honers," I said.

"All women are honers, it is just as Arnulf said."

"You said that you Norsemen are such great and strong warriors because Norse women hone you to be so, and you said it is not like that in other places."

"You could say that Norse women tend to be particularly good at it," Thióðolf said, "on account of having cultivated the art for thousands of years, and because no Norsemen have yet been so stupid and cowardly as to try and forbid them from honing us. They learn it from girlhood and it runs in the blood. Our women are the greatest honers left in the world, and we worship them because of it. But Zivah is doing well also. I look forward to the next test she makes for me, when she understands that she will not be harmed because of the first."

"Are they difficult, the tests?"

"Women speak in the language of gods and norns! Of course they are difficult. We must decipher their signals like we decipher poetry and hidden runes. It is a challenge what makes a warrior's heart sing, just as Arnulf said." He was looking at Zivah who had begun to approach. She was a little cautious, but, being met with the smiles of Arnulf's concubines and the feigned indifference of the men, she slowly approached. Thióðolf leaned down and whispered to me, "Zivah has a great talent for honing, and she will not go easy on me. But you should know this well already, Thordís."

He made an artful pause, and I drew my breath in anticipation.

"We Norsemen know well how to hone the honers," the big scoundrel whispered into my ear before he grinned at me and winked, conspiratorially.

Civilized Men

I was a pampered noble maiden, and nobody required me to work at chores that slaves could do well without me, and even as I often stayed close to the women to hear their many entertaining conversations, and did my share of spinning in the evenings, I much preferred to work with medicines and plants, leather, fur and bone. Else I preferred to be with the men and ride and practice the bow and the battle arts and all sorts of games that engaged my body and honed my alertness. My brothers told me that I did not need to learn the common arts of women, because I was never going to become a common woman.

"You, Wolfling, you are going to become one of them other kinds of women," Njál had once explained, and said no more. Yet, I was the only actual Síf of the whole court, and all the adoration due to a precious Síf befell on me, and made me very conscious about being female, surrounded by a small army of admiring and protective males.

Among the men of Arnulf's court, I felt maidenly indeed, and they all told me that I was very maidenly. I enjoyed being maidenly more and more, especially as I was beginning to grasp all the benefits. I had begun to realize that I liked the fact that I was a maiden and that I was going to become a woman one day, and that I would always be surrounded by great and well-honed warriors who adored me exactly for being different from them, and who, I began to suspect, I was going to like in more ways than I did just now. I was looking forward to that. There were limits to how exciting it was to torment Ivarr every time he crossed my path, but I was dutiful as ever in that regard also.

Although I kept running around in boy's clothing most of the time, I had begun to enjoy getting all dressed up like a proper noble maiden sometimes and wearing my hair loose, just to enjoy the praise and attention they all gave me. It was still just a play for me, and I could not walk around in a dress looking pretty for more than a little while before I was bored and got more sensible clothes back on, but I had become very conscious about my gender and very proud of it also, and was rather surprised the day I met some men who, contrary to the men I was used to, seemed to think me less than maidenly.

They were Franks, and they were Christians, and they thought that noble maidens ought to be like flowers. What a strange notion! They even thought that maidens ought to be given flowers from men, rather than tokens of true manliness. Hróarr Freysgóði came by one day with a company of newly arrived visitors, some representatives from the first ship to reach Aldeigjuborg after the Solstice. The crew had to be divided into groups each living in different halls for the duration of their stay, and now Arnulf's court was receiving our share of foreigners. They came from that land in the south-west which they called Frankland.

I was very curious about these men, knowing that they were the first Christians I had ever met. I remembered what Arnulf had told me about the Franks, that they looked similar to us and that they spoke a similar language, and yet they were also very different. The first thing that struck me was exactly what the Heri had once pointed out, namely that they had very boring hairstyles. Their hair just hung there and never further down than to their shoulders, as if they were slaves. One of them, their leader, had combed his hair, but the rest had not even bothered to do that.

Their beards were a mess, as if they had never taken care to comb and trim them, and there was not a braid among them. The leader had hardly a beard at all, but a pitiful little mustache, and none of them were tattooed. They were somewhat smaller than our men, and did not have the same dignified postures, and chatted away when they walked into court rather than stopping to take in all the new impressions in silence, like true warriors would. They acted more like dogs than wolves, in my opinion.

I wondered if these were also civilized men, and decided to ask Aziza later. Now that they had entered our court, they looked around with darting eyes and were of course on guard, although everybody acted friendly. For some reason, all the Franks looked a bit embarrassed when they discovered that one of our men was having a little go in the hay with his Sheath, Saxa, in the stables, where the doors had been left wide open for view. Saxa was shrieking with delight. I gathered that the Franks were not used to seeing such things in public, seeing as some of them were rude enough to stare and even gape until Arnulf caught their attention.

"Ah, my friends," Arnulf said, and I thought I detected a trace of anxiety in the Franks when the giant Viking approached and patted the back of their Heri. "We would have you well provided for. My concubine, Aziza, has made ready a bath for you, which I must say you sorely need, my friends. You cannot have had the opportunity to bathe all the way here!"

The Franks looked incredulously at each other, but said nothing. It was true that they stank, and I remembered what Arnulf had once said about Christians being afraid of water. I could not wait to see how they would react to the bath and immediately ran up to Aziza, volunteering to assist the girls. She said it was fine, and I leaned close to her and whispered, "Are these men civilized, Aziza?"

"I dare say they think they are," Aziza whispered back, "But to us from the Caliphate they are almost as barbarian as the Rus."

"Oh," I said disappointedly. I still wanted very much to study those legendary civilized men. At least these people thought of themselves as civilized, so it was better than nothing, I assumed, and so I proceeded studying them carefully.

The Franks appeared utterly uncomfortable in the hamam, surrounded by slave girls who tried to pull their clothes off, what they seemed to dislike for some reason, and one of them shouted something which apparently meant that I had to go out of the room altogether. I sneak-peaked from behind a curtain instead, of course, wanting to see whatever it was that they were trying so hard to hide. But once their clothes were off they looked pretty normal, so I was not sure why they were so ashamed. Maybe it was the lack of tattoos.

They had particular trouble taking off the garments that hid their Freystones when the slave girls tried to get them out to have them properly cleaned. They refused the attention and to Aziza's great dismay, they insisted on wearing these dirty undergarments into the bath, what made me finally conclude that there must be something seriously wrong with their Freystones. I pondered if there would be ways to get a look at those. Even if I was not allowed to play with men myself yet, I had become quite an expert in these matters, seeing as I needed to be informed about all things that might become useful to me later, what everybody always encouraged me to.

Aziza seemed to find this situation difficult as well, and went up to Arnulf with her head bowed apologetically, showing her dismay in the manner of a slave.

"What is it, my dear?" Arnulf whispered.

"They do not want to wash their Freystones, House-Bond," she whispered back, still with her head bowed.

"They don't?" He asked and frowned.

"House-Bond," Aziza whispered, "the girls already think they stink. We can only imagine what it will be like beneath those undergarments, when they do not wish to have them washed. Bathing with those garments on and without soap is hardly sufficient. Heri, I beg of you that I know it is customary, but, I will not offer these men slave girls for comfort," Arnulf said, "It is not in their customs anyway, at least not in that way. Do not worry about it, Aziza, dear." Aziza's shoulders relaxed, and when she returned to the bath she nodded silently to the other slave girls, who all seemed to release their breaths.

The Franks finally bathed and did seem to relax a little, although they were a little upset when they were offered new, clean clothes to wear until their own had dried, for the slave women had already taken their stinking clothes to be washed also. When the Franks were finished bathing, they went to the men's Hall, and now the slave men emptied the bath of water, since it was always their job to carry water. When evening fell, I had also bathed and had my hair washed. I was dressed up nicely in the same blue silk dress I had worn for the winter Solstice celebration.

I was given my belt and all the ritual gear, for the mead serving ritual would of course be held now that we had guests from abroad, and they had to be included into our gathering for the time they spent here. Apart from the special rites to call back the Sun Maiden and invoke the power of Thor to help her, I went through all the procedures walking on the table as before, serving the men according to rank, and the Franks with them.

They seemed quite familiar with the rite, even though they revealed that they did it a little different at home. They failed to lower their eyes to me when they thanked me for the drink, and they kept calling me Dame instead of Freyia, but I was told it was the same thing, except a Dame is never a goddess also. It would be against their faith to acknowledge my divinity. They were very strange folks. I sat down between Thióðolf and Arnulf's High Seat. The guests had been given seats of honor as well, as they were seated on the other side of the table at the top end, their leader sitting directly opposite me and next to the High Seat.

The slaves served us and did not sit at all. While we ate, we talked little, but as soon as bellies were filled, everybody relaxed and drank and chatted. The Franks talked about a king of theirs, whom they called Karl Magni, almost as if he was named after the Thunder Lord's son, although the way they pronounced it made the name sound almost like Charlemagne, and they were obviously very proud of him.

He had been the king of Frankland, but now he was also the king of Saxland, that land south of Denmark where I remembered that the legendary Queen Yrsa had been from, the captured girl who had charmed the Vikings who abducted her until they made her a queen, and she had become the mother of the legendary Skioldunga king, Hrolf Kráki. This Karl Magni had also conquered a place called Bavaria and was thought to be the rightful king of Italy, and was threatening the borders of the Iberian Emirate in the south, as well as those of Denmark in the north.

The Franks said that wherever he went, Karl Magni spread the word of someone called Christ, which I understood had to do with Christian people, and it was indeed true that these Franks were Christians, what made me very curious about them. Thióðolf was not very impressed, however, making a comment about how the word of Christ had in fact been forced upon the Saxons after destroying their sanctuaries, raping their priestesses, and beheading 4500 of their warriors in one single day, but the Franks shrugged and said that war is war, what no man around Arnulf's table could really dispute.

Hallgrim exchanged glances with Thióðolf and let him know in that silent manner that it was better not to speak of such things now. Like the men and the slaves did, I listened intently to Arnulf's conversation with the Franks, whose way of speaking Norse was very accented. But even as they spoke among themselves in the Frankish language did I soon begin to pick up meanings and words, for they did indeed speak a language somewhat similar to the Norse. The differences in words were also matched with a difference in their very way of speaking, a way that seemed more direct and less poetical, and without references to the gods and goddesses all the time.

They did refer to other things, though, such as the names Christ and Madonna. Thióðolf whispered to me that those were their chief deities, their one god and his mother, although there was apparently also a son and that nasty god what sucks the souls out of Christians who they called Dee-ah-boh-lus and gave their crosses to if they thought they saw him in a man. I was very curious about these matters, and Arnulf seemed to sense it, for he asked the Frank leader, whose name was Sir Gottfred, if he could tell us who this Christ was. All the Franks beamed proudly, and Sir Gottfred began to speak.

"Our lord, Jesus Christ, was born into this world 791 years ago. He was born to a maiden whom we call Madonna, but whose name was Maria. But even as she gave birth to our lord, the Madonna had never known a man..." He paused artfully to let that fact sink in, and we were all duly impressed.

"Where did she live then?" I asked.

"She lived in Nazareth, young Dame," Sir Gottfred said, and when I met his eyes I thought he was a nice man, and he looked as if he was pleased to be talking to me.

"Did they not have men in Nazareth, Heri?" I asked curiously, wondering what kind of place that would have been. Sir Gottfred looked amused.

"Yes, of course they had men there. But the Madonna had not known any of them," he explained, what only made me more confused.

"Did she never go out then?" I asked, "Did she have no clansmen?" The entire Hall began to giggle, and I tilted my head to the side and looked up at Thióðolf, who was grinning very broadly and patted my back encouragingly.

"She did have clansmen," Sir Gottfred said patiently, "and she was most probably allowed to go outside. What I mean was that she was a maiden, as in... the word for it is really virgin, but you know not this word in your language. It means a maiden who has not been with a man."

"Oh, you mean she had not played with a man's Freystone yet?" I asked, trying to use easy ways of speaking since I had begun to suspect that these men would not know what riding Freyia's path meant. They clearly understood what I meant now, and I wondered why they blushed and looked so surprised and so embarrassed.

"Yes, that is quite my meaning, young Dame," Sir Gottfred said, looking a little uncomfortable.

"Did she get to play when she was older, then?" I asked, and the whole Hall burst out laughing. Even the Franks looked like they had trouble keeping their guffaws back, although they all looked anxiously at Sir Gottfred, who appeared utterly embarrassed.

"Young Dame, this is the Madonna we are speaking of. She is most holy to us," he said gravely, and I looked confusedly at Arnulf, who smiled and winked encouragingly at me.

"I understand, Heri," I said patiently, "I just wanted to know if she ever got to play with a man's…"

"Stop!" Sir Gottfred interrupted me and looked around the table, where men were getting all red from forcing back laughter. The Frank looked so upset that I bowed my head apologetically, although I had no idea why he was angry with me.

"The Madonna never did that!" He growled angrily.

I wondered if he was feeling very sorry for her, being so upset about it. I said nothing but bowed my head again just to make it clear that I was sorry for whatever it was he was angry for.

"She is a virgin," he wheezed, even though I had not said anything.

"I am sorry for her too, Heri," I said compassionately, but when that only made him look ever the more angry, I whispered, "and I am sorry if I offended you. I meant no disrespect, Gottfred Heri."

I was indeed feeling truly sorry for unknowingly having offended Arnulf's honored guest, and a tear fell down my cheek. I wept as easily as other maidens now, just as I could laugh also. Immediately, I felt Thióðolf's hand pat my back reassuringly.

"You must excuse the maiden, Sir Gottfred," Thióðolf said, "She is of our people and has never met Christians before. She knows nothing of virgins, or of goddesses who cannot engage in matters that are in fact holy to us, even if they are not so to you. She meant no offense."

"Then I am sorry also, Thióðolf Skald, I meant not to offend the Dame of the Hall," Sir Gottfred said and bowed his head to me.

The matter of religion was suddenly left, everybody probably thinking it safer not to speak of such matters seeing as the Christians were very upset about their goddess still being a virgin even after 791 years, and I decided that I would be careful about reminding a Christian of that sad truth again.

Soon the conversation grew merry once more, until Sir Gottfred, having had a few cups by now, once more turned to me, this time obviously trying to win back my favor. Strangely enough, he had now somehow strained his voice to sound very gentle, as if he was talking endearingly to a small, frightened kitten. I regarded him curiously, having never once in my life being spoken to like that.

"You are such a pretty little maiden, young Dame," he said, "The men must be giving you flowers all the time!"

"Flowers?" I said, astonished.

"They don't? Well, maybe not yet, but soon enough I am sure these noble men will be picking flowers to give you all the time," Sir Gottfred said, as if he was trying to reassure me. I looked down the table at Arnulf's warriors, who were all regarding me expectantly. They were at their very sweetest now, looking proudly and affectionately at me, and yet, the image that now presented itself in my head made me burst out in giggles.

"What is so funny?" Sir Gottfred asked, still smiling.

"I am sorry, Heri, but I was just, I was just imagining any one of these warriors in the act of picking..." a giggle overtook me for a moment, "... picking flowers!"

The Hall went quiet for a moment before my men threw their heads back and roared with laughter, making jokes and simulating the act of picking flowers as if they were little maidens making a flower crown for the midsummer celebrations. I laughed so hard my tears began to roll, and even Sir Gottfred looked a little amused amidst his obvious confusion. When the commotion had settled a little, everybody looked expectantly at us again, and Sir Gottfred cleared his throat.

"So, I understand that the Rus warriors are not of the kind what picks flowers to young and pretty maidens. Surely there must be some other tokens of admiration or affection that they can give you? What would you rather have than a flower, young Dame?"

I looked uncertainly at Thióðolf, who had gotten that look of profound amusement in his eyes while still managing to keep his features straight. He nodded lightly to let me know that I could speak freely. I thought about these tokens of admiration and affection that the Frank was speaking of, and remembered the one token once given to me by the warriors what had truly made me feel cherished and cared for. I blushed at the thought and smiled as charmingly as I knew how.

"I would rather have a head," I said demurely.

There was an awkward silence while the Franks stared at me, jaws dropped. I lowered my eyes, trying my best to look humble and inoffensive lest I had unknowingly insulted them again. I peered uncertainly at my brothers, and felt relieved again when I saw how much they adored me now. They had my back all the while, I realized, and somehow, I was speaking for all of them what men could not freely say to each other without causing offense. Women and maidens can speak words that men cannot speak and live, Arnulf had once said to me, courtesy to the soft. Oh, yes. I would speak for my men.

"Excuse me, Maiden, did you say a head?" Sir Gottfred finally asked.

"Yes, Heri," I said gravely, "I would very much appreciate a head."

Sir Gottfred looked at Arnulf and then at Thióðolf, uncertain if he had understood me correctly. "I am not altogether certain if I understand the young Dame correctly, Arnulf Heri," Sir Gottfred said after some consideration, frowning. The Frank clearly wished to avoid another unintended word duel with a maiden, and opted for a little humility.

"She means that from a warrior, she would rather have a gift of the severed head of an enemy what has in any way offended her or her kind," Arnulf explained cheerfully, and the Franks all went pale.

"That is an unusual wish for a young maiden," Sir Gottfred commented, looking quite astonished, if not aghast, hardly daring to meet my gaze.

At least he did not speak to me as if I was a frightened kitten again.

"You clearly do not know our Sífs," Hallgrim chuckled, and the other warriors cheered.

"They are blade honers, our women," Sígtrygg added, and my brothers cheered again, beaming as they looked at me now, all appearing immensely proud of me.

"Proper spear enticers, they are, our girls," Njál grinned.

"Our Sífs are axe-wielding arm-raisers," Agnarr said, being a man who aimed at learning the art of poetry, and so often experimented with poetical cover words, what now earned him another round of cheers and a thumbs up from Thióðolf Skald.

The Franks exchanged glances.

"Where I come from, young maidens are given flowers, not heads," Sir Gottfred finally said, shaking his head as if he was a little disturbed.

"What do they do with flowers then, Heri?" I asked curiously.

"What do they do with them? What do you do with heads?" Sir Gottfred asked incredulously, and all the Franks, albeit somewhat shocked, looked not offended this time, but sincerely curious.

I recalled all the things that I now knew had been done with Hialti's head and proceeded dutifully, "I would make a poem about it and spit on it. That was what I did the last time I received a head."

I glanced over at Miri and Zivah and the other slave girls, who were all having trouble keeping their laughter back. I met Miri's laughing gaze and proceeded, "And then I or my handmaidens would perhaps later piss on it, kick it and stomp on it until there was nothing left of it. Then we might bury it," I frowned, wondering if I had remembered everything, and added cautiously, "If there was anything left to bury, of course."

The Franks just gaped at me as if they did not understand a word I had said. I thought they needed further explanation, remembered other things I had heard being done with heads in various legends, and added helpfully, "If I was not quite so angry with the head's owner, I might just boil it and take the skull to a silversmith, perhaps. Make it into a beautiful drinking cup and present it to the warrior who gave me the head in the first place, as a way of rewarding him. Or if I was very angry with the head's owner and his kinsmen, I could send the silver skull cup to them as an anonymous gift or pretend it was a gift of friendship, and then I could have a good laugh when they drank from the skull of their own clansman."

Even when presented with such a detailed and easily understandable description of the usefulness of severed enemy heads, the Franks still sat speechless, and their eyes betrayed a lack of comprehension. I also thought I detected a look of disgust, and realized that the Franks might think the actions I had just described were in fact dishonorable.

"Well, I am not a man, Heri, so I hope you understand that I am powerless to settle such matters in the direct ways of men," I explained, hoping that an appeal to their manliness as opposed to my vulnerable position as a female would placate them. "So, I would have to go about my vengeance in clever and hidden ways, the way that women do." I concluded, quite satisfied with my explanation.

When they still failed to respond intelligently and instead kept gaping at me, I thought about the fact that the Franks seemed to have very novel views on certain basic matters and added, inspired by Thióðolf's words earlier, "It is honorable enough for a maiden to proceed thus, among our people, even if it might not be so with yours."

Sir Gottfred only nodded respectfully to that. His eyes were still a little wide. The Franks began to talk between themselves, and I heard them say a foreign word, "savage," several times. Aziza, who was just walking behind me to serve more drink, whispered into my ear that the word "savage" meant the same as "barbarian." They clearly meant me. I beamed with pride, as well as anticipation, for if they thought me barbarian, they must be civilized men after all.

Civilized men were funny.

"Maiden, do you like to receive heads?" Sir Gottfred finally asked.

"Of course I like it," I said, frowning, and looked to Thióðolf and Arnulf for help.

"It is a great honor paid to a maiden, Sir Gottfred," Arnulf Heri said, "It is a very noble gesture from a warrior, showing favor to a maiden and a willingness to avenge slights against her. He shows himself a man worthy of her respect.

You don't find the severed heads of enemies all around, it takes some courage and manly skill to get that, not to say dedication. But flowers? What do flowers mean? Anyone can pick a flower. It does not prove a man's worth, picking a flower."

I nodded my agreement, as did all my brothers.

"Well, it is not meant to prove a man's worth. It is a gesture to the maiden, a way of admiring her, and saying that she is like the flower," Sir Gottfred said.

"Why would she want to be like a flower?" Thióðolf asked, sounding a little outraged at the notion. We all were.

"Because the flower is sweet and beautiful," the Frank said defensively.

"Tell me, Thordís, would you like to be a flower?" Thióðolf said, turning to me. I tried to imagine that kind of life and slowly shook my head thoughtfully.

"It sounds boring, being a flower," I replied, "A flower only stands there all its life unless someone picks it, when it begins to die slowly. I would rather not."

"Ah," Sir Gottfred said, "what would you prefer to be then?"

The Franks looked expectantly at me, wondering what a maiden who wanted a head rather than a flower would actually want to be. But that was an easy question.

"I would rather be a she-wolf," I said and smiled my sweetest smile, what made all the Franks widen their eyes for a moment, "Then I can run wild in the forests and hunt and play and have all the fun I would like to have," I concluded contentedly. What I had said about being a she-wolf sounded exactly like my life.

"I see," Sir Gottfred said and leaned backwards for a moment, shaking his head in disbelief again, exchanging glances with his men. Then he leaned towards me again, "I think that men would be rather frightened of you, Maiden, and that they would not woo you, if you were a she-wolf," he said, "whereas a flower is always desirable."

I regarded the Franks incredulously for a moment before I let my gaze pass over all the warriors of the Hall, the Franks, and my brothers the Rus. Suddenly I knew the real difference between these civilized men and we savage barbarians. For there could be only one reason why a man would need his woman to be no more challenging than a flower.

I would not offend my Heri's guests again, but there are always subtle ways of saying things. I drew my breath and spoke from my heart, knowing well that my verdict was holy.

"It is possible that Christian men are frightened of she-wolves, Heri," I said, and let my gaze pass all the Franks in the most neutral and inoffensive, yet also clearly uninterested way that I could muster, before I nodded approvingly towards Arnulf's warriors and concluded my verdict with a loving smile, "but as you can see, Gottfred Heri, any man who woos me will be a he-wolf."

The Franks graciously began smiling even as they had been defeated by a maiden's words. My own men looked at me with broad smiles and light in their eyes. It was my first proper word-duel, I suddenly realized, and I had won it, and to perfection, where I had never won a duel with any man before. Not only had I won it, but I had won the duel on behalf of all my men. My brothers were bursting with pride and Thióðolf squeezed my hand beneath the table, and like all the men he was trying hard not to look too triumphant in the faces of our humbled guests.

"You have earned another nickname, dear Thordís, our Síf," Hallgrim chuckled, being the first to speak after my splendid victory on behalf of our hall, and the one to pass out rewards, "We shall call you Serpent Tongue now, along with all your other names."

"What sorts of names does she have now?" Sir Gottfred asked, smiling gracefully as he acknowledged his defeat.

"Blood Drinker!" Sígtrygg called out.

"Heart Devourer!" Agnarr shouted.

"Liver Gorging Hare Huntress!" Runarr cheered. The hall roared like never before. My warriors rolled on the floor from laughter, and I blushed a little, remembering when I was given a freshly killed hare to skin a few days past, and had felt just a little hungry.

"She-Wolf and Blade Honer," Njál said when he could be heard again, "and I am pretty sure she will become our greatest Spear Enticer! Look here, Sir Gottfred, she made me this lovely rabbit skull necklace, is our Síf not the most diligent little maiden you ever saw?"

Sir Gottfred looked seriously pale and whispered the name of their god of below, Deeh-ah-boh-lus, the one that sucks the souls out of Christian folks. Njál grinned broadly with his fanged teeth and nodded politely, "Oh, I am quite content with drinking my enemy's blood only, Sir Gottfred. And I have really never been that particular about my enemy's faith, to tell you the truth."

"You all owe me name gifts now," I reminded my brothers, and had to move quickly to catch all the rings and trinkets they now threw to me. The Franks wisely refrained from commenting on my reward. Arnulf hugged me, kissed me on the cheek and let me sit beside him in the High Seat, as if I was truly the Hall's Freyia. Each one of my warriors came and hugged me and hurled me up in the air, calling me the best blade honer ever.

Njál flashed his sharp fangs at me while he held me and asked if he looked like a proper he-wolf to me, what I laughingly acknowledged and was rewarded with another flight towards the roof of the Hall, while the Franks buried their sorrows in more ale and mead and kept casting worried glances at us all. After a while they cheered up a little, though, seeing as it was next to impossible for even the most civilized kinds of men to sit glum in a hall full of Vikings having a party, and the rest of the evening was only merriment.

Once, I overheard Njál saying to Ivarr that he would be able to get me a head one day, no worries, while patting the young boy reassuringly on the back, and Ivarr, not aware that I was watching, smiled so adorably and blushed. After that night, I noticed that Ivarr was furiously practicing head-chopping almost every day, mutilating one sack of hard-packed hay after the other. The slave girls complained, because they had to stitch the sacks together every evening, but I thought it sweet and made no mockery of it.

WIDUKIND AND CHARLEMAGNE

The Franks stayed in court for a whole week before they left. Every day, the men ventured out with them and stayed out, and in the evenings they ate and drank in the warriors' Hall. I was not privy to their councils. But the day before they were supposed to leave, Arnulf Heri and Thióðolf were tired of the Hall and stayed in the Hold with us, and there was a knock on the door. One of the Franks entered, the one called Siegfried.

He was rather old, I thought, as old as Arnulf at least, and he had darkish hair and a very full beard, what after a week among the Rus had been washed and combed and styled so that he looked as barbarian as the rest of the men. Siegfried was followed by Hallgrim and now the men sat down around the table. The slaves left the table at once, seeing as there was to be a men's council, but when I got up to leave with them, Arnulf told me to stay. He said that I might as well start to learn about the greater world of men out there. And then he gestured for me to come over and placed me to sit on his great knee in the High Seat.

I felt so very honored.

"Arnulf Heri," Siegfried began, in his heavily accented Norse, "now that I find myself among friends, I would like to convey a truth about myself. I am not a Frank. I am a Saxon. I am also a Heathen like you men here. For some time I have had to hide and pretend to be a Christian, and when I heard Sir Gottfred wanted to go and see the Rus, I offered my services on the way. But I am not sworn to him. And now that I have seen how you all live here, I have nurtured a growing wish to stay. I have heard that there is one man missing to the warriors' Hall. I have not told this to Gottfred, but I have spoken to Hallgrim and the others in his group of six in secret, although they are presently only five men. I have even spoken to the Sheath, Miri, and she, uhm, she said she would not mind if only I could wash myself like a proper savage."

Siegfried the Saxon grinned when he saw that he had made the rest of us laugh already.

"What I would like to ask you, Arnulf Heri, is that you let me show my worth and see if you will accept me into your band. I am willing to swear myself to you for as long as you wish it. I really have no wish of going back to Sachsen where the Franks have now made a nation of slaves out of my people. I have lost everything I once owned, even my good name. I have nothing to return to."

"If Hallgrim and the other men… and the woman too agrees," Arnulf chuckled a little, "I can see nothing wrong with that proposal. We can let you stay and see if you get along, and then I will take you on as my sworn man, Siegfried."

"I am eternally grateful to you, Heri," Siegfried said, and they cheered on that. "Now that you are here in the Hold with us, perhaps you could entertain us a little with a somewhat less… Christian approach to what has been going on in your lands of late, Siegfried," Arnulf said, "I must say those Franks keep me well befuddled."

"Indeed. Let me tell you this. I have five and thirty winters here on holy Earth, and most of my life as a man grown has been a long and hard battle. When I was a young boy, there was still hope, still thoughts of glory. Now all that remains are desperate refugees fighting to maintain the last vestiges of a once most beautiful land. Great Widukind has been a Christian for five years now, and with him lost to the cause, the armies have dissolved and given way to hopelessness."

"What did he go and get himself baptized for?" Arnulf asked, and I nudged him discreetly in the side. When he paused to look at me, I whispered, "Excuse me, Heri. What does baptized mean?"

"That is a way of converting to the Christian faith, Maiden," Siegfried said. "The baptism involves a rite where you are dipped into water and then a spell is spoken what ties you forever to Christ. They think that if you have been baptized you have a chance of getting into Heaven."

"What heaven?" Arnulf asked.

"Oh, you know, Heri, they think there is only the one," Siegfried replied, and we all laughed.

"At least it seems you have to get a wash before you get in," Arnulf snorted, and had us laugh even more. Even Siegfried laughed, and I cleared my throat again.

"You may speak, Thordís," Arnulf said.

"I was just wondering why the Franks are so afraid of washing, if they have to wash to even become Christian," I asked politely.

"Christian priests believe that washing leads to sin," Siegfried explained, and when we all looked dumbfounded at him, he continued, "You see, they think that when a man and a woman wash their bodies, they become lustful."

We all nodded. Even I knew that. And when we continued to look expectantly at Siegfried to complete his explanation, he suddenly exclaimed, "Oh how fortune has blessed me to come among people who do not even know of what I spoke just now!"

Arnulf frowned, not liking to be thought ignorant, but Siegfried quickly explained, "You see, Heri, the Christian priests believe that lustfulness is sinful. They believe that the pull of Freyia is sinful. They believe that the games of Freyia are sinful, and that the human body is sinful and dirty and soiled. Especially the body of woman. They believe that we ought not to engage in lustful games at all, and when we do so anyway we are supposed to repent our sins and flog our own backs and beg forgiveness from the Lord and Christ."

Now that it was explained to us, we all grasped it. I had already heard some stories of such notions, and so had the men, of course, it was just that it was hard to grasp that anyone could seriously think such thoughts. The men were frowning and shaking their heads dismissively.

"They make dirty all that which is holy," Hallgrim said darkly, and they all nodded.

"The strangest thing about these civilized people," Njál the Foolish said, "is that they are actually upset about the fact that we have bodies and need to please our bodies with the bodies of other people. They think that is a bad thing, for some reason. They truly are upset about that fact. The Big Tunic Men keep washing themselves all the time because they think they are soiled from all kinds of things, especially the games of Freyia, while the Christians appear to think they are doomed and dirty in any case and often refuse to wash altogether. It is hard to understand."

We all nodded gravely to his speech.

"But why are they so upset about having bodies and feeling Freyia's pull?" I asked.

"Honestly, Maiden, I have never truly understood that part. Those times I have asked a priest he has started to splutter, as if the very subject upsets him so much he can hardly speak of it," Siegfried said and shrugged.

"I do know that there are runes written down in very holy books that seem to tell them it is so, or so they believe, and they keep feeling dirty," Thióðolf said, "It is not a reasonable thing, but a lot of the things those civilized people do and believe in are far removed from reason anyway. My impression is that they are terribly frightened about everything. A man needs only stick his tongue out and roll his eyes a little and they swoon. Like the way they are terrified of Hel as well. Maybe their fear blinds them and makes them thus skittish? I heard they even fear their own god."

"It must be very tiresome to be so easily upset about the most natural things," I said and felt sorry for all those poor civilized people. It must be so hard to feel dirty all the time, even if you were not. And by goodness it must be hard to walk around like a stinking turd also. When I said as much, all the men laughed and the slaves with them. I could not help but notice that even Shumayl laughed.

"Admittedly, all folks do not think in those terms even if they are Christians," Siegfried said, "but the very pious ones are rather strict about it, and I have heard of ancient public baths what have been closed down on that account. They say that you know a saint by his or her stench. A saint is a holy man or woman, in case you wondered."

"I have a feeling that their holy women are not quite like ours," Arnulf mused, creating another round of shaking shoulders and snorting men. After some amusement, Siegfried was urged on to tell his story.

"It has now been eighteen years since the sanctuary of the Irminsul, that is Saxon for The Great Sage, was destroyed by the Christians. I remember it as if it was yesterday, for I was there at the sanctuary that day. I was still a very young man, and although I had been a warrior for two years I was unarmed that day, because it was the custom of my people the Saxons to not enter the sacred grove while still armed. In that way we show our submission and our slavery to the great lord. I know that you all call him Óðinn, but we Saxons refer to him as Wodan as of old. That shrine is ancient and very important. Folks used to come from all over the homelands on pilgrimage to this grove of the Breath-Giver for hundreds of years. And that day was a day of ceremony. Men and women, young and old, had gathered to pray and show our reverence to the Lord of Winds, and the ritual was presided over by the holy women who have dedicated their lives to the god. Nobody had expected an attack on the sanctuary. But then they came, the Franks, they rode fully armed into the shrine and began slaying everyone. It mattered not to these men if their victims were children, or women, or old people, or cripples, they slayed everyone that they could reach with their blades. I had a sister and two of her children to protect, and strove to get them out of there unharmed. What I saw before I managed to flee from there was a gruesome sight. They pulled out the entrails of men still living. The Christian soldiers raped the priestesses of Wodan right there on the altar. They stabbed little babies and put them up on stakes, and when their priests entered the grove they told them that these were our Heathen sacrifices to the god. While their soldiers tortured and raped and killed, their priests and their priestesses walked around the pillar of the Great Sage and sang hymns to Christ before they tore down the holy tree and desecrated it, pissed on it and laughed while the raped women wept. And then came Karl Magni, the king, and declared that this sight was most pleasing to the lord – to their lord. The Franks had invaded our lands, and now began a battle that has lasted my whole life since. We warriors met up in the woodlands and elected a war leader by the name of Widukind. His name means Child of the Forest in our language, which is not so far removed from yours. He was indeed a woodman and it was his idea that we fight this battle where our strength lie; in the woods and the hills, for the Franks are better at open field battles, and use strategy as a way of planning to act dishonorably. For years we fought them, attacking the enemy from unseen and unexpected places.I went with Widukind to Denmark thirteen years past, and we talked there to Sígurð Ring, the king of the Danes, and he was willing to receive refugees and support us to a certain extent. But rather than adding men to our Saxon forces, the Danish king said he had to think of his own. He decided to strengthen the great wall that separates his land from the southern realms, that wall they call Danevirke. It had already been begun a long time ago, but now Sígurð Ring had men start working harder to make that wall stand strong, and he worked out the defense of channels and coastlines. He has also realized that the Franks can never be defeated in open field combat. They have to be stopped by fighting in the way of shadow walkers, by seemingly random attacks and swift escapes.'"

"Like in a Viking raid," Hallgrim mused, and the men exchanged thoughtful glances.

"Yes, like in Viking raids. But my tribe has not been sea-born for many generations, Hallgrim," Siegfried said, "Where you are the masters of the ocean steeds, my people were the masters of the forest hills. But the Franks responded to our strategies by burning down great stretches of ancient and holy forests. We had not imagined they would do such things. These forests had oaks in them that were surely thousands of years old. They were very sacred. But the Christians do not seem to believe in anything sacred, apart from their lousy book."

"What about the Danes," Arnulf said, "they are sea-born, are they not?"

"Yes, but the Danes have been hesitating for a long time. They have worked on strengthening their defenses, and they have been friendly and helpful to those of us who have come to ask for shelter and supplies, but they have not wished to partake in any battles. They are biding their time, hoping that through diplomacy they will not have to fight the Franks. They even received Karl Magni at their court a few years back, when he tried to make them refuse more Saxon refugees. To Sígurð Ring's credit, he refused. Saxon refugees may still come to Denmark. Even I went there, to safely deposit my sister and her children. But it is no life for a man, being a refugee, living at the mercy of your betters. I returned to my homelands and tried to continue the fight, and I fought next to Widukind many times. A great warrior, a great sage, and a great man and leader of men."

"Who went and got himself baptized," Arnulf said grimly.

"He did that for his people, like a sacrifice onto them," Siegfried said, "and if you had been at Verden and seen what happened there..." he turned to me and frowned, "How old are you, Maiden?"

"I am seven and a half year," I said.

"Seven. Yes. This happened some eight or nine years ago, I think. Karl Magni had won a very decisive battle, and our army had to acknowledge defeat. I was among the scouts of the forest and had found a hidden place for myself, close enough to watch the field and hear the shouts. The king rode across the field and screamed at my tribesmen that if they wanted human sacrifice, then they should have it. And he declared that all men who did not let themselves be baptized immediately should make ready for beheading. Then, as one man, my tribesmen fell to their knees in acceptance of Death. The Christian king was furious, and as if just to mock us, he made his priests walk about and baptize the Saxon warriors anyway, and then he had them all beheaded. There were four thousand five hundred men what had knelt to Death and what were sacrificed to Christ on that day."

We were speechless. Even though the men knew about this event from before, it was something else to hear the story spoken from an eye-witness.

"Now began the real horror," Siegfried proceeded, "for with all those great men gone there was hardly anybody left to protect the women and the children. Karl Magni let his soldiers run wild. That is how he finances his army after all. His soldiers of Christ raided our land like Vikings: stole, burned, raped, tortured and killed. Whatever was left of our people eventually were either sold as slaves or made into serfs, that is a sort of slave too, but land-bound rather than man-bound, and force-baptized, of course. All of us men who had owned land and estates and titles, all that was taken from us, and Frankish noblemen were set in our steads. We owned nothing left of our own land, and people have had to work like slaves for their Frankish lords ever since. Our sacred parliaments were dissolved. We used to be twelve tribes, twelve Saxon tribes. We had sent three men from each tribe, one war-leader, one nobleman and one commoner, and they used to gather for parliament and make the laws and the decisions for the common years, each representing their tribe and their class. It was a good and sacred and time-honored way of ruling a tribe. But our parliaments were crushed, and all we have had to go by since then are the cruel dictates of Karl Magni. And his dictates continued harshly and cruelly until Widukind acknowledged our defeat. He realized that there was only one way to placate the Christian king, and that his own death was not that way. He knew that his death would only fuel more combat and more suffering to an already broken tribe.

"So Widukind made a spectacular entry into the royal congregation of Christians, by walking into their midst and letting himself fall down on his knees before the cross, and speaking a whole bunch of inanities that he knew would make sense to the Christians, if nobody else. Karl Magni was so moved by his old enemy's humble gesture that he made a great show of Christian forgiveness. Since then, he has paraded old Widukind around like he was some sort of exotic puppy, behold the old enemy of Christ who has now seen the truth and changed his Heathen ways. It is a sad sight. The old warrior has borne that humiliation for as long as it has kept his people from suffering even more. He was baptized five years past, and since then the Franks have tried to make a more peaceful reign in Sachsen. But the truth remains that all Saxons are now second-class citizens in their own land, and many of us kept fighting little battles here and there until it no longer seems to make any sense. The battle is lost. I made myself useful as a mercenary for the Franks then, when my band of brothers was utterly dissolved, but now there are rumors that all Saxon men are going to be forcefully sent to battle the Avars in the east on behalf of Karl Magni. I have no wish to fight against other Heathens for the sake of that Christian king, even if the Avars were never any friends of mine. I sold my battle hand to Gottfred on his journey here, for the sake of seeing a different land, and I cannot say I want to go back to my own," Siegfried said, and added jokingly, "Unless I had with me a fleet of Rus Vikings, of course."

Siegfried spoke those last words as a joke, but the Rus Vikings did not laugh. Arnulf and Hallgrim exchanged glances, and looked from Siegfried to Thióðolf.

"It seems that our Rus Viking services are about to be in high demand of late," Arnulf mused thoughtfully. "Young Thióðolf there has suggested similar things. He is from North Way, you know, and says his people are rather concerned about the events what are going on down in Sachsen, seeing as this Karl Magni appears to be on a mission to baptize everyone else. Now that Sachsen is falling, Denmark is next, and if Denmark is taken, there is only so much what separates the lands."

He paused, and Thióðolf shrugged to confirm the truth of Arnulf's words. "Then I can say that I am truly among friends," Siegfried said and raised his cup to cheer with Thióðolf, who cheered back. And then there was a silence.

"We are moved by your story," Hallgrim said finally, "and more than pleased to have you with us. But as to Viking fleets, we shall have to think about it, naturally."

"Naturally," Siegfried and Thióðolf both said in unison. The following day, the Franks left our court. They looked rather disappointed when Siegfried declared that he was staying with the Rus, and Gottfred looked veritably hurt when Siegfried waved his goodbyes with one arm, holding his other arm around Miri. Miri, on her side, smiled sweetly at the Christian lord, only to have confirmed that a man like him would not smile in public to the likes of her.

We talked about it later and were all rather certain that those Christians preferred women what could stay virgins for 791 years on end.

THE SPEAR-WIELDER STRODE

The months after Yule were often merry as the days grew longer and the world still shone white with snow. We frequently went skiing, and, when Thióðolf and I went alone, I was always dressed like a boy, and being so good at all the manly arts, I passed well as long as my hair was tucked beneath a hood and my face half covered. In any case, few men used the hills for sports and we hardly ever met anyone.

We both felt that our adventures together were protected in some way, that higher powers would make sure nothing ever happened, and surely we never felt threatened at all. Both he and I had always known the protection of our Full Troths. Between his goddess and my god, we were well taken care of, and we had many proofs of that. He taught me how to ski without the use of a staff, and then how to shoot with bow and arrow while skiing. It was very challenging, but my body always seemed to be able to copy the movements of others, and so I studied him and copied him until I reached another level of perfection.

One day in late winter, we were out with Zivah and some of the men, Hallgrim, Runarr, Njál, Sígtrygg, another warrior called Síggeir, Ivarr and Búi the slave boy to take care of the horses, and, it seemed, for whispering ceaselessly with Runarr. That day, Zivah surprised Thióðolf by approaching us while we were shooting at target from a still position. She looked a little embarrassed but stood there, studying his feet carefully.

"Zivah," he said gently, as he always did when she approached, signaling that she could speak.

"I wondered if I might try the bow, Heri," she said, still with her eyes locked at his feet.

"Do you shoot, Zivah?" He asked, surprised. The men around were looking all other ways, pretending absolute indifference and temporary deafness with very little success.

"I am my mother's daughter, same as she," Zivah said, "I mean same as the Maiden, Heri. Our mother taught us both." She cast a nervous glance at the men, knowing that their presence meant that she had to be careful, and added, "Please excuse me if I offend, Heri."

"You do not offend, Zivah, you surprise. I like surprises. I fear this bow is too heavy for you, but you can try it, and if you like, I will make you a better bow. Or perhaps Hallgrim will, is that not so, Hallgrim?"

"I can do that," Hallgrim said amiably, "Only the law states that slaves may not own weapons."

"Well, we can say that I own the weapon and that I have ordered my slave to use it, because I take pleasure in seeing a beautiful woman shoot with a bow," Thióðolf said and winked at Zivah, who went very red.

"That is a very good reason, Skald," Hallgrim said, smiling, and all the men made sure to turn another way while they grinned broadly and exchanged knowing glances. Thióðolf gave the bow to Zivah, who felt its weight and agreed that it was too large and heavy for her, but that she would like to try nevertheless. She aimed and shot, and hit the target straight. We had both inherited a sure aim from our mother, and the men were duly impressed. Thióðolf looked so proud and happy I almost thought he was going to hug her, but he managed to control himself when he saw Zivah cringe from him.

"That was a great shot, Zivah. You have earned a bow," he said, and I saw that she was smiling when she turned away from him.

The next time we were out, Zivah was presented with a bow of her own as soon as we were well out of town, and she shot so well that the men cheered her on, and after that she often accompanied us outdoors and practiced her shooting.

Then there was that one time she forgot herself completely while she stood among the men, and met Thióðolf's smile with a big smile of her own, an action of her own part that still surprised her so much that the men almost toppled over laughing when they saw how she tried to compose her features back to her usual sullen mode as swiftly as possible.

She was so upset about them laughing at her that she suddenly slid off on her skis, and for once, Thióðolf followed her and stopped her by touching her arm. She remembered her place and stopped stiff, apologizing with her head bowed, and we all heard the small sound she made when she winced out of fear when he touched her. It was clear that she still did not trust him not to beat her, for she looked terrified.

I saw Thióðolf's face turn sad at the sight.

"I will never hurt you again, Zivah," he said softly, and when she still stood there all stiff and anxious he added, "I just wanted to say that we did not laugh to ridicule you. We laughed simply because you were so sweet when you tried to hide your smile. So sweet. We could not help ourselves. Please, do not be angry with us."

She nodded slowly and seemed to relax a little, but tears were lurking in the corners of her eyes, and her fear had been all too real. Thióðolf sighed remorsefully, and then suddenly something changed in him. It was the skald in him that seemed to seize him, and when the change was complete he spoke a poem with his deep bard's voice, what seemed to reverberate through the hills:

"The River Goddess wept
And the Spear Wielder strode
Up steep mountains
And down deep valleys
River wolves stole the goddess
May the Tribeswolf bring her back!"

The goddess. Bring her back. The goddess. Bring her back.

Those words echoed, over and over. We all stood awed at the poetry, and I could see that Zivah struggled to decipher the verse, but it was not at all that difficult. She knew that Thióðolf's name meant Tribeswolf, even if he had used different words for both than those what made up his name, and that a spear wielder was a way of saying both warrior and lover. The river wolves who stole the goddess were of course the Vikings, and the river goddess, that was herself.

When she realized that he had made a poem about the two of them and how he wished to restore her to former glory, she broke down in fits of sobs and tears. The men could not interfere so I went and hugged her instead, holding her while she wept, and the men, out of respect, pretended not to notice. When she had finished weeping, we sat together in silence for a while.

"I am tired of fighting him, Thordís. I want to accept my fate and have peace of mind. I like him, I really do. I wish I could yield to him now," she said finally, "but there is still something missing. There is still something within me that cannot forgive."

"What is it you need, Zivah?" I asked.

"Freedom," she said quietly, "I need freedom, sister. But that is too far-fetched, is it not? I would be nothing but fair game. He is the best Heri I could hope for, and yet he is my Heri, and I am not free. What a beautiful poem he made, Thordís. I do not hate him anymore, I even like him, yet still I cannot help but resent him. How can he bring me back? My people are gone, and there is no place in the world where I can be free. How can he ever atone for that?"

I had no answer to her speech.

Later, when I spoke to Thióðolf alone, I said that I thought I knew what the final test was about. When he asked me what that would be, I said it would be about Atonement.

"How can I atone to her?" He asked.

"How would I know, Thióðolf?" I said dismissively, "You are the poet here. Invent something. I just gave you a clue."

"Ah, you little norn," he said smiling. "We are within a sacred song."

Then came spring, so suddenly and powerfully that it was as if all nature wept the coldness away in one great seizure.

THE SÍF WITHIN

One bright early spring day when I was out riding with Thióðolf, we found a place to sit out, and I decided to breach a subject I had long been pondering. I opened my mouth to speak, but Thióðolf shook his head to signal that he needed a small break, took out his comb from a pocket and began combing his hair. I gently took the comb from him, stood behind him while he sat and began grooming him.

When I had finished doing his hair and beard, I sat in front of him between his crossed legs and enjoyed the feeling of the comb as he brushed my hair with it and finally made a little braid to keep my hair away from my face, the same kind that he liked to wear himself. I leaned back against his chest when he had finished, and we just sat like that for a while, enjoying our closeness.

We often worked with combing and braiding his hair and mine when we were sitting out together, since doing something with the hands was a good thing when learning through words, according to him. It also felt good to be close in this way. Finally, he gave me a nod, and I spent no time waiting.

"Thióðolf," I said, tilting my head to look up at him, as I was still sitting there in front of him. I saw how he smiled warmly like he always did when I did that. I liked the way his eyes often seemed to be brimming over with love when he saw me.

"I heard Hallgrim say that you had been trained by blade honers and that they taught you, uhm, they thought you about how to rule people the right way."

"Yes."

"So what does that mean? To rule people the right way?"

"The best way to explain these things to you is to tell you my story," Thióðolf said, "so that you will understand how ruling can be a way of serving." I nodded eagerly, always curious about people's stories, and particularly Thióðolf's, who rarely spoke about his own past except in a few fragments.

"Do you remember when I told you, when you first came to us, about how my sister honed me and made me a warrior?"

"Yes, Thióðolf, I remember it very well," I said.

"Good. And you might remember that my trial of manhood came when we had a squabble with another clan over the matter of a Síf's honor, and that it was nothing too serious, so that it did not merit death."

I nodded.

"Thordís, we never have real squabbles with other clans that are not serious enough to merit death. What we do have are mock-squabbles. We make them up."

"What?" I gaped.

"Ours is a warrior's world. But that does not mean we have wars all the time. On the contrary, years and decades can pass without serious incidents of any kind. For the most part, we live in peace, at least where I am from. And we prefer it like that. Even most warriors do. Peace is what brings joy and prosperity and good times. But our people long since learned the hard way that if we allowed ourselves to go soft and unprepared, we would become, we would become like your mother's people, Thordís. We would become easy prey."

I could agree with that. My father had said that the River People were very wise in their gentleness and the way they dealt more freely with ranking, but it was also true that we had been unable to defend ourselves against Vikings.

When Thióðolf saw that I was not offended by his assessment, he continued, "and so we hone ourselves for war all the time, knowing well that the better prepared and the more strong we appear, the less chance there is for us to have to risk our homes and our Sífs in war. But it means that we need to be constantly alert and constantly trained. In times of peace, we make up squabbles and little feuds just to keep ourselves well honed."

"So," I interfered, "do you actually kill each other?"

"We try very hard not to. It is excellent exercise, Thordís. It gives us the training we need to partake in a war or a combat, and it also exercises our self-control, because even as we have to fight for real, we will attempt not to kill or seriously maim our opponents. It does happen, but the whole thing has been sanctified first and witnessed, and so nobody will blame a man if an accident happens, unless it appears to be no accident. Then we might have a real feud going on. So we tend to be careful."

"Oh." I thought I could see how it made sense after all.

"This tradition is particularly important when a young boy is of an age and skill to prove himself in battle. I was fifteen years old, and had trained since I was three, and I very much wanted to join the King's fleet the year after, but I had to prove myself first. Our land, Hálógaland, was simply too peaceful for me. All the clans there are friendly with each other. Ours is a happy land, Thordís, it is very different from here. Even slaves are freer than you, as a maiden, can ever be here. To a young lad, peace can be difficult. Everybody could see how I suffered because I could not get a chance to prove myself, and so my clan made a deal with another clan, what also had a young lad in need to prove himself. The Sífs of our clans were made privy to the plans, and one day a young cousin of mine came into the hall and complained that a certain young man of the other clan had invited her to dally with him the whole afternoon, but that he had left her waiting in the grove where they were going to play and never turned up. When she had confronted him, he had laughed at her and told her that she was desperate for his Freystone in public! It was very insulting to all of us, but of course not the kind of insult that would normally lead to a proper feud. If it had been real, her brothers or some other clansmen would just go and beat the offender up, and not even his clan would have reacted, knowing him to have offended a woman. I was very young still, and knew not that it was all a pun, and when all the clan acted seriously outraged, I was too, because the idea of a Síf of mine being humiliated was what I had been brought up to always want to avenge."

Thióðolf smiled broadly at the memory.

"All the women of our clan demanded that we do something about it lest they would all become objects of ridicule to men who thought they could slight them and scorn them, and they howled and tore off their clothes to show us their breasts, reminding us of how they nourish us and what we have to protect. They beat their chests and tore their hairs and carried on so terribly that the men shrugged and ignored them utterly and promptly left the settlement to plan an act of vengeance on behalf of all our Sífs." Thióðolf smiled broadly once more.

"For the first time, my clansmen brought me with them, telling me that this was a great opportunity for me to prove myself. I was told to give our enemies a good beating, but not kill them, since our Síf had not been raped or beaten or anything else so serious as to merit death. No boys ever learn about these games until they are grown, so I believed every word, as did the other lad from the other clan. He had been served exactly the same story, you see. We were both a bit perplexed when the word duel that always initiates a fight indicated that the other clan was just as outraged as we were, but we young boys were too excited about the prospect of entering real combat to really pay attention to that fact. We fought well, and both parties thought they had given the other a good beating. I earned my first scar, and became a man, as did the other lad. And that was really the whole point of the fight even from the start."

"They all tricked you? Both your own clan and the other clan?" I asked, confused.

"They did not trick us as such, Thordís. They helped us. Can you imagine the love and the care they must all have felt for us, to create such a risky spectacle just to allow us two young boys to prove ourselves? They were all in on it, both my clan and the other clan, men and women all. Our Sífs put on quite a show for our benefit. And the men of both clans risked both lives and limbs, Thordís. And they did it all for us, and they let us think it was for real so that we would really fight well. It was profoundly moving to realize after."

"Oh," I said, awed, gathering still new knowledge about my father's people.

"I also told you how my sister greeted me as a warrior and lowered her eyes to me, and that I swore to protect her," Thióðolf continued, "After having lived through her mockery all my boyhood, it was a great feeling to finally see her submit to me and respect me as a warrior and her protector. I was a proud young man, Thordís, and I am the kind of man who is better at ruling others than at being ruled. I do not have the chant of submission in my soul song, if you understand."

"I understand that," I said, smirking. Thióðolf was definitely not the kind of man what let others rule him, but he was always very good at taking the command in all kinds of situations.

Even when it came to his Heri, Arnulf, had I noticed that albeit the fact that Thióðolf always paid Arnulf all the proper courtesies, he was never really submissive, and Arnulf never asked him to do anything that he did not want to do himself. When they were the only two free men in the house, they acted as equals, and they both respected each other as men born to rule.

Thióðolf proceeded with his story, "Well, the new rank I had assumed got to my head at once. I liked nothing better than to boss my sister around, secretly avenging myself for all the years that she had tormented and bossed me around. I kept ordering her to serve me in this way and that way, until one day she replied with a yes, Heri."

Thióðolf chuckled, but I frowned, not quite understanding. All the grown women I knew always addressed free men as Heri and obeyed their orders. Then, all the grown women that I knew were slaves. It was just that they were the only women I could compare myself with, and seeing as I was as bound to obey the men as they were, I often forgot the difference. Thióðolf shook his head when he understood my confusion.

"A sister is not supposed to address her own brother as Heri, Thordís. That is to imply that he is far above her. It is not so. Women and men of the same clan are equals except for the fact that the man ranks a little higher and may command the woman in all matters of security and similar. I was not commanding her for her own safety or benefit. I was commanding her because I liked commanding her. It was impermissible, but I could not help myself then. The new authority I held as a warrior and as a man was intoxicating."

I frowned again, quite unable to understand his position.

"You do not understand how it felt for me because you do not have the ruler's chant in your soul song, Thordís. You just have to understand that a person who has that chant will want to rule, often just for the sake of ruling. I have that chant, and that is why I am so good at making people obey me."

"Oh," I said, musing. It made sense, and it was true that I did not recognize that desire to rule in myself. I had never wanted to rule anybody. I was rather better at obeying. "Is that a man and a woman thing, Thióðolf, to have the ruler's chant or not?"

"Not at all. There are definitely women who have that chant also. They are always the best House-Freyias, well fit to rule a great estate, or to marry a man whose power is so great that they will also get power through marriage with him, even if they have to obey him formally. Else, such women often turn to sacred professions where they can exert authority. Many women are easily submissive also. As to men, most men, even warriors, are better at following orders than making them. Apart from Hallgrim, and perhaps Sígtrygg, all the men at Arnulf's court are like that, really. They like nothing better than to be ruled by a stronger man. They are just as submissive as most women are, even if they act more manly about it."

He peered at me and nudged me in the side, teasingly, "And before you start to think that you are very submissive, I will tell you that you are wrong. You may not have the ruler's chant, but you have not the submissive chant either."

"I have not?" I objected, "But I am always very obedient, Thióðolf, do you not think so? I can even imagine all kinds of things if you just tell me to, and after you told me to imagine things all the time, I even do it on my own sometimes now."

"Indeed," he chuckled, "you are very obedient and very well-behaved, and your daily courtesies to all the men in Arnulf's court make their heads spin very pleasantly, which is partly why you are doing it even if you are not aware of it yet. But you only behave like that because we are ruling you the way you want to be ruled." He chuckled.

"The way I want to be ruled? How do you do that?" I frowned.

"Well, Thordís. Let us use me as an example, since I am really the only one who ever actually commands you despite all the eye-averting and eye-lowering you bestow on other men. I am in truth the only one who really rules you. Do you ever feel bullied by me, Thordís? Have I ever abused my power over you?"

"No, Thióðolf, never," I said, shaking my head determinedly.

"Good. Because anyone can bear a lower rank if only they feel heard and seen, and are liked the way they are, and allowed to do things they like to do. Have you anything to complain about at all?"

"Nothing," I smiled, "You always know what I need and want and if I ask something you always comply, and you are kind to me and very respectful towards me."

"Sometimes I refuse you things you want," he said.

"Yes, but you always explain why or say it is a security matter."

"And so it is, and you believe me because?"

"Because I trust you know best in those matters. Because you have always shown yourself worthy of my trust."

"How does it make you feel, then, that I often tell you what to do and sometimes what not to do, and always take the lead?"

"It feels nice," I admitted, "I feel that I can relax and learn and do my things in peace. I feel safe and cared for," I added thoughtfully, because I had not realized these things before.

"That is how I rule well, little She-Wolf, and that is how we make our people strong, and how we hone the honers. I serve you all the time. I anticipate your needs, I try to imagine what you would want, I read your signals and your responses to know if I should pursue a path or not. I listen to your soul song and do my best to let it resound freely even within the sphere of my protection. I serve you, Thordís, that is how I rule you."

He paused and smiled at me. "You are a blade honer born, Wolfling. You love to be ruled, but only if you are ruled well. The only reason you are so obedient and respectful is because you are being ruled well, and so you can relax and feel free from both ruling and serving. But you are only compliant because you feel free when we rule you. If we had ruled you poorly and made you feel abused or restricted...ah! You would never have submitted. You would have been our Night Mare!"

I beamed, knowing that the Night Mare was a goddess out of Hel who could ride men to death at night. I also knew that Thióðolf was right. I had never been ruled badly.

"Would you rather rule yourself, Fierce Eyes?" He asked.

I had to think about that.

"Would that mean I had to make all the choices and all the decisions?"

"Yes."

"It sounds tiresome," I said, "like a burden. I feel exhausted, just thinking about it."

"Why?"

"Thióðolf, I spend all my time trying to take in everything I see and hear around me and understand all of it and it just seems a little too much if I have to take charge all the time also. Just the thought of it makes me feel tired and sad and a little angry," I said, and wiped off a tear.

"I know, little one," he said and patted my back gently. I did not know why I was feeling so upset, but there I was. Thióðolf just smiled and let me carry on.

"If somebody tried to make decisions about me that I do not like all the time I would be very angry as well," I said, and wiped off new tears, seeing as the very thought of being ruled badly angered me even more than the idea of having to do all the ruling myself. And then I realized that if I was ruled badly, I would have to take care of all that ruling myself. The thought of being ruled so poorly that I would have to take charge myself made me feel very angry. I would make misery for anyone who forced me into something like that, and I knew it already. I told Thióðolf and looked so outraged that he laughed.

"It is as I said, Thordís, you may not have that ruler's chant what also women may possess, even if you have not seen such women among the Rus yet. You have something far more precious, and, I suspect, something far more enjoyable. You have the blade honer's chant singing strong in your soul song. It is your loudest chant, it overrules all others. It is the very beat of your song."

"It is?"

"Yes, my little Flame-Head. You may not even notice it, because it is such a strong chant in you that you take it for granted. You hardly need to do anything at all to hone others. Just by being you are making other people in your proximity, both men and women, not to say little boys, aspire to ever expanding greatness. Everybody has changed for the better after you came to Arnulf's court."

"Perhaps not Hialti," I mused.

"Well, we could say that in his case, being dead is a great improvement," Thióðolf said, what made us both shake with laughter.

"Shall I resume my story?" Thióðolf asked after a little while. I nodded eagerly. "It was clear to all my clan that I was the ruling kind of man, and it was also clear to them that I was abusing my power over my sister. When she publicly addressed me as Heri after I asked her to get something for me that I might as well have gotten myself, ordering her just to have her obey me, everybody heard it, and I felt shamed. She had begun to hone me again, but this time in the less direct manner that a woman can use to hone a warrior, by thus subtly making it clear to everybody that I was dishonoring her, trying to make a slave out of her.

"Not long after, my mother's oldest brother approached me. It is usually a maternal uncle, or else a man from the mother's clan who makes these arrangements. He had already made a deal with two Wand-Witches, Huld and Sígrún, what I did not know yet. But these two holy women had agreed to hone me into a good kind of ruler. Now my uncle came to visit, and took me apart. He said that he knew that I had the ruler's chant in my soul song, and that nobody who cared for me would ever try to crush that chant in me, for it is a good chant to have. But if I was going to rule, I might as well learn how to rule well, and if I was to rule well, I would have to become not just a Heri, but an Einheri."

"What is an Einheri, Thióðolf?" I asked.

"It is a man who rules but one. It is a man who rules himself, Thordís. When a man can rule himself, he will be able to rule without even trying. When a man rules himself, his desire to rule others vanishes. When he has no more desire to rule others, he can rule well. And that is when he also rules with true authority, for others sense that he is in control of himself, and that it means that he can rule justly. That is the kind of man other men will want to follow, and women will want to... he... respect."

He grinned a little, and I raised an eyebrow.

"I was told to seek the old Wand-Witch who had named me, some sixteen years earlier when I was born, the woman called Huld. She is a very powerful Seið-woman, and advanced blade honing was among her skills. My father gave me a gold ring, and my uncle gave me another, and they told me to give her one ring when I sought her for apprenticeship, and to give her the second when my apprenticeship was concluded. We must always pay for such service, and it is always worth it, although it was hard for me to see at first." He laughed a little at the memory.

"I traveled to see the great Wand-Witch, and came to her abode. It was a terrifying place, what with stakes all around, on top of which were placed the skulls of various animals. There were large and vicious hounds there, looking more like wolves than hounds. And the place was a wreck! Everything was falling apart and there was litter everywhere, and I felt sorry for the old lady, who lived by herself and had no man to take care of her. Little did I know that the witches had wrecked the place themselves, just to give me something to do. And the old lady herself was not at all kindly!" He laughed again.

"Is she like the Kindly Ladies?" I asked.

"Not exactly, but she could be quite like them, if she wanted to. And now she certainly wanted to. She scared me so much I almost shit my pants many times! She has power, that one, and great Seið. I offered her the gold ring and she made me swear to obey her without question and serve her every need. She made me work for her, bossed me around, made me know exactly what it feels like to be ruled unjustly and abusively, and treated without respect. I hated her, but every time I tried to stand up to her, she crushed me."

"How?"

"I will not go into details, child. Suffice it to say that she could go into your mind and paralyze you and pull all your deepest fears out to the surface. Oh, how I suffered, and how hard I had to work to hope to please her even a little. It went like this for weeks, until I was thoroughly subdued. I wept when I was alone, Thordís. I felt so powerless and so shamed, but I could not return to my clan without having gone through with the apprenticeship. That would have been an even greater shame. Then one night, as I was in her cottage, she said that she felt lustful and that I was handsome young man, and that I should take my clothes off."

"Was she not old, then?" I asked. Thióðolf threw his head back and laughed.

"She was very old! She was a terrible-looking old hag! I was so terrified I hardly knew where to put myself. And yet I could not refuse her. I felt like I was going to be raped! I had not power over myself, or over her. She had utterly broken me.

I felt my tears flow as I took off my clothes and stood there, and even more shamed I was when I realized that her Seið was powerful enough to make my Freystone stand, as if I wanted her. She leered at me and drooled and laughed viciously, saying that she was going to fuck me like I had never been fucked before. Not that I had.

In my land, it is bad custom to command a slave woman against her will, and all the slaves I knew were people I had grown up with, and folk would think ill of me if I made such a command without being encouraged by the slave herself. No girls, whether slaves or free, had encouraged me yet, having been always told by their elders that young lads are lousy at it until they had been properly taught by an older woman. So I was still utterly inexperienced. But that did not matter to the old hag! I was standing there naked and weeping, and then she took off her own clothes to reveal the old and shriveled body of a hag, and I wept even more as she told me to lie down."

I gaped, but suddenly I knew why Thióðolf understood so well what it was like to be raped, and why he found it so despicable.

"I lied down and braced myself for the rape. Huld came and stood over me, with a leg on either side, letting me see her rather shriveled gate of Freyia. I closed my eyes and wept again, and she asked if I was going to beg her to let me go. I shook my head and said she could do whatever she pleased with me, for I had no power anymore. Then she suddenly moved away and threw a blanket over me, saying that she had just been pulling my leg to see how obedient I was. I was so relieved I thanked her for it!" Thióðolf laughed again. "The day after, Huld was gone. In her place was a beautiful young woman, some six years older than me. I knew her to be Sígrún Wand-Witch, an apprentice to Huld and a very well-known blade honer and spear enticer. I knew what that last thing meant, and felt suddenly hopeful, thinking that last night might have been a test and that the reward was Sígrún, and that she would perhaps order me to do what Huld had the night before. I would not at all have cried if she did. When I got up from bed, Sígrún was acting all meek and impressed by me, lowering her eyes and fluttering her lashes, serving me breakfast and telling me how strong and manly I looked. I felt so proud again, flexed my muscles and pranced around, trying to impress her, and with every move I made she almost gasped and whimpered and said she was feeling powerless against me. She said she was sorry about the way Huld had treated me, but that she was as much of a slave to Huld as I was, and that she hoped that I could save her from the old hag, but we had to be careful about how to proceed. She also told me that Huld would be angry if I did not do my work for the day, but that the old witch would be out this evening doing her terrible sorcery, and when I returned at sunset, I would find a surprise in bed, and she would give me exactly what I wanted. How well I worked that day, Thordís, anticipating the night's pleasures... ha!" His shoulders shook again with laughter.

"I returned at sunset, having bathed and being so excited I could hardly control myself. I entered the house and saw that the curtains had been drawn before the bed, and I thought I heard some whimpering from behind the curtains. I walked cautiously towards the bed and pulled the curtains aside and... you would never have guessed what was there..."

"What was it?" I asked eagerly.

"A bitch, Thordís. A small female dog tied to the bed, only too happy to see me, waving her tail and whimpering for me to caress her. And to make matters even worse, Sígrún suddenly entered the house, pointed at me and laughed and told me that I had gotten exactly what I wanted. By the gods, I felt more stupid than I have ever felt in my whole life, before and after."

"... Was it a dog you wanted then?" I asked, a little perplexed.

"This is one of the ways in which women speak in the language of gods and norns, Thordís. The blade honer showed me that I did not really want a woman at all. I just wanted something only too happy to be tied down to the bed, ready to serve me and obey me. I wanted, in short, a bitch. I was being shown exactly what I really wanted."

"Oh," I said, wide-eyed, and allowed myself to laugh when Thióðolf did. I would remember that trick, I thought deviously, just in case Ivarr tried to get back at me when he one day achieved a higher rank than I had. I laughed gleefully at the thought until Thióðolf resumed his story.

"Sígrún was just as powerful as Huld, and just as merciless. She made me do all the same kinds of works as Huld had done, and she was even less easy to please. I suffered terribly again, and this time even more, because Sígrún was a young and beautiful woman. It was far worse to be treated like a turd by her than it was to be treated such by an old hag. Old women are supposed to be obeyed anyway, but a young woman, ah, that was different. She treated me as if she despised me utterly. This time I had begun to grasp that the witches were teaching me something, and I recalled that I had come to this place to learn how to rule well. And so after a while I began to do all my chores even before she could order me to do them, and I always did my best. I tried hard to anticipate all her cravings, and did everything as soon as I understood what she wanted, trying to do it before she could ask, so that I would not have to feel the humiliation of being ordered by a woman. Weeks went by, when I not only dutifully obeyed without complaint, but also tried to read all her signals and anticipate all her needs. One day I realized that I had not been bossed around or treated harshly for many days on end, simply because I had become so good at observing what had to be done and how to please her. The very next day, something awesome happened." He sighed happily.

"I got up early in the morning, and the first thing I did every morning was to gather the buckets and go to fetch water from the nearby stream. Then I saw Sígrún Wand-Witch seated naked in the stream, and she was so very beautiful. But I knew this was another test, and did not want to be humiliated as I had before. I hesitated for a moment, and then I pretended not to see her and went to fill my buckets. I went back to the house, and nothing was said, so the day went as before. I had made Huld's farm splendid with all my works now. I had begun to do all kinds of things that nobody had ever even asked me. I had fixed sheds and walls and tended the garden and made order out of the disorder I had encountered when I first came there, thinking that the old lady lacked a man to care for her. Now that everything was fixed, I set out to make the place even better than it had once been, all on my own accord. I was making a new fence that day, after the water-carrying, and Sígrún actually came up to me and looked approvingly at my work and said that I would make a fine man someday. I beamed, wanting nothing more than to be thought a fine man! The next morning, I found her in the stream again, this time she was laying spread out on a rock with her legs apart so that I could see right into her gate of Freyia. It was not at all shriveled. I was utterly embarrassed, knowing it to be another test, and so I did as I had the day before, ignored her and filled my buckets, having a hard, I mean a hard time walking back from all the excitement. My goodness."

He laughed so hard he was shaking violently, and I with him.

"On the third morning, she was doing the same thing, only even worse. She was naked and she had, she had knelt down on a rock with her back to me and looked as if she was trying to get something out of the water, and, uh, I could see her behind very explicitly. She looked like she was ready to be taken like, well, like a beast. I thought I would die from excitement. I had a very hard time looking the other way, but I managed, fearing the ridicule she would bestow on me if I did anything else. I filled my buckets and was about to leave when she turned around and smiled at me in a way she had never smiled at me before. She asked me if I would not want to join her for a bath. I was afraid that she would trick me again, but I acted very submissively and entered the water with her. She was taking the lead and told me what to do, and so I relaxed. I knew she would not humiliate me as long as I didn't assume anything. To my great delight, I got what I wanted, only not quite in the way I had imagined."

"How, then?" I almost clapped my hands.

"'Suffice it to say that she ruled me utterly. I was a slave in her hands. She took me. I went with it the first time, seeing as it was my first. But after that we played Freyia's games day and night. And she kept ruling me, telling me what to do, how to do it, when to do it, and generally ordering me about. I enjoyed it, and learned a great deal about women, but it was difficult also. I kept thinking of the way she had displayed herself before, ready to be taken, but that was not at all the way she acted.

As I told you before, I have not the submissive chant in my soul song. I wanted to be the one who took her, but she ruled me mercilessly. Sometimes it was as if we were fighting for supremacy, more like being in a combat than being with a woman. I always lost. Not because she was stronger than me. I was only sixteen, but like all warriors who have trained daily from the age of three, I had already developed great strength and skill, and if she had been any other woman I could easily have subdued her. But Sígrún has the power of Seið, and she could not be subdued. I was feeling more and more humiliated, even as I was drooling after her all the time.'

"'Then one day it occurred to me once more that I was supposed to learn how to rule, and how to rule well. I contemplated how it had come to pass that she even deigned to be with me that way, and realized that it had happened only when I had learned how to anticipate her wishes. One day as she was ordering me to undress, I refused her. She sat down and asked what the problem was, and I just kissed her. I began to caress her in manners I knew she liked, and to my surprise, she simply surrendered. I kept following all her signals, trying to anticipate exactly what she wanted, and followed the paths that appeared most appreciated. Suddenly I got what I wanted, and I was allowed to rule her, but only because I ruled her well, because I was in fact serving her. I began to realize that ruling is a way of serving, and so it should be. And as I became better at it. It came to pass that she reached Freyia's Frenzy, and pulled me with her into the experience.'"

"What is Freyia's Frenzy?" I asked. I had heard about Freyia's waves, which I had by then guessed was what happened when the women tended to go all squeaky.

"It is a divine state, Thordís, a state of utter peace and utter rage, two polar opposites coming together as one. It is a state that brings about great wisdom, purification, healing and stamina too. It is impossible to describe with words, really. Only a woman can reach the frenzy, but only if she truly trusts the man to hold her through it all the way. And if she trusts him, she can take him with her, and then he will know that state too. This was what Sígrún did for me. Then, Thordís, then I not only knew how to rule well, I also knew the goddess. This was how the goddess came to be my heart's Freyia, and how the art of poetry became a part of my soul. It was after this that I became a skald, and an Einheri, and a worshiper of the great Freyia, who makes men into true rulers."

We sat in silence. I was rather stunned, and thrilled too.

"So..." I said after a little while, "who, what is the goddess to you, then? Is it so that you serve her by ruling her? Is that how you worship her?" Thióðolf sighed, but not from exhaustion, only to take in breath and release.

"You mentioned that you had pondered about what Shumayl said about his god being present in everything, and how I had said we have such mysteries also. It is the truth, Thordís." He made a sweeping gesture towards the hills and the woods and the river below, "To me, all this is the goddess. And so I am in awe, always. I worship her, and I adore her, and I would lower my eyes to her if she appeared in human form before me. But as you say, I also worship the goddess in women, and not just in women, but in everything, even in myself, and just as I rule myself, I rule the goddess. Just as I use the forest and the hills as I like. Yet the goddess awes me and gives me life, and I would be nothing without her. Ultimately, my goddess and I are equals, Thordís, just as you are equal to your god."

"I am not equal to the lord of Thunder," I said, shaking my head.

"Yes, you are. All beings in the whole world are in truth equal even as we have ranks and rules to get by," Thióðolf said, "We are all the same thing, made out of the same stuff, whether great or small, every being is the same, a tune within a chant within a greater song, and yet even the greatest songs are made of the same stuff as the tunes themselves. One day you will also know this, even if you cannot grasp it now, and then you will know that you and your god are one."

I did not know what to say. This was even more complex than the matters of rules and all the other kinds of rules and different ways of ranking in different situations.

"I don't understand this, Thióðolf. Maybe I am not that clever after all." I felt a little disappointed, for everybody had been telling me that I was unusually clever and wise beyond my years.

"You are very clever, Thordís, but you need to match words with deeds, and for the time being these are still just words for you without substance because you have not yet experienced what it means. You will understand these things when you have more experience, and you will probably know all of it when you have known the frenzy. Be patient, little one. Now, you have grasped that I worship the goddess in women and in maidens. But I worship her not by obeying her, but by ruling her. Yet, that is how I serve her. Just as I serve you even as I rule you."

I opened my mouth to speak, but he continued, "It is not the truth that I always rule women. I have been taught by women, as I have just told you, and I still regard both of them as my mentors. When I was apprenticed to them, they ruled me utterly, as they still rule me. I have always sought these women for counsel ever since they released me from my apprenticeship to them."

"So they ruled you," I stated.

"Yes, but what you may understand from what I said before, it is that one of the things they ruled me into learning was how to rule women the right way," he said. "These women are very wise. They know that warriors rule in this world, and so they have found ways to make warriors rule well. They honed me mercilessly until I knew how to rule even them the way they wanted me to rule them. And then they told me to always rule people by learning how people want to be ruled."

"So you ruled them in the end?"

"No, no, no, by no means! They are Wand-Witches, Thordís, they are the freest kind of women in the world. The freest kind of people, I should say. No men and no women are as free as they are. But one of the reasons they are so free is because they do not rule at all."

"You said they ruled you!" I protested. I thought it confusing, what with all the rules and all the other kinds of rules, what to Thióðolf was so natural that his mind was being sharply honed in his attempts to explain it all to me.

"They ruled me only because I asked them to. The truth is I asked them to teach me, and you know that we must always lower our eyes and obey those who have offered to teach us at any time. And so they taught me, and I submitted to their teachings. That is how they ruled me. I chose to, so it was not as if they rule me the way I rule Zivah, or the way I rule my sister, since I had and will always have an option to be ruled or not."

"Why would they want to teach you how to rule women, if they are free women?"

"As I said, they want to teach warriors that because they know that warriors rule the world, and warriors hold all the might. In this age of war, there is no other way, and most women and other soft folks, they depend on warriors to protect them. Since that is the way of Fate, the witches, who are the last truly free women in the world, do not try and change that, but instead they teach rulers how to make their subjects happy even as they rule them, just as they teach kings to rule their kingdoms for the purpose of peace, justice and prosperity, and a joyful and mutually rewarding co-existence.

In the homelands, the women are very strong, and we men cherish that, although we make ourselves even stronger so that we may match them, to be he-wolves to the she-wolves, and that is exactly why we are so strong. We have not the humility of the men of your mother's people, Thordís, who could let women rule them. It is because we are warriors, it is impossible for us. We would be weakened if we were to accept a lower rank. Warriors must rank higher than those who are dependent on warriors to protect them, whether the warriors are men or women, actually."

"So if a woman is a real warrior she ranks as high as any other warrior?" I asked.

"Yes, of course. And it is common enough for women to learn a deal of battle arts. But it is very uncommon for a woman to prove herself that way. Even you, if you continue your training in the warrior's court until you are grown, you will be pretty battle-skilled, Thordís, and you could surely be a match to many men from other kinds of tribes. Compared to our training you would not stand strong against Norsemen and it would be rather unlikely that you ever got to prove your worth as a warrior. To be honest none of us think that you have that kind of soul-chant in you. The battle art is like a dance to you. You wield arms as well as any boy but you lack the ferocity you would need to actually use your arts in a combat situation."

I said nothing, knowing well that he was right. I had no wish to ever enter combat, but I loved the wielding of blades and shield nevertheless. It was, as he said, like a dance to me.

"We who spend our whole lives honing our warrior skills in order to protect must be able to expect respect and even a degree of obedience from those we protect when it is needed," Thióðolf said, "and most warriors are men. Our women do not complain about our higher rank because they understand that we must stand together against slavers and rapists and greed-ridden conquerors. We do not put our women down like other folks do, because we understand that men are weakened in their souls and minds by false humoring from subdued women. To be as strong as we have become, we need our women to support us and stand with us in this battle that is life.

"The only way to make our women stand with us the way they do is to prove to them that we merit the power that we have, to honor their soul songs and include them in the way of the warrior. We have made our women into blade honers, women who can see our weaknesses and hone us into greater men. We are a happy people, back in North Way, and we have our witches to thank for that. And we have yet to become Vikings. We are true warriors there still, not pirates and slavers."

"What about the Wand-Witches?" I asked, "You said they are free, and that they don't rule. How is that possible?" As far as I had understood, ruling and being ruled were the two options, and those who ruled appeared freer than those they ruled in all respects.

"Thordís, I think you know this in your heart. You are still a child who must submit to your superiors, but when you grow up, you will be as free as a Wand-Witch. Perhaps you will be one. But you will not be ruling anyone either. For the time being, since you are a child, you are being ruled and you have absolutely no control over what happens to you, to tell you the truth. Do you feel that, Thordís, do you feel how utterly in our power you are?"

I looked thoughtfully at him. There was a time when I would have said yes, but that time had passed. I was in their power but it did not feel that way, like with the rules and the Contrary rules.

"Thióðolf," I said, "I honestly feel that I am freer than any of you."

He just looked at me for a while before he spoke again.

"You are wise beyond your years, child," he said fondly. "You lower your eyes to the men, and you are being ruled by me and by Arnulf, and yet you feel freer than we do. Do you understand how that works?"

"Not exactly," I admitted. I knew in my heart I was free, but I did not understand why.

"Ruling is the same as serving," Thióðolf said, and looked a little sad, "Those who rule are never free."

I knew not why, but tears were streaming down my face and his, and we sat in silence for a long time, listening to the lazy buzzing of bees, and watching the butterflies until one landed on Thióðolf's arm. I watched it fascinatedly, thinking that it was a sign, but said nothing.

"Do you know, Thordís, that I had never been a proper Viking before last summer?" He said quietly, and dried his tears. "I did not partake in the raids, but I was there, I was with the Rus Vikings, and I made poetry to praise them. All the things I saw, it was not like anything I had ever seen before. I have been to many fights and many battles, and there was that scouting trip, but not one that involved the large-scale raping and enslavement of women and children. This, you have not seen the homelands yet, you have only seen Aldeigjuborg, and so you might think the world is like this. But it is different at home. We are warriors, yes, but we hone our honor just as much as we hone our courage and our skill. Our women remind us of our honor at every turn, because they are free women."

He turned to me, looking intently at me, "This is a very sick place, Thordís. Almost all the women are slaves, or might as well have been slaves. Living like this - it hardens the heart. You cannot stand by and watch these things happen without hardening the heart.

Last summer I hardened my heart, so that I would not succumb to the grief and the dishonor. I hardened it and suddenly I forgot the sacred trust, and thought that I could force a defenseless slave girl to like me, forgetting that she had no reason to trust me at all."

"Are you men not supposed to harden your hearts?" I asked, after thinking through his words. It seemed to me that the hardening of the heart was all they did, the men.

"Our hearts? Why should we harden our hearts?"

"Is that not what you do, every day? To be warriors?"

"No, Thordís. We harden our bodies. We harden our minds. We harden our spirits, so that we may be strong, and able to protect all that is precious and vulnerable. The heart, Thordís, the heart is precious. It is vulnerable, and in that respect it is the same with men and women. It cannot stand hardness. The heart succumbs to hardness and becomes no heart at all, and so it cannot be honed. The heart is what we protect. The heart is where the goddess resides. The heart is the Síf within. The heart is like a maiden. It should never have to be hardened."

"Why not?"

"Because if the heart is hard, it is no longer a heart. It becomes like a raped woman, like a slave, an empty hole to be used by other forces."

"What other forces?"

"The first is Fear. The second is Greed. The third is Hatred. Those forces will enter the heart, rape it and enslave it, and then a man loses his honor, and becomes a slave to these forces. No matter how hard his body is, no matter how hard his mind is, no matter how hard his spirit he is nothing but a slave, for his inner Síf has been taken, and his soul has left its abode in the heart. He is a lost man, his household is empty, his Sífs are gone. He is protecting an empty house. He is protecting his enemies. He becomes deluded." He looked at me and touched my cheek gently, "We have many songs about this, Thordís. Songs about the abducted goddess. It is all about the heart, and how to retrieve it, how to heal it. Do you know the story of how Thor lost his hammer?"

"Yes," I said, nodding eagerly. It was one of my favorite stories, and always made me laugh when I thought about how my lord, the manly god, had to dress up as a bride and pretend to be a woman.

"It is about the loss of the heart," Thióðolf said. "The hammer is the symbol of his might and manly power. The story is about how all the manly might of Thor was lost when his mind slept, and when he was willing to give the goddess away to lower forces. Then the goddess had to become hard, and she withdrew her favors to him, and he found himself with neither heart nor hammer. He had to go into that space, where the heart resides, and become soft like a woman before he could retrieve his hammer of might. It is exactly the same as when we hone a boy through humiliating him and making him feel what it is like to be weak. He must learn how to protect and cherish the heart. A man must be strong, but if his heart is hardened, he becomes weaker than he can even realize himself. He may go through his life believing himself a big and strong man, yet when he dies and reaches the seat of judgment at the shores of Hel, he will find that the ones who judge him are women. The norns are like merciless sisters, Thordís, sisters who hone their brothers through ridicule. They will show him all his weaknesses, and he will be nothing but a weak little boy, succumbing to mockery and dishonor. But in that seat of judgment, it is often too late to prove himself worthy, on account of being quite dead."

I fought hard with myself not to ask whether the Kindly Ladies were not also like merciless sisters, but he had forbidden me to speak of them, and so I did not. Instead I looked at the butterfly that had returned to sit on his hand a second time.

"Will I be a spear-enticer when I am grown?" I asked, suddenly thinking of something Njál had once said. Thióðolf went a little red at first, but then there was amusement in his eyes, and finally he grinned broadly and patted my back affectionately.

"I think you will be the most insufferable spear-enticer in the known world. Thunder and lightning roar in your veins. Yours is a power yet to be awakened, but even now it can be felt," he said.

"When will it awaken?"

"It will awaken the first time you experience Freyia's Frenzy."

"When will that be?"

"Some time after you have bled the first time. Another seven years before you bleed, and then some more time before you walk on Freyia's path."

"Will you take me to the sacred frenzy then?" I asked.

There was only a stunned silence behind me.

I turned to look up at him again, meeting his eyes. Thióðolf looked so surprised. And he had gone a tad bit red. At least he did not laugh. He opened his mouth to speak a few times and almost stammered when he finally replied, what I had never heard him do before.

"I would be very honored if you asked me. But I am twenty years older than you, sweet Thordís. I think that when the time is due, you will find me too old, and too much like a father for you. You may find that a younger man will please you more."

"Oh." I went silent, wondering if that was really true. I already thought him beautiful in every way. He was my warrior and my poet and my closest friend, and he held me close every night already, when our hearts always beat the same rhythm against each other.

I could not imagine any other man I would rather have to lead me onto Freyia's path the first time.

"Thióðolf," I said, after a little while, "I love you. I think your heart matches me." I saw a tear run down his scarred cheek. I looked out at Aldeigjuborg and let my fingers run through the soft spring grass before I turned to him and spoke gently, meeting his deep blue gaze, "Because, you know Thióðolf, it is as you said before. I am free. I will always be free. I feel it in the men's hammer. They tell me the truth, my fathers. I think I am the freest person in this whole place. I have seen men who need to own the women that they love, but you, I think you will love me even if I am free. You have the heart of a Thunder Warrior. And I trust you, Thióðolf. I trust you with my life. I would never close the gates of my divinity to you."

I turned to look ahead again, to allow him his private reaction to what I said. I heard him draw his breath behind me, and felt the beating of his heart against my shoulder blades. I heard him swallow, and take a few deep breaths before he could reply.

"Thordís," Thióðolf said gently.

I turned to look up at him. His face looked so mild, and his touch was so gentle when he made me turn to sit facing him. The butterfly had settled on his hand a third time, and we both looked at it together before he spoke again.

"I will show you my goddess," he said, "Look into my eyes. Just look. See."

He locked his gaze with mine, then, wolf on wolf.

I looked, and saw the warrior's weathered and scarred and bearded features soften before my eyes. The change happened so subtly and yet so dramatically, for he had changed, the skald. Within moments he had transformed, and it was an act of Seið.

He was very manly, Thióðolf, like all the warriors. His beauty was a manly beauty. He was ferocious and strong. His wolfish soul was wild and free. He was no slave to his baser needs or to those of other folks. He was an Einheri, who ruled himself. And yet his features had somehow become blurred, and I could no longer see his beard or his scars or his traces of hard life. All his manly features had now become transparent and something else had emerged from within. His heart's goddess was watching me through him, and her shine outshone even the warrior.

"The goddess is the Síf within," I thought I heard his voice reverberate through my mind, even if he had not spoken.

She was living within his soul-stone. As I looked into her deep blue eyes, I knew that she is within everyone, and that she spins our fate as we walk on holy Earth, and that she is different to all that she inhabits, one being with countless minds, countless hearts and shapes and names.

She was awake, Thióðolf's goddess, awake within his heart.

When I saw her, I knew that she is often made to slumber when men and women's hearts are hardened by Fear and all his sons, and then she weaves fate as randomly and often as harmfully as a sleep-walker walks. My soul song stirred, and a chant rose from it, one that I had not known yet. I knew that when my heart's Síf would wake up, when the goddess would rise in me and seize me, and when I could embrace her as the whole of me, I would rule her and know how to spin my own fate. For I was her. We were equals, and we were powerful beyond measure.

It was all clear to me then, why the goddess could be ruled, and how it was possible to rule her at all, and why both the why and how of it were good things. The Fate-spinner is the greatest of all blade honers. She wants to be ruled, just as we want to rule our own fates. Fate can only be ruled by those who know how to rule her well. It was clear to me, and yet overwhelming. My most important insight then was birthed from the fact that my Tribeswolf had turned inside out and become his own opposite.

My man had created a womb by Seið.
My warrior looked like a maiden.
Everything was possible.

Five Silver Skull Cups and a King

One evening, everybody had been enjoying the telling of true and less-true stories from many places in the world. Aziza and Shumayl had been entertaining all of them with stories from Big Tunic Land. Thióðolf and Njál, who were the only free men present in the Hold at that time, listened attentively. Zivah had to go outside to tend to some outdoor chores. By the time she had reappeared in the Hold, Shumayl felt familiar enough to ask Thióðolf a question.

"Heri, please excuse me, but would you tell us some story from your own homeland, perhaps? I have heard that your land is quite different from here even if you speak the same tongue as the Rus."

"That is true," Thióðolf said and paused when he noticed that Zivah had slowed her pace and appeared to be straining her ears. He smiled.

"Zivah, come here and sit down," he said. It was the first time he had given her a direct order since he became her master, and Zivah's eyes widened a little before she promptly obeyed and sat down next to Shumayl, looking curiously up at her House-Bond.

"Are you going to tell a story?" Thordís asked, and as soon as he nodded, she and many of the slaves gathered round expectantly, to hear a story from the Land of the High Flames, which they said lied to the northernmost part of the world.

"There are nine great tribes that make up the kingdom of the Háleygir," Thióðolf said, "and my mother's tribe is known as Nauma's tribe. Nauma is the name of our ancestral mother, just as Thordís was the name of the ancestral mother of the Thunder Priest line. In the valley of Nauma there is a great river, and that river is also called Nauma, after our ancestral mother, and it is said that her spirit is still alive, running in that great river. Thordís, Zivah, my mother's people revere the mother river much like your mother's people did. Now, back before I was even conceived of, my father Grjótgarð was elected king of the Háleygir."

"Elected?" Shumayl asked.

"Yes, a king has to be elected by the parliament of the tribes, obviously," Thióðolf said, and then shook his head. "I am sorry. I should know there is nothing obvious about that to you, but I did not think of it. Zivah, your people did not even have kings, did they? I heard your tribe was ruled by way of council too."

"We had no kings and we ruled ourselves by council," Zivah said, and blushed a little at being so directly approached after all this time, "but our people descended from other people who did have kings and towns and all sorts of things that we remembered in our songs and tales, and we also heard lots of tales from other lands. It was always my impression that a king becomes king if he is the first son of a king."

"Yes, that is the custom in many places, although it is hard to believe," Thióðolf said and shook his head dismissively.

"Imagine that. The king's first son turns out to be an idiot or a coward, and yet he is still made king," Njál exclaimed and laughed.

"The tribes of North Path Island will either rule themselves by council just like your folks did, or else they will elect a king to rule them, mostly to be in charge of the army, of course. There is little point in having a king at all unless it is to lead the army. The man who is elected is often the son of a king, but any son of a king or any man even related to a king may be a candidate if he so wishes and if he has enough people to support him. He must have shown his worth through various trials and tests and be able to convince folks through eloquence and action. The king who now rules in Hálógaland, King Grjótgarð of Borg, was one of the twenty-five known sons of his own father Sígurð, and the only one to be elected by the all-parliament of the Háleygir."

"Twenty-five sons, no less," Njál said and whistled to show how impressed he was.

"A king must have many wives. A king must make sure to be allied with all his people, and among us that means a king must ally himself through marriage with all the nine tribes. And so, after his election, he had to go on a very long round of proposals. He had to travel from tribe to tribe and woo a woman of that tribe, any woman of his choice who would have him, of course. Needless to say, people were quite eager to get the king to marry one of their women, the women themselves in particular. Everywhere Grjótgarð went, women were throwing themselves at him and making the most alluring and imaginative shows to attract his attention. And then he came to Nauma's valley.

"By that time, the young king was so fed up with eager women that he went to sit by his campfire one evening rather than going into the settlements. Then there was this aged woman who came by and asked if she could share his fire."

"Wait, Heri, are you saying that the king was traveling alone, outside, at night?" Shumayl asked, frowning, and Thióðolf said, "Yes, of course, what sort of king would he be if he was skittish?"

Thordís and Njál just nodded as if that explanation was totally sensible, and the slaves exchanged glances and shrugged. Thióðolf continued his story, "The king told the old woman to take a seat, and shared his food with her. When she asked why he looked so gloomy, he said that pretty girls were raining down on him and made it really hard to choose which ones he wanted for his wives.

So the old woman asked if he would rather want a woman who was hard to get. The king said that there were many women who were trying that approach too, knowing that he was looking for something novel, only hard to get was not that novel to him either. Then the old woman smiled and said that she knew of one woman who was actually hard to get, and the king asked her if she could let him know more.

"The old woman said that she knew a young woman who refused herself to all men. Her name was Almveig, and when she had been only fifteen years old, she had been herding cows in the mountains all on her own when five strange travelers approached her and told her that they wanted to play Freyia's games with her right away. She had told them that she did not want to and that they should go their ways, but they refused and told her that she could fight or not, but they would have her anyway. Then Almveig had told the men that she saw no reason to fight if there was no chance of winning, but that she would regard this as rape. The men did not care, not even when the first of them discovered that she had never been with a man that way before at all. They cared nothing for her pain, and all of them had her, one after the other.

"Afterwards, Almveig pretended that she was happy with the whole thing. She said she had only been frightened because it was her first time, but now that she had seen what good men they were she had changed her mind, and she offered them drink. The men were stupid enough to believe that she did not mind, drank and partied, and while they were drunk she stole one of their horses, rode to the closest neighbor and told them what had happened. She rode to one settlement after the other and let everybody know about the five rapists, asking her tribesmen if this was how they protected their tribeswomen, letting men such as these travel freely through their lands.

"So the tribesmen mustered, found the rapists, blood-eagled them and came to Almveig with their heads. She spat in their faces and spoke the holy words, and then she had the heads boiled and took the skulls to a silversmith. She got five beautiful cups from these skulls. She declared after that because of what these men had done to her, she would not accept any man unless he passed the test of the silver skull cups. After that, many men had tried to woo Almveig, for she was not only of good lineage and great beauty, she had also become famous on account of her ferocity and her courage, but none of them could pass the test of the silver skull cups, and had to go their ways. The king asked the old woman what sort of test it was, and the old woman said that nobody knew, and that the test might solve itself if he could find out what the test was at all. The king smiled and said he would test the woman himself, knowing that the most determined of women often changed their minds in the presence of a king. So he made sure that all the people in Almveig's vicinity would be aware of his presence in their lands, and surely enough women came from near and far in the hope of snatching the king or even getting him in their beds for just one night, seeing as the King's seed is holy. But Almveig did not appear. After seven days, Grjótgarð decided to go and see her, and was well received by her kinsmen and her Sífs, but still, the maiden had not appeared. They told him that she lived on her own in one of the houses there, and pointed to the house. King Grjótgarð went into the house and stood by the entrance while waiting for her to ask him in. It was very dark inside, and he heard a young woman's voice tell him to enter and sit down. He sat down, and a silver skull cup was shoved across the table towards him, filled with beer. The king took the cup and drank his fill, and asked if he could see the one who had served him such fine brew. The woman went into another room and then returned carrying an oil lamp, which she set down before him on the table. Now he could see her in the light and knew that she was a beautiful she-wolf of a woman, who besides knew how to brew the best sorts of beer, and then he saw four other silver skull cups on that same table, all filled with the same beer. He looked at the skull cups and asked if she was expecting more guests. She told him that she was not, and that he could have them all. So the king took one cup after the other and emptied them, each time commenting upon her excellent brewing skills. When he had reached the last cup, he said that it would be unfair if he did not share the cup with her. Now, Zivah, you may not know this, but the sharing of a cup is a very important symbol of marriage. Grjótgarð could see that the girl hesitated. She arranged the cups so that they once more stood facing him, letting him see the faces of dead men beneath the silver coating. These are the men who raped me,' she said, 'and I have held my enemies' heads in my hands. I always have them with me, their skulls. I drink from them daily and serve them to my visitors and keep them on my table and next to my bed. Most men flee from me when I give them my special treatment, but here you are, still seated and ready to share one of my cups with me. Do these skulls not bother you, King?' Grjótgarð smiled at the girl, raised the last cup, and drank a sip before he offered it to her and said, "Almveig Freyia of Nauma Valley, you are the queen of all good brews, and the only thing that bothers me about these skulls you keep so close is that I was not the man what gave them to you.'"

Thióðolf stopped talking, and to Zivah's astonishment, they all fell over laughing, even the children. She looked from one to the other and finally dared to admit that she had not understood the punch line at all. Thióðolf turned to her, smiled and said, "Zivah of the river lands, I do not blame you, for you know not all the customs of our people yet. Grjótgarð passed the test, and Almveig Freyia became the Nauma queen of Hálógaland."

"They say a man often loves women who remind him of his mother," Njál mused, and everybody looked at Zivah and giggled. She frowned, not understanding either the comment or its relevance to herself, and bowed her head since a free man had spoken, but peered suspiciously around, having the oddest sensation that everybody else knew something that she did not.

A ROYAL COMPENSATION

It was one of those early and sudden springs that often bring about an almost unnatural heat which is felt when the winds are quiet, and it made everybody feel light and happy. Something had changed in Arnulf's court since I first came there. It was as if everybody were simply more comfortable with each other and more familiar, even across the borders of rank, and the slave girls were beaming just as the warriors were. Maybe it was true, I pondered, that somehow my arrival had made them into more than just a Viking band and their slaves. We felt more like family now, like a proper clan. Even Zivah looked as if she felt at home, and sometimes she even smiled and talked to the men.

It was an early morning, the Sun shining brightly, and it looked to be another hot day when Zivah came up to me and said nervously, "Thordís, my House-Bond wants to take me for a, uhm, for a ride today, he said."

She blushed, and I frowned. We were not unfamiliar with the men's riddle-speech anymore.

"He asks that you come also," she added, as an afterthought.

I nodded, relieved, donned my riding gear and met with Thióðolf and Zivah at the stables. Frost-Fax was already saddled and ready and I thanked Búi the stable boy before I mounted the little horse. Thióðolf mounted his own horse, and then bent down and whisked Zivah up to sit behind him. I did not ask where we were going, and Thióðolf did not tell, looking serious as Zivah cautiously placed her hands on his sides to keep her balance.

She had never been riding a horse before and looked anxious, but kept casting glances back at me, as if to make sure that I followed, being even more afraid that her House-Bond might demand that they should be alone together. We rode out of town, away from the river, towards the rolling hills of the west. We rode for a good while, I think, Thióðolf regularly making sure that nobody had followed and that nobody were around. Finally he led us through a narrow trail into a grove, where we found a beautiful clearing. There we unhorsed. Thióðolf checked the area while we waited by the horses, and I asked Zivah if she knew what we were going to do here.

"I don't know," she whispered. "He just told me that we should go, and he did it in front of several other men, so I could not question his orders." She lent down and whispered into my ears, "I think he did it on purpose, to make sure I could not ask any questions."

"Maybe he has a surprise for us," I whispered eagerly, and Zivah looked a little pale. When Thióðolf returned, he said nothing, but signaled to me to stay put while he led Zivah to the middle of the clearing by a great rock and told her to wait there. Then he returned to me and did the strangest thing. First, he unfastened his sword and gave it to me. I stood with it in my hands and felt how heavy it was.

"You can put it down," he said, "on the ground. But I will ask you to guard it." I nodded solemnly, completely amazed at this strange act. I had never once seen a Norseman willingly give away his weapons for safe-keeping. They always wore them, like they were a second skin. Even when they slept, they kept them next to their bodies, in their beds. Among the men, only slaves went without weapons. To my amazement, Thióðolf next took out his battle-axe and gave that to me. It was also too heavy for me to carry for much time, and so I put it down on the ground next to the sword. Finally he gave me his dagger. His spear was the only weapon he did not wear at all times and he had left that one at home, as he had his shield. "I charge you with my weapons, Thordís. Guard them with, well you are not a warrior so I am not going to ask you to guard them with your life. But guard them with that gaze of yours, and call down the Thunder Lord if necessary. Or just call me, and I will come. That might be a little easier."

"When should I call you?"

"You will call me only if you notice anyone approaching. Keep watch, Priestess. I charge you."

"I accept the charge, Skald," I replied formally, and he smiled. "I am going to talk to Zivah now, over there. And I ask that you stay here and look after the horses and my weapons and that you keep guard and call me if anybody approaches."

"If you are going to be over there I will not hear what you are talking about," I objected.

"That is in many ways the whole point, Thordís. I need to talk to her privately. I just thought that she would feel less frightened if you were around. I am sure you can find something to do out here what with all the trees to climb and all those herbs I know you like to study endlessly. Just keep an eye on my arms and keep watch."

"I see," I said, feeling a little disappointed. I also had very good hearing, and decided to strain my ears to listen anyway.

Now Thióðolf went over to Zivah, and to my surprise, and hers, he began to take his shirt off, and then his tunic, until he stood there with his torso bare. He was looking quite magnificent, I thought, but that fact was still lost on his slave.

Zivah bowed her head and clenched her fists, and it occurred to me that she thought he was going to finally rape her after all, but I was not worried. Instead of raping her, Thióðolf sank down onto his knees and bowed his head before his slave girl.

I gaped, and so did Zivah. He was much larger than her, and she could not possibly have been a match against him, yet he was at least unarmed and half-naked, and he was kneeling on the ground before her and bowing his head, as if she was the master and he was the slave. He had taken exactly the same posture as he had forced my sister into on that terrible day in the market when we first came to Aldeigjuborg. He spoke to her then, and I could not hear what he was saying, but I saw Zivah looked bewildered. She looked at me, and I shrugged. He spoke again, a little louder, but I could still not make out what he was saying.

Zivah shook her head violently and I think I heard her whimper. Finally his voice carried loud enough for me to hear.

"I am the Viking who destroyed your village," he almost shouted at her, "I am the Viking who killed your mother. I am the Viking who raped your friends. I am the Viking who abducted you and betrayed you. I am the Viking who beat you bloody and made you kneel in the mud. I am the Viking who almost raped you. I am the Viking who owns you and makes you call him Heri. I am everything you hate. Beat me, woman! Beat me now!"

When Zivah still stood, looking upset, he almost shouted, "Beat me! It is an order! Beat me or I will beat you!" Zivah did the unthinkable and slapped her master across his face. She was terrified and looked like she was about to turn and run, but he just sat there on his knees and told her to beat him harder.

338

She gave him another slap, and he looked up at her and asked mockingly, "Is that all you have got? Are you really that weak?" Suddenly she came at him with surprising ferocity. She beat him, first hesitantly, then with steadily increasing courage, and anger. She really struck him then, in the face, on the body, she even kicked him in the chest. She began to wail as she struck him, each blow producing a loud whimper from her, but she did not cease now.

Her fists rained down upon him, yet all he did was to sit on his knees with bowed head, his hands protecting his tender areas. He was almost unmoved by her blows, taking each one in silence and without losing balance. The warrior had been through far worse ordeals throughout his life, but it was clear that she was leaving marks on his skin now. Finally Zivah discovered blood on her hands and saw that her House-Bond was bleeding from the nose. She stopped then, staring at him, and then took a few paces backwards before she let out a strange howling sound and threw herself to the ground.

Her whole body was shaking and trembling. It reminded me of how I had seen animals react when they have just escaped a dangerous situation. They always tremble like that, as if to shake off the turbulence of the recent fright. Afterwards they are as calm as they were before. Thióðolf was a warrior, and like all warriors, he knew well the great tremble and how it heals the soul-wounds caused by terror. And so he did nothing while Zivah trembled on the ground, just sat there in the same humble position and waited until Zivah began weeping for real. Then he slowly, carefully approached, crawling on his knees until he got to her.

With the utmost care and gentleness, he lifted her up and held her as she cried, rocking her like a baby in his arms. He did not try to stop her from crying, he just held her for as long as it took her to cry all she needed to. To my surprise, she did not cringe from him at all. Instead, she seemed to burrow her head into his chest and relax into his arms, just like I used to do. He kept holding her until she no longer shook, and for a good while all they seemed to be doing was staying there, all quiet, and together. He was holding her. Zivah was waking up from her dream and yet he was still there and it was true. Thióðolf held her.

It was so strangely soothing, as if she had always trusted him. His deep blue eyes were so full of love she thought she must still be dreaming. She reached out and touched his cheek and traced the lines of his face with soft fingers. Thióðolf said nothing, but smiled fondly at her. His arms were so strong and it felt safe resting in them, and his chest was so warm. She heard the beating of his heart, steady.

"Thióðolf," she said quietly.

"Yes, Zivah," he said.

"Heri?"

"Just Thióðolf," he said, "The title is just for show. We can be true, here and now."

"Why? Why did you do this for me?"

"Because you are worth the effort, and I could not bear to see how you suffered anymore. Because I love you. Because you needed Atonement and I needed to provide it. Because I love you. I love you."

"You love me?"

"Yes."

"Oh." She frowned and looked into his eyes, searching. He smiled.

"I suppose 'oh' is as good an answer as I could expect."

"Yes," she said and smiled a little, what made him smile even more.

"For now," she said.

"I know, Zivah. My love, I am so sorry I hurt you. I am so sorry that Arnulf's men hurt you and your people. I am so sorry that this was the first thing you saw of our people. I am so sorry you have been a slave."

"I am still a slave," she said and touched her collar thoughtfully.

"For now," he said, "I see no other way until we leave Aldeigjuborg. I am so sorry but you will just have to be my property a little longer. It is safer that way."

"We leave Aldeigjuborg?"

"Of course. I am not leaving you behind here. I said I love you."

"Where are we going?"

"To my home. To Hálógaland in North Way, on North Path Island. We can leave within two years, when I am no longer bound to Arnulf Heri."

"And I will not be a slave there?"

"No. As soon as we get there I will free you, if not before. Then you can choose if you want to stay with me or if you want to receive compensation money for the years you have been my slave, and then you can do whatever you like with your life."

"What if I am noosed?"

"The men of Hálógaland do not noose women, Zivah."

"They do not?"

"We are not Vikings, Zivah. We are warriors. We protect women, we don't raid for slaves. A man tries to noose a woman in my country, he ends up as a silver skull cup on her dinner table."

That made her smile, but she was still curious.

"No slaves?"

"Yes, we have slaves, but not in the way they have here. We can speak of that later, if it is fine with you. You are not going to be a slave there anyway. You are going to be my Eastern Princess, if you like. Or whatever you wish to be. We can make up a great story for you. If it is entertaining enough, nobody will care if it is not true. My tribesmen love nothing better than a great story."

"Yes, Her, I mean, Thióðolf. That is fine with me. Thióðolf…"

"Yes?"

"You are not a Viking? At the raid?"

"I am not. I just happened to be there with them because I had to swear my service to Arnulf, I had a mission, that is also something we can speak of later, Zivah. Please."

"What are you?"

"I am a skald and a warrior," Thióðolf said.

"And..?" She peered closely at him. She just knew there was something more. Something nobody had told her about him, something she needed to know. He smiled.

"Zivah, in my country there is a king called Grjótgarð of Borg. He rules the land, and when he took the High Seat of Borg back in the days, he married nine women."

"Uhm, I think I heard that story before…" she said uncertainly.

"Indeed. Only what you did not know is that Grjótgarð of Borg and Almveig of Nauma valley are my parents," Thióðolf said, "They had two sons and a daughter. I am her youngest son and one of my kingly father's eighteen sons."

"Your father is a king?"

Zivah could hardly believe what she heard.

"Yes. Uhm, Zivah, this is probably the right time to tell you..."
he smiled deviously, "I was to give you a message from Arnulf and
Hallgrim and all the men of the court."

"What?"

"Yes. Uhm. They said they were sorry for what they did to you.
They wanted you to know that."

"They are sorry?" She asked incredulously.

"As hard as it is to grasp, yes. They are sorry," Thióðolf said. Zivah
was speechless, "and, uhm, they also said they hoped that you would
come to like their gift, even though they know it could not possibly
ever atone for what they did to you."

"What gift?"

"Me," Thióðolf said, "I am, apparently, their gift to you. As a way
of Atonement." He was actually blushing.

"What?"

"Well, as I said, they were sorry. That night in the tent, when
Arnulf almost raped you and then thought better of it, well, he
realized that he felt really sorry for what he had done to you. He
went to Hallgrim and they talked about it and decided to give you
something as compensation. Something that you had wanted all
your life. Thordís had told me that you had always prayed for a
prince to come and whisk you off into some exotic foreign land, and
I told Hallgrim, who told Arnulf, and seeing as I am a prince, they
gave me to you."

"They gave you to me?"

"Yes. Arnulf was being the Contrary when he gave you to me, so
even if you belong to me by law, in sight and view of the gods and all
that is holy I really belong to you. Even if you call me Heri, you are
in truth my Freyia, and not the other way around. That is the law of
the Contrary."

"The Contrary?"

"It is called the Ritual of the Contrary, a very ancient and sacred
game of perception for the purpose of Atonement or teaching, or
in our case, both. Hallgrim and Arnulf made the rite and Arnulf
became the Contrary while Hallgrim took care of the path of the rite.
That was why Arnulf tried so hard to corrupt me, because they had
to see if I was truly worthy of you. They tested me out through the
Ritual of the Contrary."

"They wanted to see if you were worthy of me?"

"Yes, of course. You see, after Arnulf... uhm, you know, when he felt sorry about what he did to you, the men thought that sort of remorse in a man like him was in itself so miraculous that you could not possibly be less than divine. You are a goddess to them, Zivah."

"What?" She almost screamed it.

"Yes but you are a slave too, so the courtesies must be observed nevertheless. You have no idea how hilarious the men think it is to have a goddess bow her head to them all day long and not even being aware of how dazzled and in awe they really are of you. Now you know. For when you bow next time. Courtesies, you know. They are very important to us Norsemen, the courtesies. In any case, they had to make sure that I was a true prince in every way before they let me know because for as long as I did not know, I was just a pending gift that could be withdrawn. They did not tell me until I had passed the third test of not, uhm, not raping you, basically."

"What, what if you had raped me?" She spluttered, feeling angry.

"Oh, they said they knew that would not happen on account of your divine nature. If Arnulf could not bring himself to rape you, then I would surely not. I had to prove myself nevertheless, so they made sure I would be hard-pressed and tempted, and even made to think that it was the right thing to do. I passed the test, and when I declared publicly that I would not touch you unless you really wanted it yourself and that no other men were allowed to touch you, then they made the gift real by telling me."

"What about telling me?" She wheezed.

"Obviously, they could not tell you until you were able to perceive me as a gift at all. If they had told you then you would have thought yourself mocked. They knew I would have to work hard for the sake of convincing you that I was a worthy gift to you, if I were to honor them. I really do want that for my own sake too, because I love you, Zivah. The men never doubted that the day would come, and instructed me to tell you then. I really hope this was the right time."

"How. How..." she kept opening and shutting her mouth, unable to utter another word.

"They wanted to give you a prince and they had one to give, so to speak," Thióðolf said amiably. "Not that I was told until after I passed the tests. So I had no idea until after that first night in the Hold. I was quite shocked that night when Arnulf said you were mine, when truth shall be told. I had never owned a slave girl before and you were so utterly miserable and so damn attractive at the same time. I have never felt more conflicted and disturbed in my whole life, which was good seeing as that is the sort of situation what hones a man's soul sharp."

"All the men... they knew?"

"Not at once. The game must be played carefully. It is very holy and powerful. The berserkers were the first to know, and later some of the other men were let in on the truth. After Hialti died, they told the rest of the men. Well, some knew about it before, but all in all. All the men agreed and wanted to partake in the apology and now they all seem to think they have given me to you. They are very proud of having been able to offer you such a gift, seeing as they all like you and hold you in very high regard, and besides recognize your divinity. Not that they are going to lower their eyes to you or anything. You still have to do the bowing part. They just want you to know."

"I do not. I..." Zivah almost spluttered, looking very red and somewhat angry.

"I know," he said in mock regret, "I am never going to be king, Zivah, on account of having seventeen brothers, but on the other hand, I will always be that which you dreamed of. I will always be a prince. I belong to you, it seems. Not that I mind at all."

"You. You... you Norsemen are crazy!" She snapped, outraged.

"I suppose we are," he said, and cocked his head teasingly to one side, with an expression of concern, "but we do not bore you, do we, Zivah?"

Zivah could not help herself. She laughed and laughed and laughed.

THE POET'S ATONEMENT

If they talked, it was too low for me to hear, but they seemed to be, and when I heard Zivah laugh from her heart I could not bear to be left out anymore. After some consideration, I decided that this was certainly one of those situations where completely different rules applied, and so I could afford to be disobedient. I got up and collected the weapons. They were too heavy and big for me to handle them well, and so I struggled and partly drew them with me as I moved towards my sister and my mentor. Finally I reached them and placed the weapons on the ground beside me before I sat down, looking expectantly at the couple.

"I think I mentioned that this was supposed to be a private moment between me and Zivah," Thióðolf said reproachfully.

"I know," I said, "but I could not hear what you were saying." I lowered my eyes as if I was being obedient, which I clearly was not. I had no intention to either, but I could at least go through the ritual moves of respect and obeisance.

"That was the point, Thordís," Thióðolf said, "You were supposed to look after my weapons."

"They are too heavy for me," I said, "Better to leave them with the only one here who can actually wield them." Thióðolf sighed, but smiled, and to my surprise, I noticed that Zivah was also smiling, and then they both giggled. I often thought adults laughed at the strangest moments, but since their conversation was supposed to be private, I made no comment. They decided to just ignore me.

"Zivah," Thióðolf said, "I cannot say I am sorry for beating you that day in the market. I would have apologized, but the truth is that I had no other option. I really did my best to save your skin, even if you did not know."

"He invented a whole new eastern kingdom for your benefit," I said, forgetting myself, and then placed my hand across my mouth to silence myself. Zivah nodded.

"The Eastern Princess," she said quietly and smiled shyly up at her man, who was still holding her in his arms. He released her gently and she sat down in the grass before him. Thióðolf cleared his throat and looked very solemn. But I thought I saw a glimpse of humor in his eyes.

"What I would like to apologize for, Zivah, and for this I am truly, deeply sorry..." he paused, looking so serious that both my sister and I became very solemn and leaned forward to hear him better.

"I am truly sorry for buying that ugly dress for you. So, very sorry. I should have known you would not have liked it. It was not worthy of you. I will never buy an ugly grey dress for you again. Never. Please forgive me."

Zivah stared at him for a moment in disbelief, but then her face broke out in a sweet smile, and she began to shake again, only this time it was with laughter. "I can forgive that, Thióðolf," she said between the laughter. Thióðolf smiled and exchanged one happy glance with me. I smiled back.

Then Zivah seemed to become aware that he was bleeding from the nose and from some other scratches that she had recently caused, and leaned forward to touch his face. "You are bleeding, House-Bond," she said anxiously, "I have hurt you."

"I think I can handle it, Zivah," he said, "You are not exactly Arnulf." They smiled at each other again, and once more I forgot myself and said, "He has been through worse, you see," a statement which mysteriously caused them both to roar with even more laughter. When they had calmed down a little, Thióðolf said that she did not have to call him House-Bond or Heri when they were alone together or just with me. His name was enough. As Zivah agreed to this, I remembered something she had said before and blurted, "Zivah thinks that you want her to call you Heri when she spreads her legs for you."

They both looked shocked for a moment, and then Zivah began to turn a bright and burning red. She glared at me, speechless. Thióðolf, however, looked amused.

"That is not entirely true, Zivah," he said to her, looking very grave, and she shook her head affirmatively, burning with embarrassment. He winked at her and said, smiling, "I would much rather you call my name when you do that."

Zivah blushed a deep red then.

"Only if you want to do that, Zivah," he said gently, "I have never claimed you like that and I never will, unless you wish it so."

He locked his gaze with hers then, wolf on doe. As she gazed back at her man for the first time without averting her eyes, in my sight at least, something passed over Zivah's face, a change. It was as if a darkness that had long held her face in shadow was lifted, and something else and new was lit in her eyes. As I looked at her, I thought her eyes revealed the existence of a secret well within, a fountain of sorts, one that was just about to be discovered.

She seemed to try and speak, but not a word came out, and she blinked her eyes several times. I thought her lips trembled. The cautious smile she offered him now was different. I had never seen her smile that way. Before the raid, all her smiles had been carefully premeditated; the smiles of a mask. The smiles she had later bestowed on other members of the court had been more genuine, but restricted.

Zivah had no masks anymore, and this was the first time I ever saw her real face, and her true smile. It was a smile that came with a silent question and a silent acceptance of something she had so far feared with all her being. Thióðolf reached out his hand to her and their fingers met in the grass, touching carefully, curiously. Her hands were so small and delicate next to his, what seemed to fascinate them both as they stared at their hands, touching one another in the grass. That moment it was as if they were the only persons present in the whole world.

When the touching continued and made them draw closer, I realized that they were about to venture onto Freyia's path, and that there was certainly no reason to call down the wrath of Thor in this particular situation. I remembered that it would be impolite of me to stay and watch, and so I dutifully walked away to spend time in the field, climbing trees and exploring the ground for herbs and roots and other useful things.

It had been so delightful to kiss him, so lovely to touch him that she almost forgot that Thordís was still present. But when the girl suddenly left, Zivah experienced a surge of panic, as if she was being attacked by something invisible and threatening. The possibility that he would suddenly turn into a violent beast and rape her brutally became such a real one that she almost screamed. Before she knew what had happened she was sitting several feet away from Thióðolf, crouching on the ground, panting, almost gasping for air.

She looked at the man who still sat exactly where she had left him all of a sudden, and noticed that he was not looking at her but was squatting, all calm, pretending to be studying a flower right in front of him, his side turned to her. It was such an odd response to her little flight that she calmed down immediately and began studying him, wondering what to say.

"Zivah," he said, "have you seen what a beautiful flower this is?" She got to her feet and walked cautiously over to his side and squatted down next to him, looking at the rather ordinary pretty little flower. He did not turn towards her but kept looking at the flower as he spoke to her.

"Zivah, I will not hurt you. Not ever. If you say stop, we stop. Any time. Whatever we are doing, I will stop when you say stop. I have the self-control of a warrior and I can stop the moment you tell me to. Please trust me. Can you do that?" He said quietly, still looking at the flower and not at her.

"It is so hard, trusting," she whispered. She felt like crying, because it hurt so much, the way she could not bring herself to trust him even now. "I know, beloved," he said. No more. He did not even press the issue. His acceptance of her distrust in him made her feel as if she could actually trust him. That, and the way he did not confront her neither with body nor words. He continued to watch the flower while he listened to her and just confirmed what she said.

"I am afraid that you would suddenly turn on me and become like someone else," she said and forced back a sob.

"I know. I am so sorry that you feel that way."

"Are you not angry with me for not trusting you after all this time?"

"Of course not, Zivah. How could you just trust any man again after what you have been through? A man has got to earn your trust in him, and that is just as it should be anyway. A woman ought never to trust a man unless he has proven himself to her."

"I am afraid of your strength," she said quietly, "I have been so afraid of the strength of men."

"Nobody blames you, sweet one. You are very delicate also. We must seem rather imposing to you."

"Yes," she said and smiled. He smiled and peered at her from the corner of his eye. She was starting to feel relaxed again, starting to remember how delightful that kiss had felt.

"Two years before you came, before the raid, I was attacked by a man who had, he had tricked me into thinking that he was passionately in love with me and wanted to take me somewhere and let me wear lovely silk dresses…" She paused and felt her eyes widen with fear at the memory.

"What happened?" He said slowly, and she saw his eyes fill with tears.

"He seized me and I was so, it was so terrifying to realize how much stronger he was than me and that I stood no chance against him. Then more men came."

"Oh, Zivah, I am so sorry." He really was. She could see how deeply her words affected him.

"They could not finish what they started," she whispered, "Father, Thorbjörn, my stepfather, he just appeared out of nowhere and before I even had time to understand what had happened he had killed them all. He just sliced all six of them into pieces within the blink of an eye."

"Was that when you received your head gift?" Thióðolf asked, smiling again.

"Yes. That was when I learned the rite. That was how I knew the words."

"Zivah," Thióðolf said, "that rite is very powerful. It has a way of repeating itself. Men who try to hurt you will probably end up more hurt than you. Men who may have thought to harm you but who still have a core of honor within will suddenly be moved to remember their honor in your presence. Your father made a spell of protection for you on that day. He made you the sort of woman who gets to hold her enemy's head in her hands. He did that out of love for you, just like we did that for Thordís, and now she has the same protection."

"You did it for the rest of us," she smiled. He just smiled too, in response. He never spoke of hidden rites, just as he did not speak of the hidden honer. She was starting to know. "And yet, all this time I have been frightened of you Rus, Norsemen. You are so big and scary and too strong for you own good, Thióðolf."

"I assume your Norseman father was strong too."

"Very. Almost like Arnulf."

"He used it only to protect you."

"Yes…"

"That is what a man does, Zivah. That is what he is supposed to do. That is how I was taught, and all the men of my tribe. Please do not fear me. I will never use my strength against you, not ever. I would only use my strength and battle skills against anyone who tried to hurt you."

They sat quietly for a little while and looked at the flower together. She found that she felt safer the longer they sat. The anxiety that he might suddenly become violent abated, little by little. She wondered how he could understand her so well, this crazy Norseman prince.

"How do you know how to be with me?" She asked, "How do you know how to not frighten me?"

"The men of my tribe know the runes of the goddess. We learn of women's mysteries. We are taught by women. We learn what it is like for a woman who has been raped, among many other things. We learn how to approach her and how to let her know that she is safe."

"Oh. But Thióðolf, nobody actually raped me."

"Yes we did. We all did."

"What do you mean?"

"We took you from freedom to slavery. You saw too much violence and too many rapes and lived too long under the constant threat of being raped and mishandled by all of us. Even when it was not a real threat anymore, you could not know that. I saw how terrified you were on that ship and at the slave market in Khazaria. It does not really matter whether somebody actually stuck it in you or not in the long run of things. You carry the same wounds and the same fears as the women who actually were raped.

It has been clear to see for everyone, and it has been such a painful thing to acknowledge, day after day after day, how we are all but rapists and killers in your lovely golden, amber eyes. Of course that is true also. If there is any comfort it is possible that your case actually has made some of us into better men."

"Why me? You, not you, Thióðolf. I do not think you do rape and kill and enslave people anymore. The Rus. The Vikings. They do this for a living. Why would my case be any different to them than that of any other girl?"

He met her gaze now.

"These men never bring the girls they abduct to their own homes, Zivah. They always buy them from men worse than themselves, and then the girls are always happy to discover what nice sort of men they have come to and are actually grateful to be with their new masters. You have seen what they actually do. You did not disappear into one of those countless lost stories that are only sung once and only on raids. You came along, carrying your whole story of pain and loss with you into their court and everyday life. That you made it past Khazaria and into their court made of you a constant reminder of what they had done to your people. There was the grace and courage you showed. Even when you had been beaten, you stood there like a queen, like a goddess, albeit in shackles."

"Oh," Zivah said, suddenly not wanting to think about these things.

"We do not have to speak of this now," he said.

She nodded and looked at him. Zivah was not so afraid of him anymore, but she was afraid that she would be again. She did not want to flee away from him and feared lest she do so anyway. But she wanted to touch him. He is my prince, after all, she thought. In the eyes of the gods and all that is holy, he belonged to her.

He is a gift to me.

"I am at your service today, Freyia," he said and smiled charmingly. "You can order me around all you like, now. I don't even demand that you be kind to me. I am your gift, you know. Apparently the men think that I am perfectly suitable to stand in their stead when you wield your vengeance. They were very cheerful when they let me know that they expected me to represent them."

Vengeance. Their eyes met again, as if it was a challenge.

"Take off your breeches and stand up," she said gravely. Thióðolf Skald obeyed immediately and stood naked before her. She drew her breath. She could not allow herself to see how beautiful he was. Not yet. She wanted him to feel vulnerable also.

"I like to see you standing naked while I am still dressed," she said testily.

"I never liked to see you that way, but I am sure I deserve this anyway," he said jovially.

"You do," she agreed, but she did not mean it so much anymore.

"Seeing as you are at it, what do you think of your gift?" He asked, and frowned a little, as if he worried about her verdict on his naked body. He was not embarrassed at being naked at all. And he was awesome. He was so very beautiful. Even his scars were so. Even that which she had thought of as his most dangerous weapon, and which was now saluting her quite enthusiastically; even that was beautiful.

"Glorious," she said, "My gift is glorious. I think my gift is a god."

"Prince is more than sufficient," he chuckled, "but you can worship me any time. I like libation offerings, if you need a tip."

Zivah was starting to feel very well entertained.

"Your, uhm, your Freystone is standing up." She giggled.

"It is on account of your presence, I imagine. He probably wants to have a look. I really cannot blame him, seeing as you are rather pleasing to the eyes. Even in your grey dress and tight bun."

She refused to laugh at his joke. Not yet.

"I used to think it was a weapon," she said, sounding grave, and glared directly at him. The prince looked sad and asked, so very cautiously, "Zivah, did you never have a nice man do this with you? Not ever? Or have you not, uhm, have you not been with a man at all?"

"Yes, I have. Not so many as people thought. I liked to talk and kiss a little, but I always withdrew. But then there was one young man who was my sweetheart for a year. He was nice. It was nothing at all like anything I keep seeing here. It was a bit more, quiet, perhaps. Did not last that long either. I liked to have him close but I thought it was a little boring."

"Hmm," Thióðolf grinned, and there was a light of amusement and mischief lit in his eyes. She knew what he was thinking and forced herself not to smile. Too soon, she thought. He still deserved some trashing, seeing as he stood in the place of all the Vikings.

"When he wooed me, I rejected him, and he was so angry. He went to my stepfather and learned some of the battle arts after that. He even fought against the Vikings when they came. He was one of the men they hanged," Zivah said challengingly, "Do you know what he said before they hanged him?"

"No, but I would like to know."

"He called my name and said that he would die a man now because of me."

Her tears streamed down her face. She had not expected the memory of it to move her so. But now she remembered the boy who had once held her in his arms, her first man, and how he had died while she watched, a young sweet man, being hanged and stabbed. Her former lover had not screamed or cried.

He had just spoken those words to her and died like a warrior. Her first lover had been so very courageous, and she had never thought that he would have been, before she saw him die.

"You made a man out of him," Thióðolf said quietly, "and he died an honorable death, which is more than a man could ever ask for. But I am sorry for your loss, Zivah, I really am."

He bowed his head, and somehow, his Freystone also bowed.

"He bows to me," Zivah said, so impressed that she dried her tears.

"A wise man learns how to let his Freystone apologize for him," Thióðolf, grave-faced, declared ceremoniously, and Zivah went from tears to laughing sobs.

Then she started touching him. She moved around him as he stood passively while she touched his entire body and traced every line, and smelled him, and tasted him with her lips. Then she let fall her hair, took off her dress and let him look at her and touch her just the same. It was such a soft and trying and subtle game, like a dance, so careful, so tender, until she felt an hitherto unknown heat glowing from within and she wanted to feel him closer and closer. She felt her mouth twitch, so strange, and realized that she was experiencing real passion for the first time ever.

She wanted him. She really did want him.

It was a good while after that she found herself on the ground with him above her, but he was still not taking her, just playing with her, getting to know her, enticing that new and growing passion in her with every tender touch and firm grasp, and his lips seemed to burn on her skin a long time after he had moved to a different spot. Suddenly he whispered into her ears that he would like to kiss the pearl of Freyia, and when she nodded in surprised agreement, he did, and did it so well that she soon heard herself scream as she rode the waves of pleasure.

Oh gods, she thought, I am squealing like a slave girl. When he came up to kiss her face again he told her that he could do it again because he could never have enough of her pearl, but she pulled him close and whispered, "I want. I want..."

She could not bring herself to say it.

"What do you want, my Freyia," he asked mildly and kissed her ear. She could feel his lord stone pressing against her inner thigh and groaned a little, in case he got the drift of what she wanted all by himself. He looked innocently at her and waited.

"I would, I would like to, that is... oh you know," she said.

"I do not think I know, my golden goddess, but I am yours to command."

"I want you inside..." she blushed.

"Inside what?"

"Oh gods, Thióðolf..."

"The gods are surely watching," he spoke piously.

"I want you to ride Freyia's path," she whispered.

"You do?"

"Yes."

"Are you sure?"

"Yes."

"Because we do not have to, Zivah. This is all about you. What you want."

"I want..!" She felt a little upset now. She had a feeling that he was teasing her.

"Are you absolutely certain?" He was enjoying himself and only casually pushing his stone against her thigh. She thought it burned there and had never thought she would ever want it so much.

"Yes," she whimpered, "I am certain!"

"I think I forgot, what was it you wanted again?"

"Thióðolf," she snarled, exasperated, "Zivah wants to fuck!"

"Oh, good," he said compliantly, "that was what I had in mind also," and obliged her with a very deep push.

The Sun Maiden moved high in the sky and a long time passed. Sometimes I heard those strange little shrieks that women tend to utter when they enjoy the games, and I wondered if I would ever squeal like a girl in a man's embrace. They kept playing Freyia's sport for so long that I began to wonder how it was even possible. I was used to hearing Arnulf and his concubines playing in their beds at night, and I had often seen men and slave girls having a rather swifter go during the day, even outside in the courtyard although they mostly kept to the stables, and even if the slaves appeared quite content about their men, I knew that the time that went by was usually not that impressive.

Even Arnulf, whom the women called a stud, which apparently meant that he was playing it well, never played for such a long time as this. But my sister's shrieks of abandon kept coming at almost regular intervals, and the Sun was moving towards its abode in the west. They were lying side by side on the soft grass while they looked at the clouds together. It was not the first time they had been lying like that and she had felt satisfied and content and happy and then joyfully discovered that it had only been a break. This time it was surely over, she thought, actually starting to feel as if she could not take anymore. Then she spied a movement down below and saw his Freystone rise again, as proud as ever. She reached out to touch it.

"Do you never tire?" She giggled, playing casually with it. It had a funny way of bouncing back every time she pushed it over to one side.

"I reckon there is a lot of apologizing what needs doing here today," Thióðolf said, "seeing as I am atoning for the whole damn court of Vikings."

They both laughed.

"I reckon Aziza was absolutely right about what she said about you on my first day in Arnulf's Hold," Zivah said thoughtfully as she kept playing with the back-bouncing wand. She had grown rather fond of it for the last few hours. She simply loved to touch it. He observed how she was now using it to make circles.

"It is sometimes disturbing how similar you are to your feline fosterling," he commented anxiously, and Zivah smiled gleefully.

"What did she say about me then?" He asked curiously.

"She said that Thióðolf Heri is a very good fuck," Zivah said, "and I second that. So did Tana, if I remember correctly. You got it from three sources now, House-Bond."

"Ah!" Thióðolf grinned and gave his chest a proud beat, "Your verdicts honor me."

"Thióðolf," Zivah said, "How is it possible? I did not think it was possible for a man to keep going and going like that."

"I am blessed by heavenly Freyia," he said, "and I have been taught how, Zivah. A very long story to be told on another occasion. My stamina stems from a particular sort of art that I happen to master quite well."

"I do not doubt that," Zivah said dreamily, "what art is that?"

"It is an art of divine frenzy. Zivah, do you still fear my strength?"

"No…" she smiled, "I have found it rather useful of late." He smiled at her words but looked thoughtful all of a sudden, and when she stopped playing with his lord stone he did not even seem to notice. It looked as if he was considering something and weighing the possibilities. An image flashed before her mind's eyes, a memory almost forgotten.

"Thióðolf," she whispered, "I do not know why but I feel I need to tell you something that may be important."

"Do tell," he said and rolled over on his side to caress her breasts.

"Once, when I was very young, I went to spy at my parents, that is, at my mother and stepfather when they were playing Freyia's game. And I was so frightened by what I saw. It looked so terribly violent. Thorbjörn looked like he was furious, raging, completely out of control, and he was so hard. Not like you."

"You did not find me hard back there?" He asked, raising an eyebrow.

"Not like that," she said, smiling, "not like that. It looked like he was hurting her over and over. She, my mother, she was so gentle, Thióðolf, so delicate, so beautiful and sweet. She always cared for everyone and never demanded anything in return. She never scorned me or anyone. I loved her so much, and I admired her, and she was so graceful and elegant and noble, but then I saw her like an animal, being crushed, losing her mind. She looked like she was fainting from the pain, her mouth was open and her eyes had just rolled back and there were tears streaming down her face, and she was utterly limp. I thought he was abusing her. I thought it was rape."

"What do you think it was now?"

"I confronted her with it and she said it was not the way it looked, and that she was happy with him and when I told her I would never surrender to a man like that she said that I would be missing out on something great and powerful and holy, because there is power in surrender, she said."

"Do you believe it now?"

"That there is power in surrender? I suppose there is. It took me a long while to realize that Thordís fought for me and won exactly because she surrendered utterly. She used her surrender as her sharpest blade. This is that night, Thióðolf, when you came to the bed and I thought you meant to take me, I surrendered. I surrendered not to you but to a flowing river that runs through my heart. It is my place of divinity. I went into that place and then it did not matter what you did to me, I thought. I never got to find out whether it would have mattered or not, though, because you did not take me then after all."

"It would have mattered, Zivah."

"Yes." Their hands met and closed around each other. It almost hurt to know how much that had mattered. How close they had been to never meet like they now had. "Why do you speak of this, Zivah?"

"Because... I want to know what it was. What it was that my mother knew and I do not," she said, "and I think you know what it is, Thióðolf. Is that not so?"

"Yes," he said simply.

"But I am also afraid. I am very afraid of that," she whispered. He sat up a little to rest on his elbow, looking down at her while he caressed her belly gently. He met her eyes.

"It is possible that it would be better to wait," he said, and saw how disappointed she was. "If you think you are ready, we can," he said, and smiled when he saw the conflicting feelings that offer created.

"You want to face your fear," he suggested.

"Yes," she replied.

"That is on account of your warrior spirit, my beloved, my goddess of a woman who owns me for her gift. If you can handle me being your Heri in public for a while longer I will pay it up to you by never denying you any pleasure when we are alone. This particular pleasure that you want now, it is one that does requires that you let me rule you. That means you really need to trust me."

"I suppose I will have to call you Heri when I spread my legs for you," she snickered.

"Yes," he said, grinning, "I would actually recommend that you do. It would help the mood, so to speak. Or you could use an older word. You could think of me as your Freyr."

"Is that not the god of, uhm," she giggled.

"The god of all growing things? Exactly," he grinned, but went serious at once, "Zivah, we can only make this work if you truly trust me. We can only do this if you trust me enough to surrender utterly."

She suddenly did not mind anymore. He could be her Heri any day, now that she knew who he was. Zivah relaxed and lowered her eyes. He took her hand in his and caressed it a little before he pushed it gently down towards the ground. Then he rolled to lie above her and took her other hand, caressed it too, and pushed it down towards the ground. His big hands closed around her hands and wrists and pressed them firmly to the ground at the same moment that he entered her holy parts. She tried to push against and found she could not move at all. He was inside of her and he was holding her firmly against the ground, and she was powerless. She met his gaze. There was only love in his eyes.

"Shall I let go," he asked, but already knew the answer when she shook her head slowly.

"What do you feel?" He asked.

"Like you are holding me," she whispered, quite astonished, "I feel, supported. Safe."

"This is one of those things your mother knew, Zivah, and yet it does not look that nice from the outside, does it?"

"No," she whispered, realizing that it probably just looked like he was pinning her down.

"When we touch each other it is the intention within the touch, the deeper intention that matters," Thióðolf said slowly, "and you know that my intention is to hold you and support you, and love you and please you. I am not pinning you down. I am letting you know with your bodily self that I have the strength to hold you. You know that. You trust me."

"I trust you."

"It is going to go deeper and it is going to look bad and then worse, Zivah, if we go down this path, but it is only going to feel better and better. Because all the way you will feel that I can and will hold you and that I will never let go, and that I will never stop until you stop. I will carry you all the way. All the way. Do not doubt it for a moment. I will take you through the whole thing and all the way I will hold you and rule you and I will not let you down. You can surrender in trust."

"What happens when I surrender?"

She had to know first.

"Then you will find that it is not to me that you have surrendered, but to that flowing river within, to your divinity," he said, "and the best thing about that is that I will be right there with you and help you stay within that divinity for as long as you are able to. I will never stop before you do. I will beat the rhythm for you while you flow. And the more powerfully and the more wide you flow, the harder I must hold you because you need to feel that I can still hold you. You need to feel held so that you may surrender to that flow. The violence you saw, that was not violence. That was a way of maintaining her flow and channeling it into divine power. The greater that power flows, the more violent it will appear from the outside."

"What if Thordís sees us like that?" She whispered, suddenly fearful, "What if she thinks that you are raping me?"

"She will certainly see us, you know her. But she will not see what you thought you saw, Zivah. Your little sister has the eyes of a she-wolf. She will see this for what it is."

"What is it?"

"It is the waking of the goddess, my love. It is called Freyia's Frenzy. We will flow like water through the great river mother of all the worlds, and come out purified and full of stamina the sort of which you have already found very useful. All the way I shall carry you, Zivah. You must surrender. You are the flow that comes from the beat. You must let me rule the beat. You must give yourself up if you are to flow. That is when you know the power of surrender. Will you do that, my Freyia? Do you wish it?"

"Yes, my Freyr, my prince, my love; I wish it."

Zivah let go of herself.

When I had eaten all the food we had brought, feeling unusually hungry and a little lonely, I noticed that the shrieks had stopped a while before, yet I knew that my friends were not finished. I knew it because something strange appeared to occur now, an almost eerie silence that seemed to fill the entire clearing. The birds had stopped singing, and even though the silence was almost deafening, the ground seemed to reverberate with a deep tremble. I knew that something magical was transpiring and decided to sneak up on the lovers to see what they were up to. I went through the woods so that they would not see me.

What I saw made me stand gaping. I instantly knew how Thióðolf worshiped his goddess. There would be no lowered eyes before a sacrificial altar, unless the goddess herself was laying spread on that altar, and he lowered his eyes to look at her. Zivah seemed to be lying in mid-air upon such an invisible altar, while Thióðolf stood on his knees, supporting her lower back with his hands and taking her so furiously that I thought I had never seen the like, and I had seen a lot of the stuff. He looked as if in battle-rage, seized by holy fury, utterly wild, even violent, yet completely in control of himself, and of Zivah.

She on her hand had surrendered utterly, her neck and head thrown backwards in the air and her long hair flowing towards the ground. Her whole body appeared to have relaxed. Her arms were spread out to the sides, hands touching the grass. Her eyes were closed, and her mouth was open. My sister's face was so peaceful that I knew that she was free in her seizure, and that she was freer there than she had ever been.

He had taken her to a place where she could know her own freedom after all, and found that it existed within. Tears streamed down her face, but they were tears of release. She uttered no sound at all, yet the whole world seemed to be brimming with unheard thunder and unseen lightning. Even as they seemed to play absolute opposites, even as they appeared lost in their seizures, one seized by blissful peace and the other by relentless fury, there was a deep communion between the lovers. There appeared to be a spell of power created between them, growing into enormous proportions, surrounding them with an ethereal, golden light.

Together, they were a divinity.

I retreated, stunned and awed, knowing that I had beheld a mystery yet beyond my grasp, but so thoroughly beautiful that my heart almost wept with both sadness and joy. I had witnessed Freyia's Frenzy, and knew it for a most holy thing. I just sat down on a rock close to the horses and thought of nothing at all for a long time, until the birds began to sing again.

It was very late in the day before the lovers finally reappeared, dressed and looking happy. They both seemed to radiate with a peculiar, intensely bright light, as if they were keeping a Sun within them, an inner Sun with rays so bright and strong they had begun to penetrate the pores of their skin, glowing on the surface. They both looked many years younger than they had been before they met as god and goddess. And they were holding hands, I noticed. The secret hearts of men and women cause the strangest turns of events.

We were all hungry again, and went to the horses. Zivah sat in front of Thióðolf this time, leaning trustingly towards him as they rode the horse together, and I asked curiously, "So, uhm, did he make you feel like a goddess, Zivah?"

She blushed, but Thióðolf pinched her in the side and asked jokingly, "Did I, Zivah? Did I make you feel like a goddess? Did I?"

He bit her ear, even. I frowned, but Zivah, beaming, threw her head back and laughed.

To be continued in....
Book Three: The Hel Rune's Claim

BIBLIOGRAPHY

Maria Kvilhaug was born in Oslo, Norway, in 1975. She studied History of Religions and Old Norse Philology at the university of Oslo. She has written several non-fiction and fiction books concerning Old Norse pre-Christian culture and religion.

<u>NON-FICTION:</u>
The Maiden with the Mead (2004/2009)
The Seed of Yggdrasill (2013/2018/2020)
The Poetic Edda, Six Cosmology Poem (2017)
The Trickster and the Thunder god, Thor and Loki in Old Norse Myths (2018)
The Goddess Iðunn(2022)

<u>FICTION</u>
(Blade Honer novel series about the life of the Oseberg priestesses):
The Hammer of Greatness
My Enemy´s Head
The Hel-Rune´s Claim
A Twisted Mirror

http://www.bladehoner.wordpress.com
http://www.youtube.com/user/ladyofthelabyrinth

The Three Little Sisters

The Three Little Sisters is an indie publisher that puts authors first. We specalize in the strange and unusual. From titles about pagan and heathen spirituality to traditional fiction we bring books to life.

https://the3littlesisters.com